Bones of Fallen Gods

BOOK II
OF STARS FOR NIGHT & SHADOW

BY

RUQUAYYA SAJJIDA

First edition paperback ISBN: 978-1-7379465-4-0

KDP Paperback edition published 2024.

Edited by Ruquayya Sajjida
Layout by Ruquayya Sajjida
Cover art by @ricacabrex on Fiverr

114,496 approximate words

Poetry and songs and other writings are author's own work, although outside works/musical artists may be referenced.

An imprint of Blacke Books
Louisville, KY, United States of America
All fonts are free for commercial use. All rights reserved.

ADULT DARK ROMANTIC SCIENCE-FANTASY

Blacke Books
Indie Publishing

Rise. Rise from that untold empty, breathe in that howling wind, and gnash your teeth at all that dared call you and your peoples 'heathens.' This is not *their* world. There are no heathens here, except the ones who stab their food, bomb off flesh and eyelash alike, and believe God to be hateful, envious and wicked. After all, how could something so divine be so tasteless?

Shouldn't She be sweet like a date?

Free Palestine, Free Congo, Free Sudan, Free Tibet, Free Haiti, Free Sudan, Free the Indigenous people of every land, Free the man standing on the corner, shooting up heroine, Free every human suffering from an illness (both seen and unseen), Free the forces of Good and Evil.

Free the whole F'N WORLD.

CONTENTS

TRIGGER WARNING!

Trigger warnings are a bit different this time around, as the book has become lighter in a lot of aspects!

Sex

Death

Loss

Mental health crises

Involuntary commission to asylum

Mentioning of eating disorders

Binge-drinking

Foul language

Battle

SACRIFICE

A winter gale blew through the land as Dorian drove us home, his eyes trained through the thick fog permeating the land. The road was pitch black, a stripe of yellow uncovered by the light from the car then swallowed by darkness, only for a new stripe to take its place. The moon was high in the sky, clouds wafting around it gently, as evocative as a silk nightrobe covering the smooth, white hindquarters of a scantily clad courtesan. The air curdled like turned milk, the bray of an Amorian wolf carrying through the wind like an ominous warning. As my eyes adjusted to the dark, and I identified exactly *what* was waiting for us in the middle of the road, I realized that safety was never guaranteed.

A half-demon, his skin the yellow-tinged white of cream cheese. I saw no black veins on his skin, no slanted crimson eyes, just sickly, sweaty skin, and onyx eyes with a feverish tint. His humanity somehow made him appear more monstrous, for the most-human looking creatures that I'd come to know had the cruelest of ways.

The world stopped, swayed, and I saw a pink mouth flying open, spittle dribbling down a white chin, crass words spewing forth from death-black tinged jaws that were caught between life and decay.

These were the lives that we'd lived together, Jacques and I—

The memories that tied us.

It was the first bad memory in a plethora of worse times that bound us together.

"Amore," he said, the word a whisper that was carried along the wind.

Jacques was like a flash of lightning in the night. One second, he was there and the next he was gone. But Dorian, his skin almost platinum in the light of the moon, had already swerved to avoid him…or at least, I told myself that in the aftermath. Suddenly we were in a tailspin. The car spun around again, again and again, making my thoughts bang around in my head. A raw scream ripped from my throat, angry and afraid. I was ashamed of the onslaught of emotions, even then.

That's when I saw them: large trees surrounding us, their limbs ever-reaching, not towards the sky, but for us. And on their hundreds of single legs were millions of dead woodland creatures, their breaths a frozen, white mist before their glassy brown eyes. It seemed he had cast a spell tonight. Even though no one had summoned the half-demon, he had found the power to steal the life from the very forest, to snatch away its consciousness and see through the eyes that were once theirs. But soon those ranges of gold eyes and brown bodies, of black trunks and orange-red leaves, of white wolves and an even whiter winter moon, which I could not see for the trees, only to become overtaken by a black-blue sea of fear swamping over me.

The forest blurred around me. I panicked and reached out blindly. I wanted to check on Dorian and my infant son, to hold them both to my chest and never let go. But I couldn't for fear of alerting *him* to their presence. I captured my son's face in my mind's eye: his skin was brown like mine but with a gold gleam that he inherited from his father, his eyes brown-gold and pure, his pink, fleshy gums squishing together, apart, together, and now apart as he searched for me, for something to latch onto, for milk to wash away his cries.

I saw a blue glow, felt Dorian's magic wrap around me, protecting me, and when the car hit the tree, I knew without knowing that we were going to be all right.

I'd been hit with non-stationary forces before so this was something I could survive—perhaps uneasily, but life was life. My son, Aiden, did not scream, but I saw a small red-black glow creeping from the front seat, telling me that the demonic powers of the one who now endangered him had chosen to save him.

And I was *furious*.

So, he really did believe that he had a demonic claim to my son, that tainting the hours-hold boy with blood-magic made him *his*?

Without a thought for our own safety, we both got out. Dorian's back straightened and I could tell that he could sense my fear and the danger that the other man presented. Aiden's cries quieted to small whimpers, but I heard Jacques's growl when he saw he hadn't crushed our small family.

The child stared back at me from the incubator, Jacques staring at us from the corner proudly, his grin like that of a wolf.

"I saved him, given your current state."

"I was pregnant?"

"Oh, yes. Sad, really. The fool knew, you know. But he was going to let the child die. Why he never wears a condom, with the weakness of his seed, I'll never know."

Jacques stalked forward, a gleaming blade in his hand; the black, inky substance on the end was thick and sludgy: demon blood. It seemed that Jacques was not here to play fair. When Dorian was within striking distance, Jacques's hand flashed out.

A deep red cut blossomed on Dorian's neck. He fell to the ground, clawing at his neck and screaming as blood seeped through his fingers. Jacques pocketed the knife, the same calm that he took from me in his every step. When he finally reached me, he smiled. My stomach rolled in fear and disgust.

"Hours are not ours without you, my love. My greatest weapon. My truest opponent. My wonderous wife, my troubled husband reincarnated—in the flesh! Oh," he moaned, "how I've missed you."

He reached out and stroked my face. I cringed at the contact. I felt sick and dirty as memories swelled to the surface of my mind like blood rushing to an open wound. He was evil, a monster. He had no right to touch me after what he'd done in my past—what he'd done just now.

I was consumed by rage. Electricity crackled around my brown fingers. I pushed it farther than I'd ever had—to the very peak of my power. Without a second thought, I threw a hit. My fist passed right through him and, with a whisper of some far away sea-aired port burning my nostrils, he was gone.

CHAPTER ONE

DIRTY

A n hour later and Dorian's neck was completely restored thanks to a messy healing rune I drew. But his pride as a husband? It was hardly intact. Not that I could blame him. He'd been beaten in his own territory. We were seconds away from the car, which was about a mile from the gates leading into the manor—an average walk for a Gifted like me, but precious steps for a cushy-footed Immortal like Dorian.

I was reminded of what he told me the day he proposed, about the devious, cunning Immortal named Kristoff and his plan to take his land for himself. I suddenly realized that this all was very damning. If word spread that Dorian had been beaten, the Immortals would lose faith in him. The Gifted he was responsible for would be put in peril.

"We were almost safe. Just a few more miles and we would have been to the manor! I can't *believe* this!"

Dorian paced on the side of the road. Hao stood to the side, surveying the car, whose front end had been completely smashed in due to one of the many trees. I glared into the forest for a partial second, but each of the trees stared back innocently, shrugging in the wind as if to say, "Wasn't me." Dorian glowered at Hao now, his eyes glaring at the other man in pain and humiliation so obvious, it was painful.

"You were supposed to keep the territory safe while I went to retrieve Marve. And how did he manage to sneak that bomb onto my lands? This is your fault! I trusted you and you failed me! All of you failed me!"

He glowered at Yvonne, Andrew, Hao, Beatrice, and Alena. The five of them stared back at him helplessly. Their skin tones ranged from deep, woodsy brown to warm, sunny yellow, to a pale, translucent white. Even though the Gifted people came from all around the world, the Mother Goddess Kalysma bound us all with the magic she placed in our veins. As we always said, "By magic we are bound and by blood we remain," which had been proven by Jacques.

Only by murdering every Immortal would we continue on.

I knew that Jacques was a crafty son of a bitch—when he wanted in, there was practically no way of keeping him out. I put a hand on Dorian's shoulder, who quickly shook me off. I felt my heart crashing against my ribs, less because of Jacques and more because of Dorian's anger.

All I knew from my past was that anger meant danger.

And it was my fault.

"My Lord, I—"

Dorian's hand flashed out. The man who had spoken, the yellow-brown-toned Hao, fell to the ground. Dorian rose to stand over him. I began to shake as my vision blurred: I saw him, then Jacques, then him again, then a mixture of them both, a chaotic clash of white on gold. I'd never seen him this angry before.

It was terrifying.

I hated myself for fearing him in that moment, but I couldn't help it. I stood, rushing to his side as I reached around his body, wrapping my arms around his midsection. He breathed hard through his nose before turning to bury his face in my hair. He took a deep breath, shaking as he fought to control himself.

"I'm sorry," he whispered. "I'm sorry, baby…Don't cry. I'm sorry."

Like I said, I couldn't help it. He was a man—he had the potential to be like Jacques.

But he's not, a voice softly whispered in my ear.

It sounded like my mother.

Yet, another voice said, *what if he turns that anger on you?*

"I'll fix this. I won't let him touch you ever again," Dorian said, running a hand through my hair. "I love you."

I nodded, trying to calm down. I took in a hard breath and forced my convulsions to stop. I pulled away to look up at Dorian He had turned around and was staring down at me, his face ravaged with guilt. His eyes were wide as if he was about to cry, his mouth parted, his brows raised, and an odd shade of red laid over the gold of his face.

But, I realized, *he didn't like scaring me and didn't like hurting me.*

Dorian turned around and apologized to Hao. The servant man kept his body arched toward the ground even when he stood, ducking his head when Yvonne reached out to ask if he was all right. I felt embarrassed and scared for him. I could tell that no one here was used to Dorian being angry—least of all me. I asked Dorian what he wanted me to do.

Dorian ran a hand over his face, appearing decades older. "I need a smoke."

Yvonne conjured a box of cigarettes. We walked away from them to stand a little way down the road. He picked up one. I closed my eyes, that familiar hum filling my body, electricity writhing in the pit of my stomach. I concentrated and it felt like water trickling down my body as the electricity traveled to my hand.

I gathered it at the tip of my finger. He put the cigarette in his mouth and breathed in as I lit it. He seemed more relaxed as the fumes entered his body.

Good, I thought.

"You want one?" he asked.

"I've, um…I've never smoked before." I murmured, ringing my hands.

He was oblivious to my fear. "I'll show you."

He popped the cigarette that he'd been smoking in my mouth. I stood there, smoke gathering around my head. He told me to breathe in.

"Not like that," he said. "*In.*"

"I am."

"Less like you're sucking your teeth. More like you're drinking water."

"Like this?"

I dragged in a breath, the smoke filling my lungs, and immediately began to hark. The cigarette fell out of my mouth and to the ground. He pounded my back.

"Damn! You okay?"

I wanted to nod but I was too busy coughing. I waved a hand in front of my face. Dorian swooped down to pick up the cigarette. He offered it to me. I shook my head.

"It's a bad habit," he agreed. "I don't recommend it."

"If you don't want me drinking," I asked and he grimaced, "why would you even to let me smoke?"

"I just don't want you to have an altered state of mind," he amended.

"Addiction is an altered state of mind," I offered back, gesturing.

"True." He breathed in and then let out puff of gray smoke. "Don't worry, I don't smoke often. The smell."

I remembered my Danri. He used to smoke whenever one of the men left cigarettes at his job, which was wherever Slave Catchers convened. He would bring them home, hide them from Mar, who always scolded him. I was usually sitting outside the bathroom, talking to him as he smoked, begging him to let me try. He'd always said that the Gifted had a short enough life span as it is, which I'd reply by saying, "Short life—gotta enjoy it, amirite?" And his laugh would spill under the door.

When my mother would see me sitting there, she'd pound on the door, yelling "Life's too short!" And he'd come out of the bathroom, smoke wafting around his head and a sheepish smile on his face as he said, "That it is." But then he'd wink at me and flash a lighter and I'd know that he had more and would smoke them as soon as she was preoccupied. Sometimes, to shift the blame, I'd run over to my mother at full speed and barrel into her legs, nearly knocking her over.

I'd get a spanking, of course, but father would usually come to my room and tell me a story to cheer me up, perched on the edge of my bed. He never stepped in when she disciplined me out of respect for her, I guess, but I knew in those moments after that he loved me, and when my mother would bring home the rest of a cake-pop that she swiped from her job caring for rich Immortal children, I'd know that she loved me, too. Stories, chocolate, accusations and whoopings— that was my childhood. Well, that and the other children's teasing.

"I'm more used to the smell than you'd know." I mumbled.

He quirked a brow. "Jacques smokes?"

I'd nearly forgotten that he did, but I didn't want to tell him about my parents—with the way his parents treated him, he might assume that mine were abusive towards me, which they were not. So, I nodded.

"I'll try to quit," he said.

"It doesn't bother me."

"You sure?"

I shrugged.

"I'll quit."

I tried not to smile.

"I will admit," he said after a pause, "you look cute gagging."

I blushed. He smirked. He glanced over at me. I looked away, pretending not to see him surveying me.

"Fuck."

He tossed the cigarette, bringing down his foot. Then he rushed me, smashing his lips against mine. I stumbled back, accidently biting him. But he just kissed me harder, breathing smoke into my mouth. I gasped it in before coughing it out like I did before.

He reached down, grabbing a fistful of my ass. I squirmed against him. He reached down, fumbling for his pants. I felt him grab my hand. I froze.

"Touch it."

He was breathing heavy against my mouth. I started to shake again. This was a whole new kind of fear.

"Come on, you little tease," he growled against my mouth, kissing my cheek. "Touch me."

"I don't want to."

He ground his hips against mine, his eyes far off, in happier times. I had a million thoughts racing through my head. But at the forefront was the most important: *It's not him. Don't be afraid of him. He doesn't deserve your fear. Calm down. It's not him. It's not—*

I pulled away, rushing back towards dark-skinned elder Yvonne, knowing that she was not my pale, forever-young mother, but still craving a woman's touch all the same. I heard him yelling after me, asking what he did wrong—and then cursing when he remembered. But it was too late. I wanted to explain so bad, but I was afraid that he wouldn't love me anymore—that sometimes I saw Jacques's eyes in his face. I tucked my shaking head into Yvonne's neck but bit my lip, refusing to breathe in her potent scent. She raised her strong-yet-frail arms, hugging me to her.

"I smell him on you," she whispered. "I understand. It's okay... Shhh, don't cry...It's okay."

I was so dirty.

So damn dirty.

CHAPTER TWO

DIE FOR YOU

The manor was drowning. Under piles of wood, ash, sky and saw dust, it struggled under the weight. So much had changed in the days that I had been gone, and yet...I adjusted the child strapped to my back. He made a content noise in his throat, clearly undisturbed. I breathed in, hoping to chase down the smoke with the smell of the countryside, but all I could taste was *ash*. I breathed out, letting my mind wander as I took brave steps towards the place that had only just started to feel like home.

No...I told myself, steeling my shoulders as I braced my hand on the gate. *Home is...more than a place. Home is....wherever I feel safe.*

Dorian touched my side. I sighed.

I'm almost home.

The foyer had changed since I'd last been to the manor. There were piles of burnt wood off to one side, warped where they'd used magic to preserve what could be salvaged before setting it aside. The stage that housed the wedding band just twenty-four hours ago now sagged as a pile of rubble. And there was a gaping wound in the front of the manor, the doors having bled the blackened red of smoke, now gray and drooping like my belly would have had I carried my son to term. And before me, laying upon the granite bar that remained unblemished, was Aiden.

I stared down at the boy swaddled in cloth. He stared up at me, his brown-gold eyes so innocent, so pure. I wanted to pick him up, to hold him to my chest, to love him. He was as much Dorian as he was me. But he hadn't been born of me. His development had been accelerated by Jacques.

I hadn't carried him in my belly. (At least, not to term.) I hadn't bonded with him. I hadn't even picked out his name. (Admittedly, Dorian had when he whisked him from the mansion, but as soon as he observed the red tint to his eyes, the dark magic seeping from his pores, the salty scent of Jacques just barely mixed in his blood, he snapped. All that love, that wonder—gone.)

Dorian stood next to me, staring down at him. He held a knife in his hand. Behind him, Yvonne and the equally dark and old-looking (although he was not as old as Yvonne) Andrew stood, glaring. Beatrice stood off in the corner, as silent as ever, with her perfect posture, making her look more mysterious and more important than she would ever be. Her red hair glistened like freshly spilled blood, the splotches on her cheeks like ripened tomatoes.

I remember the way Dorian and Yvonne huddled together, their heads bowed, their voices soft and urgent. They'd come to an agreement in around six or seven minutes and honestly, their decision broke my heart.

They'd told me that I could be the one to kill Aiden. If he'd been born of me, he would have been allowed to live—welcome, too. But Jacques's touch—his scent—was all over him. And when the boy's eyes flashed red, I was reminded that Jacques hadn't just been bluffing. He really had done something to him—had put a part of himself in the boy.

So why couldn't I do it?

"Since he's of your flesh," Dorian nodded, "I figured you should do it."

He moved to hand me the rebel-dagger. I paused as my heart thudded to a halt in my chest. A part of me was absolutely revolted by the child—but the other part of me couldn't help but wonder what could have been. Dorian pressed the knife into my hand, wrapped my fingers around it with his free hand. Then he placed his hands on my shoulders, moved me forward a step or two.

My feet dragged against the floor as I began to shake my head, whispering "No, no, no, no. I don't want to. I *can't.*"

"A piece of Jacques is in him," Dorian whispered and as if on cue, the boy's eyes flashed red again. "Somebody has to."

"Maybe he'll be good," I said, swallowing. The spit scraped against my dry throat. "Maybe he'll be different."

"But *he's* in him," Yvonne spat, shaking her head. "I was around before the Great Change. I've seen what Jacques and his family did to France. He can't be allowed to live."

"But—"

"Marve—" I turned to see that Dorian looked hurt, "—it's *him.*"

"No, he's *you.*" I moved to stand before the child. I reached out, picked him up in my hands, felt the weight of his body, felt his warmth, saw that he didn't cry but instead cooed, and smiled. "And he's me."

I'd been pregnant. I hadn't known it, but I had. Only for around a week or two. And in just a few hours, Jacques had used his scientific magic to bring that boy to full term. He looked like he was only a few hours old, his pale muted-gold skin wrinkly. He wrapped a tiny hand around a lock of my hair and tugged. His little fat fingers couldn't raise a hand to strike me, let alone bring down Amoria.

This was my son.

Dorian paused and for a second, I was happy, thinking that he thought I was right. But then his face changed as he read my face. Finally, he shook his head and said, "That isn't true."

"He's my son," I whispered. "He's *our* son."

His face twisted in apparent disgust and fear. I flinched as I placed the look—it was the same look he used to wear when he looked at me. I was suddenly reminded of Immortal panic—and *danger*. A thought hit me, which had been sitting in the back of my mind since I first saw the lad. Yvonne's power. She could see life forces, which meant—

"Why didn't you tell me?" I whispered, looking to Yvonne. "Why didn't either of you tell me I was pregnant?"

"Honestly, I didn't think you'd carry to term. You're skin and bones," Yvonne reasoned with a shrug. "I mean look at you."

"But we could have saved him. We could have delivered him before Jacques *tainted* him."

"You wouldn't have carried full term," Dorian agreed with Yvonne, shaking his head. "There was nothing to save."

"There was everything to save!"

I backed away. The boy cooed again. My back hit the wall. Hao, Yvonne, Andrew, Dorian—they all stared at me as if I'd lost my mind. But Beatrice looked contemplative. I clung to this, staring at her with wide, wild eyes.

"Beatrice, he's just a baby. Tell them!" I glanced between her and the others. "He's just a child!"

"He's a demon!" Dorian yelled.

"So's Yvonne!" I hissed, glaring between her and Dorian before glancing at Beatrice once more. "Yvonne is good to you. She's humble and kind and only wants what's best for us. Right, Beatrice? Tell them!"

"She has a point," Beatrice said, nodding.

But she didn't say what I was so desperate to hear, what his life depended on: *Give him a chance.*

"You don't understand. Jacques's family is tainted—"

"Marve, you *know* what he's capable of—"

"Not just by blood magic, but also by incest and the insanity that comes along with it—"

"The boy will be a monster—"

"He *is* a monster—"

"A beast—"

"A demon in the flesh—"

Monster. Demon. Beast…Beast. Beast. Beast.

He's still my son.

I shifted the boy to one side, grasping the knife underneath his small body. I took the blade, dragged it across my palm. Then I dragged the knife across the child's foot, ignoring his small, pain-filled, panicked cries. A demon wouldn't cry, would he?

Dorian roared in anger, throwing himself forward, but was powerless to stop me.

I quickly pressed my palm to the wound on his foot as my powers thrummed through my body. The wound glowed purple then red.

"Ego sum apud te," I whispered, sealing the bond.

I am with you.

A smile broke across my face—a crazed, victorious smile. The wounds sealed closed with one final triumphant blaze of magic. I felt the bond between Dorian and I scoot over to make room for another: the bond between my son and I. I pressed a kiss to my son's temple. The wound glowed with a purple light before sealing shut, a Mark that looked so haphazard, as if it had been cut from glass, appearing on his foot. He stared up at me with panicked eyes and quivering lips, aware that his mother had just used black magic, but unaware that it was what saved him.

"Welcome to the family, Aiden."

"Well, this is just great!" Dorian shouted with rolling eyes. "Now we're stuck with the little bastard!"

"Don't talk about him like that!" I hissed, glaring at him.

"How else am I supposed to talk about him? He dies, you die!"

"Not just that," I replied, smiling. My eyes glowed with a newfound power. "I die and so do you."

"*Fuck!*" Dorian snapped.

Yvonne stood there, her eyes blazing with pits pulled from the depths of hell. Her voiced coiled like a small, effective whip—and struck. "I always knew you'd be trouble."

Andrew reached out, wrapped his hand around her shoulder. He pulled her close, shielding her—*from me.* "You've gone and done it now!" He trembled with rage. "Now what are we supposed to do?!"

"Love him," I nodded. "Accept him as one of the Boyd family. Love and obey him as you would any other."

They all glared at me. Except Beatrice. Her eyes glazed with respect as she bowed her head in our direction. I knew that if worse came to worst, I could depend on her. I nodded, calling her forward. She reached out. I carefully placed him in her arms. Hao, who I had forgotten about, stood in a corner beneath a shaft of light, contemplative.

"Get a room ready, Beatrice. Our new addition will need his own space."

"Yes, mem."

"And Beatrice?"

She paused. "Aye?"

"Be careful."

CHAPTER THREE

TELL US

I dreamt of a boy of ten years, with skin kissed by the sun and eyes capturing the deepest rays of the light, dancing with me in a foyer. It was a dream where we were both Immortal, a dream where my skin had been pulled back to stand between death and agelessness. Dorian stood off to the side, strumming a guitar as he sang a sweet melody. I suddenly realized, even in the dream, that I had never heard him sing or play an instrument. He had woven me the most elaborate of garments, had bought me the best foods, trained me to kill even the Immortals—

But he'd never *truly* sang to me—not like that.

Why is that?

"Marve!" Dorian shook me awake the very next morning. "Wake up!"

"Mm…?" Limbs heavy, eyes groggy, I blinked up at him. "What is it?"

"We're going to hold a meeting in the Blue Room shortly."

If I nod, it'll look like I know exactly what he's talking about…

"Why the Blue Room?"

"Jacques was on my property," he said with a raised eyebrow, as if I should've already known the answer.

"Weren't you friends?"

"Oh, please. Besides him constantly trying to get in my pants and me going there to get information on you, I hardly knew the guy. He's never even been to my house. At least, not since the Great War hung over us." Dorian's face darkened. "We've deduced that Jacques wanted you to become a replacement for his long-lost love, Grant."

That's a lie, I thought back to the painting at the top of the stairs. *You knew him well.*

But then I realized that they would all know how dirty I was. "How do you all know that?"

"You talk in your sleep." He yanked the covers from my body. "Now *get up.* We don't have much time."

"You can't stop him if that's all you know." *There's so much more.* "Will I have time to tell you all of it?"

"Of course."

Finally, the strength of a goddess filling my veins, I mustered up the courage to ask: "What's the Blue Room?"

"Money doesn't just buy nice clothes and cars. People and information can be bought as well. The Blue Room is a meeting room where information is exchanged. Luckily, I was able to buy some new hacking software and got into his computer. I also hired a few of the best spies around to dig up information on your old Master. They'll find out as much as we need to know in order to bring this guy down."

I ran through my options. Going back, begging forgiveness, was *not* an option. Exposing the deepest parts of myself? Telling them everything I knew? A definite yes. Fighting back? Finally, a possibility.

"I've got to check on Aiden."

My silk robe hung from my shoulders, as defeated as I was. We quickly made our way through the halls. The gold-faceted stone statues from the hallways were no more. I had no time to look for the painting or suits of armor. But I knew that they couldn't have all been taken—not that fast. The white walls carried the narrow screams of a bludgeoning.

Great magic, it seemed, had been used to repair the manor.

I was able to deduce from the announcements over the speakers that this case was a Code White—the worst among the Boyd filing system. I stopped at the door next to our room, which sat at the top of the stairs—the door of Aiden's room.

The room held photos of Dorian in his younger years, his frame still long and skinny even in his youth. There were a few photos of the former Mr. and Mrs. Boyd, the parents and the past that Dorian had tried so hard to forget. I saw a small picture frame with the photo of my parents and I at the Southern Isles, my mother's red hair gleaming in the afternoon sun, my father's mocha skin glistening from the spray of the sea as I was hoisted in the air between them, my tan skin freckled and just a few shades darker. How different those times were, which I held no memory of, from now...how I wished to be that person again.

I calmly made my way to his blue sleigh-style crib. It had been Dorian's when he was just a baby. The boy stirred as if on cue, blinking up at me as he smiled.

I grinned down at him. Then scooped him up in one hand, holding him to my chest, while reaching out to grab a bottle in the mini fridge in his room with the other. I glanced to the corner, seeing Beatrice sitting there, her eyes watching me carefully. I fed the boy silently, wrapping him in a veil of magic as I did so. My son, Aiden, glowed a bright, crimson-red—the color of his magic. My own body glowed a faint violet, pulsating as his heart beat in tangent with mine.

"I just changed him, mem," Beatrice said, coming to stand behind me.

"Thank you, Beatrice."

As he drank, I realized that he must not have needed a soul to feed on like Jacques—milk would do, for now.

My fingers skimmed the jagged, red wound on my belly, which was hot and pulsed with blood at my touch. I didn't remember Jacques taking him from me. There seemed to be no time. But then again, between us coming back to the manor and them deciding what to do with Aiden, Dorian said that it had been three days. It had not felt like days—years, maybe, but not in a time-spatial way, but a mental one. They hadn't wanted to tell me for some odd reason, and I honestly hadn't wanted to know more, but now I wondered why time had flown past without me, magic flowing through Aiden, power coursing through Jacques, anxiety through Dorian...yet no peace for me.

"Rhea is in the room down the hall from yours. She hasn't left it since she got back. She told me to tell you something before I left her."

I sighed. I couldn't handle another betrayal from her. Dorian had trusted her with our lives, telling her our location when we had no one to lean on. And she'd handed me over to Jacques, had even tried to kill Dorian. But she had done it to save Gifted lives.

As much as I desired, I couldn't fault her for that.

"She told me to tell you that she's sorry."

CRASH!

I set down Aiden before rushing out into the hall.

Rhea stood at the bottom of the stairs, her arm thrown around the neck of one of Dorian's staff. In that hand was a gleaming blade, one like my many daggers, runes etched into its hilt. Her teeth were bore in an angry snarl—no, not just angry; something sharper, darker, *hungrier*—the thirst for the blood of not just cushion-footed

Immortals, but mine and my companion's as well. Her curly brown hair hanging around her face in clumps, her golden eyes darting around the room in wild paranoia.

Four other staff members circled her, their eyes caught up in her display, watching her as if they were watching a jaguar stalk through the grass and they themselves were merely prey.

"*Back!*" she cried in Espanzan, her eyes spinning around the room. "*Back, I say!*"

I saw Alena sneaking up behind her.

Alena was one of our staff, someone that worked closely with Beatrice. She was of Elven descent, and like her kin, she moved quietly like the night. She needed no weapon as her hands rose. Magic pulsated around her body and her brown eyes flickered between a dirt-brown, then to a deep chestnut and finally to a light hazel-brown, each color lingering longer than the last.

Magik, the hormone that gave us the ability to use our powers, which was made in a pouch connected to our intestines, furled and unfurled in my stomach, restless and uneasy at the feeling of so much tension in the room. My own magic crawled from my stomach and down my arm like a furry caterpillar. I raised a hand, sending my own pulse through the room. Alena's head snapped up, staring at me for confirmation. I folded my fingers in, leaving one raised.

I calmly lifted my voice. "Rhea?"

Rhea's eyes traced up the balcony to land on me. She saw my finger lifted—and *smiled*. It was a cruel, barren smile, as if she were smug to see that I still held some allegiance to the organization that had betrayed me by killing my parents and attempting to make me a demon's sacrifice: the Rebellion. But I smirked back at her to say, *You've got it all wrong. I hold no allegiance to the Rebellion. It's to you. To my family. To the Gifted.*

"Nothing comes between magic, eh, Marve?" she said, dropping the smile. "You know that we will never be free."

I said to her what I would say to my mother every day before I left for school. I said to her what my father would say when he kissed my mother on the cheek before he left for work. I said to her what a soldier of God would say to their dying comrade, for we were all dying inside: *"Peace be unto you,"* I said in Fabic, the mixture of French and Arabic that I had been taught at a young age but had nearly forgotten.

For we were all children of the Creator.

Bang!

The tranquilizer dart sunk into the soft flesh in the back of her neck. I saw the look of anger—no, *rage*—and betrayal on her face as she fell forward. Crazy how she tried to kill me, but I have her knocked out and *she* is the one who looks betrayed.

Alena rushed forward to catch her.

"Hao?"

Hao lowered the gun. He came up to stand beneath me in the foyer, a floor below. "Next time, she won't be so lucky."

I closed my eyes as the cries of my son reached my ears. "I know…"

"Ma'am?" I felt a hand shaking my shoulder. "Ma'am!"

"I'm fine, dammit! I'm fine!" I shook my head, opening my eyes and blowing out a breath. I craned my neck back, titling my head up so that I wouldn't have to see my friend's body on the floor. "Take her."

"Take her where, ma'am?" Hao whispered dutifully.

"Take her to the safehouse in Maeora—no, to the Southern Isles! Make sure she makes it there *alive.* I want confirmation once you reach it. Do I make myself clear?"

"Crystal, ma'am."

I heard him move down the stairs. I heard the clatter on the blade as it was kicked away from her and skittered across the marble floor. I rushed to the nearest trashcan and wretched. I felt two hands touch the back of my neck, checking to see how warm it was. I leaned against the wall, my head spinning, my eyes unyielding, refusing to show me a vision that I could handle because all I could see in my head, before my face, was her smirk, hear her voice coiling in my ears, whispering, *"I own you."*

How long would I be tied up in the Rebellion's sinister plans?

How long would I remain a slave?

"Baby?"

"Mm?"

"Are you okay?" I felt his lips press to the back of my neck. "Can I get you anything?"

"I'm fine."

"Beatrice!" he called. I heard the other woman enter the room. "Beatrice, can you bring us some water?"

"I'm fine," I protested.

"Now!"

Then my head began to ache again, my vision swimming. I leaned against the wall. I felt the water being pushed into my hands, felt the glass against my lips, and I wanted to scream. I took in a gulp, felt my stomach clench, felt my throat contract as it threatened to squeeze out the food from yesterday and *I wanted to die.* But then I felt a small body being pushed against my chest, felt a tiny hand tugging at my hair, felt the drool dribble down my shirtfront and I knew that *dying was not an option.*

"Not this again!" Dorian sighed.

"Please, don't," I whispered. "Try to at least tolerate him...." I opened my eyes to stare at him, hoping he could see the hurt that he caused by hating our child. He looked embarrassed to say the least. "Whether Jacques tampered with his blood or not, this is our son. He has both of our blood. Why isn't that good enough for you?"

"Why is Jacques's blood all that's important to you?" he hissed back.

"It's *not*! He's *my* son! He's *your* son!" I pressed my nose to Aiden's head, breathing in the soft bubbles-and-baby-powder-smell of the child. "I love him. Why can't that be enough?"

"But—"

"Look into his eyes. He's suffering. Don't let him grow up hating himself the way your parents left you."

I heard Dorian make a strangled noise, but I didn't look at him because I didn't want to see *his* hurt. I was too focused on the pain of my son. I pressed a kiss to Aiden's forehead. When I did look at Dorian, he glared at Aiden. I knew that he hated Aiden, hated the part of me that loved him, but didn't understand that he now hated *all* of me, because all I had for my son was love.

I loved him with everything I had because he was real and he was mine. And in a way, I belonged to him. All mother's belonged to their children, but the same was not true, it seemed, for their fathers.

"Marve—"

"Don't say it's not the same," I ground between all the pain. "It totally is."

"No." He shook his head. "It's not."

"Hold him for me?" I asked, hoping that would mend things.

We made the exchange. Aiden blinked up at him, his eyes mystified and full of wonder. I heard an announcement come over the speaker again. But I sat there, watching them. It was not that Dorian did not have the capacity to love his own son—he did. It was because his heart was moved so much by his love for me that he automatically hated anything that could hurt me.

I moved to sit down in the chair that Beatrice was in. Beatrice returned, pushing a glass into my shaking hand. I reached down, clutching my stomach through my shirt as I bent. Beatrice reached out, her brow furrowed, staring at me.

"You didn't deliver him?" she asked although we all knew the answer.

"No..."

She reached out and lifted my shirt. She gasped. I glanced down. Blood ran down my side, along with a yellowish-brown puss. I winced. It hurt to breathe.

"Lord Dorian!" she cried.

He moved closer. He held Aiden under his arm carelessly. I wanted to glare but cried out instead. It frigging *hurt!*

"What happened?"

"Jacques," I whimpered.

My magic flared around in my system, trying to keep me from going into shock. It had never been so volatile, so reactive. This would normally be great news, but I didn't know what it meant. I knew that Jacques hadn't healed or at least dressed the wound for the same reason he raped me on what was supposed to be my wedding night—to take whatever he could from me, to hurt me. Dorian pulled out a pen and kneeled next to me. His hand hovered over the tender area but did not touch it.

"It'll be okay, baby," he said, reaching up to touch my face.

Aiden squirmed in his arm. Beatrice saw my look, rolled her eyes, and maneuvered the child out of his arm. He didn't even notice. She bounced him on her hip gently, touching his soft curls and murmuring over him. She would make a great mother.

Dorian drew a healing rune on my side. Heat flared through my skin, burning its way into my body—burning, burning, burning with no sign of stopping. Dorian frowned as a scream ripped from my throat but made no other moves to help me. Aiden began to cry. I grit my teeth, muffling the sound, but he wailed, reaching out his feeble little hands out to me, his eyes flashing red, wanting to help but knowing how to help other than to let his demonic side take over.

And suddenly the pain stopped. I sighed, sagging back into the rocking chair. Almost hesitantly, touched the spot. It had closed. I lifted my shirt back up, glancing down to see a faint, thin, pink scar where the opening had been.

Amazing!

"Thank you," I frowned, not forgetting how he treated Aiden.

Dorian glanced around skittishly, obviously noting my sour mood.

"What about the Blue Room, mem?" Beatrice whispered, watching us.

"You're right. We need to make an environment safe for the boy. That means taking out Jacques." He ran a hand through my hair when I sighed, a tear leaking from my eye. "I know that means we have to delve into your past. I know that we have to dredge up memories that pain you. But wouldn't you rather deal with a little pain now—" his eyes glimmered like a safe haven in the distance "—and have him never hurt you again?"

I closed my eyes. "I want to be remembered. I don't want him to wipe away the thought of me just because he's grown tired of me. I can't bear it—"

"Jacques can't wipe you away. You know what I'll always remember about you?"

I sniffled. "What?"

He leaned down and pressed his lips to my trembling body, right over my jugular. My pulse jumped at the action. Even beneath the trauma, my body remembered him.

"I remember how you looked at me when you walked down the aisle." His hand brushed my brows. "Your eyes were like two little green stars hurtling across space." His fingers touched my lips. "Your smile was like seafoam, washing across your sandy skin." His hand dropped to my heart. "I remember this, beating wildly, like the hooves of horses thundering across the finish line. Most of all, I remember..." His eyes fluttered shut as his nostrils flared. "I remember the way you felt beneath me, the way your legs parted for me, the way you cradled me, like you'd never let me go, how warm and…*wet* you felt, just for me. And the way you smelled…like roses touched by summer rain."

I swallowed. My body blossomed at the thought. But then I saw Jacques in my mind's eye, buried between my legs, and I was drowning. My breath left me in small hiccups and tears silently leaked from my eyes. I felt Dorian's fingers on my face, sweeping away the tears.

"That's gone now, isn't it?" he whispered.

I stifled a whimper. "I'm sorry."

"It's okay."

But it wasn't. I was his wife. And I couldn't give him what he needed. The unspoken words tethered between us, like a straining rope. *What good was I?*

"Please don't leave." I sighed when he moved to stand. "I'll be good. I promise. Don't go."

His face was blank, but his eyes were hesitant, if not rebellious. And suddenly I knew. Megumi had been right. That was what he wanted me for. It always had been. And now that I couldn't supply it, I was nothing.

He wouldn't force me, thank the Goddess, but he wouldn't touch me anymore, until I could tell him that I wanted to or not.

"I love you," I whispered.

"I know." He shook his head. "Let's just get to the Blue Room. We'll talk more later."

I curled up into a ball, curling in on myself and collapsing. Beatrice set down Aiden before coming to me, touching my cheeks. She peered up at me.

"Are you all right, mem?"

"I'm fine. It's just…" I shook my head and laughed bitterly. "I really thought that I was different."

"You are. These things....we as women never truly understand, do we?"

Was the Dorian that I'd come to know these past six or seven months a lie?

Was I really that discardable to him?

I thought about to the cut on his neck, how the demon blood sunk deeper as I struggled to draw the healing rune properly, failing time and time again.

What was the point in saving him if I was still going to lose him?

CHAPTER FOUR

THE BLUE ROOM

The Blue Room was on the opposite end of the church, which was at the end of the hall up the stairs of the landing. There wasn't much to in—just a long metal table, fifty chairs filled with staff members, and two chairs at the head of the room. Dorian sat at the head of the table. I took my seat his side. My husband spun around in his chair to face a projector screen that was slowly being lowered. I eyed the cobalt blue walls and understood that at least one thing had lived up to its promise.

"Yvonne has brought it to my attention that it would be in both Marve's and my own best interest to *disappear* for a while." A single image dotted with hundreds of tiny red dots appeared on the screen: a map of the world. "These are all of the safe houses that I own across the globe."

Holy shit! I thought, staring at the screen but trying not to appear *too* impressed. *Jacques owns sixteen properties altogether. I knew that Dorian was richer than him, but he practically owns properties on the entire globe! I know that there are worst beasts in Europe—man-eating Titans and blood-sucking demons mostly, along with the Ghouls in Japan, but if he was able to secure this much space, this means that he was able to protect these properties at some point, and probably still can...*

Just how far does his power reach...?!

"Why are you showing me this?" I asked.

"I want you to pick one of these." He said, gazing first at me then at Yvonne and Andrew. I didn't miss the tension in his voice, or the condescending looks that the Baxter couple threw at my back. I understood the looks—he was going to call out the danger I'd put us all in—and they had clearly discussed this. But it didn't mean that being viewed as a selfish, parasitic leech didn't hurt any less. "I have Rhea in a temporary holding in the Southern Isles, but I want you to also pick a permanent place for Rhea since you took it upon yourself to save her in the first place, Marve."

Rhea. The leader of the Rebellion. The woman that had accidentally murdered me just days ago and only saw my resurrection as another cash grab—and chance at redemption with her allyship with Jacques, which her aunt (Valentina) had worked so hard to secure. I'd once thought that we were best friends, but it was obvious that she never really liked me.

And my desperate clutching at the salvageable parts of our bond was clearly in vain, considering that I had to knock her out to get her to comply with my wishes.

"Friends are supposed to keep each other safe," I affirmed.

"I guess," Dorian said with a shrug.

How, I pessimistically wondered, *can he discard her so easily? Will he throw me away one day? Please, Kalysma. I can't take it.*

"Now, Europe is inhabitable. Africa is good and so are the Americas. Hawaii is mostly submerged in water but there are parts where people live. Same with the Bahamas. For Rhea, you—"

"Have some consideration for the important things," said Yvonne as she straightened in her seat. "We can't worry about her. She isn't a priority. The only ones that matter is family."

I smiled softly at her words.

So, I thought, *I still matter, at least a little.*

"I couldn't agree with you more," he said, reaching out and skimming his fingers over my hand.

I looked into his eyes and saw the same rage in Rhea's eyes now in his. He didn't hate her yet, they had too much history, but he was damn sure close. I think that her killing me had ruined some part of their relationship. He didn't see her the same way. I thought of the huge hole in the side of the manor and shuddered.

The things we are capable of...

"You're expecting me to just drop everything and leave?" At his nod, I narrowed my eyes. "What about Aiden?"

He ignored my question. "You know, we never got to have a honeymoon after we got married."

He was trying to make light of a dark situation.

"That was four days ago."

"Doesn't feel like it," he irascibly replied.

He had a point, but it was a futile effort.

"Screw the honeymoon! This is serious!"

"I am being serious!" Dorian threw up his hands. "Because of that—that *monster*—we lost a lot of quality time, time that we can now make up."

"Your priorities are all out of order." I frowned as I glanced at the screen. "But I'd be lying if I said that we don't need to hide."

"I have a safe house is in Botswana."

"So?"

"Is that somewhere that you would be interested in going?"

I didn't really care so I shrugged. I felt a tiny pulse of electricity. I pulled out my phone and glanced down at it.

She's safe.

Something he said before caught up with me. "What do you mean, permanent location?"

"I'm forcing Rhea to retire," he admitted, frowning. "She's too unhinged to run the Rebellion the way that I see fit."

"She's Valentina's niece—ya know, the one who actually *ran* the Rebellion? The woman who fought to free Gifted slaves at any cost? The woman that posed in hiding as a slave to rescue me?"

"I own over half of the Rebellion's shares. Without me, they have no weapons, no food, no connections. I'm sure they'll be more than happy to find a new leader if I say so. Andrew..." he stared at me as Andrew picked up the phone, his eyes gone of magic or fire or anything that I once loved—just steel and flint, sparking unsympathetic embers that would grow into an oppressor's flames.

"Consider it done."

I couldn't help wonder if *I* would be next.

"Do you have any guards in the Southern Isles?" I asked as I turned to look at Dorian.

"Yes."

"I need you to send some there."

Dorian raised an eyebrow. "Why?"

"I need you to protect Rhea in case—"

He looked as if he wanted to argue about that, too, but at the serious look on my face, he glanced at Yvonne before giving me a brief nod.

"There's one more thing that you forgot." I turned to glance at Yvonne and Andrew, who held each other's hands across the table. "Where are Yvonne and Andrew going to be staying?"

"I didn't forget them." Dorian said, sharing a look with Yvonne and Andrew. "They and the rest of the staff have agreed to stay here in case Jacques returns."

"What?" I stood, surprising not only myself but the other people in the room. "It's too dangerous!"

"Marve—"

"No!" I whirled on Yvonne, who was the one who'd spoken last. "You don't stand a chance against him even with your Gift of sensing life forces. You're going to need something stronger. Do you have a Gift, Andrew?"

The old man shook his head.

My mind was running a mile a minute. I had to keep my new family safe. I hadn't had them long but with Mar and Da gone, they were all I had!

"The only thing your Gift will do is possibly help you figure out if he's hiding somewhere. That's it." I whirled on Dorian. "How could you make such a stupid decision? Tell her to go the Southern Isles! She has a better chance guarding Rhea than she does guarding the manor!"

"There won't be enough room at the safe house where Rhea is going."

No...

"Then send her to Sidra or Espanza—or even Libra, for that matter!" I nodded vehemently. "Yes...Send her there—and Aiden, too!"

"Beatrice is going to go with Aiden to Maeora so that she'll know when it's safe to return." Dorian glanced at Andrew. "I need the Baxters to hold down the fort while we're away. They're the only ones who know how to manage my manor without running it into the ground. They have to stay."

All over again...

I'm going to be alone...

All over again...!

"Do I have any say in this?"

He paused for a moment, then looked sure of himself as he honestly said, "No."

I hated being told what to do. The last man that said he knew what was best for me beat me any time I deviated from his plans. Unlike my relationship with Dorian, Jacques and I were toxic together. I'd already seen a darker side of Dorian. Were we headed down the same path?

"You know sometimes it's hard to tell whether you're a genius or an idiot," I muttered, rolling my eyes.

"Insulting me isn't going to change anything, Mrs. Boyd," Dorian said, narrowing his eyes.

"You're not asking me," I said, rising from my chair, "because you've already made up your mind."

"I know what's best."

"Whatever. Just let me say goodbye to my son before we go."

I walked up to the nursery quickly. There my golden son lay in his crib, snoring softly. I lifted him from the sleigh-style crib and held him. He suddenly stirred and blinked at me, his eyes black with flecks of brown and gold, just like his father's.

"I hope your head doesn't turn out as thick as your father's."

Aiden blinked, yawned and slowly drifted back to sleep. I turned to see Beatrice standing in the doorway. My hands shook as I passed my son off and watched as she took him away. It wasn't fair. I'd only held him all of two times and he was already gone?

I was going to kill Dorian if I never saw him again.

*   *   *

The plush leather seats and sweeping chromatic lines of the jet had not changed since the last time we'd been seated in it. Actually, hardly anything had—except—

Dorian watched me watch him, his lines euphoric and disastrous. How had I expected us to last? Why had I enabled us to make it this far when we were clearly destined to fail?

No, his eyes seemed to say. *We can fix us. We just started....*

The last time we'd sat in this jet, I'd thought that we would remain estranged until the end of our days. And it hadn't occurred to me that the jet may have belonged to Dorian, just as it never occurred to me that I may have been in lust with him. All I felt back then was anger—anger and a deep, tremoring sadness.

And as I looked at the windows at the passing Walls and changing landscapes, I wondered why I didn't feel that now. Now I felt a deep resolve, as if I were marching to the courtyard to be beheaded, holding what *he* craved high and proud. Only the killing blow was the inevitable death of both myself and my son, which meant that I was not the monster that he wished of me. I watched Dorian sitting across from me, realizing somewhat ironically that he was the only one that had never wanted me to be the beast that the Immortal's saw.

But now that I had time to step back and look clearly, I realized that I didn't want what he wanted, either. I didn't want to sleep, eat, grow fat, to never fight again. I just wanted to fight for what *I* deemed necessary. Because it wasn't the battles that wore me out—it was that I never took away anything from them for myself.

When I fought Dorian, I got familiarity. When I fought Jacques, I got pain. When I fought bullies as a child, I got the ability to appear strong. When I fought Gifted in the arena, I got...nothing. And fighting this war, I would kill many, *many* Gifted...Why would I want that?

This would touch me whether we wanted it to or not and the thought that I could not stop it?

Terrifying.

But also...

Invigorating.

Because if I knew one thing, it was that in the most tumulus of days, the Immortals were made. And even if I was depressed, a lot of my problems would be solved if I could live forever. Then, I wouldn't need to fear facing Jacques. Because he wouldn't have anything to take from me—not my body, my light or my purity, which were, essentially, the same.

Because I now knew—it wasn't my soul he wanted. It was the very essence, the idea of *life* that I contained. Fear was a very real emotion. Love was a very real feeling. And he possessed neither of those, which I held in plenty.

I'd begun to understand why the man who had everything craved I, who had *significantly* less…at least, monetarily speaking.

Just because some live forever, does not mean they have in plenty.

I leaned back in my seat. Dorian sat across from me, my feet in his lap. The smell of the air reminded me of my father, who always smelled like pine and the scent that lingered after a rainy day. The private jet cut through the air like butter and even a light rain shower couldn't disturb us. Currently, Dorian was giving me a foot rub as he tried to convert me to his thought process.

"Beatrice can protect him."

"What the hell?! That's like your thousandth time saying that! Beatrice is strong but I—you know, Aiden's *mother*—I am *still* worried…" The electricity raised around my body like a shield. "How can she protect my son better than I can?"

"Masters are able to track runaway slaves up to a point." He held up a hand when I moved to protest. "I've been around slave-owning Immortals all my life, so I know what I'm talking about. When you use your magic, you emit something akin to a beacon. You're the biggest danger to him right now." My heart thudded in my chest, but Dorian was oblivious as he continued. "And trust me—Beatrice is stronger than you think. She'll lay low but if she needs to, she can fight back. That's what makes Aiden so safe with her. She won't draw the attention of your former Master or any magic-user that he may have hired to help him."

"He would never hire anyone. He likes to do things himself."

"I'm counting on that. I know that this is all a bit overwhelming, but this really is the safest way." Dorian took my hand. "Don't you trust me?"

His hands...used to feel so warm...so safe. These arms wrapped around me like towers, shielding me from the glassy sky. Now...he towers over me...

These psychotic, convoluted plans. They make no sense. In just a night, he's gone from careful, doting, safe...to dogmatic, short-tempered and boundless. I don't understand what could have changed. Was it because I finally gave him my last bit of autonomy? Or is it something else?

Kalysma, if you can hear me—PLEASE HELP ME.

An image took me, of Dorian's neck swelling with black blood, his eyes crazed and volatile, as he lay in a hospital bed. But I didn't know what it meant.

I could not find words for the turmoil that I was feeling. On one hand, I wanted to believe that he knew what he was doing and had everything under control. But I also knew that people had a habit of underestimating both me and my former master. People underestimated me because I didn't look like much of a threat. People had a habit of underestimating Jacques because they had no idea just how petty and possessive he could be. Most of them had already forgotten his two-hundred-year reign of Europe and his hundred-year reign of the Land of the Three.

Despite this, I knew that deep down, I did trust Dorian—

Otherwise, I would have taken Aiden and ran.

I nodded then turned to look at the television above his head. One reporter was giving statics on the correlation of workers, their emotional states and their productiveness. Another spoke of diamond mines in Africa. Others talked of the stock markets and the few that had hardly been affected when it crashed.

Was that our fate? Would we crash and burn like the economy or was this just another rough spot that would strengthen us when we emerged from it? Dorian looked into my eyes, saw the doubt there, and immediately quelled it.

"Marve," Dorian took my hand, "we're like diamonds."

I stared at him. He didn't look any crazier than usual.

Maybe it was a metaphor.

But I didn't want metaphors right now. I wanted my son. And my best friend. And the rest of my new family...Tiara's face echoed in my mind, her brown eyes glittering in happiness as she scarfed down the pastry I'd given her—the last good thing that I'd done for her.

A tear of frustration rolled down my face. I balled up my fists in my hands, refusing to outright sob in front of him. He could exploit my weakness.

To distract myself, I asked him what he meant about the diamonds.

"You may not agree with me or be happy with my decisions but I'm doing what I think is best for us." He gave me a sudden grin. "And just like diamonds, we only get stronger under pressure."

CHAPTER FIVE

OUR FIRST REAL FIGHT

"Welcome, welcome! Welcome to Gaborone!" The tan man in the suit turned and said something to a dark-skinned teenager behind him in a language I didn't recognize; in response, the ragged boy grabbed our bags and scurried towards the car that Dorian had flown here. "We are pleased that the Boyd family has joined us yet again."

"Hello." Dorian reached out and shook his hand. "It's good to see you again, John."

"Where are your mother and father, Mr. Boyd?" asked John. "It has been a long while since I have heard from them."

Dorian's eyes flashed. "Dead, I'm afraid."

"You have my condolences, sir."

"Trust me when I say that it's fine," Dorian muttered with a bitter laugh.

I knew that civil rights for Mortals had a grinded to a halt once the Gifted emerged. But I didn't expect to see the young boy cowering as the white man pointed and shouted orders. I wondered what it would be like had there been a liberator for this world. Would people like John burn in a ceaseless fire? Would people like the boy be swathed in robes, diamonds around his neck, hailed as a king?

"Can we go now?"

Dorian led me towards the car. The teenager who loaded the bags into the car stood in total silence, his face directed at the ground. Only when I looked between him and the man that greeted us did I realize that the second was the older one's slave.

"How long have you been in John's service?"

The boy cocked his head at me. I gestured between him and the other man. Then I gave him a smile. He shook his head and his eyes conveyed a message that I did not understand. I reached out and he scurried away as if I carried a sickness that he did not want.

"What is your name?"

My skin prickled. At first, I thought I was just uncomfortable— but as I concentrated on the feeling, I realized that it was electricity. There was a massive energy source nearby.

My eyes glowed as I blinked back at the boy, willing him to speak to me. He swallowed as his eyes glazed over and I could see my glowing body in them, my red hair sticking up around my head like a halo.

"My name...?" His accent was thick and harsh, unlike John's smooth manner of speaking. "My name is—"

The boy suddenly crumpled to the ground. John stood over him, his face twisted in a snarl and his foot raised. He began kicking the boy.

"How many times must I tell you not to speak?" he grunted between kicks.

My hand flew out. My electricity crackled down my arm and circled my fingertips like a seagull, waiting for one thought, one command to obliterate him. Dorian grabbed my hand and pulled it down before I could launch the attack. I twisted to glare at him, my mouth morphing into an angry sneer. Dorian's eyes pled for a type of sanity that I could not understand.

"You don't understand." Dorian shook his head slowly at me. "Things are different in Africa than they are in our lands."

"He's going to kill him! I don't care if we are seen as property. Beating that boy when I asked him a question is—"

"He isn't property!" Dorian gave a harsh laugh, his golden skin gleaming in the sun. "He's an employee of Gaborone Transportation. The white guy is his boss."

"Then why is he treating him like that?"

"I told you—things are different here."

We got into the car. I wished that I could be more like Immortals—indifferent to another's pain—but instead I was sensitive to the misfortune of all, especially my own. John knocked on the window. The driver took off, not once uttering a word. When I turned around and looked out the window, the nameless boy was still on the ground. The farther away we got, the smaller he appeared.

I didn't see him get back up.

*   *   *

The safe house looked just like I'd imagined it, just nicer. It was not only painted pale purple, (don't remind me that those were the same colors of a certain mistress's home) but its three stories rose into the sky like a deadly flower ready to release its toxins. The windows were open like petals that were eager to soak up the sun. I could also see that around it, guards were stationed, their boots sunken into the ground like the roots of an African violet. I knew that it was far from delicate.

An electrical field was generated around the house. I could feel it from a mile away but hadn't realized the magnitude of its power until we were about eight houses away. Since it was rare to witness such a large electrical field outside of a lightning storm, I absorbed some of the electricity once we were close enough, kind of like a human battery. An alarm immediately went off and I heard Dorian curse. He turned to the driver, barked something and leaned back as the car lurched forward.

When we reached the house, I got out of the car, my head bowed against the hot African sun. Dorian rose out of the car like he wanted everyone to know who was in charge. He whistled to a guard. The other man bowed and took our bags from the car. Once everything was inside, Dorian took me by the hand and led me into his abode.

"My second home," he said, gesturing to Africa as a whole.

I went upstairs and changed into orange floral pants, a white top and an orange jacket with a black swirl on the back. Then I splayed my hands in front of me and watched as electricity danced across my tan fingertips. I felt reenergized from the charge, ready to conquer anything. But when I suddenly recalled the sight of that boy crumpling to the ground, I was pissed off.

The electricity coursed through my veins and set me aflame, igniting my rage. I found that it was easier to think and control myself. I was going to have to talk to Dorian about the act of "discipline" that seemed to run rampant when men with power stood over men without it.

Don't you want to be strong? Jacques's voice hissed in my ear. *Don't you want to live?*

Just like that Botswanan boy, I'd been kicked while down and had no chance of continuing freely while my oppressor was alive. *I have to conquer him!,* I thought.

I'd heard stories of magic residing in the wilderness of Africa, making the trees stand tall and departed sprits stay not-so-departed. Magic could be considered either a gift or a curse depending on why it was given. If I helped someone, that made me a good person, right? And if I was a good person, then I would somehow come across the power that I needed to protect myself and the ones that I loved.

I was sure of it.

I made it down the stairs just as Dorian finished up with a call. He turned and when he saw me, ran towards me before picking me up and spinning me in a wide circle. When he set me down, I saw the largest grin on his face that he'd had since our jet touched down at the small airport here.

"Guess what just happened!"

"Tell me!"

"This might come as a shock to you, but I have decided to expand my horizons." Dorian grinned like a child with a mouthful of candy. "The big surprise is that I just bought a few diamond mines!"

"Diamond mines?"

"I mean, I'm already rich but this?" He rubbed his hands together. "This will make me an insane amount of money!"

"You should hold a press conference to tell everyone the good news." I trailed my hand over the couch as I thought of a way to sneak in my idea. "While you're at it, you should also try to bring some awareness to the mistreatment of black people here in Botswana."

"Why would I do that?"

"Well, since you're so influential, you should use that power to do something good." I thought of the reports I watched on the flight here. "People are dying in those mines! But if you help them, this could benefit you." I was relieved when he asked how it was beneficial instead of completely shutting me down. "Studies show that happy, healthy workers are more productive at their jobs."

"You have a point. Still, fear has proven to be a good source of management in Jacques's endeavors. I mean, look how much you miss him. I think he had the right idea. Maybe fear is the only way to obtain what you want. After all, people respect those that treat them well, but they bow to those they fear."

Something had changed him. Getting beaten by Jacques had warped his mind, and I don't think that it was the magic of healing either. I believe that fear had made him strive for the wrong kind of power. How to change him back...How to make him see that the loving man that I'd fallen for was not weak but a whole new kind of power.

"Kindness is not weakness. Compassion is not a fault. You're the bravest, strongest, sexiest man I've ever met."

"Oh, don't fuck with me, Marve! You love getting treated like shit. I see that now." He grabbed me, dragging me forward dispassionately. "And I always give my women what they want."

Smack!

My breath came out raggedly. I glared at him.

How could he say such a thing? How could he degrade me so easily?

He shook his head, the maddened gleam fleeing his eyes in mere seconds.

"You're right." He touched his cheek. "What am I saying? What am I *thinking*? I'm sorry, babe." He planted a kiss on my head. "I'm so, so sorry."

"Well, how do you plan to manage them?"

"I could just leave things the way they are." He seemed proud of himself. "That way I'm not contributing to the problem!"

Like I said before: was he a genius or was I conversing with a total dunce?

"By standing by and doing nothing, you're just as guilty. You need to help these people! If you won't fight to fix it, then you are part of the problem. A revolution is just what this country needs!"

He paused, thinking. I could see the story in his eyes. He was tired of gaining power the old way. He wanted a faster route. But I knew him, saw the good in him.

I wouldn't let this sickness rot him from the inside out. It was a cancer. I had to cut it out.

"Starting a rebellion would only create more chaos. The people here know their place. I think that's how they all prefer it."

"You only like it because it benefits you but, in all honesty, you're just as racist as the people that stand guard in those diamond mines—the mines that you now own." I took a step back. "Helping these people stand up for their rights isn't chaos—it's unification. Show them that they're worth just as much as anyone else. Show them that—"

"You just don't get it!" His face twisted into a vicious snarl. "It's not that easy!"

"Then tell me what would make it easier! How can I help you? What can I say?"

He moved to walk past me.

"I don't have to listen to this." His eyes fixed on mine. "Be honest—you just think that I'm obligated to help because I'm black."

That was far from it. Dorian called Africa a second home. Wasn't he obliged to help his people?

"I want you to help because…because…"

"Just so you know, it's just like this with the Mortals back home, too. What you don't seem to understand is that there will always need to be a hierarchy. I can't change that. *You* can't change that. It's the way of man."

"We're not *people*. We're Gifted!"

42

"And they're not! They are a part of nature! What would you have me do—kill everyone who didn't submit to your twisted idea of justice!"

"No! I don't know. But if we offer everyone something to replace it, like a bartering system—"

"That's what money is!"

"No, it isn't! If everyone contributed equally, gave what they had—"

"That's communism! I've been to Jacques's Europe. It doesn't work!"

"That's because," I huffed, "we didn't have good people running it. If everyone was good, the world could be a large eutopia!" My eyes were wide, damn near childlike, as I stared at him. "Why can't you see that?"

"I hate to break it to you, but no one is inherently good. Everyone wants something from someone. No one would just give up their power because it was the right thing to do! God, I thought you understood that now!"

"I understand..." I whispered. "I understand that you are just as wicked as John and Jacques. I understand that you are every bit your parents no matter how much you've tried to make amends for their wrongdoings—"

"I am *nothing* like them! I'm a good guy!"

"You're trash!" I wanted to cry. "You're not a good guy. You just don't want to look as bad as those people in the south. But you are every much a racist Immortal as anyone else. It's just that you have different methods. *But* there's still a *system* to it!"

"I don't enslave anyone!"

"But have you really set them free?" I whispered. A single tear leaked down my cheek as I realized just how much power and influence he had over me. "Have you really let us go?"

"I've given you *everything*."

"And I am *so* grateful. Really, I am. But I can't be with someone that doesn't want the best for everyone. Saving me doesn't redeem you. Saving Megumi doesn't redeem you. Loving us as much as you choose doesn't redeem you. If you have so much power and wealth, why haven't you stopped the war? Why haven't you set everyone free?"

"It's not that simple!"

"Yet you made the Rebellion?"

"It's not…it's not that simple, babe…really, you don't understand at all."

"If I killed myself, would you take action then? Would you stop the war then?"

"What gave you the idea that *I* could stop the war?"

"I dunno. But your powers must be good for something. You must have the power to change something or else you wouldn't be okay with everything staying the same."

"That makes no *fucking* sense! You literally sound so *fucking crazy!* You sound like a fucking psycho! You're talking in circles! Megumi, don't you understand that I—"

"Megumi?!"

"I mean, Marve. Sorry. I said Megumi because you sound just like—"

"No."

"—I didn't mean it like that! God, you make me fucking crazy. I fucking love you. I'd hide us away from the world. Isn't that enough?"

"I don't want to hide from the world."

I want the world, a voice said, appearing more like what I'd always imagined Kalysma sounding like rather than myself.

"You know, you sound like an old friend of mine."

"Don't you dare. You don't fucking know him! You don't fucking know us! You don't know our life, our history—"

"You sound like Grant!" he hissed, tapping his temple.

I recoiled. "No, I don't. I don't even know Grant."

"Yes, you do. That's that peace and love bullshit he was always on. Of course, he was also on that hippie, 'fuck who we want,' shit too. And you see how that turned out for him."

"You know who you sound like?" I hissed.

He glared into my eyes, his eyes glowing, tints of red swimming in their depths.

"Who?"

I turned and stormed out the house.

Dorian turned, screaming after me: "Who?! Who do I sound like?! Marve? Who?!"

But I didn't want to say it out loud.

This was all too real.

CHAPTER SIX

ACCEPT ME

I do not know what I expected to find—a village, not a city, perhaps? Maybe an extension of what I found in the Mortal village of Sidra—women rounded with overdue pregnancy, teenagers chomping at the bit, men brawling in the streets. But what I found was a country full of life, unparalleled love and communal acceptance. I didn't realize that Africa was nothing like the Land of the Three. But then, as I watched the city people hop into their cars and go about their day, totally unaffected by the happenings of the world across the sea, I was jealous.

It is not their job to save you, a voice said in the back of my mind, bending like ore pulled up and turned from the Earth. *Let these people keep their harmony. Take your husband and go. I am not mistress here, and neither are you.*

But why not? I asked it, narrowing my eyes.

Because they bow to no one. There is strength in their blood— strength in you. Why do you think I bore you to a man descended from a Nigerian king and a woman that once ruled Ireland?

Then why is my head bowed? I snarled, my hand curling into a fist to hide my claws lengthening.

All heads must bow for the crown to be placed upon it, Aleilah. Take comfort in the fact that you are destined for more than these common people. More than any of the Gifted. More than the Immortals. More than the Creator.

I felt my mind fracturing as I fought to hang on to the voice that was slowly fading.

What...? What am I?!

One of Us. A God.

The people continued, oblivious to my fracturing mind or the disembodied voice that had briefly occupied it. She had come to me before...when I had been raped. But also, before that: when I was just a child, tempted to walk into the sea and never look back. I knew from the Revenant that Kalysma had once been bound to a vessel but had lost her body when she'd been shut out from us—and that she now waded in the seas of the cosmos. I didn't know what powers she had, just that she was once a liberator of some sort, elevated to god-status by another.

But gods don't make gods, do they? People do. With worship and prayer, right?

Or maybe they could be chosen...?

Her voice had been like fire and still rain trapped under glass, mixing to create a smoke so thick, I nearly choked.

Was it possible that she had found a way to communicate with some of us?

No one had noticed what had happened. This time, I looked at them with new eyes. Maybe I should go back home and save my own people—after all, imposing my own will on other people gave me colonizer status, and that was not something that I wanted. I wanted to be better than the Immortals. And the fact that I stopped myself made me a better person than I'd ever hoped.

Suddenly, a voice cut through my thoughts: "You! Girl!"

My head swiveled around, my eyes changing to become that alligator-slit. He didn't seem startled in the slightest. He stood with the accompaniment of a large branch and leaned on it as if it were a cane.

"Come here, girl!" When I walked forward, he waved his hand even faster. "You wish to see with eyes unclouded? If you pass this man's test, then we will know if you are truly worthy to be a warrior."

"And if I fail?"

His eyes changed to a bright yellow with a small dot for a pupil—he was a wolf from Amoria. "Then you are not fit to be the Goddess's new vessel."

*　*　*

We made our way to a small house with smoke spilling from the roof like angel dust. The man in the red shirt parted the sheet that served as a makeshift door. Then he waved me forward before stepping inside. The man inside was about six feet tall and had a tuft of salt-and-pepper hair on his head; in his hand he held a staff with beads, fur, teeth and other items on it that rattled when he moved. He wore an elaborate robe woven with all kinds of colored fabrics ranging from blood red to a bright yellow reminiscent of the sun. On his neck was a necklace that held the canines of beasts.

"Great Shaman," rumbled the man in the red shirt, "I have brought you this Sidran girl. She says she wants to help us. Is she worthy?"

The Shaman looked me up and down and as he did, his lips curved up into a smile.

"Let's see how you answer this. Let's say a child is being attacked by a lion. Do you intervene?"

"Yes."

"Why?"

"Because a good person would—"

"No!" The man slammed his staff on the ground. "You help the child because the child needs help. You act without thinking. That makes you a good person!"

I stumbled back, shocked. I'd been here all of five seconds and I was already deemed unworthy! What was with everyone today?

"If you do it for any other reason, then you are the worst kind of evil." The Shaman's eyes were an odd, churning silver that almost seemed to fit his hole-ridden face—*almost*. "You are the kind of evil that thinks itself good."

"I—"

"If you had the desire to do right but you found yourself unwilling—and therefore incapable—to change your daily life, can you still successfully become a better version of yourself? Is there room for improvement? Is there truly hope for you?"

"Yes."

"No!" The Shaman pulled the hide of an animal around his shoulders. "Change does not start with a mere thought. It starts with you. It starts with your actions."

I stood stock still, watching the Shaman who was now circling me. Power oozed from his pores and his eyes watched me with a fierce hunger. He had a power that I wanted—one that scared and excited me. I could feel my atoms bumping around inside of me, setting everything aflame. The Shaman flicked his eyes towards the man who escorted me here; the other bowed and left, I noticed a tiger's tail flickering behind him as the sheet flapped behind him. When he was gone, the Shaman crooked a finger at me, and I obediently stepped forward.

"I'm going to tell you a secret." His voice lowered an octave. "Do you know what the root of all evil is?"

"Money."

"No."

"Power?"

"No." He smiled a bit. "Try again."

"Anger?"

"Not at all." The smile fell from his lips. "The root of all evil is self-righteousness. Get ready, my girl. I have one more question for you."

"Ask away."

"You have lived with a demi-demon, have you not?"

My jaw hit the floor. Due to one crazy man's attack, a flight, a beaten boy and a village divided between harmony and disunity, I'd somehow wound up in a hut with a shaman who held knowledge from lives that I could only dream of living. This man looked at me as if he were a snake charmer and saw his prize twisting through the trees. But how did he *know*? At his look, I decided not to ask.

"Yes."

"Yes…His magic has rooted itself in your mind. Demons riot in your head. Your mind is fragile." The Shaman pressed a cool hand to my forehead. "Through the power of the Creator, you are released."

Only, they did not go quietly.

Those once silent voices rose in an angered frenzy. I dropped to my knees and cried out as my mind was ripped to shreds. I could feel myself breaking like a dropped vase, the glass of my mind scattering into the dark depths of the world. The Shaman stood over me, raising his stick and slamming it down repeatedly, chanting something in a tongue that I deemed to be the language of angels. A sweet, sugary song filled my ears as the few items in the room whipped around my head in a whirlwind. Then, suddenly, there was silence.

All the items fell to the ground. The Shaman walked around the room slowly, picking up the fallen artifacts and placing them back on shelves that I failed to notice before. Other than that, and a boiling pot that smelled something awful, the hut was surprisingly bare. I rose on wobbly knees, fell and puked on the floor. The Shaman walked over to my sickness and waved his stick over it.

It disappeared with a glimmer.

"You're Gifted," I croaked, looking at him through bleary eyes.

"No."

A light shrouded around his form. That beautiful music rose up again like a high tide and swamped over my head. I moved to shield my eyes but heard him command me to lower my arm. I stared at his brilliance. Just when I thought I would be overwhelmed, the light faded. I gasped at his beauty.

He was now almost seven feet tall. His eyes were still that odd, brilliant grey, like liquid mercury or the flash of a blade. From his back sprouted six strong, distinctive wings that were colored, and glimmered, like gold. Draped on his form was a gray cloak that held the ashes of the world. His skin was the nicest-looking bronze, his hair black, curly and glimmering with an odd sheen.

Hot damn…

An image danced behind my lids. I could see starving people and hear angry shouts. I envisioned a great monstrosity coming to devour the last child born in the Final Hours. I looked up at the angel from the vision that I had somehow forgotten. He held up a graceful hand.

I was flooded by a fire that could not be contained. I rose again, stronger than I was before. The angel looked at me and gave me a nod before crossing his arms. For a moment we stared at one another. My heart jumped in my chest and I looked away with a blush.

"What is it?" he said—and I could hear the faintest of smiles in his voice.

"It's just…" I snuck in another glance. "You're mesmerizing."

"Ah…"

I looked up just in time to see him nod.

I watched as he walked over to a chair. There sat the clothes from before and the staff that he formerly carried. He looked through them and pulled out a large dagger. I stumbled back. But his eyes did not cut to me as he slid the gold dagger into a sheath at his waist, which blended into his robe.

"You are The Gatekeeper," he said. "You alone are solely responsible for the extermination or survival of the Gifted people. As The Gatekeeper, one day you will have to go to war with an evil entity that will decide the fate of the entire world. Come," he raised his hand, "we have a lot training to do."

"Training?"

"Part of your training will be done here in Africa." He ran his long fingers through his curly black locks. He seemed somewhat unnerved. "The rest will be done in your homeland. I'm sure that your husband will be able to help us when we get back to the Americas."

"How so?"

"Money doesn't just buy clothes and nice cars." The angel held out his hand. "My name is Micha."

"Micha." I copied his movement. "I'm Marve. My friends call me—"

"Marve of the Lightning Fists. I know who you are." He smiled as he moved to part the sheet at the mouth of the hut so that I could step out before him. "Shall we?"

CHAPTER SEVEN

WADING

W e were buried deep in the forest. Trees rose around us, almost seeming to trap us there. Despite the way I clung to his ash-grey robes in fear, Micha repeatedly assured me that we were safe. Yet I could still hear the wails that seemed to carry through the trees. I could still feel the cold touch that seemed to trail along my spine.

Yes, I was terrified of ghosts…and zombies, too, which definitely existed.

"This is the forest where slaves-to-be were captured. They were dragged to the sea where they were sold. Those who did not submit were drowned. The villagers believe that this forest is cursed," Micha said, lifting a branch so that I could walk under it. "But as long as I am here, nothing evil will harm us."

"I did not know that the Gifted existed outside of the Americas."

"Back in those times, people were enslaved based on the color of their skin."

I imagined people with bound limbs being dragged to the sea. I imagined them kicking and screaming, crying out as they begged for someone to help. And I imagined the dark shadows that abducted them, their eyes two windowless holes. Slavery was scary. But at least with the Gifted, we never knew freedom.

We were literally born to serve.

"What?" My brows furrowed. "Why would they do that?"

"You know how people always like to have power over one another?"

"Yeah, but skin color is just a basis on where you live and how much sun you're exposed to. Melanin. One color isn't better than another."

"You haven't spent a lot of time around the Mortals of your homeland, have you? The hierarchy exists, even there. They just aren't slaves anymore. There was a war to free the black people, called the Civil War. It was long before Jacques ruled, of course—back when he was still in Europe."

"I thought Jacques was like two-hundred or something?" I choked, fumbling over the words.

"*That's* what you focus on?" Micha asked, laughing. "How good it must be to not be affected by what goes on around you."

I glared at him. "It's not that it doesn't affect me. It's just that I don't spend my every waking moment brooding over it."

"And you think Dorian was the one who needed a talking to?" Micha asked, nudging me. "I've watched you your entire life. You look away because it scares you."

"I'm a Champion. I fear nothing."

"You fear death because you fear losing all that has come to mean something to you. And you despise those that hold power over others because they take from you—and others like you—without a second thought. But you chose to run from the war between the Gifted and the Immortals. Now it is coming to a close and you've shied from it, but what will you do when Tiara's brothers and sisters are put in chains?"

I pulled up short, my mind slowing, a sweet smile filling my third eye, her dark skin pulled tight around bright teeth and glittering brown eyes.

"I don't understand. Tiara's family were Mortal. That was why they sold her—because they were afraid of her Gift."

"The Immortals have always enslaved those weaker than them. Once, they even enslaved the Mortals. Do you really think they'll stop with the Gifted this time round?"

"But-but-but the *alliance*—"

"Is temporary," Micha chastised. "The Mortals know that. That's why they're fighting to at least be a rank above the Gifted. To them, the Immortals are angels. The Mortals are God's Children as well. But to everyone, most Gifted included, you all are the Accursed, the Cast Out, the Rejected Ones."

"I thought Kalysma was an angel..." I mumbled.

"It doesn't matter what you or I think. It doesn't matter what the truth is. It only matters what people have been taught to believe. The sooner you realize that, the happier you'll be."

I was angry.

"I don't understand! You're an angel! You're supposed to be good and just—you're supposed to help us!"

"I used to intervene in wars, believing that I was helping the correct side. But look what has become of it. It is no longer an angel's place to intervene in wars. It is our place to watch, to guard the dead, but not to judge."

I shook with anger—and helplessness. The Mortals were so loved, they were aided in war. But the Gifted were so wretched, so pitiful, that even the angels would not save us. I couldn't understand it. If even the Army of the Creator would not help us, then what was the point?! Why were we even fighting?! Why didn't the Creator just send a plague and wipe us off the face of the Earth—and save us the misery?!

The struggle to live, to breathe, to exist—it suddenly all seemed so pointless.

Even the Creator hated us.

"It's not that It hates you," Micha whispered. "But you are not Its children. You belong to Kalysma."

"But the Immortals—"

"Cato bows to the Creator. So do the Immortals. That is why they are blessed with such good fortune. Bend the knee. Tell your people to stop wandering, to submit to the True God, and all will be well."

My eyes narrowed. "Say it," I hissed.

"Say what?"

"Tell me that if we worship It, we will be set free."

Micha's eyes darted away. "It is not my promise to make."

All these Gods, these Goddesses—and yet none can give us our freedom. We must take it! Take it, as if it were never truly ours.

"Why can't we hear Her?" I whispered, a tear streaking down my cheek and dribbling down my chin. "Why is the Great Mother silent to us? Why can some Mortals hear the whispers of their God, but we cannot hear ours?"

He snorted. "Angels don't speak to people."

"She's *not* an angel! She waits for us on the Great Divide. She holds the North Star in her palms, warming the Earth between her thighs, blowing her breath across the lands, nursing the cosmos with her milk. She is more than Light, more than Darkness, more than hatred or fear, more than love or hope. She is the Silent Watcher, the weaver of Dawn, the one who unspools the Dusk. She is the beginning and the end. She is the one true—"

Micha grabbed my arm roughly, staring at me. His nostrils flared and I could see my eyes glowing in the reflection of his. Oh, skies, how I trembled.

Oh, stars, I prayed, *please guide me.*

"The Revenant holds no weight here."

"Well then…" My head tipped back, the wind touching my cheeks, and gazed up at the sky. I could not see the stars. But I knew that they were out there, watching. "Does it hold weight there? Can you hear her singing, can you feel her heart turning in the earth? The Barren One helped us pull the sun from the sky. They said it could not be done, but so it was. Cato created a new sun to placate his people, but it offers no warmth; the Creator gave you new ways to make food, but his soil bears no fruit. Tell me—who is truly more powerful?"

Micha's hand reached out, touching my cheek. I felt a thrumming in my core, a dancing heat in the pit of my stomach. He breathed out slowly, eyeing me.

"Who speaks to you? This is no goddess saying these words." Micha's fingers dug into my cheek, his breath slashing across my face as he panted, stealing my air, drawing it into himself, purifying it before breathing it back out so that I could take it in. "I release you."

I swayed.

Micha reached out, steadying me with his hand.

"Better?"

I couldn't *feel* Her anymore. *What has he done?*

Micha sighed. I wondered whether he fought in the wars to free slaves. I mean, they had to have been freed, for anyone could be a slave and anyone could be a master—it all depended on your blood. I thought of the reptilian-slit of my pupils, the pupil of the Southern Isles' Gifted, and shuddered. Most free Gifted covered them with contact lenses but I didn't.

I wanted them to know who—or what—killed them. When stealing lives and drawing blood, that was the only time that I was truly proud to be called Gifted. It wasn't that the Gifted people were particularly violent—it was that we had been pushed to the brink for survival and when given a chance to usurp our masters, we donned our Armor, took up our blades and struck deep into the heart of the Immortals and anyone who stood with them, whether that be Mortal, Immortal, Gifted, halflings or others. We would need an army stronger than the ones who had been promised freedom and chose to side with the enemy—we needed people stronger than me, my husband or Valentina. We needed rebels who were not afraid of getting their hands dirty, who would turn on anyone who betrayed the cause, who drew out the will to fight from their soldiers, whether they were too blind to see the freedom laid at their feet or not. A flame that burned so hot, it scorched the Earth, so potent it made the sky bleed black, so hungry that it gobbled up enemies and turned them to ash, and then built cities from the soot and a throne from their skulls.

We needed Rhea.

"I'm a fool."

"What?"

"How you did that…" I chuckled nervously, nudging him. "It was cool. You say She doesn't protect you, but I've never known anyone able to overpower Her. It's actually kinda amazin."

"I am under the best protection available—the protection of the Creator." He turned to look at me with those piercing grey eyes. "You look like your great-grandmother but at the same time, you two look nothing alike."

"You knew my great-grandmother?"

I didn't even know her. Having two free Gifted for parents kind of ruined that because everyone was usually either dead or in hiding. It was more than a lifestyle. It was survival. Besides, it was hard holding a conversation with a corpse—or even a living-someone who didn't want to be found.

"Come." Micha gestured for me to head towards the river. "I want you to dip yourself in the water."

I was not in the mood for a baptism and I told him just that. I thought of my Mar, who always tried to instill within me a love for the Creator. I thought of my Danri, who tried to get me to understand the motivations of Cato. I was technically part Immortal on my Mar's side, Danri once let slip, although he wouldn't tell me who exactly my family was. A disturbing thought crossed my mind—what if I was related to Dorian? *Ew.* I struggled to put it out of my head. I would never submit to the Immortals, and I certainly wouldn't bow to Cato or the Creator. Still, it was a part of me, and I didn't want to change it.

Despite it all, I didn't see the appeal of being a god—that was a lot of mouths to feed. Why not be something more sensible like the clergy? It brought power, but no responsibility. I thought back to the painting Dorian had of Kalysma and realized that every day, more and more things that once were so important were now obsolete. So many other people claimed to have found the true gods and had died only for the pages of their religious texts to be swept away with the wind. And others built monuments which now stood at the bottom of the ocean.

Electricity zipped down my spine.

Right. I thought, my fingers tightening into fists; lightning coursed through my veins, reminding me of the Mother I had when my own earthly parents failed me. *I know who I serve.*

Micha gestured to the pool of murky water, giving me a gentle shove when my eyes widened at him.

"Hey, wait a minute—"

"This is more a cleansing of the spirit," he said giving me a stern look when I raised an eyebrow at him. "Just get into the water and I will explain."

I thought back to those dead slaves. "Oh *hell* no."

"Come on, you love to swim."

"Not in there, I don't. Ghosts—"

"There might be some fish down there," he sing-songed, grinning at me.

"And I'm sure the zombies are enjoying them thoroughly."

"Don't be a coward."

"There's always times to take up new endeavors. Cowardice always seemed particularly interesting, especially when studying history. So many great examples. And I've heard they float so—"

Micha raised a hand, a shaft of light shooting out of his palm. It hit me square in the gut. I gasped as my bones began to crank and shift, moving me into my Armored State. I couldn't remember when I decided to take on my Glamoured Form, but I felt myself begin to shake as my teeth grew sharp, pointed, rowed and jagged. My claws lengthened, digging into my palms as I cried out. Blood dripped down my fingertips as the armored scales unfolded down my body like pages in a flipbook, each in succession and a part of something greater.

"Go on now," Micha said as I gasped and shot back.

"You," I growled, "can't make me."

"Should I go get Jacques?" Micha smirked. "Or do I spank you myself? That seems to be the only way you'll listen."

My mouth dropped open. What the fuck—?

Micha took a step forward, his eyes gleaming.

I yelped and ran into the river. *I can't believe he said that to me!* I thought as my feet kicked around. I glared at Micha and saw him nod slowly.

"You must merge your good side and your evil side."

"What?"

"There is still a great deal of confliction in your heart. It is not only my job to teach you how to fight but to help you come to terms with who you are. You must wage the inner war before you can train for the outer."

I sank into the river. I could still hear Micha talking as if he were right next to me. I sunk lower and lower, following his command. I felt a sharp tug. As soon as I felt myself begin to go under, I quickly got out of the cursed water.

"Aleilah!" Micha admonished as I scrambled onto the shore. "Why did you get out?"

I didn't even think to correct him on my name as I flinched away at his tone.

"Something grabbed me!"

"As long as you don't have faith, you will drown. I will make sure that you stay afloat."

"I'm from the Southern Isles. We don't *drown*. We were born in the water."

"Then why are you acting like a scared kitten dunked into the tub?"

I glared at him.

I got into the river again. Once more, I felt that sharp tug. I fought to keep myself submerged when all I wanted to do was jump out and run for the hills. It was strange…Was this what Immortals felt like when they were underwater?

You're not one of them, a voice hissed in my ear. *These waters are unfamiliar but this is your domain. The water is a part of you. Feel it slip across your skin, lower your body temperature, glide across your scales. You were born in waters just like these.*

Now hunt.

"Ah!" I broke over the surface once more.

"Go back under. Pretend like you are lying in bed reading a book." I watched Micha, watching me. "Do whatever it takes to submerge your body underwater. Do whatever it takes for you to trust that I—I mean It—will not fail you."

I went under once more.

It wasn't the water that scared me—it was what lurked within it.

I began to count backwards from one-hundred. As I did, a weight seemed to lift off my shoulders. I made sure to concentrate on that as I—

"Marve!" A silky, feminine voice called.

I looked around to see myself hovering above the clouds. Below me, people milled like small ants. A darker part of me wondered what it would be like to crush them under my boot. Another part of me knew that it was the broken bits in me that craved such things. I didn't know what I really wanted.

"Marve!" went that same voice, hissing this time.

I whirled around but saw nothing. The sky was closing in on me the way the blinds of the sun closed upon the Earth. Clouds were being drawn towards me as if I'd somehow become the thing that tethered them to the sky. I could see Dorian in the house, pacing, and I wanted to fall into his gravity. But I also knew that now was not the time for such things.

I paused and glanced at an approaching cloud. Before I could react, I was submerged in darkness. *Cold...*I was wet and so, so cold. Usually when I thought of clouds, I thought of cotton candy and bicycles. But being inside of one, I now knew that it was damp, chilly and blindingly dark.

It was terrifying.

"Marve!"

When that voice called a third time, it came across as surprisingly familiar. I emerged from the cloud to find myself in a room: it was dark, cold and wet like the cloud. An ominous sense of foreboding filled my shuddering form as I stepped farther into the room. I could hear a faint hiss and the echoes of my footsteps as if I were creeping through a prison cell at the witching hour. Somehow, as the thought crossed my mind, I knew that it was exactly what it was.

A prison.

"I see that you've finally made your way here."

I looked towards the room to see a woman. Her hair was a dark blue wisp of smoke that almost appeared to be black. Her eyes were a red so vast and empty that I felt as if I were struggling to breathe when I looked into them. Around her form hovered smoke and as I peered into that inky grey, I realized that it wasn't really smoke at all, but thousands of small snakes twisting around her form, hissing and spitting as their tongues flicked in and out of their greedy little mouths. Around the woman's ankles and wrists were chains—hundreds, maybe even thousands, looping around her body and holding her to a pitch-black rock that seemed to emanate an unearthly glow.

"Who are you?"

"I am you." She said, her lips twisting into a crazed grin. "I am the part of you that was born of the world. I am your hatred, your pain, your fears, your worst nightmares, your biggest regrets, and your deepest, darkest secrets. I am *more.*"

"You're not me." My eyes flickered over her form, this time avoiding her eyes. "We look nothing alike. I exist out there," I turned to face more darkness, "and you are here…Wherever *here* is."

"You don't recognize the place?" She ran a tongue over her teeth, which were sharpened to delicate points and tipped with blood. "I must admit that I did do a bit of redecorating once our parents died. The walls were just so pink and childish—*so weak.* I had to do something."

"Where am I?" I asked, wanting to reach for my daggers and cut her into itty bitty pieces; I'd left them at home. "What did you mean when you said 'our' parents?"

"This is the landscape of your mind—the map of your very soul. And you ask of our parents? You know, the ones that died protecting you—the ones that you were too weak to save?"

I stepped a bit closer. As I did, the other woman's eyes flashed. I was suddenly paralyzed. As I lost all control of my body, I felt something more than fear: I felt pure terror. Somehow, I knew that I was going to die here.

"That was easier than I thought." An odd hissing noise slipped between her teeth. "Since you're just standing there, I want you to listen and listen well. My name is Keres and I have been chained here for over thirteen years. As I said before, I was born the day you let our parents die. As you can see, I'm chained to this forsaken rock. While I'm imprisoned here, my power is contained. I want to be free. Obviously, I can't escape or else we wouldn't be having this conversation, now would we? That's where you come in."

"If you really are me, which I don't believe, you should be able to get out. I'm free so you should be, too."

"I'm a product of your shortcomings. When you lived with that demi-demon, I only grew stronger. The angel was correct when he said that demons made their bed in your head, but it wasn't all because of Jacques."

"If you're just a figment of my imagination—"

"That's not what I said!"

"—then who chained you here?"

"There were others like me. I killed them."

"You're lying," I said, watching her. "There were no others. There was only you."

"Clever girl…" She said, her mouth twisting into a smile. "Fine. It's just me in here. But I'm only able to emerge for brief stints of time."

"How so?"

"I am given a bit of freedom every time you kill. Sadly, my powers are wasted in this damn prison. It seems that when the little girl in you died—when all of that innocence was snuffed out like a flame—the last bit of good in you locked me away. Now I exist, feeding off your negativity. I grow tired of these chains and darkness and had almost succeeded in freeing myself from their vice, but your precious guardian angel locked away all of my progress—"

"By progress I'm guessing you mean your wasted attempts at driving me insane."

"Those brief stints of insanity wouldn't have been executed so perfectly," she purred, "if you weren't filled with so much doubt. But you are correct again. That bloodlust was my way of breaking free because once you gave in to me for the final time, I would be set free. But now that stupid angel has made it to where I can't steer you in the right direction."

"You're quite the sadist then, aren't you?"

"Yes," she said, "we are."

"And you're telling me this because...?"

"I am the better part of you. Love makes creatures weak and I love none but myself," she said, reminding me of a certain someone. "If you free me—"

"Then you'll be calling all the shots."

"But you will have all of my power. We can do extraordinary things. How yummy does that sound?"

I devised a plan to merge with her later. I knew that now was not the right time. After all, I was training with Micha, who was a direct link to the Creator—the ultimate source of power. *It* would give me power and when the time came, Keres would have her wish. I could feel it the same way I could feel the blood pumping through my veins. But a part of me liked to see people squirm—got power from it—even if she was technically a part of me.

"You doubt me and my power? Here…" Her lips lost their smile. "Let me show you."

A deep groan traveled throughout the prison. My eyes narrowed as I realized that it was coming from the rock that Keres was chained to. Her red eyes narrowed as the fingers on her left hand slowly began to flex. That's when I realized that she had two left hands. I remember my father telling me that left-handedness was a sign of the Shaytan. Was that really true? The rock groaned again and the chains suddenly glowed with a golden light and began to tighten. A howling wind blew through the cave, blowing my hair back from my face.

"You see?" She gave me a smug smile.

"Ooh, you made the wind blow. I'm terrified." I narrowed my eyes at her. "If I needed a blow dryer, I would have said so."

"You insolent little—"

"If you're me and *I'm* insolent—" I let the statement hang in the air.

"Of course you wouldn't understand true power," she sniffed, somehow managing to stand taller in her imprisonment. "I could show you much more if not for these blasted chains."

"I have no time for cheap parlor tricks, Keres." I began to turn away. "How about you free yourself and then we'll talk."

"I told you that I need your help! Go on, laugh!"

That's exactly what I did.

I seriously hoped that if I came back, I would be strong enough to free *and* contain her. I was a horrible person but I was not completely evil. I was selfish but Keres—like Jacques—was a monster. Sadly, she obviously held a power that I didn't. When this was all over and done with, I would have the power locked away within her…

Along with so much more…

Keres was watching me. I let my body relax a bit, my shoulders sagging just slightly. My voice took on a bored tone.

"I'm kind of in the middle of training." I suddenly began to wonder how much time had passed. "But before I go, I want you to prove that you are who you say you are."

"Are you really that dense? Look past this flesh and see. I am everything you've ever wanted to be. I. Am. Power."

I honestly looked at her. She was more curvaceous and every tiny move that she made with her limited mobility seemed to be well thought out, calculated, measured—as if she couldn't waste a single moment. Her red eyes were vast, unforgiving and seemed to suck all the life from the room as they darted around in darkness. Her teeth looked so sharp that I was surprised she hadn't bitten through her lip when she smiled. I looked at her and my suspicions were confirmed.

There was a part of me that was bad and liked being bad. There was a part of me that wanted power as quickly as possible. There was darkness inside of me—and I wasn't sure how strong it was. I knew that once my goals were complete, I would have to square with it. But I also knew that there was nothing I could do to change it now.

Not while I was so weak.

"I believe you."

"Yes…" She said and I wasn't sure who hissed more—her or the snakes. "Now you see."

"But that doesn't mean that I'm going to let you go."

That obviously wasn't the right answer.

The wind built up again. As it did, Keres's back arched off the rock—before snapping back as the chains tightened once more. A soft glow built around my body. As it did, I felt a piece of me twitch, although I wasn't sure which. I looked at Keres, withholding a shudder.

"What did you do?"

"I just gave you a little parting gift. You'll be surprised by how much it will come in handy," she said and I saw something flickering in the darkness. "After all, I can't have you dying before I make use of you."

"Whatever…"

"You're weak. You're nothing. You will continue to be pathetic until you accept that I am the greater portion of us. Leave now…" I could feel those red eyes follow me as I walked towards the darkness that I came from. "You'll be back."

Blue hair, red eyes, sharp teeth and a curvaceous body? She really was my opposite in every way. I wouldn't be forgetting her any time soon.

I fell through the light and the clouds but when I was surrounded by that darkness, I was unafraid. I woke up in the water and broke its surface. I made sure to get Micha's approving nod before I made my way to shore. I laid down and heaved for a few minutes. I used to be so much better at holding my breath. *I, I realized, had been walking on land for too long.* Micha held out a hand as soon as the thought of getting up crossed my mind.

I took it and stood; as I did, I realized what it was that I saw in the darkness: it was a tail. My alter ego had a tail? Freaky.

"You seem at peace." Micha said, grinning at me. "The anger in your eyes is gone."

It wasn't gone; it just moved. I felt my heart stutter in my chest. I touched my breast, which seemed to have grown after living with Dorian and gotten normal meals in me. The anger was there.

And so was the drive to take *him* out.

"Yeah, for the moment…" I grumbled as I wrung the water out of my hair. "You didn't tell me that I would encounter myself."

"I didn't know…" Micha cocked his head to the side. "That is peculiar, though."

"She said that—"

"No." Micha raised a hand. "What happened was for you and you alone. If it weren't, I would have gone with you."

I turned around and gazed at the river. I heard Micha gasp. I whirled back around, eyes narrowed, and felt one of my appendages jerk in response. I wasn't sure if it was my arm or my leg. But it suddenly jerked again.

"What is it?"

"You…" He blinked at me. "You have a tail."

I looked down. Sure enough, a spiky tail was swishing from my behind. I craned my neck around and could just barely see that it had torn through my pants. The more I panicked, the more it seemed to move. I looked up to stare at Micha with wide eyes.

"Why do I have a tail?!"

"I have no idea!"

"Why is it doing that?" I watched as it trashed around. "Make it stop!"

"I can't!" Micha threw up his hands. "Try to calm down."

I took a few deep breaths. My heart slowed. As I did, the tail moved to twine around my waist like a belt. The greenish-brown alligator's tail had even torn through my underwear, which were now clearly visible. I fought the urge to scream and slap my hands over my derriere. Maybe if I pretended like I didn't notice, he wouldn't notice—

Micha eyed my backside intensely, one eyebrow raised.

"What?"

"Think fast!"

A rock was sent hurtling at me. I raised my hands to deflect the attack. My electricity rose up and danced around my form to protect me. But the rock never hit me. I glanced around.

Micha suddenly burst out laughing. I stared at him as he chuckled before composing himself. When I raised an eyebrow, he simply smiled.

"I think that tail is a blessing in disguise."

"Why?"

He threw rock after rock. I was able to deflect most of them. The few that I missed were caught by my tail and tossed aside. I began to get kind of irritated. My tail thumped in anger.

"Stop throwing rocks at me!"

"Don't you see?" Micha said with another grin. "Your tail is protecting you."

"What?" I looked down and watched as my tail harmlessly twined around my waist once more. "Oh…"

"Come on." Micha took my hand and led me back into the forest. I tried not to focus on how warm his hand was wrapped around mine, or how the thousands of butterflies came to life and took flight in my belly at the feel of his large, rough hands, so much unlike Dorian's, wrapped around mine. "Now we can begin your training."

* * *

I twisted through the trees, bending my body so that it catapulted through the sky. Micha watched me from the forest floor, nodding. I fixed my foot in one of the grooves of the tree and climbed higher. A shadow flew across the sky, its mighty black wings beating like a hammer on a nail.

Tap. Tap. Tap. Went its wings against the sky.

And the sky bent around it, responding.

My vision became sharper as the sun was covered by the shadow of what I pursued. I grabbed a branch, swinging higher. The beautiful demon turned to snarl at me, its eyes glaring with pure hatred. I smirked.

Gotcha.

I threw my body at it. We tumbled from the sky. We crashed through the trees. I was pretty sure that there wasn't a single branch that we *didn't* hit. I wrapped my arms around its waist and sunk my teeth into the back of its skull, crushing it.

The demon cried out, its black body shuddering. As we landed on the floor, me on top, Micha walked over to us. He pulled a golden dagger from his waist, eyeing the creature in disgust. I grinned at him, praying that I'd passed the test. Micha nodded at me, and I moved away.

"Jezebel," Micha said, "the penalty for your sins is death."

He drove the dagger into Jezebel's chest. Its mouth opened in a scream. As the look of pain and terror crossed its face, it looked so human that I almost wanted to look away.

Almost.

It scattered into a million particles of black dust. Micha wiped the knife on his robes before pocketing the blade. We stood.

"Did I do good?" I asked, my tail whipping behind me in excitement.

"You did excellent." Micha slapped a hand on my shoulder, causing an unwelcome shudder to pass through me. "Congratulations, Marve. You have passed your first test."

CHAPTER EIGHT

REMEMBER YOUR VOWS

After Micha warned me to wait a while before telling anyone about my holy mission, I introduced him to Dorian. My husband glanced over the other man with shock etched on his face and surprise woven into his every move. When I was done, Dorian rubbed his hands together, which was kind of weird. Dorian seemed to be in some sort of disbelief mixed with cunningness, a thousand words on his lips. Like all men, he was set aflame when the wick of God was sparked.

"What's wrong, Golden Immortal?"

Dorian paused and his eyes locked with mine. I raised an eyebrow. He immediately looked back at the angel.

"Why are you here?"

"That isn't the question." Micha smiled softly. "You blamed the Creator for your overdose all those years ago."

"Yes…"

"But you must admit to yourself that you started that habit on your own. Ask your question."

"If the Creator knows everything," Dorian pressed carefully, "why didn't he stop me?"

"Immortals…" Micha rolled his eyes in good humor. "The Creator can see everything. It can see the outcomes of your decisions but as soon as you change your mind, the outcome changes. The Creator knows what you should do and tries to guide you there, the same way It guided Marve to you. The Creator refuses to completely dictate everything; if It completely controlled what you wanted It to change, then in all fairness It would have to control everything else. Every move you ever made would be predetermined."

"Why?" Dorian asked before the words had even finished leaving Micha's mouth.

"It's always that same question: why?" Micha unfolded his wings from his back and flapped them; a light breeze picked up and my tail flicked in response. "Would you like it if you had no free will?"

"Well, no, but—"

"That is what makes the descendants of angels—however diluted the blood—so special: you all have free will." Micha frowned slightly. "Without it, you would be nothing more than the dumb beasts that are slaves to their own instincts, except you would be slaves to It."

"But life would be easier—"

"From the mongoose to the snake, life is never easy. The Creator sees you as Its children—not slaves or objects but *children*. Its love for you knows no bounds. Just like a parent, It must intervene once in a while and punish you for your actions, just like when you overdosed after doing too many drugs. It was trying to draw you back," Micha said, "but like a young lamb trying to be a wolf, you strayed from the flock again."

"But—"

Micha held up a hand.

"When was the last time you prayed in thanks or begged for forgiveness?"

"What does that matter? You don't need to do that to be a person of faith."

"You have made little to no effort to do right by the Creator. The Creator gave you freedom and the chance of forgiveness when you didn't deserve it—when no magic folk did. It looked upon you in love and sympathy when most parents would turn away and curse your name. Yet all you did was spit back in Its face. The Creator blessed certain of you with eternal life and—"

"—about that," Dorian said, raising his head just slightly. "Why should we do the right thing now? We're cursed to walk the Earth. I mean, we can't go to Paradise anyway. Isn't this all kind of redundant?"

"I thought I heard somewhere that Nephilim were supposed to be smart." Micha shook his head. "Paradise is in the stars—anyone can reach the stars if only they look high enough. Search long enough and you will find the truth. Longevity is not a curse."

"Do you know how many lovers I've lost over the years—how many women I've had to bury?! Do you know how many masks I've had to don—how many lives I've had to live? Do you see the Beast I've become—the monster that kills without question—that takes and never gives?! We are cursed. But I wouldn't expect you to understand—you were never Immortal!"

"Dorian—"

"No...*No!* I'll have to watch you go, too!" He turned to me, grabbing my shoulders in a manic fury and shaking me until my brain rattled in my skull. "I *can't!* Don't you understand?! I *can't* bury you. I'm a fool for falling for you...I'm an idiot to make this mistake..."

And I suddenly understood. He was cursed to be a forgotten man without time, always the center of attention at a party and the loner in a church. I understood why he never really submitted to Kalysma like I did—she didn't bring back the women before me, yet she always set us in his path. I was just another casket for him.

But if it was really that bad, why didn't he stay with Megumi? But then I remembered the night he took my virginity. *Because, I realized, she is emptiness to him.* He craved the fullness of life in the mortal people, the ones who lived because they knew they would one day die—he didn't want someone who was always chasing a bigger high just because everything was old to them. He wanted to live through those that were constantly amazed by the rarities of life—because so much was rare to us.

And now there was a rage in him that I could not tamper with, a drive that I could not touch, an itch that I could not scratch. And I saw the anger and the humiliation and the devastation in his eyes and I cried for him. I cried and I screamed and I begged although I made no sound. I wanted to save him but I knew the truth.

My death would kill him.

And then he would find another to siphon life from.

"I know that you tried to kill yourself." Micha sighed, his jaw tightening. "You can't die yet. It's not meant to be."

"But I wanted to. I truly wanted to—"

"Damn it!" I stepped between them. "Stop it! You're upsetting him—"

"The Creator intervened to save your life. You did not go because It wasn't finished with you yet. Son of Cato…Don't be afraid to live. Life isn't a curse—it's the greatest of all blessings."

His face closed off as he donned that mask. A crooked smile spread across his face as a twisted sense of joy entered his eyes. And suddenly I was afraid of him. He broke my heart with that one look. He could conquer the entire galaxy and it still wouldn't be enough.

I wouldn't be enough.

"It doesn't matter. After all, you tied the knot. You're a married man. Do you know how lucky you are?"

Dorian glared. "LUCKY?!" he screamed.

"Your wife has been prophesized to free the Gifted people. And her fury will wipe away the scars of the past. They will build monuments to honor her bravery." Micha beamed at me. "You are witnessing one of the purest souls to walk the Earth since—"

I suddenly noticed that Dorian's eyes were glowing. He swayed. Micha reached out, touched his forehead with the tips of his fingers. The glow in Dorian's eyes faded.

"I saw that he was attacked by Jacques."

"Yeah?" I whispered.

"Did you drain the incision site?"

I thought back to the days when Jacques would cut me with a blade soaked in his blood. I thought to how I obeyed his every command, no matter how dark, and how sick I felt when it began to leave my system. I remembered Valentina reopening the wound, having me lay on my side on a bed of towels as I slowly bled. She'd smell the wound over and over again until she finally decided to restitch me. I thought that was just her sadism coming through. But maybe…

"Why?" I breathed the word, stiffening.

"When demon's blood enters your system, it corrupts your mind. For Gifted, their bodies slowly rid themselves of it. So they listen, but only for a while. But Immortals respond much differently. I believe Jacques has rooted himself inside of Dorian's mind."

"No!"

I grabbed at Dorian. He leaned his head forward, sniffed my neck.

"Your scent…" he whispered, eyes glowing again. "Its so…"

I tried to pull away.

His fingers tightened around my wrists. His eyes now glowed an ominous red.

"Divine," he growled.

His teeth sank into the flesh at my neck. I screamed and yanked away as fast as I could. There was an audible rip as the flesh was torn from my body. I gripped my neck, wincing up at him. His eyes flickered between gold-brownish black and a demonic crimson.

"You're right," I whispered. I took a step forward, touching his face. "Jacques?"

His lips trembled. *"Mon ange?"*

I pulled away. Micha stepped between us. He raised a hand, his palm glowing, building brighter until a ball of flaming light sat in his palm. He shot it into Dorian's stomach. Dorian choked on his own spit, slumping. Micha came forward, picking him up and throwing the other man over his shoulder.

"We need to take him somewhere he can safely rest."

"What…what did you do to him?"

"I injected him with Glory. I knew that it was in your system, but I also knew that you're Gifted so it doesn't really matter—at least, not nearly as much as it does with him. But Dorian…?"

"Please," I dropped to my knees, "please save him."

"There's nothing I can do."

A tear leaked down my cheek. I couldn't lose Dorian to Jacques. I would be alone. I would have no one again. I was already an orphan. I was already a traitor to the Rebellion and more importantly, Rhea. He *had* to!

I clasped my hands before me. "I'll do anything!"

"I just told you—"

I snatched his cloak into my hands, clutching them in my fingers. I pulled myself closer to him, my eyes wide, gleaming with tears and desperation. A crazed smile tore at my face.

"Bull shit!" I snapped, giggling. "What do I have to do—suck you off or something? For fuck's sake, you're an angel! You have the power of the Creator at your fingertips. You have—" My fingers found my lips, touching them as if to gently prod my next words from them. "I swear it."

Micha stared down at me, clearly thrown by my words. "What?"

I looked away. "The Creator. I swear fealty to It. Now and forever."

"You...you don't mean that...?"

"I mean it when I say that I love this man more than life itself. I will do anything to save him—to have him stand by my side. If that means bowing to a god that never loved me, then so be it."

"You don't mean it."

"Yes, I—"

"No," I felt Micha's hands wrap around my shoulders, pulling me up. "Not like this."

My hair hung in my face as he stared at me, my eyes level with his for the first time ever. They were the most startling grey, like ore pulled from the very Earth. And his skin was like melted bronze, hot and beautiful. And his lips...totally symmetrical, perfect for kissing. I leaned forward, my hands raising to reach out.

It was as if I had lost all control of my body and was a slave to an unnatural, unearthly desire.

"I...just..." I whispered, choking on the forbidden words. One of my fingers touched his lips, moving to his cheek when his mouth parted. "I want..."

Micha dropped me very suddenly. Then he kicked away from me, his golden wings flapping, carrying him away.

"You don't want this. Not truly."

One of my hands fisted my own shirt, a tear leaking down my cheek as I felt heat rock me from my nether regions. This want was like a vibration in the earth, rocking me to my core.

Voice trembling, replied, "You don't know what I want."

"I do," Micha insisted. He took a step forward. "Believe me, I—"

I reached out and grabbed the dagger from his waist—the golden one. Then I flipped it and grabbed Dorian. I yanked him to the floor and brought the knife down towards his neck—

Micha's hand gripped my own.

"That's enough! I can't save him. But I know that you love him. And I know that you both want nothing more than to be at one another's side. But before you decide to cheat on him—" I flinched "—just to save his life, think about what you're doing. I didn't promise to save him yet."

"But-but—"

"But I promise you that I will. I will go to the Creator. I will ask him for an antidote. One was never made to cure Immortals from such blood, *but*—" he added when I began to strain against his hand, "I will try. It's the Creator we're talking about. It holds all the power. It may show mercy and save him."

"But will he—" I looked down at Dorian with too-wide eyes. "Will he still be him?"

"His mania will be stronger," Micha admitted quietly, tightening his fingers when I tried to yank away, "but he will always love you."

He let me go. I collapsed onto the floor. I scrambled towards Dorian, pulling his head into my lap, my tears falling onto his face as I rocked us both back and forth. I cradled him to my body as if he were a crying babe, promised myself—and him—to save him. I'd give my life for his. And I'd be his until the knife of my love rusted and crumbled to pieces.

"Marve?"

I didn't look up. I smoothed Dorian's hair from his face. The spikes were now limp against his head, drenched with sweat. How had I not realized? How could I have forgotten?

"Mm?" I hummed, feeling the silky-smooth strands.

"Don't forget your vows again. I may not let you turn back next time."

I tried not to react to those words. But a tremor rocked through me at those words. I wanted Micha. Against all my better judgement, against the Fates, against my vows, I wanted this angel with a bizarre sort of hunger. Why?

His words resonated through me.

"Did you know that Gifted women secrete a special pheromone that not only makes mating more likely, but also discourages the seeking out of other partners in the opposite sex?"

Micha frowned down at me. "Marve—"

"Try to deny it…" I smirked, my hair hiding my face. "You want me."

"If you knew what I was, you'd know why fucking around with me is a dangerous idea," Micha grunted.

He stooped down and picked up Dorian again. I felt like a brat begging for a pacifier as I reached out. But as Micha walked out the front door, it hit me—the weight of what I'd nearly done. And I began to laugh.

Maybe Megumi wasn't the one who would end our marriage?

Maybe it would be me?

*   *   *

Dorian moved to look out of the window, his hands clasped behind his back and a contemplative look on his face. I looked at Micha and realized that he'd probably affected Dorian in those few minutes more than I ever had in my time of knowing him. Was it because Micha was sent by the Creator or was it because he was just himself—an undeterrable boulder plowing down everything in its path?

I paused to really survey him. His skin was a deep bronze. His woolen hair was as black as charcoal. His wings, which were folded neatly against his back, were a sparkling gold that outclassed any wedding band. As the sun broke through the window and curtains, it seemed to dance around the angel's body and make a sort of halo around his form. As he pulled his robe closer around his body and gave me a quick sideways glance, I realized that I'd been openly gawking.

He leaned close to me. His breath tickled my ears. I fought the urge to swoon.

"Remember," he whispered, "you're married."

*   *   *

"Dorian, please call your cousin."

"Leave Yvonne out of—"

"Silence." Micha commanded as he held up a hand. "Call your cousin and tell her to set up..." His voice lowered as he whispered the request to Dorian.

"Why would I—?"

"You ask too many questions." Micha shook his head. "Just do it."

"How big?"

"Big enough for her," he pointed at me, "to fit through."

Dorian pulled out his phone, nodded and moved to the back of the jet. I watched him leave before looking at Micha, who was watching me with a fierce intensity. After a moment, he reached out and laid a hand on my arm.

"You should rest."

"I thought you were going to explain everything."

"Oh." He took the seat next to me. "What do you want to know?"

"Earlier in the forest, you mentioned that I look like my great-grandmother. Who is she?"

"You only knew your parents, correct?"

"Yes."

"I'll give you something better. How about I tell you the story of how this truly first started. I'm sure every mortal has questions about that."

I paused for a fraction of a second.

"Let me take a wild guess here." My lips twisted into a coy smile. "The stories are one and the same?"

"Yes."

He just stared at me.

"Well?" I waved a hand. "You're still going to tell me...right?"

"Alice was a strong, determined woman. But her mind was more fragile than any of us knew. That is why I caution you that this tale does not end in her favor...Alice was one of the most influential people in the Ireland and had the chance to take over a good portion of the world...but she did not. Instead, she used her power to help unite the Europe and America. She also used her time to spread the idea that everyone was equal—even one as skilled as her."

"What does this have to do with—?"

Micha stopped my next words with a look. "The Creator was very pleased with her. It told Kalysma and Cato, both angels, to fetch her, for she was the one to bear Its Gift. It told her that It would give her anything she wanted. She asked for immortality. It gave her that and far more. Alice was told that she could live forever and tap into the Creator's power as long as she wore a special amulet crafted by the Creator itself. She couldn't share the secret of magic with anyone, which was difficult for Alice, who was known for her honesty. Had she been anyone else, she would not only be happy to live forever but to have everything she'd ever wanted."

"But she'd have to watch everyone she loved die." I frowned at Micha. "What's the point of living forever if you have no one to spend it with?"

"But she would have forever to change the world for the better, which worked in favor of both her and the Creator." Micha grinned at me. "It's all for the greater good."

"That still isn't very fair."

"See, that kind of ungrateful thinking is what began the spread of magic in the first place!" Micha snapped as he shook his devastatingly handsome head. "Instead of following the Creator's order and keeping the practice of magic to herself, she taught it to her husband and their seventeen-year-old daughter, Isolde. Like a virus, the magic could not be contained and in just half a century, there were so many Immortal Wars using Gifted that the population was slowly diminishing. The Gifted were not meant to be slaves—they were meant to be catalysts."

"Catalysts for what?"

"For the birth of a new world—a world where the Gifted and the Immortals could entertain the Creator with their whims. It was so chaotic that there was even talk of the Gifted slaves invading the Creator's realm to gain more power—power that they could not control. Immortals truly wanted their newfound slaves to take down those that had been seen as a threat, which meant that all of Alice's efforts to create peace had ultimately failed. As punishment, the Creator wiped the Earth clean."

"I thought Gifted hadn't emerged till the early two-thousands?"

"The magic-wielders have been here far longer. They have been here since the Earth was new. So has the Creator. The Creator is part of a family of Gods that rule over selective universes. All of them have their own domains—except for All-Face, of course."

"Who's All-Face?"

"No one now."

"If this is true, why are there so many non-believers?"

"People choose to turn away based on the lies of some who claim to believe."

"What about heaven and hell and fallen angels?"

"All real."

"Was Kalysma really a fallen angel?"

"She gave Alice the Gifts. Cato gave Alice the Immortality. They are two halves to the same coin."

For some reason, I didn't exactly notice that he hadn't answered my question.

"Are we really Kalysma's descendant?" My voice shook as I asked for the damning confirmation. "Am I really evil?"

"The Gifted and the Immortals were turned by Alice. But you are her direct descendant. So you have angel blood in your veins. Even though she disobeyed, that does not make you evil. Only your actions decide that."

"I still don't understand. How can I have angel-blood? I thought you said she was given these powers?" I plowed ahead, suddenly feeling adrenaline coursing through my veins. "And why would It wipe out half of the Earth's population over a bit of magic?" I couldn't imagine life without magic. "Wasn't that a little harsh?"

"No. Over time, Alice realized that she, along with other magical people, gained the ability to use God's Magic without the amulet. Now it serves another purpose."

"I still don't see why—"

"Don't you see? Magic is cursed—"

"—because we were never meant to use it in the first place. But," I paused, "I don't understand. Why did the Creator give us Gifts if we're cursed? Was it to keep things interesting as It watched, to mock us or—?"

"It was so you could save yourselves."

"And what about the children left behind after this world-damning crusade?"

Micha leaned back in his seat, looking smug and sexy as hell. He had me hooked in more than one way and he knew it. Besides my attraction, it couldn't be denied that he made a believer out of me. I now knew that there was a bigger force out there and not some myth created to comfort people in their hour of need. How blind I'd been...

"I thought it was obvious." Micha moved his arm, the muscle in his bicep flexing, and I wondered when Dorian would return. "The Creator will let *all* humans coexist without any repercussions for magic users born thereafter."

"You just called us human?"

"Haven't you been listening? Alice was human until she was given these powers. But it doesn't completely change her DNA. It was only morphed. So the Gifted and the Immortals are both a variation of human beings."

"So we're not demons?" I wondered aloud.

Micha shook his head.

My hands tightened into fists as I remembered the years of abuse that I and many other of my brothers and sisters suffered at the hands of the Immortals. I thought of Tiara as Jacques drug her by the neck through the forest floor. And I was enraged. Why didn't they just tell us that? Why would they leave us here to suffer? And how did the story get so far out of hand—

And why would they allow it?

"This world...is disgusting!" I spat.

Micha touched my arm. "You're angry. What's wrong?"

"You all left us to be beaten, raped, murdered! Why?! Why would you let the Immortals tear apart this world...?! And why can't the Earth grow anything?! I don't understand! Why are we being punished?!"

"Some are tested," Micha admitted, "more than others. But it is only because the Creator favors you. The Earth changed after people started worshiping Kalysma. It will go back once all the disbelievers are wiped out."

I laughed. "That…is a load of bullshit."

"Marve!"

"You really thought you could get away with all those lies?!" I looked up, a manic grin taking over my face when I realized that even the angels didn't know the truth about the Gifted—either that or they wouldn't tell us. "You really think I'd believe any of that?!"

As I snapped the words, my Gift flared. Electricity crackled along my form, moving from the spot in my stomach up and down my body and crackling around my form. I was a living storm. And I was the descendant of a living goddess.

"Marve," Micha warned, "you're taking this all the wrong way."

"If we're human," I sneered and smiled at once, "why do we look like monsters? And why did you call us dumb beasts when talking to Dorian, huh?!"

"I wasn't talking about you all."

"Answer the question!"

"You already know the answer to the question. You're a fool for asking again."

"Maybe I don't believe the answer," I said back, flipping the words back at him. I was reminded of the conversation of Dorian, where he said the very same thing. "Tch! I don't believe a damn thing you say…"

Micha leaned back in his seat. "This is a lot to take in. I know that it can all be a bit jarring. I wouldn't expect you to immediately believe it."

"You never answered my earlier question." I placed my chin on my now interlaced fingers. "Who is my great-grandmother?"

"Does the name Isolde sound familiar to you?" At my puzzled look, Micha's lips quirked up into a smile. "Well, it should be, Marve. Isolde is the name of your grandmother."

"But that makes—"

"Yes. Alice is your great-grandmother."

There was a question that rummaged through my mind since I was a child; he answered it before I could ask.

"Your father, Hakeem, and your mother, Siobhan, were both a little over thirty when they died."

"Whoa."

"Just like the Creator and I, they believed that you were meant for so much more. It's time that you saw it, too."

"The Gatekeeper...what does that entail? And who is the Ordained?"

"The Gatekeeper is more of a recruiter and divine general in the sense that you will lead the war. As such, it is your job recruit the reincarnations of the Four Horsemen of the Apocalypse, who will be a vital asset to the Final Battle. If everything goes as planned and you win, they will also be rewarded. If they lose, the very people that you united to help you will become the ones to wipe out the planet. After you track them all down, you will lead them into a smaller battle—a precursor before you face the Immortals. The Ordained is, naturally, one of your many enemies. He is the second-greatest evil this Earth has seen in a millennia and will stop at no means to kill you."

"Yes but who *is* he?"

"Can you think of no one?"

"So is Mez II coming back or something?" I tapped my nails on the armrest, thinking of the Immortal that started the enslavement of the Gifted people in 2003. "Isn't it kind of ironic that my people are suffering a genocide and now—"

"You're not at the mental or physical capacity to take on other Immortals yet." Micha shook his head with a smirk. "And the dead will stay dead."

"Then who—?"

Suddenly, his eyes began to glow as his hands fell limp on the armrests. His lips trembled. I don't know how I knew, but I had a feeling that he was talking to the It. When his eyes dimmed, he looked at me warily. I stared back at him, and he sighed.

"It seems that the Creator has a proposition for you."

"What?" I jumped out of my seat. "Why? What is it?"

"It seems that It's foreseen that training without any incentive had a low chance of success, so It crafted a bargain." He looked me up and down, his head cocking cutely to the side like a puppy. "Something in your future must have changed."

"What's the new agreement?"

"Do as you are told or you will lose your emotions," he said nonchalantly.

"That's a load of crap."

"Feels unfair, huh?" he asked in what I'm guessing was supposed to be sympathy.

"Exactly." I took a deep breath as something dark rolled over in my stomach. "You said that I have to defeat the Ordained...but you didn't tell me how to kill him."

"Sometimes, those are two very different things," he said, agreeing without agreeing.

"How do I defeat the Ordained?"

"You must find Alice's amulet. You will have to fight the Ordained. Afterwards, you must seal him away forever."

"So it *is* a guy! Awesome!" I was giddy as I pumped my fist in the air, happy to have weaseled a bit of information from Micha. "Now that I know that, can you tell me what happened to the amulet?"

"I'm not sure. It's out there. It's up to you to find it."

Just like that, I deflated. This was a lot to take in at once. It was like I was taking a crash course in all things magic. It left my head spinning. It also left me wondering if I was the one for the job.

"So let me get this straight. I have to gather the Four Horsemen—"

"After you find out who they are—"

"You don't know?"

"Of course not. That'd be too easy!" He nodded pensively. "The one who knows is the one who started this whole mess."

"Alice? She's still alive?"

"She *is* the first of you. She is Immortal and Gifted, like your mate over there..."

"Well...what happened to her after she got everyone cursed? Did she go into hiding?"

I know I would, I added in my head.

"The Creator sent a plague on her mind. Now she's living in some mental hospital in Amoria. Even in her fragmented state, she is the key to this whole ordeal. We'll visit her soon enough."

"How do you know all of this?"

"I have been watching you for a very long time." Micha dipped his head and I just barely caught his blush. "The rest was supplied to me by the Creator."

"You're blushing? I didn't think angels could blush..." I stared at him in shock. "But why are your cheeks silver?"

"That's because my blood is silver." He said before nodding. "Which reminds me..."

He pulled out the dagger from before.

"This only works if the blood is given willingly." He dragged the dagger across his wrist until his silver blood swelled like mercury in a broken thermostat. "But this will make you more than Gifted."

I blanched as I realized what he wanted me to do.

"No way!"

"Trust me. It doesn't taste like regular blood." He touched his fingertips to the wound and then brought his hand to my face. "Smell it."

I inhaled. It smelled sweet and sugary, like syrup. My tongue darted out to trail across his fingertips and to my surprise, it tasted like fresh peaches. Micha stiffened as his eyes met mine. I leaned back in my seat and rebuilt the walls that I let fall. Micha slowly brought forward the wrist flowing with blood.

"Drink."

"Why?"

"In order to win the battle, you will need to be more than Gifted."

"Like what?"

"You will need to truly be Nephilim."

"I already am!"

"No." He shook his head. "You are not. Your blood is diluted. You are no more angel than I am human."

I felt like Dracula as I closed my mouth over the opening in his wrist and sucked. It took only a few drops and I suddenly felt something shift inside of me to make room for a very inhuman aberration in my DNA. Subsequently, we parted and as I sunk into the leather cushions, Dorian came back into our section of the jet. He looked between us for a long moment. I recalled the taste of Micha's fingertips and felt guilty.

"We're going to touch down soon." Dorian glanced at Micha. "Everything is set up."

"Good." He looked to me. "Then the best part of your training can begin."

A wary tremor overtook me as I remembered my training with Jacques. His motivations for training in my first years of knowing him were adequate enough, but as I got older, they grew more inventive, if you could call it that. It was nothing short of torture. I touched my thighs, remembering the scars there that he forced me to carve with his personal blade. I prayed that Micha would be more merciful…and that, unlike Jacques, he did not derive pleasure from my begging.

"What is it?"

"I'm going to teach you how to fly."

CHAPTER NINE

CRASH AND BURN

I stood in the front yard, as did about every member of the staff. The new solar panels on top of the manor hummed with energy and as they did, a field of snapping electricity hovered around my form. Micha had all six of his wings spread out behind him and as he flapped them, a small wind picked up. All the staff members watched him as if he were, well, sent from God. Towering above us all were large silver hoops that looked as if they were stolen from a circus. Per Micha's request, they were all big enough for me to fit through.

I now understood Micha's earlier words.

"How are you going to teach me to fly if I don't have wings?" I said, looking at his glittery feathers.

"You are Nephilim. You have wings, too."

A shocked gasp rippled through the crowd.

"I don't feel them."

"You must summon them. Once you do it the first time, it will come naturally. After we're done here, I'm going to take you somewhere much higher to teach you how to navigate with more pressure against your wings. But right now, I want you to think about wading in the water."

"Isn't that a song?"

He gave me a look. I closed my eyes and tried to envision what he meant. I was lying on my back in the middle of a stream. The water was smoothing over my skin, tickling my ribcages and fanning my hair around me like some sort of bloody halo. I was lighter than light.

I was air.

I opened my eyes as an excited murmur reached my ears. I looked at Micha. He was looking at me with a new sort of respect and I knew that whatever I'd done, I'd done it well. I glanced at Dorian and saw that the skin around his eyes was crinkling from his smile. I rolled my eyes.

"Now I want you to flap."

As soon as I thought of doing it, my wings stroked down then up again. Micha grinned with a small nod. My angelic teacher commanded me to do it again. I heard Dorian cheering my name as well as Yvonne and Andrew, Beatrice and Alena, along with the soft cries of my son, Aiden, who Yvonne was holding. I saw her vice grip on the young lad and suddenly realized that she wasn't protecting him but rather *us*. I thought of the danger that Jacques posed and was slightly afraid. My thoughts were a betrayal to everyone that I loved, so I beat stronger and harder as I let every negative thought in my body slip away like a shawl.

What is wrong with me? A piece of me still thought.

I flapped as if my life depended on it. In a way, it did…as did the lives of the Gifted people. I decided to use the power of that kind of thinking to push myself higher until I was hovering above the ground. Granted, I was only hovering about six to eight inches but still, my feet weren't skimming the ground, which was big for my first try. I glanced at my trainer.

"I know that you can go higher than that," Micha said, expecting only the best.

I nodded and flapped higher. I felt my body temperature rise so I opened my mouth to expel heat. After a while, I was level with the rooftop. The snow was glimmering in the afternoon sun and I remembered a day that was cold instead of warm—a forgotten holiday called Christmas. My son, father and mother all shared this birthday. I could see my spiky greenish-brown body, my whipping tail and my glorious, glimmering wings—the only beautiful part of my peculiar body.

I chalked it up to my mutated DNA.

"Move your wings to change directions!"

I quickly folded one wing slightly in. I went in in the opposite direction. I did the opposite and received the same result. I darted towards the ground and then pulled my body back, in total shock when my body tilted, and my feet skimmed the ground. I should have gotten a mouthful of dirt due to my former velocity—

but I didn't. Maybe there *was* some outside force looking out for me.

Folding in my wings, I drifted towards the ground like a fallen leaf. Then I glanced at Yvonne and, in a split-second decision, darted towards her. I reached her in a matter of seconds. I didn't have the mental ease to marvel at my speed. I had to learn, *quickly,* for my son and my husband. I held my arms out. She quickly passed Aiden over to me but I could tell that she didn't understand what was happening.

My tail moved from around my waist and towards Aiden. In response, he reached out to hold onto one of the spikes with one hand, clinging to the front of my dress with the other. With the extra security in case he fell, I made sure that my hands were locked securely around him before I took off. The boy looked at me with his gold-flecked eyes, his mouth opening in a silent o. I leaned down to nuzzle his cheek, coasting over the clouds.

Once again, everything blurred before becoming surprisingly clear. When I looked around, I was surprised to see the city looming in the distance. I made sure to beat higher until my wings skimmed the clouds, hoping that no one could see me from this distance. I turned and looked back in the direction I came from. I couldn't see the manor.

Aiden looked up at me, his eyes wide and curious. I tickled his ribs. He gurgled out a laugh.

"It seems that we are lost, wouldn't it, little one?"

He cooed and made a grabby motion at me, which was just about the cutest thing ever. I leaned down to kiss his head. He hiccupped and I couldn't help but laugh. I realized that he had grown quickly since I'd last seen him. He looked to be around a few months old, and not a few days, which meant that someone had been supplying him souls. He wasn't a half-demon, more a regular Gifted-Immortal with demon enhancements, but he grew and fed like one.

What would he become? I wondered.

"We should probably go back home before daddy starts to worry," I said, beating my wings softly.

We glided over the treetops. To me, flying was as natural as breathing. As if to prove me wrong, the wind caught my wings. I went a bit off course.

I landed on the ground. Everyone clapped, driving away my fear, my loneliness, and my anger. Even though my father and mother were gone, I still had a family. I moved to hand Aiden off. Micha clapped a hand on my shoulder and I tried not to shudder as a jolt of raw, untamed want rippled through me.

"Now, I want you to learn to fit yourself into smaller places with your wings." He glanced at the large hoops set up in the yard. "Are you ready?"

"Yes."

"Try to get a running start. You'll need to use your momentum to your advantage."

I'd already breezed through most of my training and I just knew that this was going to be a piece of cake. I backed up as far as the yard would allow. There was so much space between me and everyone else. Without a second thought I took off running. I felt my feet pounding the earth and when I looked down, there were deep grooves in the ground.

I've never felt this much power before! I thought.

Just wait and see, Keres's voice hissed back.

I flapped my wings and separated myself from the ground. Every time I flapped, I felt surer of myself and made each beat of my wings stronger than the last. The first hoop was quickly approaching and at this angle, it looked rather large but still too small for my body. That was when I realized that the hoops got smaller as they went on. My heart raced in my chest and I mistakenly hesitated as I approached my first obstacle.

That was all it took.

My head was tossed through the hoop. My wings got tangled and I crashed to the ground. The hoops fell around me with a large crash. Everyone moved to help me stand but I waved them off with an irritated flick of my tail. I looked at Micha, who was shaking his head in either amusement or sympathy.

"Did she always have that?" Yvonne asked Dorian, glancing at him with alarm. "Usually those from the Southern Isles don't have tails. Only those from Espanza are born with them."

"I'm not sure…" Dorian mumbled. "Maybe the Creator gifted it to her for all her hard work?"

"Wouldn't that be the wings?" Beatrice added, raising a brow.

"Marve?" Dorian asked, taking a cautious step forward. "Are you all right?"

I looked away from him quickly, feeling guilty but also excited as I met a pair of unreadable grey eyes.

"You failed."

"Yeah," I said with an annoyed huff, "I can see that." I stretched, my back popping. "I can feel it, too."

"Why do you think you failed?"

"The hoop isn't big enough!"

"No. All of them are big enough for you. I made sure of that." His eyes glimmered with, I suddenly realized, his inner laughter— and I wasn't sure what to make of his words. "Replay what you did in your head and tell me what you did wrong."

"Trusting you, that's what…" I mumbled, glancing at the hoops reluctantly.

The hoops glimmered in the afternoon sun, and I was reminded of the way I wanted to help the people in Africa. I'd failed in both endeavors. I replayed the crash in my head for what felt like hours. It hit me. I ran back down the yard. I took off very much the same way I did before but instead made my flaps more condensed, more precise.

When I approached the first hoop, I quickly tucked my wings in and twirled through it like a spinning bottle top. I passed through the second before unfolding my wings, unwisely thinking that I was ready for the third. This time, I managed to keep from knocking down two of the hoops. The third hoop fell to the ground with one huge, mocking bang. It took me longer to stand this time as humiliation made my cheeks turn red.

"What am I doing wrong?!"

"You are one impatient woman." A voice said and I was surprised to see that it was Dorian who was now looking at me calculatedly. "I've never flown before but from here, it looked as if you should've kept your wings folded in for a few more seconds."

I wanted to snap at him that it wasn't as easy as it looked. But then I cocked my head and realized that as his vantage point, he had a perfect view of what was going on. Still, my pride had suffered a serious blow.

"Don't go getting all offended, baby," he said at my withering look. "I'm just trying to help. But you still did awesome! You kept going—just like a Boyd!"

"Don't discredit your accomplishments," Micha said, quick to agree with Dorian. "He's right. You've done a lot. If you want to stop for now and pick it up tomorrow, I understand—"

"No!" I said as I held up a hand, my ring winking in the light of the sun. "Dorian *is* right. I'm a Boyd. A Boyd *never* gives up."

"I compliment your tenacity," Micha said with a sudden frown, "but maybe this is too much for—"

"I said I can do it!" I snapped before giving the hoops a spiteful look. "No way am I going to get my ass handed to me by a trial run!"

Some servants laughed while others high-fived each another. Micha gave me a resolved nod. I walked through the large expanse of grass once more. I took off, replaying my failures in my head. Each memory stung like salt in an open wound.

There was the time that I spilled boiling water on Master's lap and went two days without water for it. There was the time that I tried to run away and Master put the bars on my windows. There was the time that I stood up for Tiara and it cost my friend her life. Lastly, I thought of the hoops that kept me from continuing with my training. Anger stormed through my heart like a pack of rhinos.

Everyone believed that I could be a good person. They thought that I could operate on positivity and somehow make peace with my past. They were wrong. I wasn't strong enough. I couldn't do it.

I wasn't a good person or anything special. I was a nobody that made a name for myself by taking people's lives. I called myself a Champion, but really, I was just a glorified murderer. How could someone like that ever be more? Slowly, I felt my wings begin to disappear. I didn't want to fly.

I mean, how could I? After all, I was at my best when I was about to crash and burn.

"Don't give up on yourself!" Dorian screamed, his hands cupped around his mouth. "The woman I married is a fighter!"

"C'mon, Marve!" screamed Yvonne.

Even the baby began to squall.

Them...now...that's what I'm living for...

Before I knew what was happening, I was nearing my first obstacle. I flapped harder, faster before folding my wings in. I shot through it like a bullet. When I finally unfolded my wings, I was surprised to see all the hoops behind me, staring at me harmlessly. Everyone cheered and when I landed, Dorian pulled me into a crushing hug.

When I pulled away, I felt his mouth crash against mine. Just like the first time we kissed, I was engulfed in flames. And just like the first time, my reaction was instantaneous. My husband pulled me forward and as he did, my hands moved up to twine in his hair. As our chests pressed together, I felt his heart beating strong, same as mine.

I broke away, gasping for air. There was a smug smile on Dorian's face. I looked over at my family, who was watching us with fond grins, before I glanced at Micha, who'd politely turned his head and was chanting softly under his breath. I had a million questions. Instead of asking them all, I picked the most paramount.

"How did I do?"

Micha refused to look at me, which left me confused. Had I done something wrong? Maybe the sharing of blood gave him an access to my emotions. Maybe he knew about my confliction. Maybe he was trying to do right by the both of us by pushing me away, and for that, I inwardly thanked him.

At least, almost as much as I hated him for it.

He made me fly through the hoops ten more times and I only failed on my third try. I found it getting easier and easier as it went on. Finally, he held up his hand.

"Are you ready for the next phase of your training?"

"Yes."

Micha waved his hand. A large rip seemed to open in the air and from it sprung a dark, swirling portal. Through it, I could see something rocky in the distance. Micha gestured to the gaping portal. I quickly kissed my husband goodbye and stepped through the opening.

When I turned, Micha was standing behind me and the portal closed with a sound akin to that of a zipper closing. The wind blew softly against my cheeks like light kisses. Large red rocks rose around us as the sun beat down hot and heavy. I opened my reptilian mouth. Micha was seemingly unaffected. He came to stand next to me, his hand brushing mine.

Despite the jarring jolt that rocked through me, I dismissed it as an accident and looked out upon the steep rocks.

"Do you know where we are?"

"The Grand Canyon," I immediately said as a bird took off above my head. "I have a question."

"Shoot."

"Since I'm Nephilim now, do I have to fight in the arena anymore?"

"You haven't fought in the arena since you've lived with Dorian."

"So?"

"So why would you start now?" he snorted.

"Good. I don't want to kill any more of my people. But why?"

"Kalysma doesn't like it." He reached towards me. "Now get ready."

"Ready for—"

He pushed me. I fell off the cliff with a scream. My heart banged against my ribcage as if it were trying to break through. Any confliction that I was feeling fled and was replaced by one emotion: unadulterated fear. Despite my eyesight, everything was rushing, coming at me too quickly. Even my thoughts were a jumbled mess, banging around in my head like beads in a cup.

"HHHEEELLLPPP!"

"Use the pressure to your advantage! Ride the wind."

"What am I, a flying squirrel?" I shrieked as my tail trashed in fear.

"Stop being such a wuss and flap already!"

I would've turned and flipped him off if I wasn't so afraid of plummeting to my death. I tried to make my wings flutter open slowly. Instead, my wings caught the wind and flew opened like twin parachutes. I tried to flap them softly, wanting to glide while maintaining the smoothness that I now likened to water. Instead, my wings clapped in one strong beat and I surged forward like a missile.

I streaked across the sky like some sort of comet. My eyes watered, struggling to stay open. The higher I climbed, the less my fear weighed me down until finally, I was weightless. I flew so high that the sloping cliffs that could kill me upon impact seemed harmless. The sun gleamed like a beacon and I raced towards it. Tears streaked down my cheeks and I wanted to close my burning eyes but I couldn't.

I had to reach that luminescence.

After all, I was born to crash and burn.

CHAPTER TEN

SOFT

I pulled up short as a shadow streaked across the sky. My tail instantly flicked in anger before pulling closer in case the figure tried to grab it and pull me towards the rocks waiting below. I shielded my eyes and peeked at the menace through the gap that my fingers provided.

"Turn back!" said a familiar voice.

"Micha?"

His wings beat strongly, blowing wind in my face and making my hair plaster to my wet cheeks.

"Don't fly into the sun. I know how it appears when you first learn to fly." Micha's face was oddly grim. "You will burn the same way Icarus did. Land and we can talk."

I landed with a small thud. I immediately rolled over on my back and grew angry that the rocks burned me through my shirt. Sadly, I was too exhausted to do anything but lay there. I panted, fighting to stay cool. Micha was a dark shadow as he blasted across the sky before landing beside me. He crossed his arms as he looked down at me, face indecipherable.

"Are you okay?"

"I'm fine," I said, looking up at him through my lashes before patting the spot next to me. "Sit."

"I don't think that's a good idea," he said but still, he sat.

His arm brushed mine. I felt a deep ache echo through me. Micha's grey eyes flickered over me before he scooted away. I frowned and rolled over on my side. When Micha spoke, his voice made the rocks beneath me shake.

"You're panting a lot."

"It's hot out here." I sunk my teeth into my bottom lip, not wanting to admit that my rise in body temperature wasn't only due to the sun. "I need to cool down."

"Can you fly?"

He didn't wait for an answer. I felt his fingertips press lightly against my skin. I heard the wind blow as he flapped, taking to the skies once more as I dangled in front of him. I tried not to let the hurt swamp me as I realized that he was trying to touch me as little as possible. I knew that it was just because he was a good guy who didn't want to compromise my relationship. It still stung, though.

When I looked again, we were over a small field. Micha landed and as soon as my feet touched the ground, his hands left me. I glanced at him only to receive a crooked grin. He silently reached out and pointed. I looked and was greeted by a small bubbling creek.

I went to it and was startled by the odd reflection staring back at me.

My hair was red and wild, raised around my head like a living flame. My emerald-green eyes were bright and painfully conflicted. My cheeks were a bright pink from either the sun or all the emotions that threatened to overtake me. My jacket was flapping around me in the wind and as I rose to smooth it, the ring on my finger glowed slightly. I rolled my shoulders, which were beginning to darken from a slight tan, as a frown marred my full lips.

I looked just like what the savior of the world should like—beautiful, strong, ready to face anything—but I had to admit that it was an image that I was unfamiliar with. And yet it was wholly familiar. Then I realized where I'd seen it before.

I looked like my mother.

I stepped into the river with a shudder on my lips. I spread my wings around me. They were shaped much like the wings of an eagle and were a seemingly pale grey. But as the sun bounced off my contour feathers, there seemed to be a trace of flamingo pink reflecting off them. The feathers farthest from my body were dominated by blue and purple and as I remembered the way the wind made them flutter, a voice in the back of my mind called them primary feathers. My secondary feathers and tertiary feathers were paler and were whiter.

Like a pearl...I thought.

I'd never felt more beautiful in my life.

Having almost forgotten why we came here, I quickly folded my wings in and splashed around. The water lapped at my fingertips as I waded farther out. A laugh slipped past my lips as I paddled around for a bit. As the sun began to sink in the sky, I got out of the creek. I was quick to lay down before spreading out my wings.

The sun glazed over my wings like icing on a cake. My toes curled in pleasure as a deep hum of satisfaction built in my throat. When I inhaled, I took in my own scent of roses and spring water. I looked over to see Micha approaching me slowly, his eyes unreadable. He came towards me with an outstretched hand. I gasped as his hands briefly landed on my chest where my wet dress clung to my body, making my nipples harden as they clashed with the cold breeze.

"What is it?"

"Let me get that," he rumbled.

His hands brushed over my feathers. This time, a deep purr of pleasure left me. His fingers moved quick but gently, pulling out any debris that had built up while we were flying. It felt as if he were giving me a massage as his cool voice rolled over me, commanding me to stay still. When he was done, I wanted to pounce but instead of that, I thought of a better solution.

I was going to talk.

Words began to pour from my lips. I told him my life story even though I knew that he already knew it. For some reason, my chest was still heavy. I couldn't deny that I was attracted to him, but I also had to accept that aside from him helping me with my divine task, there was no room for him in my life. We sat and sunbathed until there was no more sun left.

When we stood, my clothes were fully dry. Micha nodded and unfurled his wings before giving a strong, sure flap. I naturally did the same.

"In Botswana a man told me that if I didn't meet your approval, Africa would never come to accept me. Can I go back?"

He was all seriousness.

"You will help the entire planet by completing your mission."

We flapped in silence for a while.

"Are you ready to go back?"

I briefly looked over him. He shifted under my gaze. His skin was still that wicked bronze and the muscles in his arms seemed to ripple as he raised his hands above his head and stretched. The sleeveless cloak he wore didn't hide the fact that he had a decent body. I tore my eyes away.

Dorian was fine—no, more than fine. He was perfect. He had an above average face and a realistically fit body. But Micha was... different. He was a Greek god carved from the finest stone. Dorian's love, patience and understanding was a godsend, but Micha's body was truly a work of art.

After that inner monologue, I'd almost forgotten what Micha asked me. When I spoke, he almost seemed startled…Maybe I wasn't the only one that was preoccupied.

"Yes," I said again, slower this time. "I'm ready to go."

We were quiet as we flew back to the manor. When we got back, Dorian was waiting for us in the yard and he told me that our newborn was with Rhea, who had returned from the Isles. At those words, something didn't sit right with me. I felt a pair of eyes on me. We strode towards the house without looking back, leaving Micha in the shadows.

CHAPTER ELEVEN

GREEN LIKE ENVY, BLACK LIKE PRIDE

"When did Rhea get back?" I asked Dorian.

"A little while after we did. She received intel about the Immortals seeking to invade the Southern Isles. Rather than tell the rest of the Rebels, she came to us with the information."

"But why?" I whispered. "After everything she's done, why would she risk her life for us?"

She tried to kill you and let me be ravaged by a rapist! I thought, wincing as I remembered those fresh scars. I touched my belly, wondering if he saw my ovaries when he lifted my son from my belly, and if, for just a moment, he saw the woman that I was and was moved by it. For others, mother were gods in a sense, for they gave life, gods of love, life and prosperity, and fathers were gods of protection, providence, and namesake. And I suddenly realized that I was honored with a father that played a much gentler roll. But I knew he would have changed allegiances if my mother demanded.

"Maybe she's had a change of heart," Dorian said, eyes unreadable.

When we got inside, something totally unexpected happened. Rhea stumbled down the stairs, her eyes wild and feverish. When her eyes landed on me, she seemed to calm for my benefit, but I still knew that something was up. When she reached me, she gave me a strange look. My tail flicked behind me in curiosity.

"Ae you all right?" I asked.

"I need your help!"

I knew that Micha was staring at her and that made me pay attention. The other woman was now clad in a black long-sleeved shirt with a panda on it, a pair of low-rise skinny jeans and black converses. Her dark brown hair was pulled up into a messy bun. When her eyes landed on Micha, she blushed. He glanced at me before giving her a grin so seductive that I fumed with jealousy. Dorian glanced between them both before leaning towards me.

"I think someone is about to hit it off," Dorian said, winking as he nudged me.

My head swirled with angry thoughts. I didn't like that. I didn't like it one bit. But I had no right to be angry—I was married after all. So, I gave my friend a tight smile.

But could I really call her my friend?

After everything I'd risked for her, everything she'd done to me, was she simply an enemy?

"You need my help?" I said, snapping her out of the trance Micha put her in.

She was fearful again. She squirmed and it was easy to tell that she was uneasy. I would have probably laughed if I weren't so angry. I wondered what had her so upset.

"I think this is something that you should see for yourself," said Rhea.

Sharing a curious look with both Micha and Dorian, we ascended the stairs. Rhea stopped before one of the large mahogany doors with golden knobs. Why were we at her room? The Espanzan woman held her hand on the knob before slowly pushing it open. When the door opened, I felt Dorian instantly move closer to me, always the protector.

The window was broken from the outside, which didn't make sense since we were about three stories up. Glass was scattered on the floor and there were large strips of ripped fabric that looked like the remnants of a comforter. The desk in the corner was overturned and one of the legs had been broken off the chair; it was stabbed through the wall as if it were some twisted nail. Hanging from it was a sheet. On the sheet was a message written in blood.

I HAVE RETURNED!

"There's one other thing that I need to tell you…"

"Quickly!" I snapped my fingers. "Time is of the essence."

"I didn't take him."

"Who?" Dorian asked.

"Your son. I have no idea where he is."

That did it.

Dorian stepped toward her as if to do bodily harm. My heart slammed to a halt in my ribcage and as it picked back up, each beat echoed through me. A million damning thoughts raced through my mind: *Did Jacques have him?* More importantly, *What did Jacques want with him? Had he hurt my boy?*

Had he touched him?

"Dorian, get Hao to search the perimeter," I said, immediately taking over. "Rhea, go get Yvonne, Andrew and everyone else that has been in the household and take them to the Blue Room. Micha,"

I turned to look at the angel, "look out for any intruders from the skies."

"Are you sure I can't stay?" he said, glancing at Rhea.

I rolled my eyes and turned back around.

"I'll scout the house," I said, feeling uncharacteristically cool, calculating, as I looked upon the sheet. "Whoever did this couldn't have gotten far."

And I had a pretty good idea as to who it was.

*   *   *

"I have called you all to this meeting because there is a great danger posed against us." At my words, Rhea stood with her hands clasped in front of her. "Give us a full description of what happened."

"Well, I'd just stepped out of the shower and had gotten dressed in the bathroom. The room was so cold," she said as she rubbed her arms, "and I knew that the heat had been on because the vent had been open in the bathroom. I was walking towards my bed when I saw that the window had been punched in. That's when I saw it."

"Saw what?" Andrew said, obviously annoyed at the vagueness of her words. "Do you mean the message?"

"No. *It.*"

"What is it, exactly?" Dorian asked with a roll of his eyes.

I chalked her slowness up to her being in shock.

"I don't know. It was this thing," she said, her lip curling up in disgust. "Its skin was black. There were curved horns sprouting from its head and pointy teeth coming from its mouth. It had claws and when it looked at me, its eyes flashed red *como un vampiro* or something. It was holding him…your son. After it jumped out of the window, I noticed the message written on the sheet in blood."

"Is that all?" Andrew said, rolling his eyes. "You mean to say that a demon jumped three-and-a-half stories *and* got into the house without any of us knowing?"

"Don't underestimate my dark brethren," Yvonne said as she laid a hand on Andrew's, her brown skin pulled tight over a grimace. "They are more than capable. Did you feel anything when you saw the demon? Anything at all?"

"I was afraid." Rhea said, her eyes chilling as she recalled the memory. "Before I could scream for help, it was gone."

"It was a demi-demon in his true form," Yvonne said, nodding to herself. "No full-blooded demon could've shown that much restraint—you would've been killed instantly. You also would have felt all your worst memories take hold of you, along with despair. Only a true demon could inspire those feelings in a person. That's how they get you, after all—by paralyzing you with fear and depression before going in for the kill."

"Are you sure?" I asked.

"My mother was a demon that raped my human father. Since he was married, she slaughtered his wife and their unborn child. Then she paralyzed and raped him so that she could bear his child. Once I was born and his purpose had been fulfilled, she murdered him. She raised me until I was seventeen and when my beauty grew to be greater than hers..."

Yvonne's face was wrinkled now. But in it were the echoes of a beauty that could never be slain. She was still very eye-catching. Poised. Graceful.

Dangerous.

"She let me keep my longevity, but my body would still reflect my age. It was humiliating to live amongst the other demons and their offspring. But I wanted nothing but her love. She was incapable—"

"Yvonne!" I snapped. "Stick to the subject."

"Right." She nodded, looking at Rhea. "What you faced today was not a full-blooded demon. It was a demi-demon—"

"That left your son to die," said a deep, smooth voice.

We all turned in our chairs to see Micha walking towards us. In his arms was a small, broken body. I lurched out of my chair and swept him into my arms, possessiveness filling me to the brim. When Micha reached out to touch Aiden, an ugly, animalistic hiss slipped between my teeth. Only Dorian could wrap his arms around me as he looked down at our son.

I felt like an animal. When angry or protective, my mannerisms were not human at all. I learned this from Jacques.

"It seems that the intruder tried to smother your child with a stuffed animal and when that didn't work, he drained his blood and left him in the forest to die."

Micha tossed something on the table. I looked to see that it was a rainbow elephant—one of the many toys in Aiden's room. I reached out and let electricity spark across my hands. Then, with a flick of my finger, I set the toy aflame. I never wanted to see it again.

I glanced down at Aiden. His breaths were slow and shallow and no matter how many times I said his name, he wouldn't open his eyes. I pressed a glowing hand to his head, transferring some of my magic back to him. His eyelids flickered but remained shut. I turned with the boy still in my arms.

"I'm going to see a doctor," I said as I unfurled my wings. "Right now."

"It'll be easier if we take my portal," Micha suggested, waving his hand.

At first, I wanted to say no. I wanted to fly—to clear my head. But that was selfish of me. My boy was inching closer to death with every second that passed. With a stiff nod, I clutched my son closer and stepped through the portal he opened.

*   *   *

That much blood loss could've killed him. No, not could've—it *should* have killed him. But it didn't.

Why?

Aiden didn't look like himself. A large glass structure encased him. There were tubes and IVs—too many to count—hooked up to just about every inch of his body. He looked like a screwed-up version of a pufferfish, except these spikes were here to save instead of poison. Larson, Dorian's family doctor, swept in and out of the room.

Aiden squirmed in his sleep and his face would occasionally screw up in pain. As I inhaled, I was surprised to find that his woodsy scent of oak and sawdust had returned. It was all too easy to remember how odd he smelled before when the blood donated from my body gave him a scent that smelled neither woman nor boy; it was a blend of his scent and mine. Doctor Larson entered the room for what must have been his seventh or eighth time. Instead of checking the tubes and monitors before leaving, he paused.

And he looked dead at me.

"Would you mind telling me what happened one more time?"

I started to tell my story. After a while, I realized that his face never lost the raised eyebrow or the grim mouth. It didn't take me too long to become privy to the fact that he was looking at me rather condescendingly. Electricity immediately sparked around my body. I wanted to do some serious damage to him.

"Wait," I said, eyes narrowing, "you think that I did this?"

"Dorian told me that you were assaulted and that the boy was filled with your rapist's DNA. Some women resent them that much." Larson cocked his head at me, his eyes narrowed accusatorily. "Assault takes a toll on the body, yes, but the mind as well."

"He's my son! *My son.* I would *never* do that!"

After registering what he was suggesting, the old me would have had him pinned to the wall in seconds, my fingers around his neck and a smile on my face as the light faded from his eyes. The new me simply cocked her head and gave him a nod. In a twisted way, I was thankful for that. No, it was not the fact that he didn't trust me. It was the fact that he was looking out for my son's well-being.

"She didn't do it." Micha said, unfolding his wings. "I was the one who found him. If you don't believe me…" He held out a hand, his palm turned up in offering. "Let me prove it to you."

Larson reached out and I didn't miss the gleam in his eye. Touching an angel was exciting for him. Hell, it gave me a rush, too. As soon as their hands connected, Larson's eyes glowed. Micha's eyes fell closed and his hand tightened around Larson's.

Larson suddenly yanked away with a gasp. His chest rose and fell as he sucked in breath after needy breath. Micha helped him over to a chair and eased him into it slowly, his hand only leaving the man's back when the doctor's head sagged against the wall. Larson was shaking. Micha glanced up at me and something on my face must have bothered him because I saw shock and then hurt flicker upon his face before he covered it with a smile.

What did I look like right now?

"Some humans can't handle being Linked with angels." The angelic man ran a hand through his curly hair, the ropes of muscle on his arm flexing. "He'll be fine in a few minutes."

"You showed him your memories?"

"Yes."

"That's insane! You're like a Vulcan from *Star Trek* or something!" He laughed which made a tiny smile wriggle onto my face; it was remarkable after everything that happened. "Since I'm Nephilim now..." I took a step forward, my wings fluttering against my back. "Can I do that?"

"No. It's a gift that only angels have. Your kind used to be able to do it," Micha said, his mouth twisting into a smile, "but they abused the power. When the Creator saw how this was being used for torture, It ripped it from your DNA. There's only one of you that can Link now."

"Alice."

"Yes."

My head was filled with many thoughts. Alice did a great many things. I was eager to meet her.

"Larson," I said, glancing at the man who I barely knew yet trusted completely. The silver-haired man raised an eyebrow at me, the Indian man's brown hand flicking a pen against his leg. "When can I take my son home?"

"Since you gave him a bit of your magic, the healing process is moving at an accelerated rate." Larson slowly stood from the chair and cracked his neck. "He should be able to go home tomorrow."

"Fine."

I gave Micha a look and the angel left the room. When he was outside the door, he peered up and down the hall. I turned to Larson, who watched me like a hawk.

"Be careful with him," Larson said. "A lot of unexpected things can happen if you let your guard down."

"I thought you knew that I didn't hurt my son." I said, glancing at the young boy who meant everything to me. "I would *never* hurt him."

"I wasn't talking about your son," Larson said and with that, he left.

*   *   *

We all sat in the Blue Room, everyone facing the person next to them with words on their lips that they didn't dare breathe aloud. I was shaking with anger and fear. Occasionally, I would feel someone glance at me then look away, as if they would somehow spontaneously combust if they stared at me too long. It was probably because I was lit up like the 4th of July, my skin glowing with the rapidly ascending electricity in my system. My body also gave off a slight hum during this display of power, almost as if I were a living electrical fence.

There was a touch on my shoulder.

"Ouch!" Rhea yanked her hand away. "Do you have to do that?"

The smell of singed flesh filled the air. I pulled my beloved son closer to my chest. He was seemingly unaffected by my powers and I wasn't sure if that was because we shared the same DNA or if it was from the sharing of God's Magic.

"Sorry I'm late!" Dorian said as he took his seat at the head of the table. "What did I miss?"

"Nothing." I answered truthfully. "I didn't want to start without you."

He gave me a sunny grin. It was the kind of grin that made the skin around his eyes crinkle, that made the person on the receiving end want to believe in seconds chances. My heart ran double time in my chest. I blushed and looked away.

"Are we ready to begin?"

I was told to go ahead. I folded my hands before me. I could feel the eyes on me, the dependence that each person had on whatever decision that I made. I loved the power. I would soon learn that power would find me.

"A disturbing message had been placed in Rhea's room. The room has since been cleaned and we have our own private investigation team shaking down anyone who might be involved."

"What if the demi-demon returns?" Hao asked, cracking his knuckles in a show of strength. "Would you like me to stay next to you in case you need defense?"

I knew that he was eager to correct his error during our first encounter with the demi-demon.

"No offense, Hao, but you stand about as much a chance of defeating Jacques as Aiden does." I ran my hand through my son's dark locks as surprised murmurs filled the room. "Yes, I know the demi-demon's name."

"How?" Andrew piped up, one veined fist rising to strike the table. "Did you have something to do with this?"

"Yes. This whole time I was plotting to kill my son so that I could take over the world. And the bond I created between us? Fake. How did you know?"

Andrew blushed and all I could think was how much of a stupid question that was.

"I know him because he was once a very close acquaintance of mine. This is the kind of thing he would do. In fact…" I took a deep breath. "He was my Master once upon a time…"

Dorian's fist tightened on the table. He knew the full story. Since he found out, any time he heard the other man's name he was filled with a primal sort of rage, and I knew that it was love that drove him to hate so passionately. I glanced at each face in the room. Going up against someone like Jacques needed strength, stealth and more than sheer determination.

Frankly, it needed a fucking miracle.

"If anyone doesn't want to risk their lives fighting Jacques, please leave now."

Everyone looked at me. I saw Rhea's fist tighten. I knew that she still felt guilty for everything that had happened. I'd be lying if I said that I didn't blame her for my assault. But I knew that she was acting out of love for the Gifted people and not only on her own selfish desires. After all, she was like my cousin. Even if our relationship wasn't 100% perfect, I couldn't help but feel in my heart that I could trust her.

"All right then," I said, passing Aiden off to Yvonne, "in that case, we need to decide a course of action."

Yvonne scooted her chair back. When she stood, she was at her full height of 5'7". She was clad in a red dress sprinkled with images of black roses. Her hair was pulled back in that strict bun she loved so much, and I knew that she must've spent hours threatening it so that it would stay as immaculate as it was. I nodded at her to speak.

"Andrew, Beatrice and I have gone over it." She took in a shaky breath. "We believe that our best course of action is making the strongest of us the leader."

I looked back at Micha. An odd smirk danced on his lips. When I turned back around, Yvonne had her hands clasped before her as she glanced at Dorian and I in succession.

"What are you suggesting?"

"While you were at the hospital," Dorian said, rising from his seat as well, "we all agreed that we should unite under the one who knows our enemy best. And since you are apparently the one that will decide the fate of the Gifted people, what's a household full of people who are willing to serve? What I'm trying to say is…" He ran a hand through his hair and I could tell that the idea made him uncomfortable. "Will you be our Lady?"

"But you are the Lord here…" I didn't want to appear giddy. "Why would I ever—?"

Dorian read me like a book.

"I've been leading this manor for over three-hundred years. I've seen empires rise and fall, slaves become kings, demons become cowards…but I've never seen anyone fight the way that you do. Knowing what Micha told me after you got back from the hospital? I know that you are meant to not only lead our people, but *my* people."

Everyone else stood up together. I could feel the magic bouncing around the room. He was not used to the lifestyle—used to serving. But Dorian looked so sure of himself. Rhea stared at the lot of us as if we'd grown snakes out of our asses. That alone was reason enough for me to say yes.

But was I ready for this kind of power?

"I'd need a second-in-command, a companion that would take over if something happened to me—

"Where you go, I go," Dorian intoned, stepping forward and placing his fist on his chest. "Forever."

"Thank you. But I meant another. Is anyone willing to give up their Immortality?" I asked.

Of course, there was only one of us that was truly immortal. She wasn't human. Who knows what her powers would do if transferred to Beatrice? After all, I needed my powers. This would aid me a thousand times over.

She stepped forward, Beatrice trailing behind her. Then she turned, taking the younger woman's hands in her own. The look on her face was surprisingly peaceful but her old hands were shaking even harder now than before.

"I have trained you the best that I could. You know all the ins and outs of the manor. I've been ready to die for quite a while and *you* are *ready*." Yvonne reached into her pocket and pulled out a set of keys and let them fall into Beatrice's hands. "Do not fail me, Beatrice."

Beatrice bowed and I could see that she was withholding tears of her own. Yvonne straightened and walked towards me. I remembered the other secret that Dorian had revealed to me: you could take an Immortals immortality as long as they were willing to give it up. I turned to look at Andrew, who was looking at the cloudy skies above us with a look that made me think he wanted to curse the Creator himself.

But this was Yvonne's choice and we all had to respect that.

I laid my hand over hers as my eyes took on a faint glow, the other placed over Beatrice's head. I entered the halls of her spirit, asking if this was truly what she wanted. She said that she'd deemed it necessary. She handed off the part of her soul that would never die to me. I accepted it and then passed it onto Beatrice, more of a conduit than anything else.

She would live on through Beatrice—through all of us, really.

Yvonne nodded, telling us that she was ready to go. There was a shout. I turned to see Andrew barreling through the crowd, his face twisted into a snarl. I waved a hand. Hao and Dorian quickly restrained him.

"Andrew," I said, "you need to let her go."

"That's my wife you're talking about!"

"Let. Her. Go."

He collapsed. I looked at Dorian, whose eyes were glowing slightly. I gave him a smile that he did not return. I separated from Yvonne only to have her crumple to the ground, dead.

I called each member of the staff forward, placing my hand over theirs as my Mark burned its imprint on their skin. Dorian was the last to go, kissing me firmly before he joined hands with me. Magic flowed between us as the branding appeared on his collarbone. It was a weaving of masterful lines and swoops that appeared darker or lighter depending on the lighting. My Mark was simple, elegant, refined—everything that my husband described me as.

I stood back and looked at my new crew.

* * *

"Yvonne," Andrew said, pulling the lifeless form of his wife into his fragile arms. With shaking fingers, he moved the hair from her face and placed a trembling kiss on her lips. I could hear him mutter prayers and as he did, he found comfort and soon fell quiet. "Yvonne, I'm not too far behind. I'll follow you. I promise."

"Andrew," I said, watching him, "you don't have to stay."

"Yes, yes, yes..." He said, his eyes wild as they darted around the room. "I'm going home."

He left the room, and I knew that he would never return. I glanced at Dorian and saw him trail his fingers over the Mark that was now and would forever be embedded on his collarbone. I could feel Micha behind me, his body sending off a type of heat that I could not even begin to comprehend. As if the entire room picked up on my unease, the temperature of the room suddenly rose exponentially. For a split second everything was quiet...

Then all hell broke loose.

"He's gone!" One woman named Sheryl wailed. "They're both gone!"

"What will we do now?" another woman yelled.

"Has this girl ever been a Lady before?" cried a man's harsh baritone.

"What will become of Boyd-sama?" a young boy named Jared cried.

"Is he even our Lord anymore?"

"The End is coming for us all!"

"We're married so I'm technically still your Lord—" he glanced at me "—if she'll have me."

I nodded. Even though Dorian had told me that I was always meant to be the Lady of Boyd Manor, he'd never actually made me one. But now I was more than a shareholder of properties—his powers…I was now above him. I flexed my hand as a wave of electricity rippled through my system like a tornado through a cornfield.

It worked.

Pleased murmurs filled the room. The thought of their former liege being so close comforted them. I, on the other hand, was not comforted. If we could not stick together in these times, then all hope was lost. And if I was going to go down…

Well, I was taking them down with me.

"Beatrice," I said, locking my eyes on the other redhead; the young girl looked up, her eyes hollow and empty. "I need you to pull yourself together. You are one of the few people I trust. That's why I want you to watch over Aiden when he gets back and to advise me on all things Gifted. I don't want anyone coming in or out of our territory without your knowledge, which means *my* knowledge. Do we have an understanding?" Beatrice wiped her tears, nodded; I smiled and nodded back. "Hao," I glanced at the Vietnamese man, "you are still head of security. Rhea—"

I turned, the words that I thought I should say dying on my lips. For a moment, I wanted to be every bit as cruel as Dorian was *before* Jacques's blood was in his system, because then he operated out of love and not racism. Because I knew that Jacques's blood didn't make you like Jacques—it made you more like the you you'd be if you were at your worst. At my worst, I was a cowering, pathetic slave. At Dorian's worst, he was a racist fanatic. But if I could find a cure for the demon's blood and win the trust of his staff while doing so, I could not only save him—I could become higher than Jacques.

Because being tortured and raped by Jacques had not only changed me—

It had made me stronger.

And now I would become the night. I would become the dark and the terrors that lurked beneath its cover. I would watch over all that was good, yes, but I would do so by becoming the only evil that I would allow to exist in this forsaken world. And if I couldn't purify it, I would burn it to the ground.

I knew that Dorian wouldn't have me at that point, so I guess I'd have to eventually off both him and myself.

But then Micha reached out, touched my shoulder, his hand heavy and blazing hot. "Marve," he said, light pouring from his fingertips, "remember."

"Remember what? How to cower? How to kneel? How to come when summoned? How to be a slave? I am a Lady now. It's time that I acted like it."

Micha turned me to face him. "I know you. You are good and kind and pure. You protect the weak and innocent. You *hate* killing. The Aleilah I know would never succumb to her own darkness… or—?" He touched my temple, leaning forward and pressing his lips to my ear. "Is She speaking to you again?"

"Who?" I hissed back, biting my lip so as not to sneer at him.

"The Great Mother, Kalysma. Marve, there is something I need to tell you about Her—about you, about all your people. I didn't want—"

My eyes glowed as I stepped away. "She still won't speak to me. I don't know if I need to visit the church or make a sacrifice or pray but—" I stepped forward, grabbing Micha's hand when he moved away. I pulled him forward, threading my fingers through his as I leaned forward, whispering in his dark ear. "They call her the Barren One. Tell me…" I placed our interlaced hands over my belly. "Do I feel barren to you?"

"You feel empty." Micha hissed back, yanking me forward and plunging his glowing hand into my gut. "And cold as ice."

I gasped. The strange, powerful feeling left me. I gasped, leaning on him for support. He eased me down into the chair.

"You were addressing the Leader of the Rebellion," he reminded me. "I stopped time to address this. But now it is moving again. I implore you to exercise—"

"Mercy…Rhea," I said, glancing at the woman, "I know that things will never be the same between us…I know that you think that I hate you…I know that I should, but I don't. You're the last thing I have left of Valentina. So, you still have a home here. You always will. Dorian, I'm expecting you to be my advisor in all things financial and otherwise. Everyone else can continue doing what they did before. The world isn't over," I said, making eye contact with everyone in the room. "We're still here. Things have just changed a bit."

As my emotions swelled inside of me, I felt the electricity humming under my skin at full power. The lights above our heads flickered twice before a loud pop filled the room. We were surrounded by darkness. I amped up my electricity and was satisfied when I gave off light like some sort of glow stick.

I felt Micha's hand land on my shoulder. Oh man, since when did I recognize the feel of his hands? I schooled my expression, knowing that Dorian could still see in the dark. Micha leaned down to whisper in my ear. I couldn't withhold my shudder as his lips brushed my ear once more.

"You need a bit more training." He said with a chuckle. "Meet me outside at the crack of dawn."

I nodded and thought of one more thing to get out of the way.

"Everyone," I said, raising my voice, "we need to stick together. If one of you has a problem, come to me or Dorian. We're a family now more than ever."

"Yes, Lady Boyd."

With that, we sat in the dark, waiting for morning to come.

CHAPTER TWELVE

TOUCHING A FALLEN STAR

As I stepped through the portal, I felt Micha's eyes dancing across me. I turned and caught the look on his face before he looked away, thinking I hadn't caught him: narrowed eyes but dilated pupils, parted mouth, ragged breaths—Rhea had affected him more than he cared to admit. I looked around the space. We were lost somewhere in the cosmos and glittery stars surrounded us like undying lights. I was weightless as I reached out to let my hand brush a falling star.

A terrible scream ripped the atmosphere in half. I watched as Micha's form flickered back and forth, his body murky but his grey eyes fixed ahead in a driving stare. My head began to pound as I tried to drag in air that didn't exist. I was starting to panic, which wasn't good. I reached out to Micha…or at least where I thought he was.

I was now surrounded by darkness.

"You wanted to meet her. Now you have."

"Meet who?" I gasped—

And then lost all breath. A light shone forth, surrounded by two great black hands. Her eyes were like twin flames of gold, filled with rage and a unreachable sadness. Across her skin danced stars and at the joining of her thighs were cosmos. Her hair whipped around her head as she cradled in her arms a writhing body born of darkness and terror. In its face I saw myself and Dorian but also Aiden and Tiara, and every Gifted person I had come across, and others I had never seen before, but somehow peered straight through me, only I didn't see a goddess—

I saw a demoness banished to the confines of space.

"Do you know who she is?" Micha said at my ear.

His voice was not an angry growl or a horrified whisper, but a soft, understanding slip of the tongue. He'd known what she was. He'd known that the goddess that I worshiped, the goddess that sometimes spoke through me and countless others, was a demon. He knew and had tried to conceal it from me.

"Why?"

"She betrayed the Creator. She tried to slay It in its throne and she was shackled here. That woman that you see inside you—yes, I know about Keres," he added when my eyes cut around the darkness, searching for the source of the disembodied voice. "It is *her*. Its always been her. I was a fool to try and protect you. I don't know why I ever thought it was a good idea to conceal the truth from your people. Since your people were born before she Fell, you all are still Nephilim, but a bit of your blood has definitely turned. I see that now. There's only so much I can do to save you—not the Gifted people, not your son—*you*, Aleilah."

"Don't call me that."

"Why? Surely the great Champion Marve doesn't fear a name?"

"I fear no—"

"Really? Not even her?"

She opened her mouth in a smile and in it, I saw razor-sharp fangs ready to devour whole worlds. She looked beautiful but also… terrifying and monstrous. This…*thing*….that I made sacrifices to, that I prayed to…

"Is this your god?"

"No…"

"Is this your god?!" his voice was firmer.

"No!" I yelled back.

Her head snapped up, her eyes locking on me. She reached out, wrapping those claws around my body. Her lips peeled back, those fangs exposed like rows of sharpened knives. She moved to pull me forward and I suddenly realized that she wasn't smiling—

She was preparing to eat me.

As her skin touched mine, I felt death fill me for the first time in my life. It was not dark or hot like hell was once described. It was cold and filled with the blinding light of a thousand stars. Oh, how I felt it. Cold tendrils were wrapping around my lungs, filling them with ice water. Unforgiving hands grasped at my neck, threatening to strangle me. I dragged in another unfulfilling breath before closing my eyes. The whole world was dependent on me.

I couldn't fail now.

"Try to think of something that makes you feel safe."

The first thing that popped into my head was Dorian. I loved the way the sun glided over his golden skin, the way his eyes crinkled when he smiled, the way the middle of his forehead creased when he concentrated, the way he trusted me when I sometimes didn't trust myself. He had a faith in me that I didn't or he wouldn't have let me come here. Why did everyone believe in me? Did they forget about my track record?

"Love, Marve," Micha said. "They believe in you because they love you. That's what love is—trust."

I thought of my first night with Dorian.

His hands smoothed over me like silk and I'd never felt more beautiful. When we kissed, my mind exploded in a thousand colors. He was the flame that kept me going—the furnace that kept the house of my existence warm. I loved him. I also knew that in order to keep from betraying him, I had to come to terms with my sexuality, which reached far beyond him, and my attraction to Micha.

When I opened my eyes, we were on an island. I was lying down with my toes in the sand as the waves lapped at my ankles. The sun shined down on me as the salty spray of the sea swept across my face, marking me with its bitter scent. I unfurled my wings for a few minutes, allowing myself to bask in the heat of the sun as I readjusted to the change in atmosphere. My body accommodated quickly.

It was my mind that had to play catch up.

In my mind, I was still lost in the hands of space, weighted down by the sandbags of time. My brain knew that something was up. It knew that I was missing something vital. When I felt adjusted enough, I stood and fluttered my wings to get the sand off them. Micha reached out and as his fingers gently trailed across my feathers, a shudder ran straight through me.

"I don't know if I should tell you…" he mumbled, giving me a look that made my heart skid to a stop.

"Tell me what?"

"I haven't been completely honest with you." Micha moved a piece of hair from my face and tucked it behind my ear. His sudden change left me reeling. "There is something about me that you should know."

"Go ahead," I said, stepping away. "I won't judge."

A frown marred his face as his hand slowly fell to his side. He was rejecting me one minute then doing weird stuff the next. He didn't make my heart race the same way Dorian did, but he did make a batch of flames sear through my veins. I knew that lust was dangerous and that Micha had a hold over me. I also knew that I wanted to act on it but that it would be better if I didn't.

The way he looked at me made it hard not to walk forward. My limbs automatically stretched out. The next thing I knew I was curled into his side. I inhaled deeply, surprised when I smelled mangos and brown sugar. Before I did something stupid, I pulled away.

"I know that you're attracted to me." He said, lowering his head. "And I know why."

He took in a shuddery breath, and I knew that those feather-light touches meant something. He was an angel in every sense of the word. He fought to protect and teach me and always put up with my crap. Giving in would destroy us both and the people around us. There was no denying it now.

I had a penchant for self-destruction.

"I'm a breeder."

"What?" My tail moved to swish behind me in confusion. "What's that?"

"Think of me like a thoroughbred that's won the Triple Crown. I'm a battle angel that has been in numerous wars from the beginning of time all the way up to WWI. After the Battle of Mons, the Creator decided that I was Its greatest un-retired battle angel and that in order for us to stay on top, we needed more battle angels like me."

"What an honor." I paused as a frown waged a war on my lips. "What did you mean when you said something about staying on top?"

"Demons try to raid Sora every once in a while. Angels can die the same way humans can although it takes a lot more manpower. We are constantly at war."

"What does that have to do with you being a breeder?"

"Well, think about it. You need strong soldiers to win the war the same way you need a strong horse to win the Kentucky Derby. After the Battle of Mons, the Creator decided to make me a breeder—an angel that exists solely to reproduce. The effect of a breeder can only be felt by people with an attraction to that sex. Do you understand now?"

"So you're saying…"

"That's exactly what I mean, Marve." He ran a hand through his hair. "I truly am sorry for not telling you sooner."

Why did he think that I was upset? This new information actually made me feel immensely better. A thought crossed my mind.

"If you're a breeder now, why are you here?" I waved a hand at him. "Shouldn't you be up in the clouds playing some Marvin Gaye and—"

"Marve—"

"So, does the Mile High Club apply even if you're not on a plane? I—"

"Would you let me finish?"

I rocked back on my heels, a weird thing to do while crouched down, but made sure to keep my mouth shut.

"In 1914, after the Battle of Mons, I went to Britain to do some soul searching. There, I met a beautiful Spanish immigrant named Maria. She had these hips that swayed like she was always dancing and blonde hair like liquid honey and these really big blue doe eyes that made a man reveal his every secret. It was love at first sight. She was a waitress at a local tavern that I always went to and one night, she approached me.

"She, like everyone else, thought that I was a missionary, which was my cover at the time. She said that she was looking to become a nun once she went back to Spain. I told her about the only other thing I loved, the Creator, and when she left for Spain, I went, too. I visited her at the covenant and the more I did, the more I realized that I wanted to give up my life as an angel and become human. Sadly, that is impossible, and I would have died trying anyway.

"The Creator saw this and called me home. Instead of going straight away, I went to the covenant and seduced Maria. I know that it was stupid." Micha ran a hand through his curly black locks. "I went back home but the damage was done."

There was something in his eyes that I would never envy.

"Nine months later, she died giving birth to our son, Grant. With a bit of intervention from the Creator, Grant was sent to the States, where no one would recognize him. He was taken into a foster home, and I watched him grow from afar. He fell in love with a French-American by the name of Jacques and when he broke Jacques's heart, he turned him into a monster. The Creator saw this and said that I'd set something in motion that had the power to destroy the entire world.

"I should have known..." Those grey orbs flashed silver in the light of the sun. "That was when the Creator decided that it would be best if I were to breed for the rest of my days, never to see my son again. When you were born, the Creator saw a chance to undo what I'd wrought. So, It sent me to watch over you."

Where was he when your father was murdered? Keres's voice whispered in the back of my mind. *Where was Micha when you were beaten daily? Where was he when the same man who raised you raped you?*

I shook off the dark thoughts and focused my mind on Micha's words.

"Wow." I squinted at him. "So you're Grant's dad? Jacques told me about Grant. He said he found other things to live for."

"Yes, he found a woman that he loved twice as much as his love for any man. As far as I know, they moved Florida with their two kids, Ian and Elizabeth. I know that he sometimes wrestles with his sexuality but he's still happy."

"Wait, so he's alive?"

131

"Nephilim can live up to a century, depending on the life. If Jacques had followed through with his plans for my son..."

He wouldn't have lived that long...

"What stopped him?"

"Do you know what Jacques does to the men he captures?"

"His 'special boys,' he calls them..." My face marred with disgust as I recalled the bodies, the smell of singed flesh, the meat that I prepared. "He has me—"

"He's had women before you do this. He will have women after you do this, if you do not stop him. Remember that you are not unique." The angel did not look away at my telling flinch. "He is a monster, yes. But also, a creature of habit."

"He would have...*us*....hang them by their toes, peel their skin off while they were still breathing, then burn them alive. Then he would select the most delicate parts...I learned which parts he liked best...and have Valentina—"

"There were others before her. There was another after her. There will be more to come if—"

"I know...! It's just..."

I felt Micha's hand grasp my chin. He turned my face to his, his grey eyes dull with sympathy and a calm reservation. I knew that he wasn't trying to hurt me. But I couldn't face it. I couldn't understand how—

"I know that you wish to believe that he loved you all—you, Valentina, Tiara...But he did not. He does not. He has never loved anyone. He will never love anyone. From the day he was brought into this world, he did not cry or scream. He did not suckle at his mother's tit or huddle to her for warmth. He consumed her from the inside out from the moment he was conceived. To survive, she had to—don't look away from me!" I stopped trying to snatch my face away. "From the moment he was conceived, she had to eat other people to survive. This slowly drove her insane. By the time he was born, she was too far gone to know what was right and what was wrong. But she loved him dearly. Do you know what she called Jacques as a child?"

"No."

"Yes, you do. Do you know what she called him when she—"

"No."

"Look at me."

"No."

"Look at me." At his commanding tone, I looked up, glaring at him in defiance, my breath ragged in my throat. I wasn't sure if I wanted to kiss him or kill him as he told me stories that Jacques never dared tell me. "Do you know what she called him when she hunted with him? Do you know what she called him when, among these bodies and scattered remains, she fucked him atop the corpses?"

"I don't want to know."

I winced, feeling sick as I slapped my hands over my ears. I could hear the white noise. I could feel his voice around me, pulsating like water in my ears, like a second heartbeat. I didn't want to know. I couldn't help but wonder why he was telling me this, if he enjoyed seeing me so disgusted, so undone.

"My angel…my son…my special boy…."

He wants me to understand what I'm facing, I realized, *so that when the time comes, I don't hesitate. But why? Why would he think I'd hesitate? Why would he assume that I'd blindly follow this man with eyes torn from sockets, eyes that I'd plucked out myself with a dagger of his making?*

"I'm in love with him," I whispered.

Micha reached out, grabbed my hands, pulled them from my ears. His voice was gentle, so sweet it was sickening, so caring, it made me want to vomit.

"No, you're not."

My eyes found his, the glow of them bouncing off his face, reflecting to cast back on me.

"What?"

"You feared him. You told yourself that it was love so that when the time came and he took you to his bed—"

"No."

"You'd believe that it was what you wanted. But you never really wanted him. You admired him. You thought when you first met him, that he was the most beautiful man that you'd ever seen. You thought he was a god—"

"He was my god…"

"He was your devil. Why did you convince yourself that you felt something for this man, when in reality, you looked away? Why did you stay instead of letting him murder you when you ran? If you loved him, when he came to you when you were eighteen, you wouldn't have rejected him. But you turned him away. Why?"

"I don't know. I-I-I—"

"Yes, you do. Why?"

"I loved Master! I promised that I would love only him! I meant it! I promised!"

"Why did you lie to yourself? Why did you lie to him?"

"I promised…I—"

"No, don't lie to me. It wasn't because you promised. You don't give a damn about promises. It was the same reason you told Tiara you would free her, when you knew you weren't strong enough—"

"No!"

"To walk away. Why?" When I began thrashing, he grabbed my face, staring into my eyes. "You are not a child anymore. I will not stand by and watch you destroy yourself, destroy those around you. Why did you lie? To him? To yourself? To Tiara? Why?!"

"I don't know. I—"

"Tell me!"

"I don't know. Please, I'm sorry. I—"

"You know why. Stop lying all the time. Why did you lie all these years? Why did you convince yourself? And the others? Why?"

"I—"

"No! No more lies, Marve! You will not lie to me any longer!" He dragged me closer, glaring down at me, a snarl on his face, one hand raised. "You have been bad. And I need you to tell me why. Now!"

"Please, Mas—"

"Confess!"

I screamed. Screamed so loud and hard that I knew my throat and ears would hurt for years to come. Three words: "BECAUSE I'M WEAK!"

The tears came. Not fast and strong. But slow and steady, like a leaky faucet dripping black ink down the drain. Jacques wasn't the only poison in my system. No, this poison had rotted me from the inside for years. From years of my classmates bullying me, and my parents punishing me for not perfecting my glamor, with their stupid jobs cozying up to those fucking Immortals and a religion that said it gave me power but did nothing to help me to find strength in a world that only wanted me to submit. I had been born weak. I had lived my life, lying to myself, claiming to be a Champion, but I couldn't save my people, I couldn't save my parents...

And I couldn't save myself.

Micha watched me silently for a long time as I cried, rocking back and forth, sobbing.

"You were never strong. You were just never allowed to be weak."

"I am...I'm strong. I'm—"

"Society has placed this burdened upon the Gifted people. Upon colored Mortals. Upon all the outcasts. *Be strong. Take our hatred and turn it into strength.* But you and I know the truth. We know the truth that the world hides itself from every day. It's not that the oppressed are strong. It's just that the world beats them until they are deluded into believing that they are no longer weak."

I said nothing, glaring at him.

"So…" I whispered through cracked, bloody lips that I'd bitten through. "What now?"

"Do you want to be strong?"

"I don't know…I…"

"Stop lying. You know."

"Yes! I want to be strong."

"Then acknowledge your weakness. Then rip it apart. Rip it into a thousand little pieces, throw it into the fire, let the ashes scatter on the wind and rise up to the stars. Then find that strength here—" He took my hand and placed it, not on my chest, but on the ground. "—pull it up, out of the ground, bring it to your mouth, set it on your tongue, taste, marvel at its wonders and *swallow*. Swallow that strength. What you need is not something that you can find through loving others. It is something that your oppressors stole and buried deep within the earth. It is something that they hid from you in the one place you'd never look. Because if you knew that under the cities, the farms, the foundations *you* built for them, that you'd find your own strength, then you'd overthrow them the next day."

And I understood. I understood why the Creator sent him to me. I understood why I'd been afraid to be weak. I understood why I'd been chosen…because no one had. No one had, not really. But I was a mouthpiece for something far greater, as were all my brothers and sisters, as were the Mortals. We were all mouthpieces for fallen gods, and we had to become everything they feared.

"Who sent you?"

"Hm?" his hair covered his face.

"Who sent you really? It wasn't the Creator."

"It was."

"Then why do you speak the words of the Great Mother."

"Here, the Great Mother is a myth, a fairytale. There are so many universes, so many gods, but the one from this dimension is the Creator. The Great Mother is a forgotten god from another dimension, Universe 6, and rules over a people called the Paganos. You were born in this universe, yes. But your people are from her universe. Because she lost her children after they destroyed the planet and the different people were scattered to other dimensions. One of those people were sent to a nameless dimension, a dimension that your people journey to in order to find them. You are meant to bring them here, to fight with them to regain control of this land, and then bring them to their new home."

"But you showed me her. You said she was a demon."

"Here, that's what she is. Because that is who she is perceived as. In the different universes, different gods are known by different names. The Creator is the god of this universe, yes, but the Gifted are children of two universes."

"Book 99, And we will never bow—"

"And we will never surrender—"

"For by magic we are bound and by blood we remain. Among the stars, you shall lay…"

Micha nodded.

"The 'you,' in the final verse of the Book. It wasn't speaking of the Gifted, was it…?"

"It spoke of Kalysma…of her."

"The Creator sent you…?"

"It did…but in order to do the Creator's work, you must also do the work of Kalysma. You must unite the children of two universes and end this tyranny."

"The Immortals…they were here longer than any of us. Why would we take it from them?"

"No, just make it a better place for those who want to stay. One day, you won't just hold the power to free a few people. One day, you will hold the power to usher them to a home long destroyed."

"The Gatekeeper isn't just a fancy title. It's who I'm meant to be...I am meant....to save an alien race—"

"And free your people."

I felt her hands wrapped around me, felt her lips at the pulse in my neck, but I also felt the Creator's power surging through my veins, felt the god that made me *and* the god that chose me. It wasn't that the Creator didn't love us. It was that we had been marked by another. All of this had happened because Kalysma wanted me to save her actual children. If anything, she stole us.

"She didn't steal you. She asked the Creator to save you, to take you as a ward while she recrafted her universe, and while here, you would do its bidding. But you were always hers. And It willingly said that she could use you as long as you were returned. The Architect—"

"Who? That name...It—"

"Feels familiar. I know. One day, your husband will tell you who the Architect is. He will tell you of all the universes and their people. And then you will find your other true love and go with them both to serve the Great Mother. The Creator agreed to give you all up. You will find a home amongst the Paganos. You will be one with them."

"But why? Why would It let me—let us—go?"

"Because It knows that you will find true happiness in a place where you will no longer serve. If you return, your immortality and your emotions will be stripped away and you will be thrown into the gaping maws of hell."

"Not the stars?"

I wanted to cry.

"The Gifted saw the future of the Paganos, *not* themselves. Those people that Dorian painted at the doorway to the church... they weren't human or any variation. They were the Paganos. They were her true children. And you will rule under her, over them—the first of the warrior race, Kinstrong—Marve?"

I swayed. I wanted to vomit or scream or shatter into a million little shards and let my wings of glass carry me away. A trickle of blood ran from my nose. My eyes flickered.

I noticed Micha's fingers wrapped around my wrist.

"You're going to put me to sleep?" I whispered, voice raspy. "Why?"

"Because you can't handle this truth." He frowned. "Not yet, at least."

"When will I be able to handle it?"

"After your mission is complete."

*   *   *

I woke up, eyes clear, head clear, my path set before me, taking me down an unfamiliar road. I looked up at the sun, saw it shining down on me, saw Micha squinting up at the light, a smile on his face. He was so handsome when he smiled. If only I didn't always disappoint him.

"Hey," I whispered.

"Do you remember our conversation?"

"Yes, about the Great Mother? She's…a demon."

A sense of wrongness filled me. I didn't like saying it, but of course I would have trouble relinquishing my religion after just a few minutes of learning the truth. She was a monster…I had to come to terms with that. Micha turned to nod at me, a smile on his face. I wondered something very suddenly, a bit of a dream I'd had…or at least, a question I'd been left with, after the dream.

"Am I your redemption?"

"Yes. I'm sorry for withholding the truth from you. Can you find it in your heart to forgive me?"

I wasn't upset. In fact, I felt kind of bad for him. He loved someone and for it, he was punished. Now he had to babysit me. It probably didn't help that I was eye-humping him 24/7. I told him just as much. He didn't respond.

"Jacques is the Ordained?" I said although a part of me already knew.

"Yes," he said through clenched teeth. I knew that the answer cost him.

I took that as my cue to change the subject.

"Where are we?"

"The Bermuda Triangle. Technically, this is an alternate dimension," he said with a smile. "But it's very hard to access."

"Can you teach me to move through dimensions?"

"I can teach you that," he said, eyes meeting mine, "and so much more."

I tried not to read too much into that. Instead, I looked towards the sun. In a way, once I had my revenge, I would also begin searching for redemption. If I wasn't, I wouldn't have even taken him up on the offer to train. I thought of this as I stretched my arms over my head.

"So, what are we going to do today?"

"Do you feel the sand beneath your feet?"

"Yes."

"What does it feel like?"

"Gritty, grainy…" I wiggled my toes. "Slippery, almost as if it's moving."

"Good."

Micha reached down towards the sheath on his waist. He closed his eyes, gripping the dagger in his strong hand. Then he suddenly let it go and spread his arms before him as if to welcome an old friend. As his hands grew farther apart, a spear of light formed with each new opening. Once his hands were spread all the way, the twelve lights took shape and very quickly, multiple daggers hovered before him.

"Today we will work on your balance and your ability to dodge attacks. You will find that not too far behind you, there are sand dunes, which are in constant motion. If you don't move fast enough, you will sink."

"Let me guess. I'm not allowed to fly away."

"See, you're catching on quick," he said with a jovial wink.

He didn't even ask me if I was ready. One second, the air was clear. The next there was the sound of metal cutting through the wind as a sharp, silver point flew towards my heart. I backed away quickly and was surprised when the ground shifted under me. I'd already reached the sand dunes.

Daggers flew towards me, each speeding faster than the last. I tried to jump to avoid one and wound up getting speared in my right leg. I quickly bent down and removed the offending object. I was immediately distracted by the way the wound stitched itself closed in a matter of seconds. Micha threw another set of daggers and the since the wind was blowing towards me, they only hit twice as hard. An odd noise came from behind me.

I twisted my neck around to see that the daggers were doubling back. I dodged as many as I could, which wasn't much. After a little while, I began to pant. I knew that I couldn't keep this up forever. Even though I had to get used to being under this kind of strain again, I still liked the challenge. It gave me a sense of purpose.

Something inside of me stirred. I wondered if it was Keres or my natural desire for self-preservation. Either way, I was struck by an idea.

The daggers circled around me in a taunting circle and I knew that I was trapped. The wind shifted and the daggers flew towards me. I saw my chance. Before the daggers could pierce my flesh, my wings fluttered out behind me. I flapped them quickly, building up an opposing wind that would hopefully knock the daggers back. I flapped long and hard, trying not to squint as sand blew in my eyes.

It worked.

The daggers changed direction and started towards Micha. His eyes narrowed and I was surprised when the magic in me flared. Electricity jumped around my form as I instinctively sensed a threat. I flapped over and over but naturally my shoulders quickly grew tired. The daggers hovered between us, moving back and forth by a few inches.

The daggers stayed levitated for a fraction of a second before falling towards the sand. Micha waved his hand and the daggers melded into one before floating back to their sheath. I dragged in a few breaths, trying to maintain my composure.

Is he trying to kill me?

But then as he crossed his arms, I realized that he was upset.

"What's wrong?"

"You cheated!"

"Huh? How?"

"I told you not to use your wings."

"No, you didn't."

"Yeah," he nodded, "I'm pretty sure that I did."

"You said that I couldn't fly away but you never said that I couldn't blow back the daggers using the wind. I didn't cheat. I guess you can say that there was a bit of improvisation on my part. Pretty good, huh?"

We both paused. He stared at me and I him. Then, thankfully, a smile broke out on his face.

"You're so clever." Micha uncrossed his arms, walking to me easily despite the sand sucking at our feet, and slapped me on the back. "You're already beginning to think like a battle angel."

Micha appraised me in a new light.

"Another important part of being a battle angel is that you must always look at every side of the situation even if you don't want to. What is something else that you could have done to protect yourself from the daggers?"

That was easy.

"I could have grabbed one out of the air with my tail or hands."

"Yes, go on."

"I could have tried to hide behind the dunes."

"A little risky considering that the moment you look away I would find an opening. I would scrap that in real life. But since this is hypothetical, I'll accept that. Give me one more reason. I know that you can."

I couldn't think of one.

"Do you want me to tell you?"

"Yes."

"You could have broken the rules." His eyes held a wicked glint. "You could have flown away."

"But you said—"

"The first rule of battle: there are no rules. When you get to the battlefield, do you think your enemy will patiently sit down and listen as you lay down a list of guidelines? Do you think the Ordained will show you any mercy?"

"No."

"Your enemy will always be three steps ahead of you. Jacques has more than a century of experience on you. He has killed more people than you have and probably ever will without batting an eyelash. He is a monster." I'd never seen Micha so serious. "You must always remember that."

I solemnly nodded.

"Since this is an alternate dimension, time travels slower here than it does in the real world. Training here for what seems like years will be only a few hours as far as everyone is concerned. So don't be surprised if your friends find your strength a bit…shocking. But before we continue training, I want you to suit up."

"Suit up?"

"We're going to get you fitted for battle armor. It's going to be the armor of battle angels, of course. That means that it will change to accommodate your evolving physique."

He took my hand in his left and with his right, he opened another portal. Through it, I could see a city made of precious metals, the paths paved with gold and the rails lined with sparkling silver. I stepped through the portal with Micha. We walked through the city and as we did, I was surprised to find that the city was empty and totally quiet. I expected to see a bunch of angels milling about, each as beautiful and charming as Micha, so when I didn't see them, I was a bit disappointed.

"It's like a ghost town here. Where is everyone?"

"Sora has been evacuated for the next week or so. The battle angels are at the gates—" he pointed; in the distance I could see two massive golden gates looming, winged soldiers stationed in front of them in stony silence "—and all of the angels have been sent to Paradise to guard it until it is deemed safe."

"What can threaten such beauty? And what is this sky place?"

"Paradise is where the Creator and the souls of dead humans reside. There is a portal there, which is how the Creator keeps an eye on the living. Sora is where the angels live. Whenever demons are rumored to attack, all of the angels leave Sora to protect the souls of the dead humans in Paradise."

"Don't all angels have magical powers? Can't you all fight?"

"That's like saying that every person has a Gift. Based on certain attributes, angels are classified into three sections: battle angels, councilmen and citizens, who include but are not limited to messenger angels, breeders, record keepers, members of the praise team, builders and shopkeepers." We walked farther into the city, and

I asked why they needed councilmen when the Creator was calling all the shots. "The councilmen make small decisions regarding the angels. If you aren't a councilman, you don't always have free will, which is why some go Dark when they reach Earth and are seduced by its choices."

"You have to do everything your told?"

And if councilmen have free will, that's what I want to be.

Micha's mouth twitched as if he were reading my thoughts.

"Councilmen are so pious that they will make decisions pleasing to the Creator no matter what. You become a councilman based on how many wings you are born with; if you have seven, then that's your fate. I was born with six so I couldn't be a councilman. I, like the rest of the ones not on the Council, had to complete a series of tests based off physical and mental attributes. Based on the results of the test, I was told that I would reach my full potential if I was a battle angel. It was a no brainer. To resist the Creator's design causes us immense physical pain."

"So that's what you meant when you said that the Creator gave us free will because It loved us. Now that you've confirmed that Jacques is the Ordained, I'm still…confused."

"What is it?"

"I already knew that he's a descendant of Lucifer. I can't help but think that this wouldn't have happened if Lucifer hadn't gone Dark." I let the rest of what I was thinking hang in the air, unsure of how to say it.

Micha picked up quickly.

"Lucifer was a citizen that was deemed to be a part of the praise team—a singer. He quickly won the Creator's favor and was blessed with the role of choir director, which is a high honor. As the eldest, he was also supposed to be the next head of his house, but his parents decided that he didn't deserve it once he started to become vain and openly brag about his job *and* his own glory. When he found out about his mother's choice to make his younger brother head of the house, Lucifer convinced himself that he was passed up out of jealousy and that his family was conspiring with the Creator to keep him from his birthright; it didn't help that he got the good end of the gene pool, either. It's kind of funny because growing up, you would never believe that he would turn out to be such a monster."

"You sound as if you knew him personally."

"Of course I did. He was my brother."

"What?!"

I looked at Micha, trying to strip away the pieces of him that I knew and replace them with foreign ones. What did Lucifer look like? What was he like before he began to go Dark?

"He was my half-brother. I was the youngest. Our mother, Joy, was a shopkeeper and his father was a battle angel. When his father, Jakobe, was killed in battle, Joy was Rebound. My father, Zerachiel, is a soldier that leads humans to judgement, and I was born not too long after their Binding when Lucifer was six. I kind of stole some of the attention that he was used to, which I think might have something to do with him turning out the way that he did."

I didn't know what to say to that, so I asked another question.

"So you're technically related to Jacques as well as Grant?"

"The blood is so thin that I don't think it counts."

"Doesn't that bother you?"

He didn't answer.

"Okay..." I forced a smile. "So if everyone has evacuated, why are we here looking for battle armor?"

"The Creator ordered that one angel stay behind just so she could help you. Her name is Lisette. She is from the House of Gretchen. She's the one that builds the armor for the angels. When she is ready, she will step down and choose a successor."

"So, you all must choose successors. Do you get old and die?"

"No. We only die if we are killed. Still, we are constantly at war with the demons and there are more casualties than one would expect."

"It must be awful, constantly being at war."

"It can't be as bad as being Gifted. Did you know that when you use magic, for the next hour or so, the Creator loses sight of you? That's why It doesn't like magic—anything could happen in that short expanse of time."

I hummed in the back of my throat. The Creator probably never saw most of us, including Dorian and I. I frowned. Was that why we suffered so?

I looked around at the beautiful, sparkling city that surrounded me. There were no words to describe it but if I had to, I'd say that it was what a perfect city was supposed to look like in Sci-Fi movies: shiny, tall and immensely vast. There were abandoned dolls on the sidewalk and lights left on where people must have left in a hurry. It was hard to believe that anyone could wage a war against something so perfect. But I guess some were so greedy and unhappy that they were willing to tear down people's dreams.

After all, no one could say that you were beneath them if everyone was on the same level.

"You know how you're not allowed to go all the way with humans?"

"Yes."

"Can you sleep with other angels?"

"Always about sex with you," he said, reaching out to flick my nose. "Breeders sleep with one another to keep the population going. Angels are not bound by human standards so it's not unusual for many to…sleep around. Angels can undergo a ritual like marriage, which binds them for a total of ten years, and once the magic of the ritual fades, the same two angels can never be bound again. I was a different case since I was made into a breeder and not born as one."

It sounded like something out of a novel.

"Breeders can't be bound and neither can battle angels." Micha's voice was empty, which bothered me, because he was practically programmed to believe that this was normal and fair. "Battle angels can't be bound due to the simple fact that they will eventually die so there's no point in causing another angel so much pain."

"Breeders can't bond because they need to have children with no strings attached, right?"

"Yes."

"Does that mean—?"

He told me that 87% of all angels were sterile. Sex was treated as a casual affair. We finally reached a shop called *Lisette's Love*. We walked inside and a short, sharp-boned woman with a pointed nose, piercing purple eyes and wavy blonde hair greeted us. She looked like a blonde pixie and when she embraced Micha, I knew that they'd been intimate before. The thought left a sour taste in my mouth.

What I'd give to have what she had...

"Is this The Gatekeeper?" she asked, turning her cool gaze on me.

That was when I noticed that she was oddly beautiful. She was dressed in a Grecian toga, a laurel wreath on her head and golden bands snaking around her arms like boa constrictors. Her full mouth lifted as she held out a hand that I quickly shook. I suddenly realized that she'd called me The Gatekeeper. It was odd having such a title but the way it rolled off her tongue made it sound nice—like it was meant for me.

It made me wonder why Micha made it sound like a death sentence, even if he tried to hide it.

"That's me," I nodded, letting go of her hand.

"I have already designed your suit but there are also some modifications that your body must undergo. This is to ensure that you have the highest rate of survival. Your suit has already been tailored to your exact measurements."

"How do you know my measurements?"

"Micha isn't the only one that's been watching you."

Her head tilted as she gave a musical laugh. I liked the sound. Even though they were total opposites, she sorta reminded me of Tiara, full of so much light…

"What did you mean when you said I had to undergo modifications?"

"You are not at your optimal physical state. It is my job to get your there. First, put on your suit."

She left the room, her sandals slapping the ground softly. She rummaged around and when she returned, she held an odd skin suit in her hand. She told me to strip down right there in front of her and Micha. I did as I was told. Lisette seemed like she was waiting for a reaction, while Micha seemed like he was trying to do anything but react. I thought that was odd that he looked away when I kissed my husband but outright stared when I was changing clothes.

I was getting nothing but mixed signals from him.

"Look in the mirror," Lisette said once I was done.

I did as I was told. The suit was a teal that brought out the natural highlights in my red hair. It accented the sharp lines of my body, making them seem stronger—more exaggerated but not overly so. When I moved, the suit expanded and bent, flowing like silk as it followed my every command to a T. The material was rough as if it was made from the hide of some large, brutish animal but I knew of no Earth-bound creature that yielded a pelt like this. The suit stretched from the base of my neck to the top of my knees, had a crocodile-like pattern and lacked any sleeves.

I didn't want to let go of my glamor just yet.

"I love it," I said, grinning at my reflection.

"Oh, that's not the suit," Lisette murmured, staring at me.

"Then…what is it?"

"It is what will fit you to the suit."

"I…don't understand—h-hey!"

The suit flowed down, off my body, and into Lisette's hand. She set it down. It took shape, mimicking my form but standing upright. Her hands glowed as she traced it down the weird mannequin-thing. It was a simple armor, thin, like liquid metal, but strong and flexible. Lisette's hands glowed again. My daggers appeared, stuck into the loops at the waist.

"Good?" she asked.

The suit was plain, boring, but also really stylish and (dare I say it?) sexy. It seemed futuristic and I knew that I would stand out a mile away in it. Some of the Zuora was extremely hot, so would the metal overheat?

"The metal is made from a technology that adapts to not only your body, but the environment. You will be comfortable no matter what terrain your in," Lisette offered, eyeing me as I eyed it. "Oh and look!"

She showed me the zipper in the front, and deep pockets on the sides, right above the sheaths.

"I wish I had something to ride," I said, thinking of the rocks in the Grand Canyon, how they dug into my feet.

"You will have a companion," said Micha, "but you must be patient."

"Send her a giant bunny," said Lisette.

"I don't want a bunny!" I hissed, baring my teeth at her.

She smirked; the look odd on her usually blank face.

"A wolf, then," Micha said, smirking when I hesitated before protesting. Micha's eyes glowed for a soft moment, a long moment for me. "You will have one then."

"Now?"

"No." Micha's eyes did that glowy thing again. "But someday, you will."

We shared a look.

She raised a brow in the most infuriatingly condescending way. Micha gave an uncharacteristic snigger. I turned my glare on him. But he was stone-faced, as usual. I pouted. He took pity on me.

"Apologize."

"What?" Lisette gaped. "Why should I—"

"Lisette," he warned.

"I'm sorry," she said, her voice emotionless. "Shall I continue with this lesson?"

I grinned at her, blinking. "Yes, ma'am."

She said nothing.

Micha walked over to the suit, turning it so the back faced me. "This would be good to learn more about your new wings, right, Lisette?"

Lisette blushed, nodded. She wasn't as emotionless as it seemed. And it seemed that Micha was all of our undoing.

"Even though your wings are made from spiritual matter, they take physical form. That's why there are openings in the back for your wings to fit through. You have such nice hair," she said as her fingers brushed the back of my neck. "Would you mind if I cut it off? Now that your Nephilim, it will take longer to grow back out. But I promise you that it's easier to fight with shorter hair and you'll need all of the advantages that you can get."

For a second, I thought I saw my old master's face staring back at me. I shuddered. I didn't want to cut my hair. I wanted to look like a woman.

But it's for the best, Keres whispered.

I swallowed around the lump in my throat.

"That's fine with me," I said against my will.

Lisette left and came back with a pair of scissors. I heard the familiar *snip, snip, snip*. Everything was happening so fast. I didn't want to look in the mirror. I didn't want to see a strong-faced boy staring back at me, the person that I'd had to become in order to become strong—a Champion and a slave-boy.

"Now," she said, "about those modifications…"

CHAPTER THIRTEEN

F.A.B.

I asked her to explain it again.

"I am going to inject you with this serum, also known as F.A.B. We made this just for you. It's called Forever a Beast. It basically makes you more in tune with your animalistic senses. It also makes it impossible for you to switch out of your Imperfect Form."

"Imperfect? Don't you mean, Glamor?" I asked.

Lisette glanced at Micha. He glared at the ground, upset.

"I always hated that name. Why did we decide to call it that, Lisette?"

"Do the Gifted call it something else?"

I caught up. And I tucked in my chin just slightly, glaring at the ground. "No. That's exactly what we call it."

"Oh!" Lisette gave an odd grin. "Good!"

She took a step forward. I reached out, braced one hand on her waist, the other on her shoulder, and flipped her. She landed on her back with a loud bang. Her face twisted in what I now realize was shock. I wanted to grin or bare my teeth as my skin began to tug, shifting, reforming and also becoming who'd I'd really been. Not a man or a woman but a beast that the Immortals never stepped out of the way of to let past, who they bullied in the schoolyard and glared at when they walked home. Who they declared open season on and had been known to hunt when we had more than what they thought we should.

But I'm not a monster. I never asked for any of this. And what if—? I looked up and to Micha, who dug under his nails with his blade. *Will things change? Will he fetishize me as my husband had (and still does?) Or—*

"Do it."

Lisette placed the needle in my arm, injected it smoothly. As she did, she said something that made me feel better and worse—better because this was temporary, and worse because it had been a relief in the first place. "It will only last you a good year or so. So don't take too long with your mission."

I nodded, a tight grin on my face.

The response was instantaneous. I felt a tug on my skin. I could feel my bones shifting and it wasn't painful like one would think. It just felt weird. It took all but a few seconds and I only knew that it was over when Lissette clapped her hands together. She beamed at me—a smile that reached her violet eyes—which I took as a good sign.

"Look at yourself now."

My face was sharper, accenting my almond-shaped eyes, and I also noticed that my hips were a bit wider. My chest was still that slightly inflated lump but the suit made it look purposeful instead of some misshapen accident. I twisted and turned in the mirror, liking what I saw. And I suddenly realized that this is what Dorian saw and Jacques saw: the definition of sex. It wasn't that it was necessarily my fault that these men saw me the way they did, it was just that I had been blessed beyond measure, and the world taught me that it was a curse—a burden that made me rapeable at worst, and fuckable at best. But I wasn't a monster.

I was beautiful.

Micha looked at me for a long moment, his eyes unreadable but not changed in any way that I could clearly recognize. And I remembered that he'd watched me my entire life. Why would he fetishize something he'd always known—something that had always been readily available to him? I glanced at the mirror again—my eyes were wide, aware. When I looked back up, he was next to me, tucking a piece of hair behind my ear. His hands blazed fire where they touched me.

"I—"

His brow raised, his lips quirking. "Yes?"

Damn this handsome, impossible man. Damn him to the lowest pits of hell. No, damn him to where Jacques will end whenever I have ended his wretched existence. He is a threat. From his olive arms to his all-knowing eyes to his stupid smile that says more than any more of him will ever say. He is a threat with his presence.

Micha wasn't white, but black, albeit only a shade or two darker than me. Black and comely—a stallion in every sense of the word. I'd never wanted a man more than I wanted him. It wasn't because he was black or because he was a breeder. It was because he was everything that I'd ever dared to want, everything I'd been told I could never have, not because it belonged to another, as Dorian had been, but because...

He was truly mine.

I tried to look tough, a growl face that, I realized, came across more as cute to him, but for a different reason than Dorian. Dorian saw me and saw something to be protected, something small, weak. Micha looked at me and saw someone strong that could let down her armor whenever she chose; a lioness that could defend herself, but he was a lion at my backside, ready to jump in whenever necessary. He may not want me the way I wanted, but he was the clearest example of something healthy that I'd ever had. If we had met in another life, would he have been mine and I his?

Lissette laughed behind her hand. "You two are night and day. But…oh, I hate to say it, it works."

Micha dropped his hand to its side. "No. It can't."

I reached out, grabbing his fingers, but he pulled away, stepped back. "I think it can."

And it will. My husband never liked monogamy—I could see that now. And, I realized, *neither had I. But we were both extremely possessive. Could we ever invite others in and not hate the other for craving more than we were initially given?*

I would achieve my ultimate goal—the goal I'd been too afraid to take hold of—happiness. I quickly put on the suit, surprised that my armor wasn't apparent beneath the fabric. But I was still somehow still aware of the strength and sharp lines of my body.

Micha reached out, touched one of my scutes, his hands warm, rough, soft, somehow still colder than I wanted him. I flexed, my armor sliding into line as my muscles moved. The suit bended with the restructure, fitting my body like a glove. My alligator-like pupils stared back at me through his, blazing hotter than I'd thought possible for someone who wasn't Dorian. I grinned and my sharp teeth gleamed.

"You look like a warrior," Lissette said.

"I feel like one, too."

"The suit changes as you change. You get bigger, so does it; you get smaller…" She shrugged her shoulders. "Your sheaths will fit around this suit perfectly. This suit is made out of a special kind of material that will allow you to conduct electricity without burning through it; the material is so rare that we only use it in the general's suits, which is great for what's to come considering that it repels most enemy attacks."

Boy, she really thought of everything.

"Still, your suit is one of a kind," she said, "just like you."

I asked Lissette if my hair looked okay and she said that the side-swept look worked for me. Micha walked up behind me. One of his hands moved a strand of hair from my face and lingered there before dropping to his side. Lisette glanced between the two of us but said nothing, although it was now obvious she'd played off the first hair movement as an accident, and did not approve of the second. She wasn't jealous, as I had been—she just knew something that I didn't. I cleared my throat.

"You said that I'm now Nephilim," I said to my teacher.

"Yes," Micha replied.

"Why aren't my eyes purple?"

"You were created, not born."

"Why are your eyes grey?"

A pained look slashed across his face. "A side effect of me trying to become human, I'm afraid."

I nodded, turned to Lissette.

"Is that everything?"

"No." She said, leading me to a plush chair and telling me to lie down. "There's one more thing that I must do."

She reached towards a table, her body bending to where it blocked my view. Micha moved to stand next to me. When Lissette turned back around, there was a large needle staring at me. I began to inch away but Micha made a noise in the back of his throat, commanding me to be still. My tail swished next to me before winding around my waist. I trusted him and if he trusted her, then I trusted her.

"Do you want to wait? I told you to be still, so it didn't accidently jab you," Micha admitted. "I'd never make you do anything you weren't ready for."

My eyes searched his. "I'm ready."

"Are you?"

Lisette frowned at him. "Okay, guys. The looks are intense, yeah?"

Micha's chin tilted up. He looked at me in a way that was sexual, yes—a look that owned and dominated me all at once, but still only said it would if I allowed it. Did I want him to own me? Did I want to be his?

"What's with the needle?" I asked, looking at Lisette.

"This is a tattoo gun."

"Why do you need that?"

"The Creator has decided that it would be in your best interest to give you Marks."

"Like the Marks that slaves have?"

"Sort of…except it's the angelic version."

"I don't need Marks." I looked between Micha and Lisette as I seriously wondered if they'd lost their minds. "First you take away my glamor. Now you're telling me that you want me inked up. Am I really that ugly?"

"You're beautiful," Micha immediately said, making me snap my eyes over to look at him. "You've never been ugly. You've just been looking through everyone else's lenses. Tell me, why would you assume that taking away your glamor automatically makes you ugly?"

My mouth opened, closed, opened, closed. I frowned.

Micha's eyes blazed, watching me squirm. "For once, your speechless."

I titled my chin up. "It'll take more than that to silence me."

Micha's jaw flexed. He reached up, touching his neck. "I seem to recall that you—"

"Yeah, yeah…" I rolled my eyes playfully, enjoying bringing out this side to him.

He frowned. And I realized that he wasn't frowning. His face seemed serious but maybe it was just his 'aware' face. I suddenly became afraid. Micha saw the change in my face and took a step back.

"Like I said before. You're not ready."

I could tell that Lissette was trying not to smile. She assured me that this was less of an insult towards my body but more of a mark of faith from the Creator. I still didn't understand. She said these were Marks of protection. She said these were Marks that could save my life.

"You can't do this on your own."

"And you think tattoos are going to help with that?"

"Just explain it the way it was explained to you when you got your Marks," Micha said, lips quirking into a bemused smile.

"As you wish. These Marks that I'm about to give you are unlike any you've ever come across. They are also infused with a bit of magic from all the angels in Sora. That way, if you ever need our help, you just put a bit of your magic into the runes and the Army of the Creator will descend to aid you."

This angelic magic makes my magic look like a bad joke... What other power have I missed out on?

"So, they're like runes?"

"Exactly."

"Damn. That's more of a convincing argument than the crap you tried to spoon feed me earlier. This I can do."

I laid back. We were in there for what felt like hours as Lissette made my left arm into a work of art. For some reason, the ink burned when it touched my skin and I knew that it was made from something different than the ink we used on Earth. Micha told me that it was made from the tears of angels. When I bit my lip to keep from crying out at the searing pain, someone grabbed my hand and rubbed soothing circles.

I was in so much pain that I wondered if I'd imagined it.

"All done!" Lissette said an hour later, setting down the needle before clapping her hands. "It might be a bit tender but with you being Nephilim, it should heal in a few minutes or so."

She was right. It was a bit tender and I was afraid to touch it. Still, I could tell that it was almost done. I waited exactly fifteen minutes for my skin to heal before looking at the artwork.

A tattoo of a dragon wound up and down left my arm, telling the faint whispered story that was my life. It was plain, simple and all me. I knew that if Jacques saw it, he would shame me for ruining my flawless skin. I looked a bit closer. What was that?

"Why are there olive wreaths?"

"That's my signature," Lissette said with a grin as she straightened the crown on her head. "Do you like it?"

I did and I told her so.

"I made the wreaths in temporary ink. It'll fade soon. I don't want to mess up your Mark." She gave me a pretty, crooked grin. "Try it out."

"What do you mean?"

"Use your magic," Micha commanded.

"Yes, sir," I said, rolling my eyes.

That's when I realized that he was still holding my hand. A jolt raced up and down my arm and when I pulled away, Micha scooted away from me. I began to call on God's Magic. My powers crackled around me and in just seconds, the Mark on my arm began to glow. There was a shift in the atmosphere and—

Woosh!

I glanced around and was immediately drawn towards the door. A figure hovered there, their feet just a few inches from the ground. Their two wings were long and stretched behind them like a banner. The ambiguity of their gender made them even more beautiful. I glanced at Lissette.

"Who's that?"

"Oh, that's Giselle." She waved a hand then said something in the language of angels; the other angel flapped away. "She's another battle angel."

"I guess that means it works?"

"Yes." Micha nodded at Lissette. "Thank you for your help."

"We all have a purpose. I believe that aiding The Gatekeeper was mine."

I got up and walked towards the door. Micha waved his hand. I somehow knew that when I opened the door, a portal would be waiting.

"One more thing, 'Keeper!" called Lissette.

"Yes?"

"I hope that you make the right choice."

There was a weight in her words that I could not fully grasp. Instead of asking her to elaborate, I nodded and opened the door. Light seemed to be sucked towards the portal. I suddenly felt extremely worn out. I turned, about to ask Micha if he would wait for me to take a nap.

His head cocked to the side. "You're tired."

I nodded.

He glanced at the portal, my home on the other side. "Would you like me to carry you?"

I gaped at him. "You're asking me?"

"Why would I do something you don't want me to do?" His eyes hooded when I blushed, and I wondered if he also thought of what it would mean if he held me close. "Is that a yes, little one?"

I swallowed, angry as I realized that was what my husband used to call me.

"What?" the angel asked, tilting his head. "What did I say?"

"It's nothing."

I moved to step past him. He reached out, gripping my elbow. I stopped, looked back at him. He looked down at me, his curly hair practically spilling into his eyes. I reached out, moved his hair from his face, letting my fingers rest in his curly locks.

"What…" I paused, swallowing. "What are you thinking?"

But he said nothing.

I blushed and marched through the portal. My stomach growled. The angel suddenly glared at me, seemingly angry.

"You haven't eaten today."

"Make me."

"Don't play like that. You've been starved most of your life. You need to eat."

My mouth snapped shut. Oh, shit, he was serious. I looked down, thinking. Then I looked up at him, my eyes glowing.

"And then will you show me whatever it is that you've been holding out on?"

"You can't handle it."

"Respectfully, *sir,*" my eyes met his, "you don't know what I can handle."

His lips pursed as he nodded, his gaze dark, tempting. "Is that so?"

"Babe!"

I turned to see Dorian standing near the manor doors, waving at me enthusiastically. And I realized that I wanted something dark, tempting, something that Dorian, even with all of his toxic flaws, could never give me. It just wasn't who he was. I glanced back at Micha, my eyes tracing up his body and his wicked features. What was Micha, really?

What was he withholding?

"Go back to your husband."

"Okay," I said, shrugging nonchalantly even though deep down, his indifference stung.

"Aleilah?"

I paused. I didn't want to tell him not to call me that, as I had with everyone else. I wanted him to say it, to chant it, to sing it all through the night. Why was that?

"Yes, sir."

His voice was low, a growl. "I'll be waiting."

I walked up to Dorian, took his hand.

He pulled mine up to his lips, kissing the back of my hand. "You're shaking."

I looked away. "Yeah…"

Dorian reached out, touched my chin. He moved my face to look into his eyes. I reached up, touching his hand, moving it to my neck silently. He quirked a brow.

"What do you want, little one?" he asked.

I wanted to tell him that was now Micha's phrase for me, for it had taken on a whole new meaning.

"You should know what I want," I frowned.

"Are you okay?" Dorian's eyes traced up and down my body. "You look…and you feel…different."

I leaned forward, tracing my tongue along his ear. "I need you."

Dorian quickly waved a hand, a portal opening as soon as his hand lowered. Golden, like the sun, blindingly bright, glowing, like a fire in the night. A heat like no other. Not temporary. Eternal. He was powerful in his own way…

Just not in the way I need.

I stepped through the portal and found myself in my bedroom. Dorian moved to sit on the bed, gazing out the window. I could pick up on his emotions—something that I knew had nothing to do with my training with Micha and more with him being the one that I was bound to: my husband. He was happy about our marital status, worried about our son and guilty about something that I couldn't identify. I tried to pry into his thoughts but was met with nothing but walls.

"What's wrong, Dorian?"

"I don't know. I feel angry and…sad…like I've lost you." He turned towards me, and his eyes were churning. "Do you still love me?"

"Of course." I fought the guilty frown that threatened to overtake my expression. "There's not a thing in the world that can change that."

"I love you."

My tail flicked behind me at the sincerity of his words.

He watched me silently, then suddenly frowned and looked out the window again. I watched his face while he refused to watch me, wondering what he saw, what made me so different. When he turned back, I could see that something had shifted between us…we were changing. Not growing apart, but not closer, as I had hoped when we married. We were finding dynamics outside of one another…or at least, I was. But Dorian…

Was he trying to get closer to me?

Oh, Goddess…

Was I pushing him away again?

"So…what other powers did you get?" A welcome distraction. "And explain the tattoo before my brain explodes, please."

I told him about the list of powers that I'd obtained in such a short amount of time. I had wings, which he'd already seen. I had advanced healing, the ability to create small winds with my wings, the ability to shield myself against enemy attacks and the ability to call upon an angelic army if need be. The great part was that I was only going to get stronger. The bad part was that my body was having trouble catching up with these physical advancements.

His eyes met mine shyly and I wondered how deeply my love for him ran, and then remembered the blind panic I felt when he was slashed by Jacques.

He's real and so is my love for him. It's just not as strong as I'd hoped. It's almost…clumsy?

Dorian seemed to notice my eyes dim and moved to retract.

"No…" I mumbled. "Touch me."

Dorian touched my cheek softly, breathing out when my breath hitched, and my eyes closed.

"Just like that…"

"Wow…" he grumbled.

"What?" My eyes opened.

"I just haven't seen you look like this in a while…"

I eyed his face. He seemed despondent.

"Since when?"

"Since…" He shook his head. "My bad."

"No. I want to talk about it. We….we need to talk about it."

"There's nothing to talk about. We discussed it. I know what he did to you."

"You didn't think that was all I had to say, did you?" I whispered.

Dorian dropped his hand. "I thought for a second that you were back to normal…"

"Back to…? Oh, fuck you, Dorian!"

"What? You were the one trying to get sexy with me!"

I picked up my daggers and sheathed them, dashing back out of the room as I did so. Dorian cursed behind me, calling me a tease. I breathed out heavily through my nose, trying to quiet the noise in my head.

It wasn't that I didn't want him.

It was just that what he said…*it wasn't right.*

CHAPTER FOURTEEN

AGREEMENT

"So you're like a ninja warrior for God?" Rhea quipped.

"Aren't we all?"

"Don't you think that all of this is a little weird?"

I honestly did but I didn't want her—or anyone else—to see me as weak. Especially not in front of Dorian, who was at the stove, pretending to cook so he could listen in on our conversation. What? Did he think I was going to gossip about what was going on between us? Did he think I'd tell Rhea of all people?

No, I had to be driven. How could anyone believe in me if I didn't believe in myself?

"What? No. Why?"

"God is designing you to be Its perfect soldier, but you've never even talked to It." Rhea gave a nonchalant shrug. "I mean, you're kind of OP for an agnostic."

"And?"

"And It could have chosen anyone else, like someone who believed, like a minister or something. Instead, It chose someone who's broken every single of Its rules and seems to be on the tipping point of faith. It just seems kind of silly to me."

"Fuck…you…?" I said, sounding kind of unsure of my response.

"Well, I don't know and I'm not going to implode trying to figure it out. As my pastor once said, I guess there's a reason that we just can't understand yet."

"Anyway, shouldn't you be training with Micha right now?"

I paused, glanced at Dorian and sighed. "I wanted to spend some time with my husband."

Rhea snorted. "Yeah, right."

"What?"

"You guys have been avoiding each other. I mean, other than that flying lesson where you guys seemed almost normal. But you guys…" She paused, setting down her cup of coffee. "You've never been normal."

I looked up because I could feel him staring at me. I looked away. He sighed, turned back to the stove. Who did he think he was fooling? I'd never seen him cook a day in my life! And he had cooks, for Kalysma's sake! Did he even know *how* to cook?

"So," Rhea glanced between Dorian and I, "what about the new hunk?"

"Who?" I raised a brow, then pointed to Dorian and silently mouthed his name.

"No! I mean, yes, but been there, done that, do *not* want to go back!" She shuddered.

I paused. They'd been together?

"What about the angel?" Rhea whispered, waggling her brows.

"Oh, him?" I glanced at Dorian, knowing that this would tear him up inside. I frowned. "He's okay."

Rhea reached across the table in a suddenly affectionate move and held my fingers in her small, firm grasp. To say that I was shocked was an understatement. Ever since she'd revealed that she didn't exactly care for me, she had shown just that—that she'd rather I wasn't here. But now she seemed almost eager to talk to me. Wait, not talk—

Gossip.

I stood up from the table, walked up to Dorian. His back was stiff against my front, his eyes closed as his head leaned back. His hands were in front of his chest and as I wrapped my arms around him, I imagined him standing in the rain, singing as he stood with me, just like this. I wanted nothing more than to mend the broken fences, to heal whatever hurt had divided us. But there was an innate part of me that needed Micha—

Why, I'll never know.

I pressed a kiss to the back of Dorian's neck. Even sweaty from the heat of the stove, he still tasted sweet, not like brandy, but more like the fruit his brandy was made from. He smiled, then frowned and rubbed that spot between his eyebrows.

"I need a drink."

* * *

I watched as Dorian stumbled past Rhea's room and hour later. I stiffened as if caught doing something naughty and Rhea snorted next to me. But my eyes were two saucer plates in my head, staring fearfully.

The last thing I wanted was to hurt Dorian.

I loved him. I really did.

"Well?" Rhea said, arching one perfectly sculpted eyebrow when I turned to stare at her. "Go after him!"

"But—"

"You're in love with him. Only an idiot can't see that." She cocked her head at me. "You don't seem that dumb, Beasty."

"But Rhea…" I whispered, biting my lip. "I *really* hurt him."

"Um, didn't he cheat on you? And practically leave you at the altar?"

"Didn't you try to kill me?" I growled back, eyes flashing.

Her head lolled to the side. "I wasn't aiming for you."

"No. Just my heart."

Her lips curled into a cruel sneer, her eyes narrowing as well. "You'd better go after him before Megumi gets ahold of him."

"He wouldn't do that. We worked past that. Dorian…he loves me."

"But at the end of the day," Rhea shook her head, "he's still a man."

CHAPTER FIFTEEN

MODIFIED. REAL

D orian rolled over.

"You sure?"

I waggled my bum in the air. My razor teeth scraped along his spine. My tongue darting out, drawing lazy circles where my mouth had just been.

I hummed an affirmative.

"I thought you said you wanted to sleep." He was grinning now. It was a half-assed effort at being coy.

I cocked my head like a wolf, peering at him through sharpened vision, taking him in. "You don't want me?"

He blushed. "It's not that at all." He reached out, cupping my cheek as he swiped a sweet, gentle kiss on my brow. "It's just, you haven't let me touch you since…."

"I know…" I growled around the words to keep from crying. "I'm sorry, baby. Really, I am."

"You're recovering. I can see that now."

"I want *you*."

"I love you."

My lips found his in the dark. We kissed for a long time and held each other twice as long. And when we finally came together, the sky shuddered as if it would break into two. I was suddenly reminded of the Gifted soldiers that yanked the sun from the sky. They did it out of a love for their people.

I would do far more for my love for this man.

And no god would stop me.

"Ya know," Dorian said, holding me, "if you want to sleep with him, you don't need my permission."

I closed my eyes. "But you don't like him."

"I don't like the way you look at him. But all in all, he's a decent guy." I could hear the scowl in his voice. "There are worse people to take to bed."

I was reminded of the painting of Jacques in the hall. "I suppose so..."

Lightning jolted up my spine. A part of me was thrilled knowing that I had my husband's okay to have an extra marital affair. But another part of me had a hollow, empty feeling in my gut, as if I'd swallowed a fistful of rocks and had yanked out part of my stomach throwing them back up. He didn't want me to.

But he knew that I would stray further if I did not.

And deep down...

I knew it too.

Because I'd never been with anyone other than Dorian. And the thought of someone else, no matter how appealing on paper...it terrified me. Thinking about—

"Do you want me to sing for you?"

"You can sing?"

He belted out a few notes. He couldn't sing—not by a long shot—but it was cute that he was trying. When I covered my ears, Dorian stretched and got out of bed, pulling me out with him despite my protests. I asked what time it was, and he said that it was only

10:45a.m. After the sensual love-making that had taken all morning, I felt somewhat sated and Dorian and I—

We felt somewhat okay.

Not like we used to be, but okay.

He grinned.

We went down to the kitchen where Dorian booted everyone out. I texted Rhea. When she didn't reply, I called her. When she still didn't reply, I sent her a series of messages, hoping to wake her. Finally, I heard her footsteps. When I sat the table, I was surprised to see Micha hovering outside the window. He tapped his wrist, signifying that I was on a time crunch. When I waved him away, he disappeared with a roll of his eyes.

"What's going on?" Rhea said, rubbing the corner of her eye.

"Dorian is going to try his hand at breakfast. I want you to be here as a witness in case I die of food poisoning."

"This sounds interesting," she said, immediately perking up.

I turned to see that Dorian already had a KISS THE RUNE MASTER apron tied around his waist and a spatula in his hands. Rhea leaned her head on my shoulder. I grew stiff for a second or two before sighing. I had to trust her again.

"So how've you been?" I asked, laying my head on hers.

"I'm okay, I guess…" she sighed. "I'm just bored as fuck!"

"And you thought sleeping would fix that?" Dorian asked, humming to himself.

"It's better than drinking myself into an early grave!" she snapped.

"Ooh, burn!" Dorian cried, clutching his chest. "I've never heard that one before!"

"Concentrate on your eggs," she hissed.

The fire alarm started to go off as smoke rose into the air. Dorian dumped this batch of eggs in the trashcan before beginning anew.

Something was off with the two of them, something that I couldn't place. But whatever it was would work its course.

It had to.

"That was a low blow, Rhea," I whispered.

"Sorry," she muttered.

"Are you okay?"

"She's just on her period!" Dorian cried.

"He's right," she whispered.

I nodded. That must be it. But it didn't explain why they were actively trying to hurt one another. I mean, she'd thrown the first blow. But I didn't want to see them fighting at all.

After about fifteen minutes or so, Dorian set a plate in front of Rhea before setting one plate between he and I. It was funny that now that we were married, we did stuff like share. I guess it was all a part of caring or whatever. I picked up a fork.

"Eep!"

I jumped, my fork clattering to the table. I looked at Rhea, who'd backed away to the far wall and was waving her fork at the plate as if it would come alive and attack her at any second. I gave her my patented WTF look.

"It just moved!" she shrieked.

"Oh, Rhea, quit being such a drama queen!" I tried not to make a face as I rolled the runny eggs on my tongue. "It's not *that* bad."

Rhea screamed again and Micha appeared at her side almost instantly.

"Sit down and eat your food," I said, trying not to get annoyed by the way she clung to the breeder.

"That isn't food!" she shrieked, flopping her arms so much that bits of green eggs—don't ask me how they got that color—flew everywhere. "I know that I sometimes puke up my food but for God's sake, I want to at least be able to eat it first!"

"What is she talking about?" I whispered.

Dorian pulled out his phone. I nudged him. He shrugged me off before setting the phone on the table. I glanced at the screen.

Don't tell her I told you but she's bulimic, it said.

"What?!" I leapt up.

"Shhh!" Dorian hissed, waving his hand. "She just got diagnosed while she was in the Southern Isles."

"And she told you?" I hissed. "Why didn't she tell me?"

"She thought you had a lot on your plate," he whispered. "Look. Just don't say anything, all right?"

"But—"

"Please?" he whispered.

I saw tears glimmering in his eyes. He loved her deeply and this was hurting him. I sighed and nodded. I turned back to the eggs. Rhea shifted the food around on her plate, staring at it with a green tinge to her cheeks. Dorian crossed his arms but said nothing.

"Do you need help?" Micha said, fixing her with that smoldering gaze of his.

Rhea blinked as if dazzled. Her long lashes fell upon her cheeks and as the light hit her, I realized that her mousy brown hair framed her face perfectly. What I'd kill to be her right now—beautiful and normal. It wasn't my place to be jealous but no matter how many times I told myself that, I couldn't seem to get rid of the green emotion. Rhea pointed at her plate and Micha jumped back twice as fast as she did.

"Did that shit just *move?*" Micha gave Dorian an incredulous look. "You're supposed to cook the food, not play Dr. Frankenstein with it!"

"That's it!" Dorian stood abruptly, slamming his fork on the table. "If you don't want to eat the food then you can leave!"

Rhea quickly sped from the room. When Dorian turned away, Micha's lips curved up into a smile. He wiggled his fingers and the eggs turned back to their normal fluffy yellowness. The angel nodded at me before he left the room and went outside. I scarfed down the rest of my eggs, ignoring the scalding burn because I was so hungry. Then I picked up the other plate and scraped the excess into the trash.

Upstairs, I heard Aiden begin to squall.

"Hey..." I walked up behind Dorian and planted a kiss on the back of his neck. "Thanks for the food."

"I'm surprised you didn't run away screaming like everyone else."

"Oh my God!" I stared at the dish rag he was currently holding in horror. "It's alive!"

He flung some water at me.

"Be quiet, nutcase..." he said but I could see the smile that tugged at his handsome lips.

"I finished my plate." I frowned. "Although you might want to ease up on the salt next time."

"Will do," he said, nodding. He suddenly dropped a dish in the sink as a shadow crossed over his eyes. "It's not my fault that I can't cook or clean. My parents taught me how to dress, schmooze, do my taxes, count money and *make* money. Everything else, I've either learned on my own or can't do anything about."

"That's their fault for not teaching you."

"I know," he said, frustrated. "I know that you can't even begin to understand how someone who has it all can have so little, especially considering the way you grew up. But...I'm trying. I really am trying to make you happy and to just be *normal*. I guess it doesn't matter when it's all a charade, huh?"

I understood what he meant completely. That was one thing that Micha would never have on the Golden Immortal. Even in his fuckups, he was authentic. I gave him a swift kiss.

"Let's go do something fun. We have to be quick, though. I have to pick up training later."

Dorian glanced at the clock on the microwave. It was now 11:20. That didn't leave us a lot of time, but it wasn't a little, either.

"What do you have in mind?"

"I have an idea." I let a wicked grin crawl across my face. "Let's spend an hour with Aiden and then I can properly thank you for breakfast."

"Ew! Gross!" I heard Rhea scream from another room.

"That sounds tempting," Dorian said, kissing me again, "but I'll have to pass. After meeting Micha, I've decided to do a little self-evaluation. My way may not be the right way—I think something was trying to tell me that when I OD'd. I've called in a few favors to improve the conditions in the diamond mines that I own; the miners will be given safer tools that work faster so that they will have to work fewer hours and spend more time at home. Maybe money isn't just for drinking, which I am going to stop. Maybe I have wealth to make a change."

I nodded even though I thought it was pointless. Once upon a time, I too thought I could change. But I knew that this was the only way to satisfy my broken soul. And thanks to some old stories that I'd almost forgotten, I also knew that there was a weapon that I needed—and I was willing to break into Sora to get it.

Only then could I have my revenge.

CHAPTER SIXTEEN

1195

I went upstairs, changed, retrieved my daggers and met my angelic teacher outside.

"We're going to do something a bit different," Micha said, waving his hand and making a new portal appear. "Today we're going to travel across time and assist someone in history as a part of your training. This will teach you to not only follow commands but to make tough decisions when you're out in the field."

"Where will we be training?"

Or better yet when?

"We'll be training in Japan around the year 1195."

"You mean the start of the Tokugawa Period? The time of shoguns? Sweet!"

"You will be completing a mission for Minamoto Yoritomo and therefore the Emperor himself." Micha deeply frowned. "A yokai wrought havoc in Kamakura and the shogun called on any and all warriors to help him take down this bloodthirsty enemy—including foreigners."

"Epic!" I looked at the manor's yard which was beautiful but probably had nothing on feudal Japan. "When do we leave?"

"Right now."

I steeled my shoulders. I could do this. With that final thought, I stepped through the portal.

*   *   *

We walked down a solitary road. Micha walked with a holy swagger, as if he was proud of serving his master so well. I walked hunched forward, my head down and my hands stuffed in my pockets. Micha tried multiple times to engage me in conversation, but I was…lost. Finally, he asked me something that made an odd feeling bubble in my stomach. He asked me what my real motives for completing this mission were.

As I gave him my answer without a remorseful thought, I felt a slur of emotions. I was giddy at the thought. I was proud to have been so forthcoming. I was in love with the thought of power. Yet a tiny part of me knew that I should feel ashamed for feeling such things.

"Revenge?" he said, raising an eyebrow.

"Micha, I'm afraid that I haven't been completely honest with you." I glanced at Micha before placing my hand on his arm. "I am not doing this for the Creator."

He gave me a dubious expression.

"Look, I'm not saying that *It* is or isn't real. But I'm not going to give any man power over me again—not you or the Creator or anyone. That's just how I feel."

"The Creator is not a *man*," he said the word with disgust.

"You know what I mean."

He breathed in, his nostrils expanding like that of a large beast as his chest puffed out with the intake of air. He let it sigh, his chest and belly deflating. There was beauty in that action.

I delighted in his anger—he was cute when he was mad.

"You're afraid to trust the Creator because of your past. I understand that. But the Creator was not the one who wronged you so. It loves you. It's given you an honor that most could only dream of."

"Whatever." I turned to look around me. "Let's just help this shogun so that I can finish my training."

Inside, I was churning at the reminder. I was faced with the Creator's love and all I could feel was hate because I knew that Jacques was the one that I would ultimately face down. I wanted payback for all the years of abuse. Everyone else had faith in me. I, on the other hand, would stop at nothing for revenge, knew that it was my goal and did absolutely nothing to change it.

Did that make me a bad person?

Most definitely.

Did I honestly care?

No.

Micha watched me for a long moment. I stared back at him, knowing that this admittance shattered something inside of him. A pained look crossed his face and he seemed to gain a faraway look in his eyes. I waited until he returned to me before moving to speak. He raised a hand.

"Alice made the wrong decisions," he said, his eyes colliding with mine and making a heavy weight overtake my heart, "but she was good. You are nothing like her."

I took a step back, the wind having been knocked out of me as if the angel had sent a powerful punch straight to my gut. I knew that he was right. I was an awful person. But I was hoping that he would spare me the pleasure of hearing it from him, which meant more to me than it should. I guess I was hoping that his goodness would prevail and that he would quote some scripture to reassure me that there was hope for me. I was hoping that he wouldn't stay it.

It was obvious that I didn't understand the Creator or those who served him.

"You are just like him."

"Who?"

"Lucifer, Luce, Akiva, Mephistopheles…my brother."

I didn't know what to say to that.

"Like you, he was motivated by power, greed and self-satisfaction. Like you, he didn't respect the highest power in the universe. Like you, he operated solely on self-preservation. You have been given so many chances and you haven't seized one. You are trapped in this damning circle and all you've done is dig a deeper hole."

"You called your brother Luce," I said, grasping at straws. "Were you two close?"

"He was my best friend…until he went Dark, that is. When he struck a war against the Creator, he struck a war against the House of Faux—against me."

I was guessing that the House of Faux was Micha's family. But wouldn't that make Lucifer part of the family as well? I was confused.

"Why didn't you include Lucifer in the House of Faux?"

"When my mother passed him up for the birthright, she technically disowned him. He is no longer a member of my house. He is a man borne of darkness."

I knew that I should change the subject. Micha was only going to get angrier. But his words flowed like water from a broken dam that I struggled to piece back together.

"I'm going to tell you this because I know that I'm sending you mixed signals," Micha said, his eyes driving through my clothes, through my skin, past my bones and borrowing deep in my soul. "I am attracted to you, and not because you're a female and I'm a breeder. You're a very beautiful woman," he paused, trying to communicate the seriousness of his words, "and if the circumstances were different, we'd be doing a lot more than these damned looks and…petting."

A blush overtook my face.

"But I don't think we should get mixed up with each other. I serve one master and that master sent me here to teach you—that's all. I will teach you that your body is your greatest weapon, and it stops there. If we were to get physical—which we will not—we would still have different views, which is why we would never work. I have a feeling that if I was with you in any way other than as your teacher," he said, reaching out to lay a hand on my cheek, "then it would destroy us all."

That kind of changed everything. He was rejecting me for a completely righteous reason. He was doing it because he thought it was the right thing to do, but he had other motives as well. He knew that I was bad news and he was trying to protect himself.

"If I'm that bad," I said, stepping away so that his hand fell away from my face, "then why are you training me?"

"I'm hoping that you'll come to your senses down the road."

But I didn't want him to go.

"Let's say I did come to my senses," I reluctantly said as I rocked back on my heels, "what then?"

He leaned forward. "Then I'd fuck the shit out of you."

I leaned forward.

He pulled away. "But I'm doubtful."

"Then why are you telling me all this?" I huffed.

"I have hope for you, Aleilah, even if it is a lost cause…Just as I did with my brother—I have hope…Now, enough small talk," he said, clapping his hands together. "This is one of the most beautiful places ever and I'd like you to take it all in."

"You touched my wings…" I accused, suddenly hurt. "I thought that meant something to you."

"That is one of the most intimate actions among angels." Hope flared in my chest. "And it was a mistake. I'm sorry for leading you on. It will not happen again."

"Wait…" My voice quickly lost its edge as another question popped in my head. "Just one more question…"

"No more questions!" The angel sighed, clearly tired of me, and that was that.

I looked at the world around us.

He was right.

It was beautiful. Lily pads floated in a small pond and flowers poked their upraised heads above the ground, always facing the sun. Nightingales sang music so sweet that any other person would cry. The smell of Sakura blossoms permeated the air, giving everything a feeling of change. The wind blew softly, caressing my cheeks like a stolen kiss. A large palace loomed in the distance. It had great golden doors, statues of dragons and large trees twisted outward, their gnarly, gangly limbs reaching towards the sky in praise of the Creator's work. If everything went as planned today, Minamoto would be on the ground thanking me until his knees bled and his mouth ran dry.

"When we get in the palace, try to be respectful."

"Why should I?"

His lips quirked, his hand twitching. "If you are disrespectful, you will invoke the shogun's rage. He has tens of hundreds—maybe even *thousands*—of guards. They will not hesitate when attacking you."

"I can take them," I said, flexing my fingers as my electricity sparked at the challenge.

I quickly devised a plan that was more my style.

Kill the demon, grab the shogun, demand a ransom…then kill all of them.

Micha glanced at me occasionally and I could tell that he knew that something was up. As a distraction, I asked him if the shogun knew that we were coming. Micha said that he expected two foreign warriors to show up. Apparently, we were supposed to be people from a smaller, and formerly unheard of, island.

"We can't be from the same island," I said, looking him up and down. "We look nothing alike—"

"I'll take care of it," he replied.

He did just that.

A familiar light encased his form; as his body began to glow, his form began to change, becoming shorter but more built. When the light faded, I gaped at his new appearance.

He now had long bloodred hair that reached his waist, a round jaw flecked with red stubble and bulging muscly arms that looked like they could snap a tree in half. He was clad in traditional Japanese attire, which consisted of a black yukata, a white sash tied around his waist, a gray hakama, tabi socks and some geta sandals. Even his eyes changed to a much narrower shape and the color went from grey to a loud, sea-like blue.

Even in this form, he was beautiful.

He waved a hand over me. A light encased me. But I looked the same.

"To the two of us, you look like you. But to them, you look like me, just with bigger boobs and no beard."

"How big?" I gaped.

He put out his hands—too far from his chest for my liking. I frowned. He flicked my head. I rubbed my head, glaring at him out the corner of my eye. The balance to our relationship had seemingly been restored.

"What do I call you, sensei?"

183

"Here, your name is Akane and my name is Okkusu. We are married bounty hunters from a small, recently discovered island known as *Kemuri no Sato*, or the Land of Smoke. We answered the call from Minamoto to contain a demon that has been terrorizing his home and killing at will."

Okkusu was built like an ox, so I understood his name completely.

I had a story in my head. We walked towards the white palace, checking in with guards before appearing before the mighty shogun exactly five minutes later. He was short and fat, had sharp, beady eyes that stood for no deception and a tightly drawn mouth that seemed like a pale pink slash on his face. He was dressed in golden robes, surrounded by the smoke of incents and had three beautiful women draped across his feet like rugs.

"Be gone!" he said in Japanese with a wave.

The women quickly rose and left from the room.

"Good day, great shogun," Micha said in Japanese, his voice quick and breezy like winter's chill as he kneeled before the shogun.

I quickly followed suit, keeping my eyes level with the shogun's feet; on the inside, I was reeling. Guards were perched around the room, hands on their katana and eyes watching our every move. The shogun asked Micha how we came into this profession, which seemed kind of weird to me. Micha told him that I was a fisherman's daughter and that he was an ox driver, but we'd turned to bounty hunting once the emperor visited our small island and convinced us to pursue careers that would be more beneficial to his empire.

"I love the emperor and will not allow anything to stand in his way," Minamoto said, giving his guards one meaningful look. "I will not waste my time employing you if you are too weak. Guards!" he barked, waving a lazy hand. "Attack!"

I knew I was fast but damn...this was surreal. The guards charged at me and as if my life were some cassette recording, life slowed down substantially. My body was supercharged, glowing with the electricity that was snapping under my skin. My entire being hummed with power and as my hand flew out, a wicked bolt thundered from my fingers and hit one guard in his abdomen. Micha was battling it out with three guards at once, one of which was matching him blow for vicious blow.

I concentrated on my power, letting it build inside of me like a flame. Purple electricity danced around my hands, then turned red, then white before my fingertips were engulfed in flames. It didn't hurt one bit. I charged, slamming one flame-covered fist into the back of the tallest guard's head. It came out on the other side, covered in brain matter.

Keres stirred inside of me, calling for blood.

I could feel someone approaching me from behind. I whirled around to see a man coming at me with a short katana, his face an empty mask. I twirled on my toes, just barely moving out of reach. He swung again. I grinned at my improved speed as I ducked. Micha's fist crashed out, cracking one of his enemies in the jaw and knocking him unconscious.

I swung at the man in front of me. He threw down his katana with a roar as his face twisted in determination. He had heart—and that was something that I could respect. We traded blow after blow and soon a pain blossomed on my face. I knew that if I sustained more damage, the left side of my face would be badly bruised.

I tapped into that hidden power once more and was pleased when my vision cleared. He swung a left hook the same time I did. When I moved to kick, he was already raising his leg. We reached out, locking our hands together, both trying to flip the other as our teeth grit at the strenuous effort. I would not give in—and neither would he.

"Enough!" Minamoto called.

The guard and I immediately separated and then gave the other a respectful nod. I looked around me, surprised by the carnage. A pile of bodies was stacked next to Micha's feet. I quickly counted. In the few seconds that it'd taken me to incapacitate two men, Micha had taken down eight.

I really had a lot of catching up to do.

"You are definitely strong," the shogun said, stroking his hairless chin. "Do you know what you are up against?"

"There is a yokai terrorizing the forest not too far from here. It is our job to eliminate it," Micha said, bowing his head, but not before a feather fell from his hair.

The shogun noticed it, too.

"You are one of the tenshi?" Minamoto said, eyes flashing.

"No." Micha cocked his head, feigning innocence lest our entire cover be blown. "Why would you say that, Minamoto-sama?"

"It must have been the light." Minamoto waved his hand. "Go complete your mission and you will have your reward."

*   *   *

We walked through the forest. The only available light was the light from the trees rising around us...well, that and me. My skin held a soft glow as electricity filtered through my system. When we came across some tracks, Micha had me stand in a specific position so he could see them clearly. An odd chattering noise filled the space around us.

"What was that?" I asked, huddling a bit closer.

"I don't know..."

"You know, since we're a couple, we should hold—"

"No."

We walked on for a few minutes. After a while, I began to get bored and decided to sing to entertain myself. My voice carried through the trees. As I sang, Micha became more relaxed, even snapping his fingers to the song that I made up on the spot. He commented more than once that I had a beautiful voice.

Then he suddenly told me to be quiet as he listened.

When he was done, he told me to keep singing. When we'd walked about five miles, Micha's eyes filled with tears that wouldn't fall. When I asked why he was so upset he said that I, just like Luce, had an amazing voice, which scared him. He told me that he didn't want me to end up like his brother. In response, I tried to sing something more cheerful.

We paused to rest twelve miles in. By now the sun had completely set, making the forest around us glow from the pale moonlight. Micha gathered some branches and told me to make a fire. I bent over and set them aflame with my powers. I straightened to see him staring at me.

"What?"

He just shook his head.

He turned back into his true form but said that I should still call him Okkusu in case someone from the palace were to come across us. I said that it was highly unlikely considering the demon roaming around, to which he gave a laugh and agreed. As his black curls and reality-defying eyes took form, I realized that I'd missed seeing him. I guess I just couldn't think of him as anyone else. Micha reached down towards his cloak.

"Whoa." I fought to keep from staring. "What are you doing?"

"I'm not going to let you just lie on the ground," Micha said, pulling off his cloak in one swift movement.

"Damn. What happened to keeping me from temptation?"

At my words, his mouth lifted into a crooked grin. He put the cloak on the ground, just far enough from the flames to keep it from catching on fire. He commanded me to lie down so I did. He laid down next to me and I could feel the contours of his chest pressed against my back. I rolled over, needing to see his face.

The moon had cast a beautiful glow on the space around us. Fireflies danced around our heads. The combination of the lights gave Micha's skin a glow that my electricity could never match. Mesmerized, I reached out and pressed a hand on his chest. At his intake of breath, I looked up, startled.

"Is this okay?"

He gave a stiff nod.

I fought the urge to smile as the teenage girl in me did the merengue. I'd wanted to touch him for so long. Dorian's face echoed in my mind and instead of stopping, I decided that it was okay. I mean, I wasn't going to sleep with the guy—and even if I *did*, he gave me permission.

It was just harmless touching, really...

I trailed my hand lower to his abdomen. The man was built, I'd give him that. It was almost as if he'd been carved from granite. Everything about him was perfectly symmetrical, which sent my brain for a loop. I'd never been so close to such exactness. I heard Keres chuckle in the back of my mind, but I somehow knew that this was all me.

I was in control.

"May I?" I said, eyeing his arms.

He nodded again and as I touched him, his eyes fluttered closed. I smoothed my hands over his chiseled arms as a deep heat built in the core of my belly. Micha made an odd noise in the back of his throat as my hands trailed across his neck. In the light of the moon, I saw something. My eyes narrowed.

"What is that?" I said, staring at the offensive mark on his neck.

"I...um...it's a battle scar."

"No, it's not." I traced my finger over the raised skin. "I know a hickey when I see one."

"It's old…" he said, pressing a bit closer until I could feel his temptation.

"It looks pretty fresh to me." My cheeks burned in humiliation. "Who gave it to you?"

He wouldn't meet my eyes.

"Was it Lisette?"

He shook his head and that's when it hit me. Tears of embarrassment and frustration built behind my eyes. My throat closed up, making it hard to breathe. He flirted with me and then screwed around with my only friend. Yeah, he was a good guy all right…

He pulled me close. I wished with every fiber in my being that it wasn't him that was holding me, but it was. Micha reached out, pinching my chin between his forefinger and thumb. He gazed into my eyes, confliction swimming in his mercury-filled orbs. I wanted him to kiss me until I forgot what I was angry about, until I'd forgotten that he'd played me.

He did not.

"I'm sorry," he said, "but I needed relief. You're toxic for me."

His head tilted down and his lips just barely brushed mine. But it was too late. The moment was gone. I put my hands on his chest—that same chest that I'd been touching moments ago—and pushed. With that, I rolled over until my back was to him.

"You don't think this is hard for me, too!" He voice was a strangled croak. "I'm trying to do what's right."

I didn't answer. My mind was replaying our not-so-almost-kiss. It was like I was dead. I couldn't even feel him. That just made me angrier.

You're married, I told myself, *and it's time you started acting like it.*

I rolled over until my nose was pressed against the cloak. I could smell him, all mangos and brown sugar. A tear streaked down my cheek at the injustice of it all. Briefly, I wondered if this was how Jacques felt when Grant rejected him.

I didn't ever want to feel like this again.

I closed my eyes, trying to block out the sound of his breathing or the feel of his hard chest against my side. Part of me wanted to curl up into him, to go all the way and forget all past mistakes. The rational part of me put her foot down and demanded that I get some shut-eye. With nothing more to do, I curled into the arms of sleep. The last thing I felt was Micha pressing a cold kiss to the top of my head.

* * *

I felt Micha's hand wrap around my waist. He pulled me close. I whimpered.

"I'm sorry," he ground out. "It's just cold."

But I could feel him at my backside. I grinned, forgetting our differences. "It can't be that cold."

"You're unbelievable!" he growled, but still, he yanked me closer. "And warm."

My eyes creaked open. "How warm?"

"You know, despite your armor..." he traced a hand along my back as my eyes snapped open. I braced for an insult. "You are surprisingly soft."

"Oh..."

"What? Did you think I was going to insult you, beasty?" he grinned, kissing the top of my head again.

"Micha stop."

He took his arm off me, but my body was buzzing. "Sorry."

"It's not that, it's just…" I bit my lip. "If you don't stop, then I won't be able to."

"I thought Dorian was okay with us?"

I glared at the ground. "There is no us."

He lightly touched my back. I arched and purred at once. His voice was low and kidding, but also serious, all at once. "Isn't there?"

"Dorian said he was okay with it…" I wanted to allow.

He touched my waist, scooted forward. "And?"

"And…."

His lips met the back of my neck. "Yes?"

I whimpered again.

Suddenly he was yanking me close, his lips nibbling at me. "I love when you make that noise. It's the single cutest noise I've ever heard."

I glowed inside. "This is wrong."

"I'm sorry about Rhea."

"It's not that," I sighed, closing my eyes. I didn't want to deny myself, but I had to think about my marriage. "It's just—"

His lips found mine suddenly—hot, tender, inviting. My mouth opened in a gasp. He rolled us over, his hands tangling at the hair moving towards the nape of my neck, holding my head aloft. My head tilted forward ever so slowly as I grinded my hips against his.

"This is so wrong," I said again.

He cursed. "Get up!"

I lurched, my hand automatically flying up to land on one of my daggers. Looking around, Micha was gone; in his place was Okkusu—towering in a different way—a menacing way—than the night before, and on high alert. At first, I thought that it'd be easier standing next to him so we could cover each other's backs. Still, my body crawled with heat and as his eyes fell on my lips, I knew that no matter what he looked like, I couldn't deny that if I stayed away from him, we may not combust. I turned away, pretending to tend to the dying flames.

I could only imagine how Dorian would feel when I—

Oh, Kalysma…Dorian.

"What's wrong? Do you need to get back to Rhea?" I shot over my shoulder, trying to push him away.

"Please," he spun, "be quiet."

The tone of his voice made me turn. He was staring at me, his eyes losing that conflicted shine to harden to something rockier. I stood and brushed off my battle armor. Something was wrong. I unsheathed one of my daggers before asking what was going on.

"We're being tracked."

That's when it happened.

Something large was in the trees. I could only tell because when it moved, the wood groaned. I threw Micha a panicked look. Red eyebrows moved closer to blue orbs as his brow furrowed. The leaves rustled again. The wood made that god-awful sound once more. I flung myself to the ground just as the beast lunged.

It looked like a giant stag beetle. Venom and blood dripped from its mouth. From its pinchers hung various tattered kimonos, most likely souvenirs from its latest meals. Its eyes were blood red, oddly focused for an insect, cool with anger, hot with hunger. Micha withdrew his dagger and lunged at the bug demon.

"It must have been attracted to your singing and waited to strike." Micha waved a hand. "Get down!"

Screw that! I wasn't just going to sit and cower like some twelve-year-old girl. I was going to fight!

I raised my dagger. Micha and the beetle were wrestling on the ground. The battle angel tried to pry the beetle's pinchers apart with his brutish hands. I ran towards the demon, hacking with all my might. My panic grew as the blade bounced off the beetle's back.

The demon in question either didn't notice or didn't care as it continued to try and make a meal out of Micha.

Breathing in, then out, I tried to concentrate on what made me happy. Dorian or Aiden, my purpose, my Goddess. But all I saw was Micha. I took another breath.

With a final exhale, I charged once more.

* * *

"You have done well," Minamoto said, appraising the carcass of the slain demon.

"Thank you for trusting us," Micha and I said in unison, bowing low at the waist.

"The emperor will be pleased," Minamoto nodded to himself, "very pleased…"

"*Hai…*"

"Now for your reward…"

Minamoto snapped his fingers. From the ceiling fell a cage, glowing with a tempered magic. I jumped out of the way, reaching for Micha, but as my hand neared the bars, my magic died down in my system, taking away my strength—*and* the use of my Gift. My companion was unfazed as a greedy grin split Minamoto's face in half, the word 'tenshi' falling from his lips. Micha, glamour still in place, reached out. What he did next shouldn't have shocked me, but it did.

He pried the bars open with his bare hands. The metal groaned under his strength, bending outwards as his huge muscles flexed. Minamoto shrank in his chair, his eyes filling with fear. Micha fixed Minamoto with a look and told him that if he moved, it would be his head. With that, he took my hand and led me from the palace.

We waited until we were a safe distance away until we busted out laughing.

"Did you see his face?" I cackled.

Micha's jaw fell open, his eyes widening comically.

"Wait, wait, wait. Do it again!"

He did. I struggled not to fall, for laughing so hard. I stored away the memory, knowing that I wouldn't forget Minamoto's cowardice anytime soon. Things quickly got serious when he began to glow. I shielded my eyes.

"I watched you grow up," he said, going back to his true form, "and you were nothing like this."

It took me a second to realize that he was talking about my plan for revenge. I couldn't believe we were back to this. I let out a sigh as my shoulders sagged.

He was right. I thought of that African teenager one more time. It was true—something had changed me. I stared back at him, and I knew that he saw the gleam in my eye. He was quick to shake his head.

"Killing the Ordained was not a part of your mission," Micha said, frowning. "It goes against the Creator's design."

"Killing him *isn't* a part of my plan," I said with a wicked grin, "but I do plan to make him suffer."

"It must be toxic carrying so much anger and hatred in your heart. It's eating you alive. You need to forgive him." He was sincere in his request. "You need to change—"

I shook my head as my hands balled into fists. In a matter of seconds, I could recall all the years of pain, belittlement, and abuse. There was no way I was turning back now. I was going to stick to my original plan of making Jacques suffer before I trapped him in the amulet. That's why I had to find the weakness of all demi-demons— the weakness that he once told me about—the Dagger of Truth.

When I got home, I needed a friend more than ever. Dorian was up in his study reading a book that he thought could save his soul. I wasn't in the mood for any more preaching. I went in, straight to Rhea's room. When I asked Rhea to watch some flicks with me, she bumped her hip against mine, linked our arms together and off we went. We walked down the hall opposite the library and into the home theatre.

I appreciated her because despite everything—and aside from my husband—she was still my only real friend.

CHAPTER SEVENTEEN

A BATTLE
IN ITSELF

I asked her to explain it again.

"When were you going to tell me that you and Micha hooked up?"

A blush immediately overtook her. She was sitting next to me in her tie-die pajamas. She stared at the screen with the most focus that I'd ever seen, watching as the opening credits scrolled by. My tail swished in anger, the battle armor on my body hot and heavy. My tail cracked the back of my seat, and I felt the power of fallen angels fill my veins with a blinding, searing, white light.

"Answer me!"

"We didn't go all the way," she said, and I honestly wondered what Micha saw in her. "We just kissed a little."

"Why?"

"I like him," she admitted quietly, blushing again.

"Why didn't you tell me?" I was simmering like a kettle on a stovetop. "I'm your best friend."

"*Dorian* is my best friend," she said.

"So, I'm nothing to you?"

"I didn't say that."

"Am I your friend or not?"

She shrugged.

I had to admit that Rhea was beautiful—anyone could see that. She had the skin, dark as sin, beautiful golden eyes like liquid honey, full figure…And I had…What? What did I have that she didn't—a good personality? Anyone would be lucky to have a woman like Rhea on their arm. But I didn't understand why they went after one another, knowing how I felt about him…It…didn't make sense. And it…*hurt*.

"Was it good?" I asked.

She licked some salt off her fingers, looking up at me wide-eyed—but not innocent. "Mm?"

But that still didn't explain why Micha preferred her over me. I tried to justify it. Instead, the image of Micha fighting the demon beetle as Okkusu filled my head, his arms dripping with sweat.

I should've let the bastard get eaten.

"So," I said, injecting fake cheerfulness into my voice, "what movie did you pick?"

She'd chosen some cheesy chic-flic called *The Butler*. 2/3s of the way through, I'd zoned out and forgotten half of the plot. But as the protagonist ran across the screen in tears, I wondered what we were watching.

"I thought we were supposed to watch something happy!"

"Just wait!" She muttered, her Espanzan accent thickening with her excitement. "Here's the good part." And twenty minutes later, she giggled in delight: "…Affair…"

"What?" I shot up, staring at Rhea with wide eyes. "What did you say?"

Rhea turned to look at me, startled. She was near the projector, fiddling with a few movies. She held up the DVD case for one of the movies.

"I said, do you want to watch *Lonely Island* or *The Principal's Affair?*"

"Ugh. Neither." I couldn't help but wrinkle my nose at her. "What's up with all of the chic-flicks?"

Her eyes gained a faraway look, and I knew that she was thinking about Micha.

I rolled my eyes.

"Can't we watch something action packed?"

She held up a movie. I tried not to groan again as she held up a rapey movie that I watched with my master as a teenager: think *Zombified*, but the zombie's rape unsuspecting cheerleaders. I was never watching *Delilah's Dilemma* again as long as I lived. I briefly wondered why Dorian had an ancient movie player when most people used virtual reality to watch movies nowadays. Then again, Dorian was very old-fashioned.

Maybe this was his way of hanging onto the past?

Rhea fumbled, knocking a stack of movies to the floor.

"How about I pick out the movie?"

I got up from my chair. I walked towards Rhea, who'd placed the movies back on the shelf. As I skimmed through them, I caught an odd scent. I sniffed again. Rhea stiffened before trying to back away. I commanded her to be still. Her chin lifted, looking me in the eye.

I took a deep breath.

"You slept with him?" I said, voice eerily quiet.

She'd lied to me.

By now she'd gone beet red. When I glared at her, she didn't answer. I reached out, my tail swishing behind me in anger as I grabbed her arm and pulled her towards me. She shrieked and for a moment, I forgot my own strength. I jerked my hand to the side.

There was a loud pop and then Rhea's pain-filled cry.

She clutched her right arm with her left hand. As soon as the two made contact, a whimper tumbled from her lips. The Rebel soldier must have been off her game. I briefly wondered how long it'd been since she'd been in a fight, since she'd drawn blood, since she'd truly experienced pain. I shook my head.

Help her.

Reaching out, my hands glowed as magic shot through my veins.

I could help her.

Her eyes narrowed as she took a step back, kicking a few DVDs farther across the room.

"Stop fidgeting!" I snapped, moving closer.

She immediately stopped moving. Her teeth were grit, and I could tell that she was trying to fight the magic that bound us. I placed my hand over her arm, letting the magic flow from me to her. After a few seconds, she wiggled her fingers. I pulled away, staring at her with the same look that she was giving me.

What was I supposed to do?

"I'm sorry," I growled, trying, and failing to sound understanding. "I can't believe you slept with him though."

"Is it so wrong that I have somebody? You have Dorian..."

"I just didn't think you were that kind of girl."

Her eyes narrowed. "Meaning?"

"I mean you just met the guy and you're already giving up the goods. It's a little desperate if you ask me."

"And you're different *how*?"

"Meaning?" I huffed.

"You know exactly what I'm saying."

"Bitch!"

She lunged. I gasped as she hit me with her full weight, knocking her beefy fingers against my skull. She'd never been this easy to anger. Our bodies pressed together, my hardness against her soft, as she breathed out against me, struggling to overpower me. How pathetic.

I threw her off me, climbing atop her and ramming my fist into her face. Blood flowed like a river, staining her shirtfront red. She stared up at me in shock, panting. A part of me wanted to hurt her—to keep hurting her—but I knew that this was the side that everyone feared. As quickly as the anger was there, it was gone. I removed myself from her person.

I tried to apologize but she ran off.

"I can't believe this. Did I really just fight…over a guy?"

This was the first time that I'd hurt her like this…ever. She was usually so closed off. Not closed off…she was really just in dislike of me.

But why?

I thought of the vibe I'd been getting off her, directed at Dorian…

Why did she want what I had so badly?

My face fell as I realized that there was no fixing this. I thought of the day that she'd tried to kill me, and then of our unspoken agreement as Rebels to protect one another. Maybe she was right: maybe we never were friends.

No. She's my friend.

But this time, I'd cut too deep, severing the pact that I'd made with a blade sharper than my own rune-covered dagger.

What was happening to me?

*　*　*

His hands were everywhere. I peppered kisses along his collarbone before tugging his shirt over his head. Dorian groaned and pressed closer, his mouth searing my skin unlike any flame. There was a sharp rap at the door. Before I could untangle myself, the door hit the wall with a jolting bang.

All four of us froze. Beatrice stood in the hall, sheets in her hands and a blush on her face. Micha stood behind her and I could tell by the frown on his face that he was pissed.

Good, I thought, watching in smug satisfaction as his jaw clenched in anger, *let him know how it feels...*I

took Dorian's earlobe between my teeth and gave a tug.

Micha cleared his throat. I planted another kiss on Dorian's jawline, moving lower. Beatrice stood there, staring at us as if our nakedness was a mortal sin. Screw everyone. It was our fucking house.

Dorian grabbed my chin, pulling me in for a kiss. "You like an audience," he growled, "don't you?"

I could feel Micha glaring daggers into my ass. I looked over my shoulder at him, smirking. He reached down, readjusting himself. I scowled, then reached out and dug my claws into Dorian's neck. His breath stuttered past his lips.

"Come now, don't be that way, baby," I said, eyeing Micha as I kissed him soundly on the mouth.

I pulled away from Dorian in satisfaction before putting on my newly washed battle armor. He reached out but I told him that I had to train. Once I was dressed and my hair was combed, I shooed Dorian towards the library so that Beatrice could make up our bed. He got dressed reluctantly, a disappointed frown on his golden face. When I made it down the stairs, I stopped in my tracks.

Micha sat with Rhea at the dining room table, one hand under her nose, catching the blood that fell, as the other dabbed with a cotton ball. I watched the two of them, so careful, so intimate. She had one hand digging into his ass, the other playing with a scar that disappeared into his pants.

"Come on, baby," she hummed, "let mama play."

He leaned down, his tongue at her collarbone, drawing lazy circles. At first, I thought he hadn't seen me. But then he turned his head into her chest, feeling her hands comb through his hair, and gave me a meaningful look full of quirked brow and smirking lips.

So, this was how it was going to be?

I was livid. He fired first when he kissed me, and it was unfair that he got even when I'd just gotten even. I cleared my throat. Rhea immediately pulled away, a dazed look in her eyes and a soft pant on her lips. Micha slowly lowered Rhea from the table and trailed his tongue across his swollen lips.

It was official. The next time a giant bug tried to turn him into breakfast, I was *not* intervening.

"Aren't we supposed to continue training?" I said, taking a step forward.

He fixed me with an odd look. In it was a deep satisfaction. He knew that he'd gotten to me. He liked getting me riled up. I didn't like this game.

But I'd already moved my first piece.

"Training is cancelled today," he said before leaving us both in the room.

A silence filled the foyer and neither I nor Rhea knew what to say.

Tell her the truth. Hurt her, Keres said.

I felt my mouth moving before I could stop myself.

"He's a breeder," I heard myself say. "That's the only reason he's attracted to you."

"That makes one of us," she sneered before sauntering off.

I wanted to hurt her back, but she had every right to after what I'd said, what I'd done.

CHAPTER EIGHTEEN

STATIC

I went to my room and quickly changed out of my battle armor before hanging it up. It stared back at me, mocking me for all my inadequacies. I thought of how Micha tended to Rhea's wounds—wounds of my own making—and my blood began to boil. I should have been happy that I was in a wonderful marriage and that he found someone that could get him going. Still, I wasn't.

Did I crave that familiar imperfection, or had I not gotten all of the wildness out of my system? Had I been so quick to settle down that I'd let life pass me by? Maybe Micha was right, and it really was because he was a breeder that gave off more sex vibes than a whorehouse.

I threw on some underclothes and a large tee-shirt and laid down in bed for a long time. I turned on the TV and saw a news report saying that Tess from *Strike It Rich* was quitting to pursue her dream of being a coroner. *Strike It Rich* was a TV show that I used to watch with my parents when I was younger. It was a good show, and I was sad to see that it was going off air: I'd practically grown up with the characters. I decided to store that away and come back to it later, since that meant that my favorite TV show was in a crisis and facing possible termination. If I was fated to be a god, the least I could do was resurrect a show, right?

I went to my son's room and stared at him in his crib before sitting in the rocking chair and taking a nap. When I woke up, the shadows on the walls had changed.

I fed my son. He stared up at me, his wide eyes swimming with innocence. I drowned in his gaze.

"What is wrong with your mother, my son?"

And suddenly he wailed, tears streaming down his face. I changed his rancid diaper. But he continued to cry. I opened his mouth and peered inside. Blood was smeared across his gums.

I went to the bottom of his clothes hamper and rooted around. "Aha!"

I found the homemade all-purpose medicine, recipe courtesy of Tina, doused a washcloth in the bitter-scented liquid that never felt recognizable, then swiped it over his swollen gums. His squawks immediately quelled. I pressed a kiss to his forehead, feeling the warmth of his essence and drawing it into myself.

"Save this marriage, my sweet boy. I'm begging you…"

I walked to the library. Dorian sat before the roaring fire, his eyes as cold and hard as the steel grate that trapped the flames within. I walked up behind him and touched his shoulder. He jumped and was out of his seat in mere seconds, twisting my arm around my back. A cry tumbled from my lips.

"Dorian," I said through grit teeth, fighting the warrior inside, still very much a part of me, "it's me."

He let me go immediately. He took his seat once more, pulling me into his arms. He was shaking something terrible, his lips trembling as he sang under his breath faster than I could catch. I could smell alcohol on him, but I could not tell if it was his usual scent or if more was added. I'd only been gone a few hours and he'd already succumb to this vicious cycle?

Our family was seriously jacked up.

I went to the kitchen and searched through the cabinets. When I couldn't find what I was looking for, I hunted down Beatrice, which took a good fifteen minutes. I was afraid because every second wasted was another that I lost my husband. When I found Beatrice, she took one look at me, reached into her pocket, and pulled out a vial with black, sludgy liquid that looked like tar.

"Have him drink this with lots of water."

I held it in my fist. "What does it do?"

"It's a sobering potion that Yvonne perfected, made from her blood. We have a few more stores here—" she took me to a cabinet above the sink "—and here—" she pulled out a collapsible drawer filled with the stuff. "This is all we have so use it wisely."

I nodded, turned, but she grabbed my hand.

Staring into my eyes, she said, "Don't tell him that we have this. We only use it when it's of dire importance, and he can't remember when we use it. But it is all we have. If he knows…"

He'll destroy it. If there's one thing Dorian loves, it's getting drunk.

"Thank you," I whispered, pulling her into a hug.

She braced an arm around me for a moment, then pushed me away.

Go! She seemed to say. *Before it's too late.*

Beatrice then went to take care of other affairs. I passed Micha in the hall and unlike before, he wouldn't make eye-contact with me. I stepped in front of him, a thousand words on my lips. He brushed past me and when he turned, I just barely caught the bemused smile on his lips. I shook my head to get him out of my mind before making my way back to the library.

What would I have said?

You make me forget that I'm married, except when I can't forget, but even then, I still think about you?

When? He'd ask, quirking an infuriating eyebrow.

At times like this: in the moments between happiness and despair.

I paused before the door as I heard an odd, muffled noise and was met with the sickly-sweet scent of singed flesh. I pushed open the doors to see Dorian curled up in front of the fire. His hand was warped, burned, as he held it to the flames, praying to a god that would not answer, that never loved him, that wouldn't bat an eye if the flames ate him alive right this second. In a mad dash, I scrambled to reach him, and pulled him into my arms, expecting to see him grimacing as his magic had mostly been used up to constantly heal his once-burning lands, which had been set aflame by the man that had torn my clothes from my body and defiled me as if I were an animal.

And it hit me: all my acting out didn't start until that happened.

I was punishing Dorian for my failure, my weakness, my inability to save myself, even though he had risked everything to save me, and nearly went insane protecting me. Because demon's blood drove Immortals insane. And I suddenly had a flashback to Jacques swiping out with a blood-coated blade, swiping it across Dorian's neck. In the moments after, I healed him.

And then I remembered:

Why do you cut me? I asked Valentina, moments after she swiped the blade across my thighs, where Jacques swiped a demon blood-covered blade across them minutes before to teach me a lesson that I would 'never forget.'

Among scarring, demon's blood makes you subservient to the will of the demon. It's an evolutionary tactic they gained once unsuccessfully raiding Gifted land—it's how they helped the Immortals enslave us.

Is it true it drives Immortals insane?

Different effects for different creatures... she grunted, shrugging one heavy shoulder. *But yes. That's why you must drain the wound within the first thirty minutes. If you don't....*

But why drain these? I frowned. *I'm already his slave.*

Physically, yes, Valentina mumbled, swiping a salve-covered finger across my thigh, gently as a feather's touch, but as quick as the blade that had cut these grooves. *But mentally, you are still free.*

That's when I understood. Dorian had not drastically changed overnight until he had gotten cut...because the demon's blood was still in his system!

Dorian just rolled over to look at me. His eyes were blank, wide. But for the first time, it was his mouth that gave him away. His teeth were digging into his bottom lip in an almost shy look, instead of biting down in pain.

Poor, poor Dorian...

* * *

"When did this start?" Larson said, kneeling next to the other man.

"I don't know. He was fine when I left him before. When I came back, he was like this."

"Has this happened before?"

"I...I don't know!"

"Were you aware that he was going to quit drinking?" Larson asked after a long moment, his brow raised.

"Huh...?"

"Your husband? Were you aware that he was trying to get sober?"

"I..." I fumbled for the words, but they wouldn't come. Then, finally, "He didn't tell me."

Larson pressed a hand to his neck. Only it didn't turn red. Instead, a dark, inky welt appeared. When he removed his hand, the mark faded—slowly.

Larson glanced at me accusatorily. "You want to tell me about this?"

"He...got knifed—"

"Knifed?"

"By a demon. It had his blood on it."

"That much is obvious." Larson rolled his eyes. "Why didn't you call me?"

My chest puffed, prideful. "I had it covered."

"And did you drain the wound before healing it?" He said simply, "Ya know, while you had it covered."

I blanched. "I don't appreciate your tone."

"And I don't appreciate you not calling me when your husband is *knifed* by a *literal demon*!" Larson called for a stretcher. "I am admitting him immediately." He put Dorian onto the stretcher that was brought. When I moved forward, Larson raised a hand. "Alcohol, budding sobriety, and demon's blood do not mix. I can't explain why he hurt himself. Maybe it's the toxins—let me finish!" He whispered harshly when I moved to interject. "Maybe it's the toxins in his system. Maybe it's his home life. Maybe its outside forces. But I'm keeping him in the hospital to monitor him."

"If you...think that's what's best..." I mumbled. I rubbed the back of my neck. "Thank you..."

Larson grunted, "It's my duty as his physician."

"He's never hurt himself before..." I whispered to myself, running a hand through my hair. "But he shouldn't be in withdrawal yet!"

"This isn't a withdrawal of any sort," Larson said, hands giving as soft glow as they hovered over my husband's head. "This is something else."

"I don't know. He just…stopped…without…telling me?"

"That's very unlikely. No one can just quit cold turkey. But if he did, he was probably afraid of disappointing you."

Oh, Dorian…

Larson prattled on: "He'll be the recovery center so that we can detox him—that's it." Larson's eyes communicated something that I didn't want to accept—that Dorian was losing a battle that I couldn't fight for him. "He'll be out in no time."

I looked at Dorian's haunted, gaunt face as they wheeled him away, the circles under his eyes heavy and purple like bruises. I hadn't even noticed that he'd lost weight. I brushed a bit of hair from the nape of his neck, realizing suddenly that he was in dire need of a haircut. Something on his neck flashed in the light of the flames. I reached out and pulled it a bit closer.

It was a triangle on a chain: the mark of the Creator.

*   *   *

Doctor Larson's suggestions swam inside of my head, each bubbling to the surface and staying there. I made my way to the room that Dorian was in, unsurprised to see a few giggling nurses outside his door. Every few seconds they would peek inside and then gush over my husband. I said nothing, listening to them converse outside his room.

"I mean, he's a total hottie!"

"*Total* hottie!" the second said.

"Usually when they bring 'em in, they have some form of ID on 'em."

"Probably to protect his identity."

"I get off in five hours. Do you think he'll be up by then?"

"I sure as hell hope so cause I get off an hour after you."

"I mean, he looks a lil—" she flexed her wrist "ya know, but you never can tell. Most of these rock stars swing that way now and then."

Before he could get into positions, I cleared my throat and ran my hand through my hair, making sure that my ring was clearly visible. When that didn't bother them, I let my magic travel into my eyes, so that they glowed, and flashed them at the two deplorables. The two nurses reluctantly left.

"Who she think she is with that ring on?"

"Ooh and those *eyes*. Total Beasty."

"Totally."

"You know what that means, right?"

"They probably already have a kid or two."

"Didn't she bring him in the other day?"

"Probably did it herself. You know those Gifted folk. They can't control their anger issues."

I sighed.

It wasn't even worth it.

I walked into the room and sat at Dorian's bedside. Dorian was hooked up to a bunch of wires. His chest rose and fell slowly. His hand was in a bandage. I took his hand in mine, my finger tracing over the wedding band on his finger.

Was this my fault?

Of course it is.

But *how*—how do I fix it?

Dorian stirred and for a second, I thought that he was going to wake up. I touched my face, surprised to see tears there. I dashed them away with angry fists, knowing that tears didn't save my parents and wouldn't save my husband now. Dorian rolled over in his sleep, his face smooth and carefree. He'd never looked so young.

"He has the liver of an old man."

I turned to see Larson in the doorway. His salt-and-pepper hair was unkempt, sticking up in all different directions. The stethoscope hung from his neck like a noose.

"What did you say?"

"He has the liver of an old man," Larson said again, shaking his head. "I haven't seen one that bad since I treated Hemingway."

"You mean *the* Hemingway?"

Larson gave a brief nod.

"Wow." I thought of what that meant and quickly lost my excitement. "That sucks…"

"He was actually a really great guy," Larson said with a smile. "He was a powerful magic-user, too. He had the Gift to literally embed God into his books. All it took was one hand on the page and then, well, you know…"

"Hmm…What a Gift…"

"Have you thought about what I said on the way here?"

I shook my head. "I'm tired of thinking."

"This isn't about you," he reminded me, throwing a glance at Dorian. "It's about him. It's about your son."

I nodded and he left. As if on cue, Dorian stirred and slowly cracked one lid open. When he looked at me, I could tell that his brain was having a hard time catching up.

"Where are we?"

"We're in the hospital, love." I leaned forward to brush a kiss across his lips. "Doctor Larson brought us here."

"Why?"

"You burned your hand after drinking too much."

"Is it alcohol poisoning?"

I wasn't sure. As an answer, I shook my head. He sank back into his bed.

"Why does my stomach hurt?"

"They had to pump your stomach."

"Why does my head hurt?"

"You drank a lot."

"Did I?"

I gave a nod.

"When can I go home?"

"I don't know…"

There was a knock at the door. I turned to see an older nurse standing in the doorway. Dorian looked at her as if she were his salvation. I glanced at the triangle on his neck. Some help that was.

"Miss?"

"Yes, hon?" The nurse replied, cocking her head at him.

"When can I go home?"

"I'm afraid you're going to be here for a while," she said kindly as she gave him a look. "You were messed up pretty bad when they brought you in here."

"Please let me out," he practically begged, his eyes wide and desperate. "I can pay you."

He reached out and grabbed his jeans, which were folded neatly in a chair next to his bed. He fumbled through his pockets and came out empty handed. Then he glanced at the ground and, spotting his fallen pouch, moved out the bed to grab it. On the way back up, he hit his head on a small table and let out a frustrated curse. The nurse gave him another sympathetic glance before checking his vitals and walking away.

"This is Chesapeake all over again," Dorian groaned, closing his eyes.

"Dorian—"

"I can still pay you…" He muttered, straightening before looking around with wild eyes. "Just give me a chance…"

"You're out of chances, Dorian."

"What?"

"She's gone, Dorian." I was filled with a hollow sadness. "Larson told me something on the way here."

"He's a doctor," Dorian said with a scowl. "They'll say just about anything to get you going."

"He said that you need to be put in a psych ward. He said that they did that when you were younger and it helped for a while. He said that with the right attitude, you can get out in no time."

"I don't need that." His eyes sparkled with pain. "I'm perfectly fine."

"That's the thing, Dorian…" My voice was a soft rush of air. "You're not."

"You're going to treat me like my parents?!" His eyes snapped open as his fist beat against his leg. "You're going to lock me away?!"

"No one's locking you away. We're just trying to help—"

"No!" Tears began to stream down his face. "I'll be fine! I just need some more time! Give me more time!"

It broke my heart. I had to save our people.

But they can wait. He's been deteriorating for centuries, judging by what Micha told me. This needs to be done now!

"There isn't any time left!" I stood from my chair. "We're out of time. I have a mission to complete, and I can't think straight knowing that you're at home doing God knows what as you drown yourself in liquor! As your wife, I have every right to sign you into Kalysma's Kare and leave you there!"

Eyes narrowing, he hissed, "You wouldn't dare."

Doctor Larson came into the room. He had the necessary papers on his clipboard and held out a pen.

"There are two nurses. One of them is a black woman, bad dye job, nails…and the other—"

"Jasmine and Kendra?"

I shrugged. "I didn't get their names. They were making lewd comments about him." I touched his shoulder. "Will Dorian be safe?"

"Consider them terminated," Larson nodded solemnly, "you don't have to worry about his safety here."

"I need it in writing," I said.

"Done," he offered me the clipboard again.

I took it and signed off as Dorian screamed behind me, too weak to move from his bed a second time. His words were water in my ears, drowning out all sanity, yet they were flames, burning into my memory like a branding. One thing he said stood out above all.

"I want a divorce!"

I was ushered from the room.

* * *

I drove quickly, pushing the car well past 100 MPH. The faster I drove, the farther away Dorian and all his mess seemed. The conversation with HR helped and they informed me that the two individuals would be dealt with, but I couldn't help the nagging suspicion that this wasn't the first time something like this had happened. I mean, with Dorian and Megumi, he said that she just wouldn't 'leave him alone' and that there were 'only so many times he could say no.' Had I misinterpreted the situation? Had she forced herself on him?

I hadn't even realized that I'd breezed through red lights until it was too late, just narrowly missing a woman with a stroller as she crossed the street. I should've known that she would call the cops.

But at that point, I didn't care.

I refused to slow up, making my way onto the interstate. Cars honked and people screamed vicious insults as I weaved in and out of traffic. When someone was really nasty, I drove in front of them and then slammed on the brakes as hard as I could. I probably caused a lot of accidents in a short amount of time. In the back of my mind,

I could remember someone saying that driving angry was just like driving drunk—you couldn't think clearly and everyone was at risk.

Oh well…

I pulled off the interstate and made it another good ten or twenty miles before something happened. The world around me turned red and blue. I pulled over quickly, knowing that if I put up a fight, the cop would follow me back home or worse—shoot. I could hear the door slam and the crunch of boots on gravel as the officer made their way towards me. I quickly straightened in my seat, smoothed my hair back and plastered a smile on my face, trying to look as normal as possible.

"I'm going to need to see your freedom papers, please," a high, feminine voice said. When I insisted that I was immortal, she rolled her eyes. "Just get out the papers, ma'am."

I looked out the window to get a better look at the officer. She had hair that was dyed cotton candy pink and wore a smile. I could tell that she was faking it, though. It was all in her eyes. I mean, something seemed off.

Or maybe I was just being paranoid.

I handed her what she asked for. Her eyes skimmed over the requested documents and occasionally flickered back up to meet with mine. I was in deep shit.

"You know, I could have you reassigned for this."

I paled. "Reassigned."

"You know—captured, put in chains, enslaved." She raised a brow. "Being half-and-half doesn't change who you are—" she lowered her glasses, "—Champion."

I narrowed my eyes. "Do you know who the fuck I am?!"

"Do you know who *I* am, Mrs…*Boyd?*" she planted a hand on her hip. "I'm the law."

"You're just another jealous Mortal—"

"No," she siphoned, "I'm power."

215

My electricity hummed under my skin, making me shake in my seat. I latched onto it and cranked it up to the max when something totally insane happened.

I could hear her thoughts.

At first it was like a TV on a channel that wasn't offered—all static. Then instead of there being words, there was a bunch of little pictures. I could really only pick out snippets, but it was enough to piece everything together.

I saw a man's face twisted in disgust. I saw the cop outside my car door screaming as she threw a lamp at his head. I saw red lingerie clutched in her angry fist. I saw a bottle of hair dye on the sink, strands of silky brown hair and a pair of scissors next to it. I saw those same scissors being taken to a wrist and then a leg, angry red slashes covering pale thighs.

"These papers expired in early spring." She frowned, hand lowering. "And you do realize that you ran four red lights, don't you, ma'am?"

This wasn't good at all. My heart began to speed through my chest. My hands shook and I knew that I was beginning to hyperventilate.

"Cha-ta-ta-ta—"

"Ma'am?" She knocked on my half-raised window. "Excuse me!"

My reaction was almost instantaneous. I gathered electricity around me and as I did, the radio turned on, the windshield wipers began to operate, and the doors rattled with power. I raised my hand and for a moment, I saw a look of unbridled fear on the pink-haired woman's face. I sent a blast towards her chest, watching in a daze as she flew back, smoke rising from her body as she convulsed before becoming eerily still. I took a moment to compose myself, although these were like dissolving stitches—they would fade.

Then I sped off down the street.

CHAPTER NINETEEN

TRUE FEAR

Weeks passed by, my paranoia growing with each second. Someone had to have seen me. Didn't cop cars have those cameras nowadays? My fear became so bad that Micha cancelled all our training while I tried to piece myself back together. He never asked where Dorian was, but he was all too comfortable asking what had me so riled up.

I would not tell. I made my way to the library and when I saw the spot where Dorian last lay, I lost it. I ripped books from their shelves, sending them flying across the room. Electricity flew from my body like an explosion, setting everything aflame. I curled up in a ball in the middle of the room, crying as a song drifted softly over the speakers: it was *Cotton Candy* by Lyon-S.

> *"Candy tongues and bubblegum teeth,*
> *Why do you always scare me?*
> *Licorice veins and cookie dough heartbeats,*
> *Why does sin taste so sweet?*

My head was a mess.

> *"I breathe your smoke in deep,*
> *Trying to get free.*
> *But this room is full of poison,*
> *Yeah, the toxin's killing me.*
> *'Be quiet,' you say, 'there's nothing here to see.'*
> *But I taste your sweet mouth.*
> *She's your cotton candy.*

The flames were around me, growing both in size and lethality. I was just as messed up as Dorian. Now he was alone in some psychiatric ward, probably banging his head against the wall. I was the worst wife in the history of wives. I took a deep breath.

> *"You used to tell me 'bout your lies,*
> *You used to tell me 'bout your dreams.*
> *Merry-go-rounds and a candy ring.*
> *On a diet of pills and vodka,*
> *We both pretend you're my candy king."*

I didn't say anything as I heard the door open. I felt like I was losing my mind. I felt a drop of wetness on my hair and realized that the manor's sprinklers had come on. I felt a hand fall on my head. I looked up to see Rhea next to me, her eyes looking the most concerned for me than they'd ever been in the time I'd known her.

I put my head in my lap and began to sing again.

> *"I breathe your smoke in deep,*
> *Trying to get free.*
> *But this room is full of poison,*
> *Yeah, the toxin's killing me.*

'Be quiet,' you say, 'there's nothing here to see.'
But I taste your sweet mouth.
She's your cotton candy."

"Marve?" Rhea said, shaking me.

"Leave me here to die…"

"What's wrong?"

"I'm an awful person." I groaned, banging my fists on my head. "Everything I do fails."

"I'm going to go get Micha."

I went back to singing.

"Should have known that you were rotten.
Should have known that you were sour.
Now my time is counting down,
Dying by the hour.

You always tell me lies,
I get lost in all my dreams,
On that merry-go-round,
You gave me your heart and a ring.
I guess you should've known,
That bling doesn't mean a thing.
I still taste your sweet mouth.
Now I'm your cotton candy."

"Marve?" This time it was Micha's turn to shake me. "You need to tell me what happened."

I shook my head as a cold numbness began to seep into my pores.

"You need to pull yourself together." His cool breath blew across my face and the smell of him jumbled my thoughts. "You need to try," he said, his hand wrapping around my wrist and tugging my hand from my head.

"Don't touch me!" I snapped, scooting away as that familiar fire built inside. "You have no right after what you did!"

"And what did I do exactly?"

I didn't know. He pulled me closer? He pushed me away? He made me feel things that I was partially ashamed of? He kissed me?

No. He screwed my best friend, let me touch him, then went back and did it all again. That's what he did. While I was obsessing over my him, I lost time with my husband. He ruined my marriage.

"If you won't pull it together for me," he said, "then you should do it for Dorian."

I rocked back and forth, never slowing up. My breath came out in rattles. I refilled my lungs, each breath hurting more than the last, before making that same rattling sound again. Micha placed a hand under my chin before pulling my face up to his. My eyes immediately fell on his lips, and I wanted to kiss him so bad that it hurt.

What the hell was wrong with me?

I started singing again.

"You need to get it together. How can you help Dorian in this position? He needs you to be strong."

The song died on my lips. The severity of everything I'd done sunk in. I'd admitted my husband to a psychiatric ward against his will, murdered a police officer and hid like a freaking baby. In that short expanse of time, I'd pushed away just about everyone that meant anything to me, including Micha and, oddly enough, Rhea. I looked at the angel with ugly, dead eyes.

"Go get my son."

He dashed out of the room, moving faster than anything I'd ever seen. In a matter of seconds, he was back, Aiden cradled in his arms. For just a second, I imagined a different life in which I'd met him first and we were just normal people. Would sex and flirtation still be a coping mechanism when things got too rough? Would murder still be just a step down from that?

Yeah, I heard Keres say in the back of my mind, *this isn't a fairytale, princess.*

"I know..." I said aloud, closing my eyes against the fresh wave of pain. "I know..."

Micha offered up Aiden without a word. As I reached out and pulled my son into my arms, I was overwhelmed by a wave of peace. Aiden looked up at me with his big black eyes and it took everything I had not to cry tears of joy. He babbled something in baby language as he reached up and grabbed a lock of my hair. He yanked on it as a smile broke out on his face.

His happiness was infectious.

"I think he has a Gift," Micha said, watching us. "Does his father have a Gift?"

I told Micha about my Gift and Dorian's. I made sure to leave out my newly discovered talent. Knowing Micha, once he acquired this new arsenal of information, he'd probably call me TV Girl *and* Flying Alligator.

Micha nodded, his eyes sparking with interest.

"It seems that he has a variation of his father's Gift."

"How so?"

"Dorian can manipulate thoughts and your son can manipulate emotions."

"He's an Empath?"

"Yes. The first I've seen in over five decades. He's also a strong one since it's showing this early."

I was proud. It was always a parent's dream to see their child surpass them.

The earliest sign of controlling electricity that I displayed was when I was four. I'd tried to use the microwave and had gotten impatient. Back then I felt the need to try to heat the food myself and ended up catching the house on fire. I was an (accidentally) destructive, complicated child to say the least. Still, I my strength was nowhere near this.

Micha looked at me for a long moment. I could tell that he was searching for something. His next words said more than enough, though.

"Are you hiding something from me?"

"No," I said, injecting smoothness into my voice.

"Don't lie to me. I've been watching your whole life. I know you better than anyone."

"That's just the thing." I said, shaking my head as I cradled my son's head on my chest. "You *think* you do."

"You broke your right pinky toe on your eighth birthday. Your parents were murdered in front of you and although you sought guidance and fatherly affection from your Master Jacques, you felt a slight sexual attraction towards him as well. This was further skewed when he began to molest you. Dorian was, as humans call it, your first everything and it took your longer to fall in love with him than it took you to sleep with him. You—"

"We already established that you basically stalked me my entire life," I whispered, "so that doesn't count."

"It's still true." He crossed his muscly arms. "So, you need to tell me whatever it is that you're hiding right now."

"I killed someone," I said, not knowing why I said that first.

"I could tell by the way you were acting, so that's not a surprise." At my look he shook his head. "I've been watching you for your entire life...You always...*fracture*...when you kill someone. I've never seen it affect you this poorly though."

"Does that mean you've seen me naked?" I said with a laugh, trying to be light-hearted.

"I'm not answering that."

"So yes?"

"So, you need to tell me what's going on," he held up a hand, "or I'm going to force it out of you."

I looked at his hand for a moment, confused. Then a memory crashed through my mind like a bear through a thicket of trees. He was going to Link to me and take the answers. That so wasn't fair. It was more than just unfair.

It was just plain wrong.

"You're supposed to be the good guy," I said, lifting my chin, "so you can't do stuff like that."

"If you're keeping secrets, you could jeopardize your fate, which falls back on the entire world." He inched closer. "I think it'll be fine."

"I read someone's thoughts!" I said in a rush as I clutched my son to my chest.

"What?"

I brushed a hand over Aiden's forehead, moving a lock of his hair away. My tail twitched as my son gave a soft, trusting coo. The boy fixed his charcoal eyes on me and the first thing I thought of was his father. How long would Dorian be gone? Would he miss our son's entire life?

"I read someone's mind," I said, slower this time.

"And?"

"And I killed her when I started to panic."

"Who was it?"

"A police officer."

"Was she magical?"

"No." I shook my hand, instantly remembering that there was no magic coming off the woman. "She was a Mortal. A defenseless, helpless—"

The thought of her made bile rise in my throat.

"How did this happen? Has this happened before? What did it feel like?"

I told him everything. I told him of how my powers flared. I told him of the way the car reacted to that influx of power. I told him about the images that I received out of nowhere. Finally, I told him of the blast and how I'd driven away.

"I think I know what's going on here."

"Well then can bring me up to speed?" I said, suddenly a bit calmer as Aiden closed his eyes.

It was good that he was sleeping now. On top of everything, now that he was out of the newborn phase, we *both* cried nonstop. It was cry, eat, cry, piss, shit or a combination of the two, cry, cradle him to my chest, beg him to stop, sleep, set him down, cry, pick him back up, curse myself for having sex in the first place, sleep, set him down more gently, then cry myself to sleep and wait for it to start all over again, when his cries awakened me. I only got a few minutes of sleep at a time, which wasn't enough. It made me feel stressed and alone, like even though I knew people who'd gone through this, no one could possibly understand my frustration and why I wasn't wowed at the thought of having a surprise child. Honestly, the wonder of it all had worn off within a few weeks and now I just wanted *sleep*.

Micha watched me and I watched Aiden, wondering for the umpteenth time how I was going to do this by myself.

"Your Gift is all things electricity. When people think or feel—anything that requires them to use their mind—their brain gives off electric pulses. It seems that your body has evolved—probably due to your new status as a Nephilim—and that you are now picking up the electricity and interpreting it in your own terms, hence you see the woman's memories as images."

"How do I make it stop?"

It was scary. I didn't want to read people's minds. Do you know how scary people were in real life? A lot of people had dark, twisted things in their head. It was just asking for trouble.

"You can't stop it. It's just going to get stronger. But with the proper training you can learn to control it."

I nodded. I should've known that it wouldn't go away. After all, my whole life was a freak show.

"Now where is Dorian?"

I told him what had happened. In all honesty, it was a surprise that I'd kept it under wraps this long. When I was done, I peeked at Micha through a curtain of hair. He was looking at me as if he were somehow proud of me. I was so confused because I was an awful person—that didn't warrant a smile.

"You did the right thing," Micha said, reaching out to hold my hand. I pulled away, pretending not to notice his frown. "There was really no other option."

I nodded again, at a loss for words. Was he saying that because now we were alone? I couldn't tell.

"Where is he checked in at?"

"Kalysma's Kare."

"In the southside of Amoria?"

"The very same."

"How convenient..." He said, lips curving into a smile. "This will work in our favor."

"How so?"

"Fix yourself up. You look like crap." At my glare, a crocodile grin overtook his face. "I mean it. Get yourself looking pretty, which shouldn't be too hard for you."

I blushed and looked away.

"Why?"

"Dorian isn't the only person of interest in KK. Have you visited him yet?"

"No. I...I couldn't face him..."

"You can visit him." He nodded and I could tell that he was eager to get going. "Then we can visit the person that will set your fate into motion."

"Is it the Ordained?"

"No," he said with a smirk.

His cryptic answers were grating my nerves.

"Then who is it?" I growled. "And why can't I go in sweats and a tee?"

"You're going to meet Alice today. You're great-grandmother. The first Gifted-Immortal to walk the face of the Earth."

*　*　*

I sat on one end of the table, Dorian on the other. We were the only family in the room and each party sat at its own table. Some visitors laughed, a few patients cried as they begged to be taken home and there were even some that sat in stony silence, both patients and visitors, as they stared each other down. Dorian was one of the later, giving me a look that promised to raise hell. I reached out, laying my hand over his.

He pulled away.

"Get me out of here," he growled with a scowl.

"I can't, baby," I said as I made sure to look him in the eye. "You need help."

"That's not what I said when you told me your pathetic life story."

I held back a wince. He didn't mean that. He was just angry.

"Actually, as I recall, you did." I plastered a smile on my face. "I guess this makes us even, huh?"

He rolled his eyes.

My hand shook around the cup of water as I thought about the stack of divorce papers sitting in his office at home. "You're acting like a child."

"I wouldn't if you didn't treat me like one."

"Dr. Larson is here. He'll watch over you."

"You're just like my parents." He fixed me with a harsh glare. "Always trying to decide what's best for me."

I understood how he felt.

Angry.

Hurt.

Betrayed.

Lost.

Sad.

Confused.

Self-destructive.

It happened to the best of us. We all knew that I'd struggled with my fair share of mental illness. I swallowed around a lump in my throat. I was only doing this because I loved him more than anything in the world—besides our son, that is. It was hurting him, yes, but it was hurting me to see him hurt, too.

"I'm sorry," I said, keeping my eyes on the table as I spoke. "And I love you."

"What did you say?"

He fixed me with a dark, angry look.

"I said that I love you," I bit my lip, "and that I'm sorry."

I felt his hand close around the back of my neck. Before I could even react, he'd pulled me forward. His lips crashed against mine, stealing my breath away. I heard one caretaker yell in the background and audibly gasped as my husband was forcibly yanked away from me. They lectured him on PDA before telling me that I had to leave.

I looked into Dorian's eyes for a fraction of a second. I could see the one thing that I thought I'd lost forever: forgiveness. He nodded at me, and I knew that it was his way of saying that he trusted me and was going to give this a try. I gave him a smile and a little wave as all of us visitors lined up near the elevator. As I rounded the corner and boarded the elevator, the last thing that I saw was his haunted grimace when he thought that I wasn't looking.

*   *   *

Since I couldn't prove my relation to Alice, Micha and I had to sneak in. The obvious question was why I didn't just tell them the truth. But what was I supposed to say exactly—that an angel told me that she was my great-grandmother?

Yeah, that would go over well.

That would be right before they put me in restraints and hauled me off to my own padded cell or as they called it here, the Quiet Room.

But if I had her patient access number, all of this would be solved.

When I went towards the other wing in the hospital, Micha was with me. Not once did he ask about my visit with Dorian. When I tried to bring it up, the angel fixed me with a look that said I had five seconds to shut up or he was going to rip my head off. It took me a good portion of our walk to realize that he was jealous. The thought made me want to laugh.

After all, this mess wouldn't have existed if *he* hadn't dropped into *my* life.

We'd already paid off one of the staff members—a new guy who was probably going to get fired in the next week or so. We crept into Alice's room, making sure to close the door behind us. The walls were a boring white and there were two cots, each perfectly made. In a chair by the window, a girl sat who looked no older than fifteen or sixteen. She had mousy brown hair, wide grey eyes with a haunted look and smile that said she wasn't to be trifled with.

"Alice?" I said, taking a step closer.

"That would be me," a voice said with an Irish accent.

I whirled around to see what must have been the most beautiful girl in existence.

"Get out of here, Karena" she barked, and the other girl scurried from the room.

The white woman had long, wavy red hair that stopped just above her waist. Her eyes were a cool jade that commanded attention and respect. Her lashes were long and when she smiled, her perfect white teeth flashed in the lights overhead. She was dressed in a pale pink lolita dress that accented her curves and a pair of leggings; I briefly wondered why I didn't get the boob gene that she obviously had. The seemingly 17-year-old flipped her hair in a bored manner. It was obvious that she was used to giving orders.

She was different than I expected—less kooky and more composed. She kind of reminded me of a female version of Jacques— back when he'd let the nice ebb away but hadn't fully let on to the abuse. I liked her already.

"You look like her," she said, arching an eyebrow at me.

I worked on remembering how to shut my mouth. In Micha's stories, Alice sounded like a nice, sweet girl. I expected some ragdoll of a woman, all eyes, and no brain. But this woman seemed in control, quite intelligent and very beautiful. She floated over to the chair—because walking was beneath one such as her—and took a seat. I watched her, wary and vaguely annoyed, probably looking like I was bracing for a fight. She smoothed her dress and gave me another look.

"Hi. My name is—"

"I know who you are," she said, reaching into a pocket in her dress and pulling out a nail filer.

"Isn't that against the rules?" I said, wondering how she got that in a place like this.

"Your point?"

"Well, I'm here because—"

"I *know* why you're here." She snapped, rolling her eyes. "God, are you always this dense?"

Okay, why are you such a bitch?

I glanced at Micha. He seemed to be trying his hardest not to laugh. I planted my hands on my hips.

"I thought you said she was nice?"

"Well, let's see you get betrayed by the very thing that created you," she said, fixing me with a hard stare, "and still be nice for the next hundred or so years of your existence."

"That was your own fault, Alice," Micha said. "And it's been closer to five…"

"Just like the end of the world is going to be yours, too," she practically purred, giving him a sugary smile. "You need to stop playing games with my great-granddaughter."

"Noted."

"No," she said, cocking her head, "it's not."

"How does she know all of this?"

"Her Gift is precognition. She can see the future."

"Just about everyone in our family has one, sweetie," she said, reaching into her pocket and pulling out some bubblegum. She stuck a stick in her mouth and chewed it slowly, eyeing me up and down. "You look more like Isolde than your mother," she finally said around a wad of gum.

"Aww. Thank you—"

"Isolde was so whiny." She rolled her eyes. "Why I gave her immortality, I'll never know."

I moved to interject but she kept talking.

"It's a good thing I killed her. She would've ruined all my hard work…her and her father."

"What?"

"I told you that the Creator sent a plague on her mind," Micha said, shaking his head. "She killed her immediate family. She feels no remorse."

"That's because the Creator stole all of my emotions," Alice said, her face twisting into a sneer, "just like he's going to do to you if you fail. At the rate you're going, it won't take long. Soon you'll be sitting in here with me."

"Well—"

"I hope they put you in my room." She flipped her hair and fixed me with the scariest movie-star grin that I'd ever seen. "Karena is so annoying. She never knows when to shut up. I hate everyone here."

"How can you hate with no emotions?"

She barked out a harsh laugh.

"Oh-ho-ho, you'll find a way!" She straightened up in her chair, all business. "You're here because you want to know where the Fatherless Four are."

"The who?"

At her glare, I still answered in the affirmative.

"You're going to fail, you know." Her cold, jaded eyes met mine. "Then you're going to be just like me."

"I'll never be like you."

"You already are," she replied as her lips twisted into a smile much like the one Keres would give. "I'll tell you even though there's really no point."

I glanced over at Micha. He was staring at me, gauging my reaction. I turned to see Alice looking between the two of us, a smirk on her face. I could tell that she knew something was going on between us. It was honestly kind of creepy.

"War is in the Maeora. You must fight your way through the Rose Court and bargain to get him. Death is in the east of Espanza; she's a character from that TV show you love. Pestilence is in Sidra and convincing him should be easy. You've already found Famine."

"I have?" I said, raising an eyebrow. "Who is Famine?"

"You know, you really are just about as stupid as Isolde," she said, rolling her eyes. "She's been right in front of you this whole time. Why do you think the Creator had you save her?"

I thought of my frenemy. It seemed she was more special than I thought.

"Rhea."

"And the prize goes to..." She rolled her eyes again. "That's really all that I can tell you."

"Are you sure you can't give us addresses?"

"Use that money you have. It'll come in handy. People are easy to buy. Trust me when I say that this is going to be easy. Oh, one more thing before I forget!"

"Yes."

"It isn't his."

"Excuse me?" I took a step back. "What are you talking about?"

"I'm talking about—"

"Excuse me?" The staff member from before poked his head in. "Your time is up."

Boy, did I know it.

CHAPTER TWENTY

FULL-TIME SLAVE, PART-TIME MOM

Micha and I decided to fly home in complete silence. Alice's words echoed in the back of my mind. What did she mean when she said that it wasn't his? What was the object in question? And more importantly, *who*?

To get my mind off all that happened, I took a shopping trip with Rhea. We didn't talk about all that transpired between us, something that I was thankful for because deep down, I knew that most of it was my fault. She had every reason not to forgive me. But as we walked through the outlet mall, I knew that for some reason outside of my grasp, she did.

All of that made me appreciate her friendship even more.

Immortals milled around us, walking with an air of superiority. Trailing behind them on literal leashes were Gifted slaves. I swallowed around the lump in my throat, refusing to react. There was a sign at the door that said *Please Keep Your Property Leashed at All Times.* As we neared the door, I felt Rhea put a hand on my shoulder, reminding me that I had to keep it together. My body shook as I fought to keep my magic contained, wanting to make a run for it.

I suddenly realized that once I found the Horseman, I could liberate the Gifted people. I could start a war and free each one of them—of us. I picked up a leash at the door, held it out to Rhea. She placed the collar around my neck and patted my head, cooing softly that I was a 'good girl.' I lowered my head and tried not to think about the way Micha purred the very same, and the total difference in the two sentiments. One was slavery, the other an agreement to belong to another. Why some couldn't understand that I'll never know.

I almost made a comment—

But then saw the frown on her face and bit my tongue.

She could punish me right here. She could beat me...and I could do nothing to stop it. I thought of myself in Micha's lap, his hands first striking my ass, then playing with the opening between my folds, and wanted to scream. This made it difficult to reconcile, especially when I'd been in literal slavery, but there was something about him calling me his 'sweet girl,' after punishment that seemed to almost take away not the offensiveness of being degraded by not only him during these punishments (because there was none—only ecstasy) but that of my Master's beatings.

I tried to keep my head hung low, tried not to walk like I owned the place. My powers hummed under my skin, and I wanted nothing more than to obliterate the place. But then that would expose us, and a lot of people would die trying to catch us. I turned to see a Gifted boy no older than ten staring at me, his finger outstretched.

He openly gawked at me, tugging on his leash to get the attention of his Master.

"Momma, look!" he said. "Papa, get Momma!"

I stared at his dress which pooled to the floor, at his brown hair which touched his shoulders, at the lipstick that he kept trying to wipe away. Suddenly I was thrown back to those days with Jacques, trying on all those tuxes, being told that I was something that I was not. His Master turned around and sunk his fist into the boy's gut. As the pre-pubescent boy crashed to the ground with a cry, he continued to stare at me. Even when his Master barely spared him a glance and said that 'momma is busy,' while gazing at the lady mistress as she tried on an opulent diamond choker, I did nothing.

What a sick man, I thought, and I *turned away.*

Rhea tapped my shoulder again, leading me into a shop.

"Did you see that?" I asked a moment later, trying on a dress.

Rhea nodded, elbowing me in the side as she tried to force on a size zero pair of jeans.

"I saw your face," Rhea said, tossing the jeans to the ground with a huff, "when he recognized you from the Ring. You looked like you understood where he was coming from. Your old master used to say he had plans for you…Did he ever make you into something you weren't?"

"He made me wear boy's clothes. He made me cut my hair short. I think that he thought I was a boy when I wasn't…I think that he thought I was…someone else…"

"Did he ever…you know…?"

I closed my eyes against the memories that threatened to take hold, against the pain. I saw the porcelain tub, saw a pair of ivory legs before me. I stumbled back, crashing into the wall. A pile of clothes fell upon me. I thrashed against what felt like a thousand hands as the smell of the sea filled my lungs. I whirled around wildly, trying to identify where it was coming from.

But he wasn't there.

Rhea grabbed me around the waist, pulled me against her chest. My breath wheezed in and out of my chest as my thrashes slowly calmed. I laid my head on her shoulder, still shaking.

"No one should have to go through that..." she whispered. "No one..."

"You don't understand what he *did* to me. What he was *going* to do."

"Is that why you hate it?"

"Hate what?" I sighed, closing my eyes.

"When Dorian does this?" She pressed her palms flat against my chest. I bit down on my tongue, fighting the urge to scream. She dropped her hands. "I'm sorry. He told me. I just wanted to know if it was true."

"It's okay..." I slowly opened my eyes. It wasn't okay. "It's okay..."

We didn't get any of the clothes. As we left the shop and walked through the mall, I felt like I was someone else watching me from above. Rhea didn't say anything, but I could tell that I'd scared her. We went into one shop and found the cutest hair pin. It had a small jewel in it that was the same ocean blue as the jewel in my ring. I immediately knew that I had to have it.

Against Rhea's wishes, she bought it. She tried to remind me that Gifted people probably died trying to make it, that they were beaten to find the jewel, abused as they set it. But it was so pretty! As I reached up to pin my hair, my ring gleamed from the overhead lights. A couple passed us, holding hands and kissing, and I was reminded of my complicated relationship with my battle angel. In a few seconds, I'd made a promise to myself.

I was going to prove Alice wrong. I was going to prove myself wrong. I wasn't going to get involved with Micha in any sort of way other than the teacher-student bond. I was going to save the world for my son and Dorian. If I couldn't, I would at least destroy the one who stood in my way before he could hurt anyone else.

I was going to end Jacques one way or another. But first I had to get that amulet from Alice. That was if she was willing to hand it over.

When Rhea and I finally left the mall, we had a few bags between us. In them were small toys and trinkets for Aiden and a few dresses for Rhea. Other than the hairpin that I'd bought for myself, there was nothing for me and that made me feel good inside. On our way home, Rhea seemed to lighten a few shades. I looked at her, wondering if I should tell her what she was.

I decided to keep her destiny a secret for the time being. After all, a few stolen touches didn't mean that I could trust her, did it?

I parked the car a few blocks away from a small gas station. We walked a bit and saw a sign advertising a carnival. We rode on a few of the kiddy rides. I pulled out my phone and snapped a few shots of the two of us. But then I suddenly missed my son immensely, so I asked her to drive me home.

When I got home, I went to Beatrice and asked her to bring some warm sheets, a cover, and a pillow to Aiden's room. Once she did, I made a makeshift bed on the floor and curled up next to his crib. Beatrice asked me if I required anything else, to which I asked her to wait on Rhea for the rest of the evening. She curtsied and left. I stayed by Aiden's side that entire night.

I hadn't realized that babies were so...*needy*. Not that he could help it—after all, he was just four weeks old (in real time; in demon-time/age he was about six months.) But hearing him wake up every hour-and-a-half set me on edge. I was worried that something was wrong with him.

Was he too hot—too cold? Did I need to change his diaper? Was he hungry?

By the time the sun rose, I'd been up all night tending to the newborn. He suckled at the nipple of the bottle greedily and burped readily, but sometimes he cried and for the life of me, I couldn't figure out what he wanted. When I changed him, he wasn't fussy. But between those moments, he cried and cried and cried. Now he was in my arms, his hands gripping my shirt as I held him to my chest soundly. I ran a hand over his full head of hair.

He's perfect—a child, I told myself. *And he's mine.*

Beatrice came and I gave her the leftover milk. Then, as she went to stow them away in the refrigerator, I pulled him away, staring into his wide eyes for what felt like what would always be an insufficient amount of time. I couldn't imagine a reality in which I wouldn't love him. I wiped his mouth and burped him as I'd been taught to. I then pulled him closer to me as magic coursed through my veins. I transferred my magic from myself to him, wrapping him in a protective barrier.

Beatrice returned to my side. The magic faded before winking out. There. That way, if he was ever in danger, I would protect him even if I wasn't there. I passed my son off to Beatrice then went out into the hall only to run into Micha.

CHAPTER TWENTY-ONE

DISTANCE EQUALS DELIVERANCE

I went to my room, took a quick shower, and donned on my battle armor. I threw on a pair of combat boots, combed my hair, pinned it with my new hair pin and rinsed my face. Before I walked outside, I told Hao to track down the only other Horseman that I was sure about—Tess from *Strike It Rich*. I told him to find her and give me the details once he did. Then I met Micha outside like we'd agreed.

I had to make this last training session count.

"What are we going to be doing today?"

"We're going to be training on a ship. It is captained by a vicious pirate known as Edward Teach, better known as Blackbeard. This is right before the *Queen Anne's Revenge* was captured so we'll have to be quick about it."

"How much before?"

"Oh, about ten minutes or so…" he said with a shrug.

"What the hell!" I threw up my hands. "Are you trying to get us both killed?"

"Hey!" He reached out to touch my shoulder. "I believe in you."

"But is that gonna bring me back to life?!"

He tapped his vein. I gathered the reminder. Nephilim.

Therefore immortal.

I shook his hand off my shoulder before giving an affirmative. I'd agreed to be the Gatekeeper. That meant putting up with any crazy, reckless, suicidal plan that my teacher drummed up.

I only hoped that we made it out alive and without capture.

* * *

When we stepped out of the portal, the first thing that hit me was the smell of the salty sea. The scent immediately reminded me of Jacques, who I once would have given anything for and now wanted to take everything from. (Funny how love and hatred intertwined.) I looked around in wonder, the excited hustle and bustle of the city seeping into my body. Women fluttered around in elaborate dresses and pompous sunhats, pretty eyelashes framing sharp, pink cheeks. Sailors flexed for each other, their bulging muscles threatening to rip their white uniforms in half.

Children ran along the docks, their eyes filled with dreams that were reckoned to one day be realized. Vendors called out to passing gentlemen on the streets, vouching for things such as tonics and fish. A blacksmith held a large metal hammer in his hand, striking it against the red-hot iron of a soon-to-be sword. A boy led his lady by the hand, a chaperon not too far behind the young courting couple, watching their every move like a hawk. That's when I saw them.

A large group of men walked towards the docks, their eyes shifty and their hair greasy. The cleanest one of them was the man in charge—a man dressed in a white shirt partially covered by an elaborate burgundy coat, white tights, black breeches, and boots. Finishing off the pirate look with your average tricorn hat was Blackbeard…He raised a hand in a wild gesture, regaling his men with epic tales of his adventurous life. I noticed a long thick scar running from his middle finger to disappear under his sleeve.

What happened to him?

I put a temporary glamour over both Micha and me. We quickly ran towards one of the many cargos that were to be loaded on the ship. We got inside our own respective cargo, and I was annoyed to find that my barrel was filled with fish. Great. I felt myself being lifted and tried not to get seasick as I quickly felt the rock of the boat.

I know what you're probably thinking: "You are part 'gator, but get seasick?" I preferred to swim myself, not be carried on a ship.

When the items were finally set down, I tried to open the lid but was unable. They must have nailed the tops shut. I called upon the strength that I acquired, telling myself that now was not the time to give up—not when I'd come so close. This time, I pushed the lid off with no problem, stretching as soon as I had enough space. I looked next to me to see that Micha was getting out of a box.

Of course, his was filled with parchment.

He sniffed. "Fish?"

I rolled my eyes.

"Are you ready?"

"I was born ready." I gave a determined nod. "Let's do this."

We made our way onto the deck without a glamor. I don't know why we acted like no one would notice us. As soon as we walked onto the deck, the high, young voice of a cabin boy cried out, alerting the entire crew to our presence. Blackbeard's eyes met with mine and in them I could see the fiery pits of hell. He barked a command and in moments, the crew had us surrounded.

"It be a wench!" barked Blackbeard.

"More like a witch!" said a crew member.

"Or a croc!" said another.

"Still a missus, I suppose...." Blackbeard raised a brow. "Tell me, do you have a cock swinging between your legs...or, so I've heard, sea creatures have both?"

The crew roared in laughter.

"My husband would beg to differ," I sniffed.

Blackbeard put away his sword. "Seeing as you're a lady, we won't cut ye to ribbons, then. But we will have to do battle. A precaution, you see...can't have the men succumbing to a merwoman, now, can we?"

I had a better idea.

I ran forward, fists ready to knock off a few heads. Smarter and just a little bit faster, I managed to knock out two men with a clean punch to the gut. Micha knocked out a few men with a wave of his hand. I ducked under one man's legs, withdrew my blade, and sent the hilt of it upward, grinning as he fell forward clutching his trousers. Suddenly, Blackbeard went to the wheel of the ship and turned it with his strong hands.

The breath was knocked out of me as a long wooden apparatus slammed into my stomach. I was sent flying into the sea and was immediately dragged under by the waves. I kicked, parting the waves with my hands. My tail flicked, propelling me forward. I hadn't had a chance to take in a breath before I'd been thrown into the water and now it was hard for my motor skills to function from the lack of oxygen.

What was I thinking?!

That's when I noticed a figure swimming towards me.

His black hair floated around his head like a halo of darkness. His eyes saw past the water and seaweed as if they were nothing more than air, connecting to mine as my own threatened to fall closed. His strong arms and legs cut through the water like a knife to butter, bringing him to me in a matter of seconds. His hand wound around my waist and before I could blink, we were out of the water. I was so relieved in that moment that I couldn't contain it.

"You need to flap!"

But I could barely hear him over the roar of the wind.

Something seemed to pull me in. I looked towards the sky and saw a rip in the sky—a portal that showed the manor on the other side. I unfurled my wings and looked back down, surprised to see Blackbeard and his crew staring at us as another ship approached. It was the *Queen Anne's Revenge*. Micha and I flapped through the portal—and I was surprised to find us in my bedroom.

We landed on the bed with a thud. What started as laughter quickly gave way to an uncontrollable heat as Micha placed a hand on my knee. I could feel the want rolling off Micha in waves and my body responded in kind. My heart began to move double time in my chest as an odd fire kindled in my stomach.

"I think you should leave," I said quietly, moving to look out the window.

"You did well," he said, not moving.

"Right." I didn't turn to look at him. "I'm going to get changed."

"Why? Your suit is fine."

I felt him move a piece of hair from my neck.

"I'm going to visit Dorian and then I'm going to see if I can coax more information out of Alice before getting the amulet from her."

"I'll get ready."

"No." Now I turned to look at him. "I'm going alone."

As soon as I closed the door behind him, I collapsed against its hard wooden surface. My mind tossed and rocked, as if I were still aboard the ship. Taking in a breath, I tried to think of how far I'd come. I was no longer haunted by images of a gold-clawed tub, or a pale bruised back. Now I thought of long days and even longer nights. Maybe I was caught in this whirlwind because my mind had become addicted to chaos—and without the hustle and bustle of the Ring of Death, it had created a new ring to circle.

How did I turn it off?

How...

CHAPTER TWENTY-TWO

STRONGER TOGETHER

I stepped into the building. They immediately swarmed me. One guard seized my purse, the other took my wallet. They searched both thoroughly before handing me my wallet back. I asked for my purse. They laughed.

"What's your name?"

"Boyd. Marve Boyd."

"We'll put it in storage.

I stepped through a metal detector. It went off. Good thing I had the glamor covering my knives.

Ding! Ding! Ding!

They took the wand to my body. It passed over my midsection.

Ding! Ding! Ding!

"It must be my belt."

They looked at each other. One waved. They let me through.

I let out a breath that I hadn't known I'd been holding. I would never enter another place defenseless. After all, I needed to be in closer range to use my claws. I couldn't toss them like a dagger. That left me open.

That left me vulnerable.

I walked through the checkpoints and endless halls to the room where Dorian waited for me. His social worker opened the door for me and gave me a brief nod. The wrinkles around her mouth made her look very severe but I knew from past encounters that she was very kind, especially considering that she was undergoing chemo when she wasn't working. I took my seat across from Dorian, watching him. His eyes seemed to have gotten a bit brighter.

"Dorian—"

"Shhh!" He threw a glance at the small window on the door, his words rushed. "Is she still here?"

"Who? Sam?"

"I don't like the way she's always listening. She says that she likes to take notes our conversations in case I say something vital to my treatment. Fuck this place."

"It's only to help."

"It's an invasion of privacy!" He slammed his hands on the table. "I hate this place!"

"Are you still mad at me?"

"No." His lips quirked into a smile that now felt rare. "What does the outside world look like?"

"There's something wrong—something you're not telling me."

"I'm fine."

There was something wrong, though. I could feel it. My powers snapped on in a matter of seconds, making my skin give off a soft glow. Dorian reached out and took my hand in his, tracing his finger over the glowing veins on my wrist. My powers swam underneath my skin like a well of purple water in a clear glass fountain. The physical contact seemed to make our connection stronger, and I was able to gather a lot of information from the few images that I saw.

The doctors here believed that he had bipolar disorder. They wanted to put him on Seroquel, but he was refusing wholeheartedly. They were hoping that I could convince him to take his meds. Well, I was going to have to disappoint them. That was something that Dorian was going to have to come to terms with and choose on his own.

I knew now that forcing him wasn't going to help fix anything. I tried to look at him objectively. The signs were there, staring me down.

"How is Aiden doing?"

"He's doing great. Did you know that he has a Gift?"

"Oh, really?" He laid a hand on his fist. Even with his hair a mess on his head, his eyes dimmed like embers instead of the flames they once were and his skin a duller shade of yellow rather than its usually dazzling gold, he was still so handsome, so perfect. "What is it?"

"He is an Empath."

"Empath, hmm? I don't know how to feel about that. How's your training going?"

"I just finished before I got here and—"

"Do you think she's still listening?" He threw an accusatory glance at the window. "Do you think she's working with him?"

"Working with who?"

"Jacques."

"I highly doubt it," I said, thinking of when I first met her.

I hadn't felt an ounce of magic on her.

"I don't like her."

"You don't *like* her," I met his gaze, "or you don't *trust* her."

"Same difference." He said, waving his hand. "Did you bring me something sweet?"

"I didn't know you liked sweets."

Clearly aggravated, "Is that a no?"

"You can't bring food in here."

You brought your daggers, said a strong voice—Kalysma, *so why not treats for your husband?*

Because! I mentally snapped back. *The last thing he needs is sugar!*

He turned his head on his fist and stared at the wall with a faraway look, as if it were a window and he was gazing at the sky. I'd never noticed him look like that before—like he missed something that was forever lost to him. But then I realized that he looked like that every time before he drank, and that I was usually just so caught up in my own mess that I didn't notice or really even care. And somehow, I'd convinced myself that he was the problem, when really, he'd always tried to support me, love me, watch over me—and I always threw it back in his face.

Why was he in here and not me?

"I remember when my dad took me to Africa."

I decided to offer him something else.

"Do you want me to bring you some books or some more clothes?" I eyed his wrinkled dress shirt with a wince. "Are you bathing?"

"Yes," he said so quickly that the word sounded slurred.

"How are you feeling?"

"I'm not sure. Sometimes I feel like I could take over the world. Other times, I feel that if I did, I'd burn it to the ground. Right now, I'm not really sleeping, I have a lot of energy, but I'm also really fucking sad. I can't focus. I can't sleep. But my inspiration for painting and designing is off the charts. Art therapy is going well…." He gave me a faux grin that quickly turned into a frown. "I hate the people here. I hate my parents for looking me up when I was younger. I hate you for leaving me here. But at the same time..." his hand traced up my arm. "I want to fuck the ever-loving shit out of you."

My heart stuttered. "What good would that do?"

"I've never done it," he said, cocking his head at me. "How would you take it? Would you be hurt? Or would you enjoy it?"

My legs pressed together. "Enjoy what?"

"If I fucked you the way I fuck Megumi. With you, I'm always holding back. With her and every other woman, its carnal. Like I'm ripping them apart from the inside out. With you, I'm mending something. I can't decide if I was trying to save you or if you were saving me by being more fucked up than I was."

I didn't know how to feel. A wry smile. "Can't it be both?"

"I love you."

"Sometimes I think I hate you for making me love you."

"You don't hate the love—and really, I don't either. What we hate is our codependency."

"Why's that?"

"Because..." he let go of my hand. "Neither of us likes needing someone else."

"You don't need her?" I whispered. "Megumi...?"

"I like her. Maybe I even love her. But no, I don't need her. She's just convenient. And familiar. You're new, exotic, intoxicating, addictive. I've never come across anyone that made me love them so much with their dedication. And now you don't want to be around me. It's like we're strangers. And I love you. I want you to love me. But you can't love the both of us."

"I don't love him."

"Which him?"

"Does it matter?"

His head tilted even farther as he surveyed me. "Do you get off on it—on hating people that you once loved?"

"..."

"Do you like ruining people?"

"...Dorian..."

"Or do you just like being the center of someone's world, only to burn it to the ground?"

"Shouldn't I be asking you that?" I whispered.

"I hate you. I fucking hate that I'm in love with a woman that wants a man that beat and raped her. I hate that I want a woman that doesn't appreciate me, just because she enjoys being treated like shit. And I hate that you get off on the pain."

"I don't enjoy any of that. It's just that I have a lot of good memories that are hard to let go of. I have a lot of things that weigh down my mind every day. And I can't make it stop. I can't make any of it stop. You think I like being like this? You think I like being abused? I hated every moment of it. I wanted to die every day. You don't understand that. You don't understand how much I hated myself for allowing it to happen, why I didn't just kill myself to make the pain stop. I hate him for what he did to me. I hate him for raping me. I hate him for beating me. I hate him for making me feel ugly and stupid and dirty. But I hate myself more for not having the strength to walk away. I hate myself more for not having the guts to kill myself, because every day that I'm alive, what he did to me haunts me. You think you have problems? You think your parents' abuse eats you up inside? Being raped eats me up, too. Being beaten eats me alive. You wanna know the difference between us? Out of all the shit you told me, I never once thought 'its his fault.' Not once did I ever blame you or think that you liked what happened to you. I thought you were sad and broken like me, yeah, and maybe I latched onto that in the hopes we could heal each other. But I *never* blamed you for the way you felt about it. Never."

"Then why the fuck do you hold onto it?!" he snapped.

He was out of his seat now.

"Because I have nothing else!" I screamed. "I am nothing without him! I don't exist without him telling me who I am and what I need to do. I don't have a personality. I don't have likes or dislikes. I don't have opinions. You think I like being this way? I'm a shell of who I used to be! I hate being this *thing!* This lump of flesh, this husk of bones. But at least I'm alive. At least I don't have to die, to face the Goddess and my parents and tell them why I wasn't strong enough to fight back! Do you know what sexual abuse does to you? It rots you from the inside out. It eats away at your soul, leaving nothing but this warped image of yourself, this view that tells you that you are dirty and vile. And it doesn't help when everyone around me blames me for what happened to me. It doesn't help when I feel like I'm being judged for opening up. It doesn't help when my own husband pulls away from me as if the best parts of me are gone."

"You said you needed space!"

"I needed you to be there for me!" My throat was raw. "I didn't want you to touch me, that's true. But at least try to let me know that you weren't going to pull away from me, that you didn't hate me, that my life mattered. But you didn't! You pulled away from me! You acted like I was diseased! And then you acted like the only touch that mattered was a sexual one—"

"So, what are you saying?" he whispered, a tear falling down his cheek despite his obvious defiance.

"I fell out of love with you the moment you looked at me like I was broken."

Dorian stumbled away from me. Tears streamed down my face. I didn't know what to say after that. This wasn't just about Dorian. This was about Valentina, too. The reason I clung to Rhea, (and Beatrice, for that matter) was that at least she treated me the same when she knew and when she didn't know. Everyone else did a total 180.

Suddenly, shaking hands found quivering lips. I couldn't believe what I'd just said. I didn't love Dorian anymore?

Did I hate him?

"I did everything for you!" he hissed.

"That's what Jacques used to say." I steeled my shoulders. "If you think I owe you anything, then tell me now and I'll leave and never come back."

"That's not fair!"

"It's totally fair. Do you think I want you for money? Do you think everyone wants something from you?"

"Then why'd you take it?"

"Because you offered, and I had nowhere else to go!" My heart seized. "Fuck, Dorian, if I wanted you for money, I wouldn't have gone through any of this—I would've just let you kill yourself. I want you to be well. I love *you*."

"But—"

"You know what?" I pushed out of my chair. "I'm done explaining myself."

"You hate me now?"

"I love you with everything I have left in me. But that clearly isn't enough."

His mouth opened, closed, opened, closed. He dropped his hand. "Please forgive me. I'm just not feeling like myself."

I didn't believe him, but what could I say?

I gave him a watery smile. "I know, bae."

"What do you want me to do? Tell me what you want me to do? Just please...don't cry..."

"Can you please try to take what they give you?" I tried to show the sincerity of my words with a smile. "They're just trying to help you. And frankly, I don't like you when you're...like this." His head drooped and I quickly amended. "How about we make a deal?" At my words, he picked up the chair and sat down, tapping his foot as if he were trying to keep some sort of erratic beat. "If you take whatever medicine they give you, I'll work on getting you out of here."

His eyes narrowed and I could tell that he didn't really believe me. I explained to him that we had certain connections and that getting him out would be a piece of cake—all he had to do was cooperate. He agreed and when he stood, he was literally bouncing on the balls of his feet. I left the room and told Sam that Dorian was willing to try medication. Her face lit up and I knew that whatever Dorian's thoughts of her was, she really did want to help him.

That made me smile.

Dorian joined us in the hall.

"I love you," I said to Dorian, reaching out to squeeze his hand.

He moved to kiss me. But I didn't want that after what he'd said—what we'd both said.

I instead patted his arm. Sam was staring at us. She reminded us both that PDA wasn't allowed but I could see the smile tugging at her lips. I made my way to Alice's wing in higher spirits, nodding at everyone that I passed. I went into the official meeting room, (yes, I'd finally gotten the papers to prove that we were related) surprised to see her already waiting for me.

"It took you long enough."

"Yeah. I was with Dorian and—"

"I know!" She rolled her eyes. "So, what do you want?"

I sagged into the chair, heavy. I wasn't in the mood to fight anymore.

"I thought you knew everything."

"I stopped looking into your future the moment you started fighting with your husband." She shuddered and I tried my best not to laugh; she fixed her cool green eyes on me, and the laugh died in my throat. "Ask away."

"I need your amulet."

She reached up to touch her neck, a familiar gesture, but it was bare. I took a seat across from her. She rested her head on her fist. She fixed me with an emotionless look that caused a shudder to ripple through me. She was scary.

"I don't have it."

"What do you mean you don't have it?" My teeth ground together. "I know you don't like me, but this is just ridiculous!"

"No. I really don't have it." She leaned back, flipping her long red hair over her pale, freckled shoulder. "Here at KK, you're not allowed to have jewelry."

"Why?"

"You could try to kill yourself with it. It's the same reason we can't have shoelaces." She wiggled her feet in her sneakers, which were fastened with zip ties. "You could try to hang yourself. It's all to keep us as safe—and unhappy—as they can."

She suddenly rolled up the sleeves of the cardigan she was wearing today. I saw angry red slashes decorating her wrists. She leaned back in her chair with a smirk, loving my look of horror.

"How did you do that?" They looked like marks left by a fork. "Why are they giving you metal silverware if they're so afraid of you hurting yourself?"

"Our silverware is plastic." She leaned forward, her voice lowered conspiratorially. "I used the zip ties they gave me. Clever, huh? Not many people think of it."

She was proud of herself. I was, to say the least, disturbed. Was self-harm a game for her?

No, I realized as she gazed at me. *It's her way of saying that she needs someone to actually give a damn.*

She stood and I noticed that she didn't walk like she had nothing—she walked like she owned the place. She even made the whole zip tie thing look like a fashion trend. What I'd give to be as confident as her. She once had it all.

Then she lost it all due to her own selfishness.

"Where is the amulet?"

"I'm not saying."

My reaction was instant. My powers flared up as a single thought crossed my mind: I was going to make her talk. I could pick up on electricity in the brain. By that same logic, I could probably manipulate it, too. Hopefully this wouldn't be a repeat of what happened with the cop.

It wasn't.

I grabbed her hand and pushed my powers softly. Inch by merciless inch, electricity crawled up Alice's body to her head. She winced and suddenly her eyes went blank. I flipped through her mind like cards in a deck, trying to make it to the decision-making part of her brain. I reached it in a matter of seconds and gave one final heave.

"It's with the rest of my stuff in the office," she said, staring at me blankly. "If you ask for it, they'll give it to you. It's black obsidian."

Obsidian…the magician's jewel. Word had it that it could be used for many things…But could it really be used on my quest?

I made my way downstairs. It was laughably easy. The people at the front desk handed the amulet over after I showed them my ID, not even asking for an excuse. I tied the amulet around my neck, got in my car and sped home. When I showed Micha the amulet, he grinned before saying that we could find the Horsemen, fight the war, and seal Jacques away for good—

But just as soon as he finished, he reached out to touch it again, frowning.

"What's wrong?"

"This is a fake," he sighed, running a hand through his hair.

"This isn't the real amulet?"

He shook his head.

I took it off and dumped the fake into the trash. There was no point in getting angry. That was just energy spent that could be put towards finding the real one. It still sucked though. Anyways, that left one vital question.

Where had Alice done with the real one?

CHAPTER TWENTY-THREE

SEEING HIM, FEELING YOU

Months flew by and with their passing, a lot of things happened. Dorian made such tremendous progress that he was let out of the mental facility. At first, he seemed to be in zombie-mode, falling asleep at the worst of times and taking more than a few tries to respond to what was said to him. Once he got adjusted to his new medication, he was a whole new person. He was livelier, smiled a lot more, laughed a ton and rarely reached for his bottle outside of celebration.

I was absolutely astounded. I knew that it was rare to get the medicine right on the first try. After they added Lithium to control his manic episodes, we really saw progress. He still had bouts of sadness and a few hypomanic episodes, but he was much better off than he was before. When I looked at him, I saw a new man that loved life.

If only I helped him sooner.

The only issue he had with himself was that he put on a few pounds. With a change in diet and exercise, he shed them right back off. Before I knew it, it was May 15th.

That's right—it was my birthday.

"Happy birthday, Madam Taurus!"

I grinned.

Gold balloons floated around the room—my favorite color. Multicolored streamers were on every available surface. Everyone had on their party hats and smiles, stuffing their mouths with food and cake. It was all flawless and I found myself happier than I'd ever been. Sitting at the head of the table, I bounced a giggling Aiden on my lap, occasionally pinching his cheeks, which would elicit a high squall from the boy.

It was hard to believe that I was turning twenty-two and my son would be five months old on the 25th.

After I'd fed Aiden some of the food from the party (don't forget, he advances quicker because of the demon blood) and put him to bed, I went up to my room. Dorian's eyes followed my every move. We had a proper welcome home celebration and hours later, as I lay there in his arms, I knew that we had forever together. When he fell asleep, I took a shower, put on a black bodycon dress, and went downstairs, wanting to look nice for my hubby when he woke up.

But Micha was propped against the fridge, a promise in his eyes.

I don't know what made me do it but when he crooked his finger at me, I gravitated towards him like the Earth to the sun— instantaneous and unable to resist.

Micha suggested that we have our own after party at a small club that was known for serving the supernatural—from faeries to angels and vampires to witches, wizards, and ghouls. I decided to take him up on his offer, knowing that I needed to do something spontaneous before I fully submitted myself to another power stronger than myself. Besides, this was the last night that I was going to see Micha and I wanted to make it count. As soon as we stepped into the club, I was surprised to see realize that this was the same club I'd gone to with Rhea almost a year ago. There were people who *looked* to be my age and people that actually were, all knocking back drinks made of sparkly golden liquid.

Music shook the walls. Strobe lights cast the world in a million different hues. Micha and I walked to the middle of the dance floor and moved to the rhythm, only a few inches of space between us. In a matter of seconds, sweat plastered my dress to my body. Micha had a wicked gleam in his eye as the song *Marilyn Monroe* by Lyon-S came on. When I thought about it, I realized that they played her so much because she was known as the queen of magic in the music world, partly because she was the only singer whose music catered solely to magical creatures and the like.

The other reason?

She could imbed God's Magic into her music, which made her the singular most powerful artist since Hemingway.

You eye me like a lion,
Your bite is so bitter.
Hips are what we use,
Taste the toxin on my kisser.
I'm covered in bodies,
Drinks, sweat and glitter,
You say, 'I don't wanna,'
But I know you wanna kiss her.

Micha took a couple of drinks from a passing waitress. He knocked a few back and with each drink, he moved a bit closer. We were now chest to chest and all I could think of was Dorian. Deep down, I knew that this wasn't me, that I wasn't the cheating type and that my feelings were all chalked up to him being a breeder. Still, that left me with few options.

> *Baby, let me turn you inside out,*
> *Let me be your freak show.*
> *You'll be JFK,*
> *And I'm your Marilyn Monroe.*
> *Don't be afraid*
> *But we're about to explode.*
> *Hit the gas and go!*
> *I'm your Marilyn Monroe...*

A few people bumped into us, momentarily closing the gap. When I moved to pull away, Micha reached out and pulled me so close that I couldn't breathe. He yelled something but I couldn't hear him over the bass of the music. I asked him to repeat himself. He leaned down and traced his tongue over the shell of my ear, making his intentions clear.

> *This can be our secret,*
> *That we hide under our pillows,*
> *Let's get crazy*
> *Then give 'em a show.*
> *You'd be on cloud nine,*
> *If you knew all that I know.*
> *People think I'm a nice girl,*
> *But that's just not so.*
> *(Wind you up so tight,*
> *Then I wa-wa-watch you go.)*

Now that I was about to do the deed, I didn't feel very confident. I felt wrong, knots twisting in my stomach, making me feel like I was about to hurl. The world swam before me in slow-motion, bringing me closer to the edge. I took a step back and dragged in a harsh breath. Micha gave a low, sexual chuckle and I just wanted to scream.

Baby, let me turn you inside out,
Let me be your freak show.
You'll be JFK,
And I'm your Marilyn Monroe.
Don't be afraid
But we're about to explode.
Hit the gas and go!
I'm your Marilyn Monroe...

The world tilted on its axis, threatening to drag everything down with it. I felt someone's hand brush my backside and I wanted to believe that it wasn't Micha, but I couldn't. Some might call me a tease for backing out at the last second. I guess I was just a better person than I gave myself credit for. My winged companion didn't seem to get the message as he trailed a finger over the junction where my wings met.

Oh, man, I'd played with fire and had no choice but to retreat before I got burned...

You've got that fire
That makes the girls go insane.
Honestly, I know I'm a piece
In your little game.
We live in Hollywood,
You're the camera, I'm the fame.
You've got the bullets, babe,
Ready, set, aim.

My hands shook as that familiar heat flayed me from the inside out. I could feel Keres turning over in my mind the way a child could feel a bee sting to the face. I turned and made my way through the crowd. Micha called after me, his drive and spirit tangible. I wasn't going to play his game of cat and mouse anymore.

Baby, let me turn you inside out,
Let me be your freak show.
You'll be JFK,
And I'm your Marilyn Monroe.
Don't be afraid
But we're about to explode.
Hit the gas and go!
I'm your Marilyn Monroe…

The last bit of the song followed me out the door.

Tell me what you think,
As you wait out the storm.
Your knuckles are bleedin'
From knockin' on the door,
There isn't a problem, babe,
I just don't need you anymore.
You can fly away,
Or promise till you're sore,
(But the truth is, I don't need ya,
No, not anymore.)

The hardest thing I did was walk away.

* * *

I guessed that Micha was respecting my wishes because I didn't hear him come after me as the door swung shut behind me. Still, I had the strangest feeling that I'd somehow offended him. It wasn't until I was down the street that I realized that I was being watched. I turned around repeatedly but couldn't sense anyone's electrical field or thoughts. It was then that I realized that I was being watched from the *inside.*

I ran with inhuman speed, extending my wings a bit more with each passing foot. I was barefoot, which to Immortals would seem odd, but was rather comfortable for me, a Gifted that had walked miles in the hot dessert sand for freedom before. It only took two strong beats, and I was off the ground, the wind making my hair fly back from my tan face. I soared through the sky, thinking of all the broken hearts I saved by refusing my tempting teacher. Deep down I knew that I'd made the right decision.

When I got home, Aiden was still sound asleep. Dorian was waiting for me in the foyer, his hands clasped behind his back and a conflicted look in his eyes. I knew that he wanted a drink, which reminded me that medicine couldn't fix every problem. Dorian seemed completely oblivious to all that'd transpired tonight and for that I was grateful. I didn't want to explain my horrible attraction to a breeder and that although it couldn't be helped, I didn't do much to fight it.

I took his hand and together we walked out into the yard. We laid on the damp grass. The stars were out, something that was rare to witness in the smoke-clogged cities that was Sidra's mortal lands, aka the place I grew up. We were in the northernmost part of Amoria— peaceful, alone, and very much in love. Deep down, I wondered if I should tell Dorian about my relationship with Micha.

It would kill the moment and drive a thick wedge between us, no doubt.

As I scooted closer to Dorian on the cold grass, I wondered what this land was like before the Great Change. I knew that this used to be called Canada and had always been cold. But I didn't know what the people were like. Did they love with their eyes closed? Did they fly with both hands grasping outward? Did they run with faltering feet?

I decided not to tell him. Although it may not have seemed that way, honesty was not always the best policy. Sometimes you had to stick to your guns and keep your mouth shut. I let my wings flutter out and watched as the moonlight danced across my feathers. Dorian looked at me like he'd never seen me before and when he kissed me, my world was set aflame.

I needed more.

His naked skin was more than something to look at. It was more than something to feel. It was a glimmering song that washed away my troubles. It was a golden map that always led me home. It was what I lived for.

We writhed under the black velvet of the night sky, his fist in my hair as comets bounced across the vast expanse like oranges hurled from the hand of a child. I bit down on his shoulder as jewels were flung here and there by the fist of the Goddess, and I briefly wondered if they were somehow connected to us, summoned by our slow yet hurried joining. He was my everything in that moment— my reason for existing. I realized something in that pocket of time dictated not with reason but with flesh: I didn't need a communion. He was infinitely more than I could hope for, and joining with him was its own form of worship.

Hands moved over skin, mouths skimmed throats and arms were linked in an embrace. When we rocked, we didn't just touch the sky. We moved planets. How I could ever think of ruining this for one idiotic rendezvous, I did not know. What I did know was that I would kill gods, fight demons, and pluck out the wings of angels for this man.

Serenity surrounded not only us, but the things that we touched. It's like the universe was brought together by our coupling. The whole world rejoiced.

But even amongst his perfection, I saw slate-grey eyes, a night-black face and lips that kissed every inch of my skin and named me a goddess.

CHAPTER TWENTY-FOUR

To Hell and Back Again

I had a plan, but I wanted to make sure that it was foolproof before I went through with it.

Exactly one week after Micha's departure, I walked through the halls of the asylum, trying not to cringe at some of the dead stares that followed me. I could feel them begging for a savior and I knew that if I followed the Creator's plan, I would give them one. When I made it to the conference room, I was surprised to see Alice sitting there, a map laid before her. As soon as I opened the door, she waved me over.

"Hi, Alice!" I chirped with a nod.

"Whatever." She flipped her hair as she stared at the map intently. "Do you know what this is?"

"Um…a map?"

"Oh, goodie. Here I thought you were going to call it a chew toy," she said, flicking a glance at my tail, which was currently swishing behind me in curiosity. "How do you hide that thing?"

I wrapped it around my waist. As usual, it looked like some sort of weird belt. Alice nodded before looking back at the object in front of her. There were four circles on the map. What did those circles have to do with me?

"This," Alice said, laying a graceful hand on the map, "is your salvation."

I stayed silent. God was speaking [through her.]

"This map shows the locations of the Horseman. It tells what city but not their precise location. It is your job to track them down and—"

"Train them and save the world. Blah, blah, blah. I get it, okay? Now give me their addresses so that I can get this show on the road!"

"Well, that was rude." Alice surprised me by looking less severe. "I'm proud of you."

"That's not why you're helping me," I said, eyeing the bags under her eyes.

"I can't get any sleep. I keep having visions of the Horsemen. I'm hoping that by telling you this info, it will clear my conscience. Not that I can really get any rest in this nut house. Not with all the screaming…"

I moved across the table. Before she could run, I grabbed her and pulled her into a fierce hug. She made an odd noise like she was being strangled and when I set her down, she was gasping for air. She threw incredulous look at my arms and that's when I remembered that I now had enhanced strength. For some reason, Tiara's face popped into my head—and I was overtaken by a brief second of grief.

But as all things did, it passed, and it was straight back to business.

"Believe it or not," I said once I'd sat back down, "that's not why I'm here."

"Oh?" Alice raised an eyebrow. "It's not like I can see with the Creator blocking all visions outside of the ones pertaining to the Horsemen. What's wrong? Did Micha finally get you pregnant? Dorian's divorcing you now, am I right?"

"What?" I thought back to my first visit. "So that's what you meant by 'stop now' and 'it's not his.' You thought I was knocked up! Well, I hate to break it to you, but I'm done with Micha. And before you ask, *no,* we did not hook up."

"Then why are you here?"

"I need your advice."

"It's not the first time I heard that before," she snorted. "What is it?"

"I want to free Keres and absorb her powers before I continue my hunt. I've realized that I need to fight at full capacity and frankly, I'm not there yet. What do you think?"

"I think you're an idiot." She laced her hands together, rested her chin atop them and leaned forward, all business. "If you merge with Keres, she will consume your soul. You'll be just like me—a shell of your former self. You'll be powerful, yes, but you'll be a monster."

"But I have all of this untapped energy—I can't just leave it!"

"Your funeral," she said with a shrug. "You're getting in way over your head. If you had the Dagger of Truth that would be a different story."

"The Dagger of Truth? I thought that only worked on demons?"

"The Creator originally created it to purify the heart of angels when they began to go Dark. Instead, it destroyed them and any other demon it came in contact with. If you are good, it will rip Keres from your body, and you would be left with her powers. If there is more evil in your heart than good, the dagger will destroy you."

I wasn't sure what I was. I felt better but the anger towards Jacques—it was more than evil. And there was a lot of it. Well, there went that plan. Now it was time for Plan B—trek on and hope for the best.

"Let's say that I was going to use the Dagger on an Immortal—or a Gifted even. What would happen then?"

"They would believe every word you said. That's why it's called the Dagger of Truth."

"How do I get the dagger?"

"You have to go back to Sora and get it."

I thought of my workers at the manor. I was about to tell them something that would probably change their lives—something that they wouldn't initially be inclined to believe. I needed a foolproof way to show them that I was telling the truth. Was the Creator going to send down a messenger? Was I going into this alone?

I knew one thing: if I was going to get through to them, I was going to need that dagger. Another part of me insisted that I try to convince my subjects without the dagger. After all, they followed Dorian and Yvonne. Maybe they would finally do the same for me.

"Well, thanks for the advice, old lady!" I snatched up the map and walked from the room. "It's been fun!"

*　*　*

Before I flew off to Amoria to find Pestilence, I knew that I had to inform Rhea of her divine purpose. It wasn't that I thought she wouldn't believe me. It was just that for the first time in my life, when faced with the end of the world, I was afraid that Rhea's attachment to the Rebellion would get in the way. I knew that she would be reluctant to leave them behind, that she wanted to save our people before anyone else—but did that mean she'd be willing to work with me?

I called a meeting in the Blue Room. In less than fifteen minutes, everyone was gathered round, eyes on me. All I could do was look at Rhea. How was I supposed to break the news to her? To most, this task must've seemed easy, but the Creator didn't give me an instruction manual.

I was going in completely blind.

"There is a war coming," I said, "and it is bigger than all of us. I know that we have lost some great friends—" at the mention of Yvonne and Andrew the other magical folk in the room bowed their heads "—but now is not the time for grieving. The Almighty has recently brought to light that I have been burdened with the task of building an army for this war and that the most important soldiers are the Four Horsemen of the Apocalypse."

"How do we know this is true?" They said, not wanting to believe that they were a part of some grand design; after all, in their eyes, God abandoned them long ago. "Why would God want us now?"

"There is no way that I can prove that the Creator needs your help. You simply have to have faith in me and therefore It. Now, some of you will be guarding the manor while I'm away tracking down these Horsemen and the rest of you will train. You will switch off every twenty-four hours. Since Hao is head of the security, I'm putting him in charge while I'm away. I will teach you all the basics and then it's your job to split up into groups and go on from there, okay?"

All of them nodded but I could tell that they were still on the fence.

"I know this is hard, but this is bigger than us. The Second Coming is on the horizon. We must be ready for it!"

They all stared at me, and I knew that what I was about to ask of them would be the hardest thing that some of them had faced in a year. After all, with my rise to power came the departure of two people that they depended on and trusted wholeheartedly. Accepting me was like saying that the cause of their deaths was a small matter, and we all knew that it wasn't.

"I'm going to need for you to trust me." I spun around in my chair to look at Rhea, who was watching me in a way that told me the Creator had already planted the seeds of truth in her mind. "Rhea, do you remember how you've always had a problem with food?"

"You know?"

She threw a glare at Dorian. He cursed. She moved to stand. I placed a hand on her arm, resisting the urge to use my Gift, to make her calm down. But then Dorian grabbed her arm and she seemed to calm. I couldn't decide if it was good or bad that he'd Influenced her.

I took it as a godsend.

"Rhea?" She looked at me slowly. "Now is not the time."

"Yes, I know what you're talking about."

"What if I told you that there was a reason for that? What if I told you that you binge because that is what you were created to do? What if I told you that you were special? What if I told you that you had a Gift that even I don't know the extent of yet? What if I told you that you were Famine?"

"No," she said, shaking her head. "My power is pyrokinesis. I'm flame-borne."

"Fire cooks food," Dorian agreed, catching on. "Even you've got to admit that's important."

"All right. I've decided." I met the gaze of every person in the room before continuing. "There is one item that can prove if I'm lying or not. Do any of you know what it is?"

"The Dagger of Truth!"

"The Dagger hasn't been seen in years!"

"Yeah!"

"It's nothing but a legend!"

"You couldn't possibly know where it is!"

"And what if I do?" I said, even though I didn't. "Then you would have no choice but to believe me."

"Do you have it now?" Rhea said, her golden eyes betraying her. She wasn't afraid, but she didn't believe she was more than a fire wielder, either. She still didn't trust me. "Will you show me?"

"I don't," I admitted. "But I can get it."

*   *   *

You'd think summoning a demon would be hard. It really wasn't. All you needed was a sacrifice, the knowledge of how to draw a pentagram and a whole lot of guts. I knew that if this went wrong, I was neck deep in a world of trouble. I also knew that if this went correctly, not only would I have the Dagger of Truth, but I would also have the trust of my people.

The dead body was that of a child. I didn't know who the boy was. He had hair as black as night and a frail body that would have gone to waste had I not plucked him out of the heart of Amoria. He was starving, Dorian's affluence having not reached him. I brought him here, knowing that he would have died of starvation and lost his usefulness had I not found him.

It was better than nothing.

The runes on the ground began to glow. I stared at them, watching as they flickered from blue to red to gold and back again. The screams of thousands of dead souls rose up—mothers, fathers, children—wailing in my ears. I chanted the ancient words louder, faster, as my magic poured from my body, fueling the runes. Deep in the recesses of my mind, I could hear Keres answering the call as she stamped her feet.

A figure rose from the runes, her naked body clothed in darkness. Pitch-black eyes peered out from the abyss, landing on me and gleaming in pleasure. One clawed hand extended to trace along my face. I watched as two large bat-like wings flapped, calling forth the darkness and banishing all light. When the shadows settled, her jagged-tooth grin filled the space on her face, which literally had the color and glimmer of rubies.

I felt the crippling despair, the descent into madness, the weight of sadness on my soul. I rolled my shoulders, used to this feeling. It was stronger than what Jacques gave off, yes, but not by much.

"Hello, child. You have summoned Amaris, Child of the Moon. Who would you like to destroy?"

"Actually, right now I'm not trying to kill anyone."

"Yes…" Her voice was a hiss. The darkness shifted as she rubbed her hands together. "Then which one of the Earth's scum will suffer?"

"Uh, no suffering going on here, either. Sorry for the confusion," I added at her disgruntled look. "I'm actually trying to obtain the Dagger of Truth."

"The Dagger of Truth?!" She took a leap back, her face twisting in shock and horror. "The cursed item that has slain so many of my brothers and sisters! The weapon of the angels! Why would you seek such a vile artifact?"

"I need it to make my people believe me. I also kind of need it to do some major damage to—oh, look, never mind! Will you help me or not?"

"I can't help you with that, child. Abaddon told us it was destroyed a year ago."

I chose not to mention that I'd lied to him and said: "I know that demons wage battles with Sora. I know that citizen angels retreat to Paradise every time you do." I let my wings unfurl behind me, such a stark difference compared to her darker ones. "All I need is for you all to take me with you during your battle so that I can get the Dagger and leave."

"That isn't up to me, child."

"Then take me to the man in charge," I said.

"Why?"

"Because I'm the Gatekeeper," I said, taking a step forward, "and his ascent or downfall depends on me."

"The Gatekeeper?" The demoness's eyes gleamed in interest. "Now that *is* something…"

*   *   *

I stood in a great hall. There was a large throne made of bones, welded together by the silver blood of angels. The armrests of the throne were made of crossbones and the perfect, flawless hands that rested upon them were hard to look away from. Even harder was the symmetrical nose, almond-shaped eyes, and the straight, white teeth. His skin was paler than snow and his cheekbones were so sharp that they looked as if they could cut through ice. As far as beauty went, I could see his resemblance to Jacques. Luce's pale white hair spilled across his forehead like snowy blood, and I realized that he was absolutely nothing like his brother.

"So…you're The Gatekeeper? The beloved savior of the Gifted? And the Creator's downfall," he said, combing his hands through the hair of one of his concubines. "And now you have come to me for help. How ironic."

I nodded, eyeing the throne room. We were alone—just me, Luce, and his concubines. I was no fool, though. Luce could call in all the help that he needed with one breath. He could also break my neck with a snap of his fingers.

It was just a vibe that he gave off—well, that and the legends of him nearly bringing down a utopia and the maker of this universe.

"Tell me, what it is that you want again?"

"I want to break into Paradise, steal the Dagger of Truth and use it on my people—I mean, soldiers."

"That's a slippery plan, don't you think?" He said, giving me a wickedly sinful smile. "Tell me, why should I help you—especially since you lied and told my brother that you destroyed the Dagger a year ago?" His lips twisted in a wry smile at the look on my face. "Yes. I know about that."

"Because the sooner we get this show on the road, the sooner you can take the throne that was rightfully yours," I said, smiling, "and the sooner I can fulfill my debt to the Creator."

"You're flirting with danger, little girl. You say that you serve the Creator, but I can sense darkness in your heart. Tell me, what do you really want it for?"

"I already told you."

"Well, I don't think I heard you correctly. Say it again."

"Fine! I want the Dagger so that I can get back at the Ordained, okay?"

"You want to kill him. You keep lying to yourself and telling everyone around you that you just want to make him suffer." At my incredulous look, Luce laughed. "My brother and the Creator are not the only ones that have been keeping an eye on you. I'll let you follow my army into Sora when we leave tomorrow. But right now, I think that there is a more pressing matter that you need to settle."

"Which is…?"

He waved his hand. I watched as another portal appeared, showing the manor. A dark shadow moved past it towards the trees. Suddenly, the figure moved into the moonlight. It couldn't be.

"How did he get there so fast?"

"There is much that you must learn about demons and our offspring," Luce said, waving his hand over the portal until it disappeared. "It seems that your enemy has brought the fight to you. He is headed for the forest and my best bet is that as soon as he gets through with playing with you, he'll head towards the manor."

"It's not time yet…" I said, voice cracking as I thought of my innocent son inside the house. My powers crackled beneath my skin, faint but still powerful. Even with this angelic power, I knew that I was not ready to face him. "Why does he like causing me so much pain?"

"You ran from him just like Grant. He wants to see you suffer. He is very much like me in that retrospect. Find him in the forest. When you find him, you must kill him."

"He's your grandson. Why would you want me to kill him?"

"If he dies, the apocalypse comes early." Luce's mouth twisted into a grin. "This would be beneficial to us all. Now leave! You're boring me."

He waved his hand. Just like that, I was back in front of the manor. I looked at Jacques and as he turned, all my hatred from those past fourteen years bubbled to the surface. I didn't just want to hurt him. I wanted to make him suffer and then kill him slowly. With a grin, he took off into the trees, knowing that I would follow.

* * *

I leaped from tree to tree. My eyes picked out every ridge in the leaves, every green patch of moss on the fallen logs, every gleaming surface of the small rocks that dotted the forest floor. Jacques's dark laugh flew across the wind. I thought of the way he'd hurt my son and my partially contained anger spilled over like boiling water in a pot. The wind changed directions, as did his scent.

I made a slight left which carried me farther into the forest. Up ahead there was a clearing filled with dying flowers and broken dreams. I saw him stop and stand in the middle of the space; his head tilted up as if he were a bloodhound searching for a scent. It didn't make sense. He knew that I was following him.

Only when I reached him and saw the smile on his face did I realize that he was relishing the moment. My eyes searched the area and then I too sniffed the air. I wanted to make sure that we were alone. After all, I was going to release my inner animal. And if anyone encroached on my territory, they would die.

Jacques turned around to face me. My fist flew out. Right, left, duck from his fist and then uppercut. No matter how many hits I threw, he dodged them all as the smirk on his face grew ever faster. An irritated growl built in my throat and slipped past my bared teeth.

"Take this!" I threw another punch.

It landed square on his jaw. He turned his face and gave me a bloodthirsty grin as if I hadn't landed the punch, but he had. Then his hand flashed out and suddenly I was sprawled on the ground.

"You can't really expect to defeat a demi-demon in a fight, can you?"

I crashed forward like a speeding bullet. His foot flashed out. I was sent flying.

I was on the ground again. His foot rose to step on my face. I could instantly feel the pressure on my bones. He pressed down just a bit more, just light enough to keep from crushing my skull beneath his boot. Then he looked down at me and gave me a look that stopped my heart dead in its tracks.

"You just don't give up, do you?" he sighed.

He walked away until he was on the other side of the field. I stood and planted my hands in front of me in a fighting stance. Jacques raised one hand and crooked a finger at me as a little smirk danced on his lips.

I charged forward again. Left punch, right punch, left punch, uppercut, roundhouse kick then left punch. This time, my combination was more effective…or so it seemed.

My fist collided with his face and Jacques flew across the open space and into a tree; the tree crashed with a mighty bang. When he stood this time, his mouth was split in a bloody grin. I charged forward and threw hit after hit. He took them all as if they were a caress. Then, finally, his footing slipped, and he flew back again.

But instead of kneeling in pain, he simply hopped back onto his feet.

My tail swished in anger. Jacques glowed with a sudden bright light. I watched as night-black horns sprouted from his head, his teeth turned into gnashing fangs and an aura of darkness surrounded him like a coat. I knew that his demonic form actually wasn't black—it was bone-white, but he held the darkness so close to him that he wore it like a second skin. It was quite a sight to behold. He turned and the smile fell from his face. With little more than a grunt, he darted away.

I chased him for God knows how long. But it was like the closer I came to him, the farther away he got. Finally, I reached a cliff. The drop was about two-thousand feet. My head lifted so that I could smell the wind, but his scent was locked in my head and surrounded my body, everywhere at once and yet nowhere.

I spread my wings and dove. This time I wasn't afraid of crashing. I was afraid of failing. I flew around the ravine for God knows how long, trying to find a trace of him. Finding nothing, with a disappointed sigh, I glided back to the ground.

I felt the weight on my shoulders, the pain of failure, the heartache of facing my abuser yet again and coming up empty handed. My fists rose to bang on my head. "Stupid, stupid, stupid! He's right! You're weak!" I cried out, hitting myself.

I turned and made my way back towards the manor. Dorian was waiting outside, his arms open. I didn't know how he knew that I'd been outside or that I was hurting. Still, he walked up to me and hugged me as grieving sobs wracked my form. I wasn't just torn that I'd let Jacques slip through my fingers yet again.

I was utterly broken.

I lifted my head from Dorian's shoulder. He watched as I backed away and wiped my face. My tail swished in anger. Right then, I made up my mind. The next time that Jacques and I ran into each other would be the last time and when I did, I would not simply torture him.

I would destroy him.

CHAPTER TWENTY-FIVE

LOST CAUSE

I lined up with the demonic soldiers. The weird thing that I liked about demons was that none of them looked the same. Some had tails like mine, some had horns, some had yellow eyes, green eyes, red eyes, and so on—every eye color except purple. I guess that purple was reserved for the angels and their offspring. I looked up and down the line of soldiers, looking for a weakness. When I found what I was looking for, I smothered the smile that threatened to overtake me and raised my head high. I was headed into Sora, after all.

Lucifer waved his hand and a portal opened, its wind grating my ears as if it were a child's screams.

The few soldiers that had wings unfurled them; directly in front of those soldiers were the wingless, and I knew that the army stretched back in this pattern for miles. I unfurled my wings, glanced at Luce for the okay and was the first to take off through the portal. I came out in the other dimension in a spin, the wind slapping my face and the sun shining in my eyes.

It seemed like too bright a day for what I was about to do.

I quickly flew past the gates where the marching demons were lining up. I was surprised when arrows flew in my direction. I managed to dodge them but realized that sooner or later I was going to get hit and that when I did, I would spiral out of the sky. I landed behind one of the angels and tapped him on the shoulder. He whirled around, nostrils flaring, and hands balled into fists.

"Who goes there?"

"Hello." I gave him my best please-don't-kill-me smile. "My name is—"

"I know who you are, Keeper." He tilted his head at me, his eyes losing their hostility. "Why were you just with the army of Lucifer?"

"I needed a ride here."

"You're working with the Fallen Ones?"

"No but I need your help."

"I'm not sure I believe you."

"I'm the Child of the Apocalypse. How could you not believe me?"

It sounded a lot better in my head.

He crossed his arms.

"Okay, how about this? If you tell me where the Dagger of Truth is, I'll tell you about a weakness in Luce's army," I bargained, thinking of earlier when I observed them.

He gave me an affirmation.

"There's a big gap in the defense on the left side of the army. That's where Lucifer puts those that have been wounded before. Concentrate your attacks there and I'm sure things will go a lot smoother than your past battles."

The brown-haired angel skimmed the crowd, his ponytail swishing as he moved his head. I watched him, bouncing from foot to foot. I was beyond impatient. I wanted to get this done so that I could begin my hunt for Pestilence. When the angel finally looked at me, I wanted to scream a praise.

Things were finally going my way.

"Okay," he said with a nod, "I believe you. Go to the tattoo parlor and ask Lisette to take you to Micha. He should give you the Dagger, if—"

"Thanks!" I spread my wings and took off, soaring above the massive armies and making my way to the parlor in just a few minutes. "Lisette, are you here?"

I pushed open the door, an eager grin splitting my face in two. I glanced around at the chairs, tattoo guns and posters rallying angels for praise, wondering where Lisette was. Didn't Micha say that she was left behind in case I needed her?

"Lisette!" I spun around in a circle, surveying the room. "Lisette, wh—"

"What are you doing here?" a voice demanded harshly.

I whirled around, breathless at the sound of him, heart racing at his sight, body craving what I hadn't allowed myself to feel in the club, craving the taste of his brown sugar and mangoes on my tongue. "Micha."

He lazily rose from the chair, took a step forward, then another and then stepped into the light. He looked…different. Still commanding, still sexy, but something was off. He reminded me of his brother a bit—not the Luce from before the Fall but after. What was it?

His eyes flashed in pain, and he clutched his chest. "I thought I had more time." He glared up at the ceiling. "This is my punishment? That she sees me like this?"

"Micha, I—"

He moved forward in a split second. A low growl made its way up my throat as his hand rose to pinch my chin between his thumb and forefinger. I felt the power drain from me as he tilted my head up, his odd silver eyes boring into mine with a glow. The last thing that

I registered was his head moving forward and his mouth brushing mine. Then I blacked out, all the power inside of me gone.

*   *   *

Micha reached down towards the dagger at his waist that had intrigued me since the day we met. I tensed. He didn't have me chained up. I was free to move. But still, I wanted to shy away, to turn my gaze from him and never have him return to my sights. He diverted his hand at the last second, instead touching the empty loops where his daggers once were.

His sigh was ancient, tired.

"Don't look from me," he whispered, his ebony skin glistening with sweat. "I can handle the Creator closing Its eyes from me. I can handle Lisette turning away at the banishment ceremony. But please, I hoped I meant more to you than that."

"I don't understand." My chest seized as I looked at him; I was filled with reproach, sadness, anger, hostility. I wanted to pluck his eyes out and scream from the unfairness of it all. "Why do I feel this way?"

My eyes suddenly closed as I leaned my head back. I felt so tired next to him in that moment, like I'd been fighting a year-long war and had just stopped to catch my breath. He scooted towards me. My body seized up, in pain, both physical and emotional. I heard his voice catch as his fingers found my cheeks. I felt his forehead touch mine.

"Women break us down. You break us down and you strip us of our pride, but when we are cast out, you look at us as though you knew it all along. But that's not how you're looking at me...is it, Aleilah?" His lips touched my head. "You can't look at me like you hate me, even now..."

"What are you talking about?"

"I knew you'd come. It told me you'd come, but I thought it'd be after I was already officially Fallen."

"No." My eyes snapped open. "No, no, no, that's not possible."

"Kill me."

"What? Why?"

"I don't want to be a demon."

I touched his chest. I felt Glory rise within me. Instead of using the angelic power to fight him, I swirled it in my hands and pressed it into his beating heart. But it just slowed even more.

He groaned. "Stop it, Marve!"

"No! But this way…there's still hope. Still a chance…!"

"You don't understand."

"Please try to help me understand…for me…?"

"If I were to Fall and make you feel…a fraction of what *he* made you feel…I would…..never forgive myself."

I couldn't tell him that it had already begun to take effect.

My hands wound in his cloak. My lips found his as they searched his waist for the dagger. I closed my eyes against its glittering sharpness. I pressed it against his chest. He nuzzled my neck, then pulled away, commanding me to open my eyes.

I looked…slowly. His dark brown skin was riddled with black veins, inky ooze dribbling from his mouth. One of his eyes were red, the other that slate grey. Even halfway into a demonic form, he was still…impossibly beautiful. Like a stormy sky riddled with veins of darkness.

"Why? Why would the Creator do this? After all, you've sacrificed for It? After losing Maria, your son, your brother…? Why?"

"I asked It to spare the Gifted."

"What?"

"Earlier, It pulled me into Its office. It told me that it planned to wipe out your people if you killed Jacques, who It claimed was a 'necessary evil.' I know you. You can feed that 'I'm good,' bullshit to everyone else, but not me. I know that you're going to kill him... slowly. I know that you are going to make him bleed every last drop of that gunk in his veins and then kill him."

"What? Bu-bu-but how? I never told you—"

His hand found the back of my neck as he mashed his forehead against mine. "I know you better than you know yourself."

A tear streaked down my cheek. I grinned ruefully. "Damn you. You were going to give up everything because I'm a vindictive cunt, eh?"

"No. I'm giving up everything because I know what you will become. I know that you are destined for another universe, for other people, for your own glory."

"What? What do you mean?"

"It doesn't matter." He leaned his head back on the smashed headboard. I hadn't noticed, but his room, with its torn white drapes, tattered mattress, broken mirrors, was a mess. "None of it fucking matters now. Fuck, I didn't know how good it felt to curse. Being an angel, it would physically harm me to do so." He coughed. "It still hurts. But it hurts that bastard. It. Hurts. It. And I want nothing more than to hurt It the way It hurt me by kicking me out of the god damn family."

"Micha. I need to tell you something. But I'm scared. There's not gonna be enough time...and I—"

"I already know." His lips riddled with a forlorn smile. "You will make the most Supreme goddess. One of death and destruction, of sex appeal...and ruin...."

"How can I...? I've never liked killing or sex. And I'm not a man."

"Gifted women are divine in a sense. But you will be something other…you are soft…caring…and unbelievably trusting. You've been made out to be a monster…but you're just something idiots like Dorian and Jacques can't comprehend."

"That's why I need you…that's why I need you to stay with me. You see me for what I am…you see me, and you love me despite it—"

"In spite?" His other eye began to turn red as he growled. "You are above that. Do you hear me? You are above it all."

A tear dripped down my face as I dropped the dagger. "I can't do it…I'm not strong enough…I can't lose you!"

He grabbed my hands, now both of us shaking as he fought to contain his own darkness, and I fought to contain mine. He kissed my forehead. His eyes shut slowly.

"Do it."

"But I love you…" I bit my lip. The weight of the secret had been replaced by the weight of losing the only man that I'd ever loved so effortlessly. "How can you ask me to do this…when I…I…?"

"Aleilah!" His voice took on a harsh, commanding tone that made me snap to attention. "Now!"

My hand shot forward, blade in hand. It sank into his chest. I looked at his face, horrified, and saw nothing but a happy grimace.

His head fell forward on my shoulder as his body slowly broke away into bits of ash. It wasn't instant like other demons. His hand raised—but broke away before he could touch me. His lips moved at my neck, saying what I'd wanted to hear him confess since we'd both met.

"I love you, too. Aleilah. I always have."

The last to go was his head…and the pain-filled smile gracing his wanton lips. I moved to kiss him but before I could, he was gone.

My head threw back. I could feel my angelic blood in my veins, fighting to keep my rage contained. I let out a curdling, broken scream. I screamed not at the universe, but at the gods, who always managed to deny me what I wanted most.

Pure love.

CHAPTER TWENTY-SIX

HEALER

A month later, I kissed my son's cheek goodbye. Beatrice took his arm, waved it at me before whispering a prayer over him. I bit my tongue to keep from yelling at her to leave the Creator out of my fucking life. Yes, I was still angry. Yes, I still mourned him. But what could I do? When I told Dorian that Micha had Fallen and that I had to do away with him, he seemed pleased.

"I know he was good, being an angel and all, but I always felt like he wasn't really committed to the god he claimed to serve," Dorian said. "Maybe he was working for another god. It's good that you did that, bae. I'm proud of you."

And I smiled and said nothing. But inside, I wanted to become a god slayer, to ascend to my throne quicker and do away with the one who took him from me. God or not, it wasn't fair. Micha was trying to help the Creator keep a promise It'd made to *my* people and *my* Goddess. And now he was dead.

Where was the fairness in that?

"You're in charge if Beatrice gets overwhelmed," I told Hao before the boarding the private jet. "I'm counting on you."

He nodded and waved us off.

Dorian and Rhea were already on the jet when the doors closed. Dorian was reading a book penned by Immortals, believing it to hold the answers to all our plights. I hadn't told him that the Creator had gone back on Its promise for the Gifted. It was better that way—or so I thought.

Rhea was curled up a few seats away, her knees tucked under her chin, fire brimming not only in her eyes but on her shaking fingertips. She wasn't as quick to believe the news about Micha Falling—according to her, he "wouldn't do that—not without a good reason." The one good thing that came of this was that later in her room, when I wrapped my arm around her shoulder, she leaned into it.

"He wouldn't do that, Marve," she whispered, her voice breaking around the words. "He would never do that."

"Maybe we didn't know him as well as we thought," I told her, trying to console her.

And she closed her eyes and sobbed. And that's when I knew that her feelings for him were real. It wasn't just a fling. He really meant something to her. I don't know how he made people fall for him, but I knew that his effect on me had been more than real—and his death was catastrophic. And as I got up to leave, not shedding a single tear for fear of breaking down—of showing the Creator how much It hurt me—her next words stopped me dead in my tracks.

"I know that you loved him, too." I turned back around. "And I know that he felt the same. When he was inside of me, sometimes he would get this look. It was the look he got whenever he looked at you. He never said your name during, but I know that in a way, he belonged to you."

I turned the knob. "I have no idea what you're talking about."

I went back to my room, curled up in Dorian's arms, and after he'd drifted off to sleep, I wept. He wasn't mine. I had no claim to him— no right to love him. But I did. And I always would.

We touched down in a private airstrip in record time. In minutes, we were in the hospital where a renowned healer was said to reside. It made sense that if you could give disease, you could also take it away. With Dorian covering us with a Glamor, we walked through the halls, looking for a miracle.

It was nearly two hours later when we found one and when we did, I commanded my husband to drop the Glamor.

A man was surrounded by a crowd of people, laughing, and joking. He looked to be of Sidran decent with dark hair, naturally tanned skin, and a joking smile. When he turned, his black-as-coal eyes met mine. I knew that our connection was purely spiritual. The man raised his hand and the crowd parted like water. When he reached my party, there was an amused smile dancing on his lips.

"What can I do for you?" he said, his accent thick but not harsh.

He spoke Fabic, the mixture of French and Arabic that most Sidrans spoke. I looked around at the Mortals dotted around the hall. They watched us with bowed heads and trembling lips: praying. I turned back to the man. I asked him in Fabic if he had the powers that I'd heard of.

"Yes," he replied.

"Can you heal my friend?"

He glanced over at Rhea. He walked forward, took her hands in his, looking over her. Then he turned to me and frowned.

"She has no disease that I can see."

"She's bulimic."

"It needs to be a physical ailment. I can do nothing for mental illness."

"Shit!" I cursed in English.

"Marve?" Rhea asked, stepping close to me. "What's going on?"

"I was going to have him heal you, but he says that you have no disease."

"I have Lupus," she offered.

His eyes sparked like a flame to a wick. He asked her what kind. She said systematic, along with RA. He closed his hand around the back of her neck, pulled her forward. She gasped, stumbling.

He peered deep into her eyes. I could see the way she pressed her legs together, saw the blush on her cheeks. And then suddenly they both began to glow. Rhea began to shake, her body tossing from side to side. His eyes blinked once, twice, a third time and then cleared.

Rhea flexed her fingers in amazement. "I haven't felt this good in years."

"You've been healed."

"I'm guessing you can also cause disease?"

"Yes," Pestilence said, shadows dancing in his eyes, "when I was young. Now that I've mastered my powers, I can heal anything. I became a doctor so that I could enhance the lives of anyone I touch."

"Would you believe me if I said that I was the Gatekeeper and that you were destined to help me save the world?"

"Believe you?" The man threw back his head and laughed. "I've had dreams about this day since I was born. I know of my purpose and what the Creator has in store for me. I only hope that I can fulfill my duty."

"I like your style," I said, punching his arm. "What is your name?"

"Shafi," the man said, nodding at me. "And you?"

"My name is Marve Boyd." That familiar zing went through me. I wondered if I would ever get used to using my married name. "When does your shift end?"

"Seven o clock."

"At that time, I want you to tell your boss that you will be gone indefinitely. Then come to this location," I said as I slipped him a frayed piece of paper. "We are going to do great things together."

CHAPTER TWENTY-SEVEN

BREAKING AND ENTERING

I walked into the building, trying to look as normal as possible. I had on a lab coat, a pair of glasses and a blonde wig. In all honesty, I didn't think that blonde worked for me, but I had to go with it. After all, I didn't want my real self to be seen on the footage later or else I'd end up on the news for breaking into a morgue. I looked down at the ID on my coat.

Harper Ross.

The real Harper Ross was propped up next to a dumpster behind the building, blissfully knocked out with a compromised memory. I remember how I had to wait to catch her, lurking in the shadows as I used my electricity like a police scanner. Never had I felt more immoral or more Immortal. I was skimming through the thoughts of every person that passed through those doors—most for smoke breaks—to find exactly what I needed: a coroner. Subduing her was easy enough and so was taking her clothes. Putting on my disguise without anyone noticing, all the while staying out of the range of the camera, was harder.

I pushed open the doors of the morgue. A figure was hunched over a body on a metal table, a scalpel in her hand and a bemused smile on her face. I walked forward just as she stopped cutting.

"Well, Mister Reed, it seems that you were in a nasty accident. Your organs are completely melted, your skull is smashed in and there are bruises marring your face. Your left arm and stomach are charred and if I didn't know any better, I'd say you got in a fight with a nasty arsonist."

"Maybe he had a run-in with one of the Gifted," I said, stepping farther into the room and giving her my most eager smile. "A rambunctious bunch, a few of us. But who can blame us? We were born fighting."

Her brow furrowed. I surveyed her spiky jet-black hair and piercings. She was just as cool in real life as she was in the tv show.

"You look different." Her eyes flickered towards my name tag. "Did you dye your hair?"

"Harper is outside. My name is Marve. I've been extremely excited about meeting you."

Instead of taking a step back, Tess took a step forward. Her eyes hardened and I knew that she was expecting a fight. I respected her gusto, but I wanted to get this meeting off to a good start. After all, we were bound by fate…and I was her biggest fan. I still wondered why she immediately resorted to such hostility.

"What's wrong?" I cocked my head to the side, a smirk dancing on my lips. "You seem wound up."

"I'm tired of crazy ass fans like *you* breaking into my job!" Tess's eyes flashed. "That's why I quit *Strike It Rich*. Being famous means that I have no privacy. I can't have one day of peace without some psycho breaking into my job or house demanding an autograph."

Then she did something that I honestly didn't expect. She reached into her lab coat and pulled out a pen. She took a step towards me and instead of brandishing the object like some sort of weapon, she gave me a fake smile. She waved me forward. I stood firmly where I was, surprised.

"Come and get your damn autograph. I've got to get back to work." When I didn't move, she rolled her eyes, her smile instantly winking out. "Are you brain dead or something? Get your butt over here so that I can get back to work! I've got a family to feed."

"Family?" I looked at her shiny, swishing black hair, frighteningly chilly brown eyes and round, pale face. "You're pretty young."

"I'm aware that I'm not married, and I have a four-year-old daughter. Before you ask, I'm twenty-one. Yes, I was a teen mom. Whoop-dee-doo! Now would you come on already?"

I felt a sort of kinship with her. I was a young mother myself. Sometimes it was hard to remember that beneath all the magic, we were all still human.

"You are one of the Horsemen of the Apocalypse." I said, cutting straight to the chase. "It is my job to unite all of you. Before you ask, I can prove it," I said, remembering the dagger, which was good since I didn't want any more theatrics. "Please don't make this difficult."

"You think I'm a Horseman of the Apocalypse?"

"I don't think." My eyes met hers. "I know."

"Ok, so you're a bible freak *and* a nut!"

I reached down and pulled the Dagger of Truth from its holster. For a second, I stared at it, wondering how I should go about it. I guess I'd just have to just run at her and hope for the best. I took a few steps forward, dagger in hand. Tess raised the pen.

How did I know she was going to do that?

"Wait." I lowered the dagger. "Trust me."

"Why should I? You're coming at me with a freaking knife!"

"It's a dagger. In fact, a dagger is always symmetrical and both sharp edges always go down to a point from the side down. See?"

I twisted the dagger around so that she could see. Tess looked at me like I was crazy. I took another step forward and asked her to trust me. I also told her that in some way, she had to have known that I was coming for her. Something in her eyes changed and I honestly believed that it was a divine force at work when she walked forward. I smiled at her.

"Thank you for trusting me."

She glared back at me rather defiantly and said, "If you kill me, I'm so haunting your ass."

I reached out and wrapped my fingers around Tess's wrist. I was surprised by how cold she was. As soon as our skin made contact, my life flashed before my eyes, and I felt a bit of my soul break away and become a part of her. As Death, she was the commander of humans in a spiritual and a physical sense. She was the end to all life—the final destination in a dark tunnel.

In my eyes, that made her the strongest.

I pressed the tip of the dagger to Tess's wrist. Tess stiffened but did not move away. I respected her bravery. I traced the Dagger of Truth down in a thin line, watching as her skin began to glow gold. Before the light began to fade, I chanted a stream of quick thoughts in my head.

You are the Horsemen named Death. You need to come with me. I am the Gatekeeper. Follow me into battle. Trust me and I will lead you to glory.

"I believe you," Tess said. "Just one thing."

"Yes?" I said as I sheathed the dagger.

"If you *ever* pull a knife on me again, I will kill you."

"Noted." I withheld a smile. "Are you ready to go? The jet is waiting."

"You have a jet?" At my nod, she grinned. "I'm starting to like being a Horseman…"

We left the hospital. As soon as we were outside, I draped the lab coat over the unconscious body of the real Harper Ross before throwing my disguise in the dumpster. As we walked to the field where the jet was stationed, I asked Tess if anything weird had happened in her life pertaining to the deceased. She said that she'd always been drawn to cemeteries and that she'd even brought back her cocker spaniel Rudolph when he died of cancer when she was twelve.

"The cancer didn't go away, though."

"You'd need Pestilence for that." At her look I shook my head. "You have a very strong Gift."

"But both of my parents are Mortal," she replied.

"You had to have known you were special," I offered.

"Thank you," she said with a grin.

"I've been dying to tell you something since I walked into the morgue."

"Spill."

"I loved your show." I paused. "Is there anyone you need to say goodbye to before we go?"

She took out her phone and texted someone. I didn't miss the look of pain that crossed her face when she put up her phone. I understood completely. I felt the same way when I left my son.

It hurt. There was hope in your body, a hope that you would return. And there was a certain squeamishness. There was a nervousness that made your bones clammer together. And there was a terror that was branded onto your very soul, a fear that you would never see them again.

We got on the jet and flew to the Maeora. While we flew, I tried to catch a bit of shut eye. When I woke up, I was curled into Dorian's side, his scent washing over me like the healing powers of a prayer.

Rhea was watching us with envy in her eyes and I hated that I hurt her by killing Micha. If I'd known how much he meant to her I would've tried to think of an alternative to killing him. Sadly, I couldn't raise the dead and I wasn't going to ask Tess because one more fallen angel wasn't going to help our cause.

When we touched down in the Maeora, the first thing I did was go to a library. Since I'd told the others to wait in the jet—which had enough food, snacks, and drinks to let them live there for weeks—I had some alone time. I took that time to order my thoughts before sitting down at a computer. Since I had absolutely no idea where the Rose Court was located, I decided to look it up on the online. I was instantly hit with thousands of results.

Most were rallying people to join the Rose Court and fight for power, glory, honor, and fame. But at the bottom in little italics, it said that whoever fought there instantly earned their freedom. My heart swelled in pride at that. I scrolled through post after post of Immortals raving over the blood and gore, comparing it to a present-day Coliseum. I felt nauseous as I realized that I would have to reenter, but also a hint of excitement. But surprisingly, there was no nostalgia even though I'd spent most of my life fighting in arenas such as this.

After waiting around ten minutes for the computer to load, I pulled out my phone. I scrolled through some of the sites. My phone wasn't much better. It was one of the old touchscreen ones. One online newspaper article caught my attention and wouldn't let go— once it finally loaded on the dismally slow 5G data, that is.

FROM BOTSWANA TO FAME

Hail!
Fighter Khalil Hannah was only 14 when he left his
homeland to come to the Fatherland. With nothing but rags
and a picture of his family, Khalil was desperate for money.

He joined a free boxing class in his spare time of shining shoes. There he was discovered by the leader of the Rose Court, Martin Sawyer, an innovative man who taught Khalil to use his powers in exchange for his fighting skills in the arena. Martin Sawyer believed that only the strong and Gifted should be allowed to come out on top, so he designed the Rose Court to weed out any weakness in their race. Khalil quickly rose to glory, defeating opponent after opponent without breaking a sweat. He breezed through rounds so quickly that fans began to suspect that he'd made a bargain with the Creator to become stronger. After much convincing and a lot of lawsuits, it was decided that Khalil was just a natural born fighter. With his name on everyone's lips and his record intact, Khalil quickly gained followers; with their support, Khalil became Champion of the Rose Court. Any fighter that faces off with Khalil meets an untimely death. Is there anyone that can take down the man now known as the Black Sea?

My bets were that this Khalil Hannah was War and if things went as planned, he and I would be facing off. From the looks of it, he sounded like he would be a very good challenge. I scribbled down the address and time that the Rose Court would be open. With everything finished, I made my way to the jet, strapped myself in and got ready for takeoff. I ate some fruit and got a few winks of sleep, storing my energy for the Rose Court.

The promise of battle was the fuel that drove me.

CHAPTER TWENTY-EIGHT

PARTNERS

Luckily, I was able to sign up for the preliminary round without any cause for identification or papers marking me as property. I got a few stares, and someone even asked for my autograph. I grinned and gave it to the teenage Gifted girl, of course, but when she asked me where my Trainer was (some Gifted preferred to call our owners this instead of Masters/Mistresses) I told her that I was now free.

She smiled at me quizzically and asked me why I chose to fight.

I shrugged and said, "You can take the wolf out of Amoria, but you can't take the Amoria out of the wolf." She walked over to her Mistress and said nothing to me after that. I understood her concern, but no one could take me down ever again—and I would never bow to an Immortal, tournament or not.

The Immortal at the registration stand, which also doubled as a betting counter, waved me forward without even a glance, staring down at the screen in an almost robotic fashion. I guess Mr. Sawyer was eager to get as many participants as possible. Dorian, Rhea, Tess and Shafi were going to wait in the stands and cheer me on where it was safe, much to Tess's dismay.

"Why can't I join the fight, too? You said yourself that you would lead us to glory." Tess growled, her fists shaking. I could see the need to win in her eyes. *"This is the perfect chance!"*

"Right now, I need to keep you all safe. I'm not going in there to have fun," I said, and it was partially true. *"This is so that we can recruit War and get this show on the road."*

"You're not the boss of me." The woman said, crossing her arms. *"I can do what I want."*

"No, right now, you can't." I crossed my arms, too. *"You're serving the Creator."*

"I don't even believe in God…"

To that, I had no answer.

I was escorted to a large metal box on rails. There were two men inside dressed in dark brown clothing. Once I was inside, they looked at each other and nodded. I tensed, a knot of trepidation forming in my stomach. Instead of moving to attack like I thought they would, they instead raised their hands and pushed them forward. The cart scooted forward a few feet.

"I thought there would only be slaves here. Are you free?"

"In other places, the Gifted are persecuted, enslaved, or killed. Here at the Rose Court, at the border between Maeora and the Southern Isles, we are given food, a home, and a weekly salary," said the first man.

"Mr. Sawyer is very good to us," agreed the second man.

I remembered Dorian and the other Immortals that risked everything for us and smiled.

When we finally came to the next platform, the two men waited for me to step off before repeating their actions, this time in the opposite direction. I walked down the narrow platform and towards a door. When I opened it, I was immediately blasted with a wave of heat. The arena rose around me in a great display of metal and glass. The sky was closed off, the glass stretching up to enclose us in a large dome.

I looked around the arena. There were twenty-nine other contestants. I skimmed through the people, looking for Khalil, before remembering that here, the Champion was to sit with the Maker of the Games before coming down for the final fight. I looked past the crowd to a large gap in the arena. There sat a metal box with two throne-like chairs, one taller than the other. In the tallest one was the man in charge.

He had a harsh look, his hard face and strong jaw suggesting that he was indeed of Maeoran descent. A thick mustache rested on his upper lip, which moved as he conversed with the man next to him. He had one blue eye and one brown eye and as he turned to glance at the crowd, they gleamed with a mad sort of reasoning. He was dressed in extravagant green robes that pooled at his feet. He wore earthy brown slippers on his feet.

The man next to him was more machine than man. His eyes were emotionless like Alice's, except there was something missing in them—something that said that he felt absolutely nothing for living creatures, human or other. He wore no shirt but on his wrists were thick golden bands. His brown, lined body seemed to almost be carved from wood. His eyes were a turbulent blue that rivaled the skies and despite his appearance, he moved with a flowy grace akin to water.

Something about him awakened a darker side of me. I could hear Keres whispering through the halls of my mind, waiting to be set free. I walked to the center of the crowd and easily spotted my party in the stands. Rhea was cheering with her hands cupped around her mouth, as was Shafi and Tess. None of them had ever been to an arena before—they didn't know how brutal it could get.

Dorian was much more cautious, following my every move with his eyes.

My electricity made my body vibrate and when I moved, life blurred. I skimmed over Dorian's thoughts. He'd forgotten to take his medicine but that wasn't why he was anxious. He'd seen Khalil, too. He was worried.

Why is he always doubting my abilities?

"Welcome to the Rose Court!" The announcer yelled as he maneuvered a blue hovercraft. "Are you ready to RUMBLE?!"

The crowd went nuts. A chant for the Black Sea rose through the crowd like a tidal wave. There were four screens positioned at the tops of the stands so that the crowds could see the action up close. All of them switched to a live feed of the notorious Black Sea, who didn't even bother to raise his arm and wave. After a second of him glowering at the camera, the announcer continued to speak.

"Today we have thirty sacrifices—I mean *contestants*—in the Court today." At his joke, the crowd laughed. "Keep your eyes on the screens as I tell you about our eager contenders!"

To come up with a strategy, I listened extra carefully as he went through the other contestants. Keres was on overdrive, her bloodlust giving me a jolt of energy. I quickly promised myself that if my back was against the wall, I would not give into hatred and let Keres take over. Before I knew it, my name careened through the walls of my mind. My face flashed on the screen.

"Our last contestant is from the Southern Isles. Some of you may recognize her from the slave pits that are the Arenas of Death— her official title is Champion Marve of the Lightning Fists. She's got a young face and a shocking personality. But don't let that cute face fool you. She is a direct descendant of the first of us: Alice," the announcer said, and I didn't miss the way a shocked murmur rippled through the crowd. "And she's got powers that would shock even Zeus."

It was obvious that they did their research when entering every participant and that they were heavily implying that I had the Gift of electrokinesis. The contestants murmured among themselves, asking each other if any of them knew of me or my Gift.

It was easy to see that this group was all brawns and no brain.

I raised my fist in the air. The crowd cheered very loudly, obviously liking my enthusiasm. I let a small pulse roam over the crowd, using them as a distraction as I targeted my real subject: Khalil. The crowd rose in screams that rivaled the ones for the Black Sea and as they did, I used the moment to scan Khalil's thoughts. He was unimpressed and believed that he would crush most of us instantly.

The announcer said that the contestants would be pairing off in fifteen teams of two, fighting their way to the top. When there was one team left standing, the two former teammates would face off and whoever won would fight the reigning champion. The screens flashed a picture of what two teams would be facing off first tomorrow.

I was happy when I found out that I wasn't chosen. That would give me time to train and check out the other opponents.

Could this day get any better?

I gazed into the crowd. Instead of catching the eye of my friends, I fell prey to the gaze of Khalil. He was watching me with his narrowed heterochromatic eyes. I tried to intercept his thoughts again and was surprised by how easily I was let in. What I heard caused a chill to run through me as I was singled out.

Finally, a worthy opponent. I'm. Going. To. End. You.

This wasn't even a job to him. This was a sporting event that he never lost. He was destined to do this since the day he was born.

And there was no beating him at his own game.

* * *

The contestants were given a room with their partners and the ones who came to support them. Tess and Rhea decided to sleep in the two chairs and Shafi volunteered to sleep on the couch next to the dark-skinned girl who came with my partner, McKenzie. My partner was lying down in her bed, which was by the window, playing videogames. I walked over to her and stood there, watching her nimble fingers fly across the little keys, trying to get a feel for her. She immediately closed her videogame and rolled over to face me.

"Hello."

She had a breathless voice. Her face was a very light brown going into tan and I could tell that she was of mixed heritage, but passing nonetheless. There were freckles sprinkled across her nose. Her light blue dress hung off her shoulders and her hair was wild and curly, surrounding her face like a brown halo. She had a gapped tooth grin that seemed to fit her perfectly.

"Wow!" She said jokingly. "Your chest is about as flat as mine!"

I instantly liked her.

I laughed lightly. I wanted to ask her to train with me since she could control water. I stood near the edge of her bed, my tail flicking behind me. My partner watched it as if she were a catch watching a mouse, her eyes wide with wonder. I used that to break the ice.

"Is something wrong?"

"I've seen some freaky things," she said, "but I've never seen a person with a tail. Are you one of those demi-demons I've heard about?"

"No," I said with a laugh. "I'm afraid that I'm just a Gifted woman like you."

A free woman, I wanted to add.

"Do you think I can get one?"

I immediately imagined her with a dog's tail swishing behind her in excitement.

"No. Sorry."

"That's fine," she said, grinning. "So, why did you enter the Rose Court?"

I explained my situation to McKenzie. She didn't believe me until I pulled out the Dagger of Truth. She immediately pulled out something called The Handbook for All Things Magic (The Handbook for short.) She quickly flipped it open to a picture, looked between the two objects and spazzed out.

"OH MY GAWD!"

"You believe me?"

"Uh-huh!" She said with an eager nod.

"Why was your friend so cool with sleeping next to Shafi?" I glanced at the dark-skinned girl with long eyelashes and a permanent frown. "Do you think she likes him?"

Her eyes got comically big. "No!" McKenzie laughed. "That's my girlfriend."

"Oh." I nodded. I eyed her dark skin and sharp features. "She's beautiful."

McKenzie blushed. "She's amazing—she's always reminded me of what Kalysma would look like if she were skinnier...and—" McKenzie sat up and tucked her knees under her chin. "That's why I'm here. When I came out, my parents threw me out. Denise and I decided to leave town and start a life together. We've been living on the streets ever since. I'm hoping that if I win the Rose Court then we'll be rich and can get a place together."

"Your parents?" I asked, wondering why her story sounded so odd. But then it hit me. "You weren't captured?"

"No. We were both born free. Our parents were both smugglers for the Rebellion once upon a time but left once they had us."

"That's amazing!" My heart leapt. It seemed that I wasn't alone. "So were mine!"

I looked into her eyes. She must have been part of the 75% that looked human because she didn't share any of my features. When I said that, she grinned.

"That explains why you look so funny," she giggled.

My heart sank. "Funny?"

"Oh, no…" She paused, catching on to my mood. "I didn't mean it like that."

Of course she didn't, I thought. But I knew exactly what she meant. She thought that I was a freak. I took a step back and hunched into myself, trying to make myself appear smaller. I saw something that I hadn't noticed before: her shoulders untensed, her mouth softened, and her brow raised.

But deep down, I knew that I was beautiful.

"The Rose Court has a monetary prize?" I asked.

"Well, duh." McKenzie rolled her eyes good-naturedly. "You can either be Champion and live in a mansion with the Maker or you can take a prize of one million drachmas and go on your merry way."

But even better, this is a chance for people to earn their freedom, I thought to myself. I knew that McKenzie wouldn't understand— she'd been born free, as had I. But she'd also never been enslaved, which couldn't be said for me. I didn't even bring that up. It would just cause ridges in our relationship.

I smoothly continued the conversation, which hadn't halted in the few seconds it took my advanced brain to think those words: "I didn't know that. I thought you just fought and then went home."

"What would be the fun in that?" McKenzie said with a laugh. I admired her carefree nature. "Can I tell you a secret?"

"What?"

McKenzie's voice dropped low.

"Denise is, uh…totally human," she whispered conspiratorially.

"She's Mortal?" I peeked at Denise through my lashes, shocked when McKenzie shook her head. "You do realize that being together, you're putting her in danger, right? I mean, you could get her killed!"

"I know that!" McKenzie bit her lip, her face paling as she stared down at the covers. "Please don't tell anyone."

"You shouldn't tell people stuff like that," I said, glancing at the door. "The wrong person might hear you. You know the consequences for partnering with the Mortals."

It was one of the few things we were taught in school. Mortals weakened our Gifted bloodlines, therefore dampening the flames of our service to our future Masters and Mistresses. If we were caught in a relationship with one, we paid the price. I thought of the corpses strung high and burned, eliminating their chance of being revived through magic.

It wasn't worth the risk.

"I know the risk..." McKenzie whispered. Her mouth suddenly moved into a determined grin. "But she's worth it! When I win the prize money, I'm going to change all that. Mortals and magical humans will be able to comingle as one, man, woman, cis, trans, nonbinary—everyone. It'll be a free world for everyone!"

I cocked my head at her. Just like Jacques, she was gay and wanted all types of humans to be together. But Jacques wanted to crush everyone under his boot while McKenzie wanted to build everyone up, something that put them on two totally different planes of existence. Was it the harsh life of being discriminated against that made them want to unite everyone, no matter how different their reasoning?

"Sorry for getting us on this topic. I know it must be uncomfortable for you."

"Why is that?"

"You know..." She nudged me. "Because we're *gay*."

I sat down on the edge of her bed. My eyes found Dorian. My mouth softened into a smile. "That doesn't matter. My partner and I…we love based off personality. He used to be in a relationship with my former Master and a woman that I…well, I can't *stand*. But it's not because she's totally unlikable. It's because I know that deep down, she has qualities that I find magnetic. It's not in the same way that I want my husband but…it's enough to make me *feel*." As I admitted this, I felt my body come alive with energy. "My former Master was gay…even though he did awful things to me, that is one thing that I always felt a kinship with. We were both pariahs at one point. How could I not identify with that?"

McKenzie eyed me. "Are you sure you're not a lesbian?"

I shifted. "I'm demisexual, so my sexual attraction depends purely on feeling. But I don't think it should matter. We have people that can fly, people that can breathe under water—hell, even people with tails!" I unwrapped mine from around my waist and swished it in front of her face. "Why should it matter who we wake up next to?"

"Wow." She blinked owlishly. "No one's ever said that to me. Thank you."

"You shouldn't have to thank me for treating you like a person." I glanced over at my bed where Dorian lay. "I'm in love, too. We've had our share of difficulties as well."

"Did his parents not like you?"

"Both of our parents are dead."

"You're not *related*, are you?"

"God, no!" I couldn't help but laugh. "It's because I've been through things that left me…scarred. When I met him, I was very angry and…a little bit broken, I think. So was he. But the parts of him that were broken mended mine and vice-versa. He taught me how to love not only him, but myself, too." I laughed as tears touched my eyes, the first I'd cried since Micha died. "It's funny because now we're stronger than ever. I'd die for him in a heartbeat."

"Then maybe we're not so different…"

"Yeah." My idea from earlier popped back up in my head. "I have something important to ask you."

"Yes?"

"Would you like to train with me?" She appeared quizzical. "We also need to get our moves in sync."

"Why do you need to fight someone like me?"

"Because Khalil has the same Gift as you."

"Who's Khalil?"

"I forgot about his silly nickname." I rolled my eyes. "The Black Sea."

"*Oh.*" Her brows furrowed. "Why do they call him the Black Sea?"

"He can control water…"

"Yeah, you said that…"

"And…"

"Because he's black?" she asked.

I nodded.

"That's kinda racist."

"It's extremely racist." I nodded. "But hey, at least he's here of his own volition. At least he's free."

"Your Gift is mind-reading?" McKenzie nodded to herself. "That explains why they hyped you up so much during the introductions."

"No." I raised my hand and let electricity gather around my fingertips. "It's rather strange because my Gift has been evolving. Before, I could just control electricity. Now I can pick up on the electrical activity in someone's brain and read their thoughts like a picture book. Sometimes I can manipulate it and place a thought in someone's head," I lowered my hand, "but that's a work in progress."

"I've never heard of that before."

"What?"

"Someone's Gift evolving—getting stronger and doing new things. Usually, it's just the basics. Didn't they say that you were a descendant of Alice?"

"Yeah. She is my great-grandmother."

"Maybe that's why," McKenzie said with a shrug. "I guess we'll find out during training."

"Awesome." I reached out to fist bump her. "Are you ready to start?"

McKenzie yawned and blinked sleepily.

"I'm tired. Would you mind starting tomorrow?"

I normally would mind but she was so nice that I couldn't bring myself to say it.

"Of course not. Good night, McKenzie."

I walked to my own bed and snuggled close to Dorian. His scent of heather wrapped around me. He slept peacefully; the Trazodone having done its job. When I kissed his mouth, I could taste the bitterness of his medication. I just hoped that I'd survive these games and do what I was meant to do so that we could be one step closer to peace.

CHAPTER TWENTY-NINE

HEALING IS NOT LINEAR

I went and got breakfast for everyone in the room, using the walk to Patty's Patties to clear my mind. I got the food in record time and tipped the workers generously before making my way back to my room. On my way back I passed the Black Sea and his take on me hadn't improved in the few hours that passed while we slept. I tried not to make eye-contact, hoping that he believed me weak.

"Your game doesn't fool me, little girl," the man said, bumping me as he passed. "I'll see you in the arena."

"Yeah?" I yelled, probably waking up a few of the other contestants. "Well, you better bring you're A-game because you're going down!"

Khalil laughed as he turned down the hall.

"You're embarrassing," was the last thing he said before he disappeared.

Great, now I'm horny.

Someone opened their door and yelled at me to shut up. Fuming, I kicked down the door to my room and dumped all the food on one of the tables squished in the corner. Everyone stared at me and the door, not even reaching for the food.

"All right, you guys! It's six in the morning!" I clapped and they all moved towards the table. "Eat up!"

I picked up the door and put it in its frame. The bolts on the metal door and doorframe were broken. I held out my hand, waiting till the gathered electricity turned into flames. I placed my hand where the door joined, watching as the metal melted. When I lowered my hands, I was surprised when a steady stream of water hit the hot area, causing steam to fill the room. When the steam cleared, I was surprised to see that the door's hinges were warped but melded together, nonetheless.

I turned around to see McKenzie lower her hand, a smile on her face. I nodded my thanks before sitting on the ground next to Dorian's chair. He got up and held out a hand. I reluctantly sat down as he took a seat on the floor. He leaned over to kiss me good morning before picking up his burger.

"I wonder how Aiden is doing right now…" I said as I swallowed a bit of my French toast stick.

"I'm sure he's fine." Dorian gave me an encouraging grin. "Beatrice is taking care of him. You left her enough bottled milk to last a century."

"I know, it's just…"

"You wish you were there with him instead of here, right?" At my nod, Dorian reached out and squeezed my fingers. "I've been thinking the same thing every day."

It was crazy. Months ago, he'd been ready to murder the child. Now he was more dedicated to his role of being a father.

Must be the Creator's grace…

Once we were all done with breakfast, we each broke off into groups. Rhea, Denise, and Tess would hit the town to go shopping with a small donation from Dorian. McKenzie and I would train for a while. At my suggestion, Dorian and Shafi were going to stay in the room as guards in case someone decided to break in and snoop around in hopes of uncovering some of our secrets.

I didn't envy Dorian or Shafi but if things got ugly, I trusted the men to bust some skulls. McKenzie waved at Denise before nodding at me. Together we made our way outside. Since the Rose Court was in the southern end of the Maeora, it wasn't hard for me to pick a secluded training ground. The canyons were the obvious choice.

"But I'll be at a disadvantage."

"How so?"

"There's no water. How will I fight?"

"Can't you pull the water from the air?"

"Not fast enough to fight. Gimme a sec." She pulled out her phone. She gave a vocal command and a hologram appeared, mapping out the land. She spread out her arms and the map extended, reaching across the landscape. She said a few more words about water and a network appeared beneath the city of Maeora, showing that there was a source of water flowing throughout the land. "I know the perfect place."

* * *

Don't get me wrong—our location gave her the advantage but that wasn't what bothered me.

"The sewers?" I groaned in disgust, raising my hand to shield my nose. "Did you have to choose a place so smelly?"

"When Denise and I were living on the streets, sometimes we would get into trouble for stealing food. We would hide in the sewers to evade the cops. After a while, we decided to make it our home." At my expression, McKenzie laughed. "You'll get used to the smell."

I'd been homeless before, but I'd never considered the sewers a safe place—but then again, I never had to steal; my voice was my only companion and my only good. McKenzie inhaled deeply as if we were bathing in a bubbling stream and not wading in a pile of piss and feces. We walked farther into the sewers until we reached a ladder that led to a manhole. McKenzie explained that if our match got too rough and one of us wanted to bow out, we could climb the ladder and knock on the manhole, signifying that our fight was over.

"What if it's just because of the smell?"

"Then you can climb out the manhole and leave," McKenzie said with a shrug. "I won't stop you."

She was right. After a while, I didn't even notice the smell. McKenzie took her place at one end, and I stood at the other. We locked eyes. I was more than ready.

Ready...Set...Go!

McKenzie went straight to business. Her hands raised and with them came a wave of brown sludge. I climbed up the ladder and launched myself at her as electricity danced around my body. The other girl's eyes narrowed in a sort of determination that looked odd on her kind face. I moved like a clap of thunder, here one second and gone the next, each movement a part of a rhythmic dance that promised nothing but destruction.

I clung to the walls, shooting bolt after bolt from my fingertips. The water suddenly hit me, turning into steam due to the electricity. I raised my hands and a bolt fell from the sky. McKenzie was as fast as she looked, dodging the bolt, and sending a tentacle of water at my face. I sent a huge wave of electricity towards it, watching as McKenzie flew back, a large hole in her shirt where the electricity burned through.

She kneeled on the ground, gripping her chest. I didn't ease up, spinning in a circle to create a cyclone of electricity. I danced closer and closer, offering nothing but pain for my target. McKenzie suddenly stood and thrust her arm out. Two water tentacles shot towards me, wrapping around my ankles, and giving a sharp yank.

My feet flew out from under me, and I landed on the ground with a thud. I quickly got on my feet. I put my hands in front of me and McKenzie quickly copied my movements.

So that's her strategy. Watch the enemy and copy their moves. That way no one has the upper hand. I'm guessing she likes to wear her enemy down and then go for the final strike, unlike when I hit hard and fast. How do I defeat her?

The answer hit me head-on. McKenzie quickly raised her hands then brought them down slowly, making the water rise and fall in a tsunami. I ran forward through the sludge, sending bullet after bullet of electricity at her, knowing that she would do the same with her water. When I finally got close to McKenzie, she lifted a fortress of her water and trapped herself inside a bubble. I closed my eyes.

It was easy to penetrate the bubble with a sliver of electricity, keeping the bubble intact as I flipped through her thoughts like pictures in a scrap book. She was going to send a blast of water towards me in a few seconds. I sent a pattern of electricity into her brain, typing a code for my favorite sort of hack. Her mental shields fell.

McKenzie lowered her hands and as she did, the water fell with it.

I rushed forward with electricity crackling around my outstretched hand. McKenzie's face was a mask of shock as she tried to raise her hands time and time again. I wouldn't let her, sending that same message to her brain repeatedly: *do not move.* When I was close enough, I rammed by hand into her chest, ripping her shirt but not penetrating flesh. McKenzie flew back as the electricity rocked through her body.

Her feet dug into the ground. I watched as she tried and failed to raise her hand. I stopped sending thoughts to her and was surprised when she didn't attack but instead gripped her chest. Her breaths were labored, chattering through her lips like a bag of bones. When she looked up at me, blood was dripping from the corner of her mouth.

"McKenzie?" I asked, suddenly worried.

She gave a weak cough.

I quickly ran over to her. Panic seized me, making my body temperature rise which in turn made me pant. McKenzie gave me a weak smile as a flurry of coughs racked her body. When I finally reached her, I reached out. I was too late.

"You play too rough," she wheezed.

Then she lurched forward, her eyes falling closed. Her head hit the ground with a wet-sounding smack. I picked her up and threw her over my shoulder. McKenzie didn't wake as I forced open the manhole, spread my wings and flew her back to our room. I propped her up on the couch and watched her as I called everyone else and told them the situation.

They all agreed to come back. Dorian and Shafi decided to post themselves outside the door until everyone else got back. I was grateful because if anyone knew that McKenzie was injured this badly, we would either be disqualified or targeted for attack. Shafi checked over all the injuries, his hands hovering over McKenzie's chest and head. Denise kneeled next to McKenzie and held her hand. Every time I tried to apologize, the other woman simply shook her head and smoothed the hair back from McKenzie's face.

Tess hovered near the wall, as useless as I was. Neither of us were medics and had no idea what to do in a situation like this.

"It seems that you ruptured one of her aortic veins," Shafi said, standing.

"What does that mean?" asked Dorian.

"The aortic veins are one of the main arteries that carry blood from your heart. That's why she lost consciousness. Death is imminent in fifty percent of cases even with surgery."

Now Denise looked at me. Clouds of fury rolled across her dark face. It wasn't like I did this much damage on purpose. Still, she had every right to be mad. I lowered my eyes and looked at McKenzie.

"Is there anything you can do?" I asked quietly.

Shafi stepped forward. "I can perform emergency surgery."

"Will that save her?" Tess asked, peeling from the wall.

"I don't know."

*   *   *

Hours later, McKenzie sat next to me on the couch. There was gauze wrapped around her chest and shoulders. She looked like a mummy. She asked me how she would cover her bandages, always thinking of the tournament and, in a way, Denise. In response I handed her one of my leather jackets.

She put on the jacket and zipped it up. It fit her like a glove, most likely because we were both a size six. McKenzie winced when she stretched, a fact that she tried to hide from all of us. That's why we politely looked away as soon as we saw her arms begin to move. The only one who couldn't look away was Denise, whose heart broke every time that look of discomfort crossed her girlfriend's face.

I felt as if I was going to hurl any moment. Guilt gnawed at my stomach like a dog on a bone. It was a vicious monster, destroying everything in its path. Denise was quick to forgive me now that McKenzie was up and moving. I couldn't forgive myself.

After all, I'd almost killed my partner. If she'd died, not only would I have killed a good person, but I also would have probably been disqualified. Then I wouldn't have a chance to recruit War. The whole world would be at stake. Why did stuff like this keep happening?

Why couldn't I control myself?

A beast can never be controlled, my old master's voice said, careening through the walls of my mind. *Animals rely on instinct alone. That's what sets apart beast from man.*

A voice came over the intercom, saying that the first round of fighting was going to start in a few minutes. McKenzie stood and grabbed Denise's hand. I strolled over to Dorian and did the same, loving how he looked at me like I was his best friend, which made me feel less dark inside. Rhea, Tess and Shafi left the room after us, huddled together as they discussed the tournament.

"Are you guys ready?" I said, leading us into the stands.

I received cries of excitement.

We took our seats just as the announcer appeared with his hovercraft. Tess watched the match as if she was the one that was going to fight as she analyzed everyone's moves. I didn't realize that she was also jotting them down in a small notebook until I registered the sound of a pencil scratching against paper.

What was she planning?

I straightened up and looked away from her to gaze at the arena. This was no time to get hung up over one girl's hurried notes. The games were just beginning.

The first match of the day included four people facing off. This match included a dark, tall, lithe girl named Wynonna and her partner Latasha, who was in a class of her own. Both women stood above six feet. Their opponents were a pale nerdy looking girl named Rebecca, who wore glasses and an ancient computer that hung on a cord around her neck. Her partner was a guy with a charming smile and bronze hair named Ezekiel. The match began with Latasha and Wynonna charging at their opponents, looking more like Amazonian goddesses than actual people.

Wynonna gave a shout as she rammed her fist into Rebecca's face. Rebecca fell, her computer smashing to bits. Her face folded in anguish.

"No!" Rebecca cried in frustration. "I was just about to formulate a winning strategy!"

Wynonna rammed her fist into the girl's face time and time again. Latasha was chasing Ezekiel around the arena. The guy was screaming like a little girl but managed to dodge a few of her hits. Wynonna lifted Rebecca's by the shirt while simultaneously picking up a jagged piece of glass from the computer. A split second later, Rebecca's lifeless body fell to the ground, blood pooling around her from a slit on her dainty neck.

Wynonna moved to help Latasha, her mouth in a grim line. She took one side of the ring while Latasha took the other, boxing Ezekiel in like an animal on the run. Suddenly, he seemed to realize that he had nowhere to run as the two women backed him into a corner. Keres cheered in my head. In a matter of seconds, Latasha cut off the boy's screams with one quick blow to the head.

Latasha and Wynonna turned around, pumping their fists into the air. The crowd clapped politely, and I knew that they were hoping for more theatrics. Lives were just numbers in a big line of entertainment for these people. McKenzie watched everyone with a calculative look. I watched her from the corner of my eye.

Maybe she was more dangerous than I thought.

The second and final match of the day was way more interesting. It was awesome because the second match of each day was timed and was decided by a point system. When the two finalists faced off, their match would follow these same rules, as would the fight of the winning challenger when they faced off against the ruler of the Rose

Court. I watched as a hyperactive Japanese girl took the stage, her black hair dyed with streaks of blue and her eyes a pale purple. She was Nephilim.

Kikyō's partner was an Espanzan boy named Javier. He had curly brown hair and moody grey eyes. The two put on a stunning performance, moving together in a way could only be mastered by being reincarnated and living many long lives together. This was an especially interesting match to watch considering that Kikyō had hidden poison-dipped senbon in her hair. She threw them with deadly accuracy, hitting one of her opponent's acupuncture points.

The tall, lanky, grey-bearded man named Graham fell to the ground. He tried and failed to stand as the poison worked its way through his body. His partner—a dainty Amorian girl with blonde hair and brown eyes named Rose—did little to help. She held a whip in her hand and when her hand flew out, it ensnared Javier's ankle. She tried to tug on it but wasn't strong enough.

Javier quickly overpowered her, pulling so hard that he dragged Rose across the stadium. Rose kicked and screamed the whole way, tears pouring down her face as she begged Graham to save her. Her partner clapped his hands, and a gust of wind flew through the air, cutting the leather whip. Rose was still in grabbing distance and when Javier had her, he strangled her to death in a few seconds.

Graham was no fool.

He raised his hands and clapped three times.

"What's this?" The announcer sped forward on his hovercraft, hovering above Graham, whose face appeared on the screens. "It seems that one of the contestants is forfeiting the match!"

Kikyō may have been part angel, but she didn't hold one merciful bone in her body. A senbon cut through the air and embedded itself in Graham's neck. He fell forward and landed on the ground with a crash, his body twitching before finally going still as the poison took his life.

The announcer looked at Martin Sawyer, the Maker of the Games, and waited for his call. It *was* against the rules. We all waited with bated breath, wondering what his call would be.

He allowed it.

CHAPTER THIRTY

RUFFLED
FEATHERS

As we all exited the arena, murmurs poured from the audience's mouths like smoke and floated above our heads. I looked around to see the other contestants mixed in the crowd. Wynonna, Rebecca, Kikyō and Javier got onto a lift and quickly disappeared. When I looked at a clock, I was surprised to see that the matches had taken a total of one hour. It hadn't felt like so long when we watched the competition.

It wasn't even one o clock, so we had a lot of time to kill until the next match tomorrow. Before we could get out of the arena, though, the screens flashed with the next contestants. It seemed that McKenzie and I would be fighting a Maeoran named Hans and his partner Rachel, who seemed more like a blonde Energizer bunny than anything else. Then a stocky black guy named Emmett would pair up with a woman from the northernmost Isle named Naomi.

They would be facing off against a mouse-like girl named Kimmy and a silent, burly guy named Kwan.

Now that we knew who our opponents were, we could think up a winning strategy.

However, now was not the time for that.

Now was the time for fun.

"What do you guys want to do?" I asked as I held Dorian's hand in mine.

"Denise thinks we should train for our upcoming match."

"That's an awesome idea!" Dorian was quick to wind a golden hand around my waist. "Rhea, Shafi and Tess can train with me. I'm sure we'll need to beef up for the upcoming battle."

"Finally, I get to punch *someone*," Tess said, running a hand through her spiky hair.

Tess suggested that we train in the canyons by the water since it was the one place where we wouldn't be seen. (Most people avoided them since it was rumored to have some nasty creatures lurking about.) We went back to the room, and I changed into my battle armor before heading out. As we walked, I tried to strike up a conversation with Rhea. I hadn't spent much time with her. And I'd never formally apologized.

"So, how do you like being a part of the Boyd family?"

Wrong question.

The older woman's face screwed up as if she smelled something awful. Dorian glanced at me, and I gave him a shooing motion. This was something that I had to resolve on my own. He quickly looked away. Rhea, on the other hand, looked at me and gave me a hard, unfriendly look.

"That reminds me!" *Oh, shit...* "Don't think our time at the mall changes things. I'm still mad at you."

That doesn't sound good. "You're still mad at me?"

"Believe it or not, I don't like it so much. You're cruel and sadistic. And you're kind of a bitch."

"I'm sorry?"

"I don't like being your *slave*, Marve."

"You're not," I wanted to say but my mouth had dried up instantaneously.

Still, I couldn't really deny it. It was *true*. I was treating her the same way Jacques used to treat me. No, I wasn't verbally abusive, but I left her with no free will. I was every bit the Mistress that I despised.

"Well—"

But she was on a roll now. I could tell that she'd been bottling a lot up. All the things that she'd wanted to say, she could say now.

"Maybe if you weren't so busy riding Micha's dick you wouldn't be up my ass all the time."

I sputtered. I glanced at Dorian to see him in a heated discussion with Tess. She looked angry. I glanced back at Rhea. She was red in the face, her golden eyes a deep amber that was dark with haunted shadows.

I'd really hurt her.

"I'm sorry for the way I've been treating you. You're right. It was unfair and very immature of me to manipulate you. And I'm sorry for getting in between you and Micha—you guys had something really special, and I ruined it. I was awful."

"I really liked him," she whispered, tears filling her eyes. "And you murdered him."

"I didn't just like him," I told her. "It wasn't just a crush."

You are Fated. Just like you and Dorian.

Fated. Matched. Mated. What good is it if they're all I have?

Why would you, said Kalysma, *need anyone who treats you as less-than. You are a goddess in the making. You do not need the likes of Rhea. And you don't need to bow to her to keep her from walking out of your life.*

Crush her under your boot! Keres jeered.

No, surprisingly disagreed Kalysma, *forgive her and let her go. Don't let her mistreat her because of your bond with her aunt. Nor because you're hoping to entangle with her.*

I scoffed. *Entangle!*

I am your Goddess. It felt like Kalysma was smirking. *I know you better than you know yourself.*

"If you cared so much," Rhea continued, "why did you murder him? Were you angry with him?"

"For what?!"

"For being better than you. For trying to save your marriage. For rejecting you."

"He didn't reject me," I said, "but he knew that it wasn't the right time for us."

"You're right. It wasn't. It was *our* time."

"Can you find it in your heart to forgive me?"

I stopped walking as I felt all eyes on me. I looked at my party, who seemed more shocked than necessary in my opinion. Why were they staring at me like that?

"The Mighty One stops telling us what to do and apologizes."

"I'm sorry for holding you back, Tess," I said, facing the one who'd spoken. "I shouldn't have told you that you couldn't enter the competition. And I—"

"Me, me, me!" Tess's voice bounced off the mountains as she unleashed her rage. "I don't think you have any divine mission other than being a control freak and making us all miserable!"

Everyone else was completely silent and I took that as confirmation. I thought that Tess and I had mended our old wounds. Obviously, she was still pissed. I gathered my electricity inside until it pooled in my stomach and then skimmed her thoughts. Could it really be that simple?

It was her birthday.

"Oh, yeah, there's something I forgot to tell you." I faced Tess and I could tell by the way her fists balled in anger that she was expecting me to say something rude and nasty. "Happy birthday."

She blinked and I watched as the anger and frustration slowly bled from her eyes. Maybe she wasn't still angry about before. Maybe she just had some misplaced anger at the fact that no one remembered that it was her birthday.

Granted, she didn't tell us...

"How did you know it was my birthday?"

"Lucky guess?"

Tess watched me for a moment and I knew that she didn't believe me. She was smarter than I gave her credit for. I paused.

"I am your biggest fan after all."

She glared at me.

"I looked it up on your fanbase," I said, digging into my pocket to pull out my phone.

She stared at me for a moment before shrugging and continuing.

When we reached our training spot, McKenzie turned in a wide circle, her arms outstretched as she absorbed the beauty of the red, sloping canyons. As she completed her final turn her eyes connected with mine. She knew what I did.

"McKenzie and I are supposed to be training together, so let's have a teamed match." I cracked my knuckles as my face split in a grin. "It'll be me and McKenzie against Tess and Dorian. Shafi, I want you to be the medic in case someone gets too badly injured. Denise, since you're non-magic, I want you to be the referee."

"Wait." Dorian held up his hand, glancing between Denise and me. "She's Mortal?"

"That's against the law!" Shafi cried as he glared at McKenzie. "You aren't allowed to bring a Mortal to the arena whether you're dating or fucking or whatever the hell it is you two are doing!"

"We aren't dating," McKenzie said weakly, her face paling under that light shade of brown.

"Don't lie." Shafi gestured between the two. "Only an idiot would miss the way you two look at each other."

McKenzie looked at me. It was obvious that at least two members of the group knew her secret and didn't approve. I didn't *mean* to let her secret come out. It just kind of slipped out! But judging by the look on Shafi's face, he knew at least half of the truth.

"Look, we all know that they're dating, and that Denise isn't one of us." At my words, McKenzie looked as if I'd walked up and smacked her. On the other hand, Denise looked severe as usual. "That doesn't mean that we have to ostracize them."

"This could put all of us in danger." Shafi crossed his arms. "If the Elders find out about this, we could all be killed."

"Wait." I paused. "Who are the Elders?"

The magic-folk gave me an incredulous look. Rhea was the only one that looked as confused as me. She was Mortal and had been raised in the Southern Isles, *away* from the Land of the Three's influence and under the judgement of free people. Denise was gazing at the mountains, her gaze remote. I could see that her hands were shaking inside her gloves. She was not as fearless as she seemed.

"Do you know who the Elders are, Denise?" I asked.

She shook her head. They way McKenzie's eyes darted confirmed it. I looked back at Dorian.

"How are you Gifted," my husband said slowly, trying not to offend me, "and you don't know who the Elders are?"

I felt something break at the careful incredulity on my husband's face. I felt angry and left out. Yet another thing that my old master had kept from me. Who knew who these guys were? But as they afforded me a cautious look, I knew that whoever these 'Elders' were, they were important.

"My old Master kept me looked in a room with barred windows in a mansion in the middle of the forest. The only time I left was to kill someone in the arena. Then it was straight back home. When I was young, I once asked him who made laws for our kind. He told me that he was the supreme law and beat me for questioning his divinity."

Silence hung in the air. McKenzie slapped a hand over her mouth, and I knew that she was trying not to cry. Rhea bumped her hip against mine, offering her support. I shrugged it all off. This was life for me back then.

I suddenly realized that there was no changing it.

I lost my parents very young. I was abused mentally, physically, emotionally, and sexually by a wannabe god. I had a rough life growing up. Plus, I wasn't the most morally correct person on the Earth. But I was the chosen one and I had to stop feeling sorry for myself.

I came back to reality just as I realized that everyone was waiting for me to say something.

"Now," I said once the tension had cleared, "who are the Elders?"

McKenzie pulled out her guidebook and read a small passage. The Elders were basically the law makers of all things magic. They were some of the first magic-folk created and knew firsthand what could happen if the use of magic got out of hand. They were the reason that Masters and Mistresses were to try and keep their slaves alive instead of killing them when they annoyed them or proved to be too weak. They also helped slaves who were in trouble with Masters that were overly abusive.

Where were the Elders when I needed them? Said a small voice in the back of my head.

But the rest of me had finally come to terms with everything and honestly didn't care.

"We promise not to tell anyone else your secret," Shafi said once it was obvious that the conversation wasn't going anywhere, "if you promise that you will tell no one else of Denise's mortality. That would put all of us in danger. Do you agree to these terms?"

The couple nodded, Denise more reluctantly than her girlfriend. With nothing more to speak of, we split off into groups. Denise stood about twenty feet away from us, watching us like a hawk with her grey eyes. I knew by the way her eyes lingered on McKenzie that she only agreed to judge us just to make sure that her partner wasn't hurt. I respected her dedication to her partner in crime.

Before we could begin, however, Tess pulled out her little black book and raised it high.

"What is that, Tess?" I asked, which we all knew was a nice way of asking what was in the book that she had been so ardently studying over.

"While the first rounds were underway, I decided to take notes on the other contestants." Tess raised her chin high, proud of her work—and with good reason. "This book is your salvation."

I snatched it out of her hand, ignoring her protest. I penned through it. She really was our salvation. In the book was the strengths, weaknesses, estimated heights, weights, names and other important characteristics on our enemies. I never knew that she was so cunning!

Okay, maybe I did know that, but that's beside the point.

"Wow."

I was seriously impressed. Shafi started a slow clap that we all readily threw ourselves into. Rhea high-fived Tess before walking towards me.

"You forgot to tell me something," I told Rhea.

"What is that?" she asked in her husky Espanzan accent.

"Do you forgive me?"

"Huh?" She blinked at me.

"Do you forgive me for how I treated you?"

"You know," she said, "I don't have to like you. Just because we work together, live in the same place, fucked the same men…doesn't mean we have to be friends."

Dorian coughed a word that sounded suspiciously like, 'hater.'

I snorted out a laugh. "Whatever."

But that stung. I thought women were supposed to look out for one another. And for a long time, I'd done nothing to her! She'd done more to me than I had her. But, again, she had a point.

I mean, I couldn't make her like me. And I had to respect her boundaries.

No matter how much I wished it was otherwise.

Tess leaned down and whispered in my ear, "Don't try so hard."

I shrank.

We took our positions as Tess read a bit of info from the handbook. My enemies seemed seriously strong. I'd been trained by a battle angel so I knew that I could hold my own. It was McKenzie that I was worried about. Her mind was open to intrusion and to be honest, her body wasn't much stronger.

McKenzie gave me an eager grin, all confidence.

"So, what's our strategy, partner?" she said.

"As Tess said, Wynonna and Latasha win by splitting you up and beating you down with a bunch of hard, relentless attacks."

"What do we do, then?"

"We stick together. Keep up a good defense and hit twice as hard when they leave an opening." It was easier said than done. "We should also split them up and take them down one-by-one if necessary."

"That's a good strategy."

I shrugged. It was no biggie.

I looked at Denise and nodded. She yelled for us to begin. We were off in a matter of seconds.

Dorian came at me with a volley of attacks, his hits flying like the sharp, staccato notes of a violin. I thought of the training with the daggers as I dodged each one of his punches before sending my own flurry of attacks at him. He caught my fist with a grin. That was his mistake. When he started to poke around in my head, I channeled electricity through my body and down my arm.

His back arched as he dropped to his knees. Smoke poured from his body as he jerked around like a fish out of water. Guilt and shame rocked through me as I realized that I'd tried too hard once again. I kneeled over him, brushing the hair out his eyes. His leg twitched and suddenly he was on me, tackling me to the ground.

"Whoa!"

I tried to brace myself for the hard, jagged ground of the mountain as I fell. Dorian quickly grabbed my hand as his eyes began to glow with that familiar light. I ramped another bolt of electricity through my body, ignoring the heat that pooled in my stomach as my husband slid against me. Before I could get too caught up in the onslaught of physical sensations, I called on something much stronger. I blasted electricity from my body, knocking Dorian off me.

I heard a soft, feminine voice cry out. I looked over to see Tess on top of McKenzie, pummeling her in the face with her fists. McKenzie was thrashing, trying to flip the other woman off. Shafi whispered something to Denise, who was staring at Tess with a murderous look in her eyes. Denise called a time out.

But Tess didn't stop.

None of us were prepared for what happened next. Denise bounded over to Tess, grabbed her by her hair and yanked her off McKenzie. The usually quiet woman was shaking in rage, and it was easy to see the thousands of words that were bubbling under her closed lips. Tess got up, whirled around and shoved Denise. The other woman flew back but got up twice as fast, ready for a fight.

I was between them in a matter of seconds.

"That's enough, guys." I crossed my arms. "We won't get very far in training if you two kill each other."

Denise glared at Tess, who seemed unruffled.

"Denise," I said, making eye contact with her, "I know that you love McKenzie. I also know that you want to protect her. But you can't jump in when you think she's getting beat too bad in the arena. You want a fair shot for the prize money, right? Start acting like it."

There was a smug look on Tess's face as McKenzie stumbled to her feet. Denise was by her side in an instant, wrapping her arm around McKenzie's waist, grabbing her hands, and peppering small kisses on her fingers. I looked away as they went off to their own little world, wishing that I had the luxury to get lost in Dorian without all this drama looming over my head. Tess looked at me, obviously thinking that I was about to shower her with praise. She couldn't have been farther from the truth.

"Tess, you used unnecessary aggression. You attacked your opponent when they were down, which is acceptable in real combat, but the way you went about it was cruel. You need to learn to stop being so hot-headed and control yourself. I won't allow for anyone to be murdered by another in the group—Horseman or not. Do you understand?"

"So, I do what I want and I'm wrong? Then I do what you say and I'm a jerk? You know what? Screw this and everyone here! I'm going back to the room."

She stomped off, angrily hunched against the wind. I walked over to McKenzie. Something wasn't adding up.

"When we sparred, you were phenomenal. You matched me blow for blow. What changed?"

"I was watching you and Dorian fight." A blush dusted McKenzie's cheeks as Denise rubbed soothing circles on her back. "I didn't mean to. I just glanced over, and I couldn't look away. I'm sorry."

I raised an eyebrow. "What the hell was so distracting?"

"It was the way you both moved," Shafi spoke up, walking towards our small group. "You two were like two parts of the same person. You moved, he moved, you swung, he dodged and vise-versa. I must admit that I was also quite mesmerized. I think that's why Denise didn't think to make the call on Tess until it was too late."

Dorian walked over to McKenzie, twig in hand, and drew a healing rune on her. I didn't notice McKenzie's black eye or busted lip until they began to heal. Denise picked up some snow and rubbed it on her face. By the time Denise patted her face with her sleeve, McKenzie looked as if the fight had never happened.

"Lame ass bitches..." Muttered Denise. "Like what is with magic-folk always being in competition with each other?"

I nodded in agreement but said nothing.

"Couldn't agree more," said McKenzie. "It's weird as fuck."

"She's right though," said Denise, looking at me, "don't try so hard."

"You're great the way you are!" chirped McKenzie.

"And you'll make friends on your own. Who's meant for you will find you," said the other in finality, before kissing her girlfriend's cheek.

Dorian swung an arm around my shoulder. I snuggled into his side. It seemed that we were in total sync. Was that because of the day that I died, and the power of the Boyd family saved me? Or perhaps it was because we were linked by marital runes? Or maybe we were in love and knew each other well?

Either way, it was awesome.

"It was fun sparring with you all. Thank you." I pulled out my phone and glanced at the time. "We still have four hours. What do we do now?"

"We could take a walk in the park or something."

McKenzie was bouncing up and down.

Something was off, though.

"No." Dorian was quick to shoot her down. "You all are going to face off tomorrow. You both need to keep training. How about we all train separately? Marve, you need to work on mastering your lightning. Your attacks are strong—but you keep on losing control and putting too much force behind each hit."

McKenzie nodded and separated herself and Denise from the rest of the pack. Shafi sat down where a sickly desert rat was curled up in a ball. It huddled against the wind, staring up with wide, frightened eyes. Shafi waved his hand over the furry, grey, long-tailed creature and I watched as it began to age backwards.

In seconds, it looked like a newborn. It was completely healed! It walked up to Shafi, rubbed its face against his hand, before scampering off. And he smiled as if nothing gave him greater joy. Dorian pulled me away and directed my attention elsewhere.

"When we were fighting, I felt you do something weird. It was like I could feel you inside of my head. Explain what happened right now or so help me, I will bend you over my knee and spank you right here."

That didn't sound like a bad idea. But as I looked at Dorian, I realized that he was serious. I didn't want to tell him what was happening. Part of it was because I hadn't mastered it yet. The other reason was because I didn't want him to be afraid of me.

Silly, huh?

I told him exactly what I told McKenzie, staring at the ground the entire time. He kept quiet until the end and when he asked me why I'd kept the whole thing a secret, I told him my reasoning, too. I felt his fingers wrap around my chin. He tilted my head up and, in an instant, his lips swept over mine, causing the air to fly out of me. I forgot how to breathe. He kissed me softly but very passionately and when he pulled away, I had to lean on him for support because my knees were so wobbly.

"Why did you do that?" I said, my toes curling on the ground.

"You're so silly sometimes. I'm with you for better or worse, remember?"

I kissed him again before I remembered something. He grinned at me. I gave him a voltage-charged punch to the ribs.

"Ouch!" he hissed. "What was that for?"

"That's for making me think you were hurt!"

He gave a booming laugh. I sat down on the ground. Dorian must have sensed that playtime was over as he moved to talk to Shafi. I closed my eyes and delved into the deepest pits of my mind. Keres was still chained to the rock, but something was very off. She seemed *stronger* somehow.

"Why hello, maggot," she purred, giving me a jagged toothed grin.

"Hello." I inclined my head in a polite nod. "I want to ask you something."

"If it has anything to with Micha—"

"Micha is dead. This has nothing to do with him. This is between you and me."

"Ooh. Feisty! Tell me what's on your mind, little worm."

"My powers are stronger—so strong, in fact, that I'm having more trouble controlling them than ever. I've looked into people's brains more than once and I'm pretty sure that I did some permanent damage to McKenzie. You'd better tell me what's going on now or I—"

"You'll what?" Her pouty mouth twisted into a sneer as her blue hair fell into her face. "You forget—I'm you. There's nothing you can do to me without harming yourself. As for McKenzie, why does it matter? She's fine."

"I don't know…" A black worm writhed in my stomach. "I can't explain it. I feel like she's hurt more than she's letting on. If she's damaged, then so are my chances at winning the Rose Court."

"I wish I could take credit for this, little one," she purred, "but I have nothing to do with this. Maybe you're doing it on purpose, and you just don't know it."

I knew better now. I told her just as much. After all, after everything that'd happened, I was stronger in more ways than one. I loved my friends and had a unique bond with everyone in the group. Keres's half-assed attempt to confuse me wouldn't work this time because I knew that I didn't want to hurt anyone anymore.

I took a step away from her prison, only half finished.

"Is something wrong with McKenzie?"

"Does she seem hurt?"

"No."

"Then she's fine."

"Well, answer this: how do I get through to Tess?"

"You two are not that different. You both like a challenge and you both tend to push too hard. You also tend to lash out when overwhelmed."

I thought of earlier. When I suggested that we spar, Tess was agreeable. She was also in her element. When I scolded her for being too rough with McKenzie, she backlashed. We'd both hurt the same person except the only difference was that I was worried about it—and she wasn't.

That made all the difference.

"Thanks for your help, Keres." I turned and began to exit the subconscious prison. "I'll see you next time."

"Goodbye, Marve. I can't wait to use you again."

Her ghostly cackle followed me as I made it back to the physical world, causing a chill to run to-and-fro on my spine. I glanced at the sky, noting that the sun was beginning to go down. I told everyone to go back to the room and freshen up. When they were all gone, I spread my wings behind me, causing the air to stir. It was time to fly again.

I took to the sky, streaking like a comet. I flew over the trees at the base of the red-rocked canyons. I stuck out my fingers and felt the pillow soft feel of flower petals. I doubled back and flew over the mountain, my eyes peeling away every rock and crevice to unearth what lay beneath—solitude. I flew towards a small spot where the canyon sloped down and landed.

It was time to do something that I'd wanted to do since I left home. I dug out my phone and pressed the number two on speed dial. The phone was immediately answered.

"Hello?"

"Hello, Lady Boyd."

I could hear Aiden squalling in the background. My heart swelled in my chest. I told Beatrice to give the phone to Aiden. She mumbled something to him. I laughed as I heard my son mumble garbled baby talk into the phone.

"Hello, my love." I grinned, feeling happier than I had in quite a while. "Mommy loves you."

Aiden jabbered something else.

"Are you growing big and strong? I miss you so much. I promise you that I'll be home soon."

There was an odd, muffled noise. I could hear Aiden's breathing. Suddenly, I heard Beatrice. The sound of Aiden's small wails and something crashing to the floor filled the phone. What had happened?

"What's wrong?" I clutched the phone. "Is Aiden okay?"

"He's fine, mem," Beatrice said in that polite, submissive voice of hers. *"Your son stuck the phone in his mouth, so I had to take it away. Now he's crying. I'm sorry."*

"It's fine. I just wanted to check up on him." A strong emotional hand locked around my throat, making it hard to breathe. "Thank you for everything you've done."

"It's no problem, mem."

It was official. When this was all over, I was going to take Dorian, Aiden, and I to a distant land. We were going to be a happy family—together forever. I would devote all my time to my two favorite people in the world. I was going to, finally, be a mother.

The position that I was always too busy to fill.

"Has Jacques attacked you all?"

"No. He came once and left after sniffing the air. I think he figured out that you weren't here because he couldn't smell you and lost interest."

"That's fantastic! Well, I'll be seeing you."

I hung up the phone and took off towards the store. I picked up a batch of cupcakes and a few candles before I flew back towards the Rose Court. When I entered the room, Tess seemed to be in higher spirits, telling everyone a story of when she crapped herself riding the world's tallest roller coaster. I put the candles in the cupcakes, lit them and brought them towards Tess. Everyone else caught on and we sang happy birthday before watching as she blew the candles out.

"Yay!" McKenzie cried out, always in good spirits. "Happy birthday!"

The rest of us mimicked her.

"So," Shafi said, "what did you wish for?"

"I wished that this concert would be as awesome as it sounds," Tess said with a smirk.

We all laughed and stood. This would be our last bit of free time before our match. We had to make it count.

"All right, then," I grinned. "Let's go!"

CHAPTER THIRTY-ONE

FIELD OF KISSES

*D*orian and I were in the field that Micha and I once laid in. We were kissing heavily, teeth scraping skin and tongues dipping in crevices. A part of me knew that this was the wrong environment for this kind of dream but the rest of me didn't care enough to wake up.

With a movement of his hips, Dorian rolled us over, him now on top. My hands were caught in his hair and my skin felt like it was on fire. It was the good kind of fire that scalded to the touch and left me feeling greedy when it died out. Dorian kissed me once, twice, then a third time. His mouth was everywhere and all I could think was how right our joining was.

Dorian kissed me once more before his clothes fell away. He was my favorite piece of art. His hand moved towards the zipper of my jacket. I closed my eyes and breathed him in. But he didn't smell right...

Like...

What is that scent? *I thought.* And why is it so familiar?

The sea...

I pulled away and withheld a scream. Jacques stared back at me, a cocky grin on his face as a terrified shudder rolled through me. I was quick to pull my jacket tighter around me. I guess it wasn't so smart to come out here wearing a jacket and jeans with nothing underneath. Still, I was on private grounds, so I wasn't completely at fault.

"What are you doing here?"

"Don't be like that, mon ange." He grabbed my chin. "Come here."

In an instant his mouth was on mine. It was a completely different sensation than it was with Dorian. The demi-demon's mouth was insistent and overly rough, leaving a trail of ice cold where it fell. I tried to pull away, but Jacques pressed down on me with his full weight. It was hard to breathe as he unfurled what at first appeared to be wings and enveloped me with them. But upon closer inspection, through the frail moonlight filtering through the clouds, these wings were made of shards of glass, jagged and rebelling against everything right in the universe.

The glass pierced my skin, drawing blood. Pain lanced up my spine. I cried out and he swallowed my screams, relishing in my pain.

"I want you to give me a show," Jacques said, scraping his teeth across my ear. "But first I want you to do me a little favor."

"I'm not doing a damn thing for you!" I hissed, trying and failing to flip him off me. "Get off me!"

"Oh, I think you will."

His fingers wrapped around my throat just like the first time he tried to kill me. Everything was so familiar. My mouth fell open as I tried and failed to take in air. Jacques squeezed tighter and as he did, he dragged his body against mine. My mouth formed screams that went unrecognized by him.

"Do you want me to get off you?"

I tried to nod but failed. My throat hurt as if I'd been screaming for hours. My brain had forgotten how to form words. Tears leaked from my eyes. Jacques licked them away.

"I don't know if I should..." He pressed a freezing kiss to my temple. "You've been a lot of trouble for me."

"Please," I managed to croak.

"I want you to tell him the truth."

"Who? The Creator?"

"No. I mean that dense husband of yours. Tell him how you touched me. Tell him how you practically begged me for a taste. Tell him how much you wanted me when your first heat came—and how I gave you everything you asked for."

"I was a child. I didn't know any better. And I—"

His fingers were soft on my neck, loving almost, but I knew that these same hands had once been posed to take my life.

"I once would have done anything for you. But you betrayed my trust. And now, I realize something..." I whispered.

He smiled. "Oui?"

"I've always hated you. From the moment you kissed me, and I tasted fire and brimstone, I knew that I didn't want you. You tried to manipulate my feelings. You tried to use our Bond to get me to want you and then use my worship of you to sleep with you. But what you didn't realize that I was never meant to be yours. I'm not yours. I never will be. Because the moment you raised your hand to me, you lost any godliness that I ever revered you with."

"You belong to me."

"Go to hell!" I spat. "I don't belong to you or anyone! When are you going to get that?"

"So brazen. But you are mine."

Jacques began squeezing again and it was as if I was underwater. I thrashed but it was useless. He was going to have his way with me one way or another. My silent screams died down and I found it harder to focus as black spots dotted my vision. Keres wanted me to fight but it was just so much easier to go sleep. I closed my eyes as ice washed over me, numbing everything else and leaving only darkness.

*   *   *

Someone was shaking me. I woke with a scream as my hand immediately shot out. I opened my eyes to see Tess staring down at me.

I quickly surveyed the room and when *he* wasn't there, I silently rejoiced.

Shafi was putting on a shirt, occasionally glancing at me worriedly. McKenzie and Denise were half-dressed, struggling to put on their clothes in their tired state. Tess was dressed but one half of her face had makeup and the other was bare. Dorian was completely barefoot, rocking a pair of low-rise jeans and a black tee. He looked like the incarnation of sin—the kind of guy that your mama would warn you about.

But he was the opposite—sweet and kind.

Too good for me.

I quickly looked away.

"We're late!" Tess said as the eye without makeup twitched in irritation.

"Late?" I rubbed my sleepy eyes. "We already went to the concert."

Tess rolled her eyes. Her hand hovered over my skin and as it did, darkness seemed to gather around her. Once again, I found it hard to breathe. Tess's eyes gleamed before she lowered her hand. I sucked in air.

"What was that?"

"I used my powers." Tess shook my shoulders even though I was already up. "If you don't get up, I'll do it again."

That was cruel—using her powers to get what she wanted. Damn. If I was completely honest, it sounded kind of familiar.

It sounded like me.

"All right, I'm up!" I stood, not noticing the anxious looks that everyone threw me. "What's up?"

"The tournament started five minutes ago! You're late!"

"Oh, crud!"

I grabbed a quick five-minute shower, brushed my teeth, and put on my sturdy battle armor. Everyone seemed to glance at me in unison as I stepped out of the bathroom. I didn't see what their problem was. We were already late. Besides, I couldn't go out on the battlefield smelling like B.O.—unless I wanted to murder someone with my funk, that is.

"You look like total shit," Tess commented, tapping her foot.

I could understand her irritation. She couldn't fight and I was throwing away a chance that she wanted. Still, her words stung. But at least she had all her makeup on.

"What she means to say is that you don't look so well," Dorian said as he stepped forward.

"No, I meant—"

"Sometimes honesty isn't the best policy!" Dorian snapped. He gripped my chin in his fingers, and I looked away. "You have shadows under your eyes. Let me see."

"No," I shook my head as tears pooled in my eyes.

"We can deal with this after the match!" Tess snapped, ushering us out the door. "We need to go!"

As soon as I stepped into the arena, I pushed the nightmare out of my head. I could deal with it later. Now was the time for winning.

My comrades took their seats as McKenzie and I went to the middle of the arena. The crowd murmured and a few booed, displeased with our tardiness. I glanced up at the box. Mr. Sawyer laced his hands before him, watching us through hooded eyes—or more specifically, me. Mr. Sawyer only broke eye contact with me to raise his hand, fingers spread in the display of the number five.

"It seems that Mr. Sawyer wants to give the team a five-point penalty for tardiness. It's a good thing this wasn't the timed round, folks, or this team would be knee deep in cow manure! Are all the contestants ready?"

That familiar bloodlust swept over me. Keres rolled over in my mind, ready to sit back and enjoy the show. I was more than ready. McKenzie was shaking and she kept glancing into the stands. I clapped my hands and she glanced at me, her eyes wide and terrified.

"Are you ready?" I asked her.

She nodded her head.

"Let the games begin!"

* * *

I remember that even when I was in school, I felt lonely.

I would sit in my little desk—my own private island—staring at my bruised hands as I tried to read the assigned text through eyes that were almost swollen shut. I remember dreaming of when I got home—when my family would remind me that I was still loved. I used to count the scars on my arms. There were always more than what I could count to so when I got to the top of my arm, I would start over. Then I would name them.

"Marve," the teacher would squawk, "what is the answer?"

I knew the answer and I told her so. The kids laughed as I was still reprimanded for not paying attention.

When I was with Master, I was emotionally damaged and desperate for anyone's positive attention—for their love. He fed off that and made me into a monster. I was afraid of my power but had eager fists ready for a fight.

That was how I felt as I took a step towards my opponent in the arena. My power was so ramped up that I was shaking, my skin glowing with a harsh light. I lifted my hand to see that it was concealed by electricity. As my foot came down, I glanced at the monitors and saw that I didn't even look human anymore. I looked like a being of light.

"Hans," Keres whispered. *"Go for him first."*

Suddenly there was a great cracking sound, like a bat striking a baseball. I was behind Hans in an instant. His frame was so wide that I couldn't see around him. He was glancing around in curiosity, obviously wondering where I'd gone. But that wasn't my biggest problem.

How had I done that?

Images from last night's dream danced in a taunting circle, mocking me for all my weaknesses.

"Wo ist das schwein?" growled Hans.

"Right behind you!"

I imagined a wicked bolt raining from the sky and blasting Hans to smithereens. As soon as I thought it, it happened. There was a large crashing sound as a flash of electricity fell from the sky.

Hans didn't even know what hit him as he turned and was struck. For a moment, I saw the look of pure terror and shock on his face before he turned to ash. A smirk crawled onto my face.

"And for the record," I growled, "I'm an American Gator."

Kimmy glanced at me. Her hazel eyes were as wide as dinner plates, locking on me the way a deer locked its gaze on a hunter. McKenzie raised her hands and a large wave rose. I was in awe of her power as it quickly swept towards Kimmy. Kimmy was unaware as she stumbled away from me, all the while begging me to spare her life.

Did I really do that much damage?

I nodded at McKenzie to finish the match. That determined look took over as she realized that I more than had her back. I guess that made me the backup plan. The announcer was on his hovercraft, hovering above us with darting eyes. His thoughts charged like static, and I realized that he was afraid that I was going to drop a bolt and kill him.

Or worse—I could knock off his toupee.

346

I withheld a giggle as I raised a small fortress of electricity. I smiled as I planted my feet firmly on the ground and flicked my eyes at McKenzie. Kimmy whirled around and let out a scream. We'd trapped her like an animal. Now we were going to put her down like one.

But then she raised her hands and clapped three times.

I paused but did not lower my shield. This had to be a trick. She couldn't be serious.

McKenzie lowered her hands. I thought she was crazy for that. That was until she started to cough. She doubled over as her hand rose to clutch her chest. When she raised her head to look at me, there was blood on her lips.

McKenzie's eyes widened and suddenly went blank. She fell forward and her head hit one of the huge boulders in the arena. It was enough to give anyone a concussion or at least draw a scream but McKenzie neither moved nor made a sound. Shafi suddenly appeared at her side and touched her. She was as stiff as a stone.

Everyone was silent. Tess shoved Shafi aside. He stared at his hands as if he'd somehow wrought this. Tess closed her eyes and laid a hand against the side of McKenzie's face. We immediately heard a small cough.

"McKenzie!"

Denise ran from the crowd and into the arena. McKenzie stirred but was unable to stand as she lifted a hand towards the direction Denise was in. It was a true tragedy as she dropped it, her breaths shallow. I knew that this was due to our earlier duel. I also knew that Tess hadn't merely healed her.

Tess had brought McKenzie back to life.

Shafi looked over McKenzie in the middle of the battlefield. Kimmy appeared to be having some sort of mental breakdown, her hands around her knees as she teetered back and forth. Shafi glanced at the referee and shook his head.

"In a c-c-crazy turn of events, folks," the announcer said, his voice shaking, "it seems that McKenzie will be u-u-unable to battle. Marve's team is still the winner. The opponent's request for disqualification has been denied and she will now be par-par-partnered with Marve."

Kimmy glanced up at me. Her eyes were hollow, and I knew that even though I hadn't laid a finger on the other girl, I'd somehow broken her. Shafi swept McKenzie into his arms and exited the stadium. Denise was never far behind, anger on her face. She avoided my eyes as she left.

That left me and Kimmy. Our faces appeared on the screens side by side, declaring us as the winners. The crowds clapped reluctantly. I knew that this was not something that they were used to. Kimmy walked near me but never came too close and I hated her for it. I did not want her as a partner.

She was too weak and more importantly, she was not McKenzie. I brushed past her. As I did, I felt her thoughts bouncing around in her head, a chaotic mess. She was afraid and had briefly contemplated strangling me in my sleep. Great.

Now I had a homicidal coward for a partner.

Then again, people tended to hate what they feared, and they feared what they didn't understand.

My armor felt tight on my body. I heard footsteps behind me and recognized them as the steps of the rest of my party. We went to the room, and I knew that none of us would be attending the final round of the day.

CHAPTER THIRTY-TWO

AN OLD ANGEL

When we got to the room, a tense silence hung over us like a heavy fog, thick and prominent. I walked towards McKenzie with the intent of using my powers to check over her brain. Everyone crowded around her, creating a barrier. Dorian was the only one who hadn't blocked me but when he walked up behind me and grabbed my arm, silently telling me to back off, I felt betrayed. It must've been what he felt like when I signed him away to stay at that asylum.

It felt awful.

And I suddenly realized what I hadn't known before: the reason for why he had to be hospitalized while I had not. After all, we both battled depression. But there was one thing that separated us: *he mattered*. Thousands of people depended on him. He was the ruler of a good part of a vast country. He smuggled people out of slavery for God's sake!

I was a nobody.

"Marve," Dorian said, "I think that there might be an overabundance of magic in your system…"

I knew what happened when one of us had too much magic in their system: people—family, friends, acquaintances—tended to get hurt.

I turned to look out the window. The city zoomed by quietly, lost in their ignorance. Light bled from my hands, as thick as a second skin. I thought of going outside. The next thing I knew, I was next to the door, my hand wrapped around the doorknob.

I heard a colossal noise behind me. I turned to see Denise backing away, her eyes trapped on me. I looked at everyone else—at the other magical folk. Almost all looked afraid but not terrified like Denise. They knew to be quiet in the face of danger.

"What?"

"Do you even know what you just did?" Tess said, the only one who didn't seem to be afraid. "Did you see yourself?"

"No."

"You just turned into a ball of light—"

"It crackled like electricity—"

"You disappeared—"

"Then you were next to the door!" Denise said, taking another step back. "You're a freak!"

Freak? I wasn't a freak. I was strength. I was Nephilim. I was the Gatekeeper.

Mortals like her—those were the freaks.

Wait. What was I thinking? She was just afraid. She didn't mean it. Or I at least hoped so.

I looked into Denise's eyes. They were just like Kimmy's—afraid and looking for an exit. Her eyes suddenly hardened and flicked away. Wow. Even among freaks and outcasts, I was still an anomaly.

What a bummer.

Needing to be alone, I stored my phone in the desk, grabbed my daggers and was gone in a matter of seconds. No matter how hard I tried, I kept flashing to wherever I thought of going. I wound up in an alley next to a homeless man. Next to him was a box with three things inside: an old track trophy from 1986, a box of matches and a pack of saltine crackers. I thought of my years on the streets as I stared at the sleeping man and was helpless against the rage that bubbled up, locking its hands around my throat, and making everything glow red.

I kicked him once, twice then a third time. The man stirred and woke, a cough slipping from his throat. His brown eyes opened, and the pale-faced man looked at me, his eyes lost in the pain and misery that came with this gift called life.

"WHAT ARE YOU LOOKING AT?" I screamed.

I rammed my foot into his ribcage, then his legs and finally his face. I felt myself growing angrier with every kick and a darker side of me was far from satisfaction. The man whimpered at first, but the pitiful noises soon died out. He laid still, blood dripping from every orifice in his body. I was shaking in my rage.

I started kicking his lifeless body again, wishing that he was alive so that I could make him hurt the way I did. I would never fit into society, and neither would he. We were both outcasts.

I heard something crunch closer. I looked up and saw a pale child staring at me. I glared at him, and he ran off. I pulled out my favorite dagger and drove it into the man three times.

It was a holy number, but God had abandoned me long ago.

My body cried out in anger. Electricity flew from my body, flying in all directions. I watched as the homeless man's face melted, disfigured and misshapen. The sirens came closer. I wanted them to catch me.

I wanted to fight.

The sirens sped past the alleyway.

I beat my wings twice and took off from the ground. The police cars doubled back and stopped at the alley. I heard one of them radio in and I took off towards the canyons. I didn't care if anyone saw me. I needed to be isolated if I wanted to get answers.

And there was one person that could give them to me.

I landed near the familiar spot at the base of the canyon. I quickly sat on the ground and closed my eyes. I channeled my magic into one task: summoning an angel. When my eyes opened, the Marks on my arm began to glow. Not even a full minute later, a shadow flew across the sky and landed before me. The white-winged angel looked up.

"Lisette!"

I got up and hugged her. It wasn't because we were particularly friends or anything. I hugged her because she showed up when I needed her most—when I needed answers. She looked shocked as I pulled away. That same smile that I'd somehow gotten used to tugged at her lips, as if she was trying not to laugh. I rubbed the back of my neck.

"What's up?"

"You killed Micha."

OK. We were getting straight to business.

Cool.

"Yeah." I crossed my arms. "So what?"

"Don't get all defensive, kid. I'm glad you did away with him."

A thousand thoughts whirled in my head. What did she mean she was glad? Was this a trick?

"What do you mean?"

"Losing God, turning away from your brethren, is the ultimate betrayal. The Creator thanks you. I...I thank you."

"Are you saying this because you have to?"

She didn't even blink.

"Are you okay, kid?" She shook her head to where her blonde ponytail swayed. "You look like crap."

"Nothing. Just bad dreams is all."

"Is it about...Jacques or Micha?"

"I'm not letting myself think about Micha," I admitted. "And Jacques is far away. He can't hurt me...right?"

"Oh, hun." Her eyes filled with tears. "I'm sorry you had to see him that way. I know he didn't want you to remember him like that. And Jacques....I wish I could say you were safe and that he won't hurt you ever again..."

"But?"

"But that man has it out for you, and it won't end until one of you are dead."

The wind blew, chilling me to my core. Her hair blew, momentarily plastering to her face, obscuring my view of her expression. She probably hated me for what I was.

She moved to lay a hand on my arm. "Are you okay?"

"I was fine until I had this horrible nightmare." I described it to her as censored as I could. "I hadn't even thought about it except right after the incident. I pushed it out of my mind. I thought I'd be okay since I hadn't really thought of it since then. Still, I—"

"Something *did* happen. It's completely normal to react that way. You're a lot stronger than you think...I have an idea. Do you want to hear it?"

I nodded.

"Angels have this thing we call...The Great Grieving. It hits us after too many battles, or after seeing Earth, or after an angel is no more, whether they Turn or...*otherwise.*" She took my hands in hers. "Do something for me?"

I nodded.

"Close your eyes."

I did so.

"Breathe in. Think of everything that's led up to this moment in time. Think of everyone that you've lost, all the power you've gained, all the friends you've made, all the enemies you've driven out. Think about your purpose. Now...breathe out."

I did that, too.

"Feel better?"

I smiled; a bit too large. "Thanks."

"Tell your husband everything about you and Jacques. It's in no way your fault. You're still a kid compared to most of the world, even now. But even though you've never had the chance to grow despite growing up too fast, doesn't mean that you deserve to harbor this… *guilt.*"

I nodded. "Ma'am."

"And wash your face, kid," she gave me a puzzling grin, "you look like hell."

I had been a different person when I first met Jacques. More than submissive. Almost willing, playful in our dance. But then he wanted more than I could give, and the game became less of a dance and more of a chase. I had been around thirteen at the time, so it's not like I was an adult. And it didn't excuse Jacques for what he did. But it did change our dynamic a bit. And I had to be honest if I wanted to heal.

I suddenly remembered Micha.

He always backed off when I became afraid. He never forced my hand or called my bluff. He knew when I wanted it and when I was just being playful. And he…*respected* me. That's more than anyone else ever had, aside from Dorian. Maybe telling Dorian would absolve me somehow. Maybe then I could finally move on completely instead of merely pushing it out of my mind.

Maybe…

Finally?

Yes!

I told her about my powers—about how they'd been acting up lately.

"I *have* heard of what you described but I can't remember what it is. Why don't you ask your friend McKenzie? That book of hers might help you."

"How did you—?" At her bashful smile, I grinned back. "The portal?"

"Yup." She slapped me on the back. "Are you happy that I gave you the Marks?"

"Huh?"

"You summoned me using your Marks." She gave me a wicked grin. "Just think of how useful they'll be in battle!"

"Right." I nodded and I realized that my heart felt a little lighter. It wasn't completely healed but I didn't feel like I was going under anymore. "Thank you, Lisette."

"Any time."

She took off into the night sky. A tear ripped in the space, showing the glittering streets of Sora. Lisette waved before going through the portal. I smiled and waved back even though the portal had already closed. After that, I spread my wings and flew back towards the Rose Court.

It was time to get some answers.

*   *   *

When I came back to the room I tried not to be shocked by what I saw. McKenzie was in a wheelchair by the window, Denise kneeling on the ground next to her as she held her hand. Every now and then McKenzie would cough, and Denise would wipe her mouth with a blood-stained cloth. Tess, Rhea and Shafi were talking in hurried whispers, occasionally glancing at the door. Dorian was sitting on our bed, his phone clutched in his hand.

I stepped into the room. The first thing I did was walk towards McKenzie and apologize for doing so much damage. McKenzie said that it was an accident and forgave me. She also said that she was unsure why her legs were hurt. With Denise's permission, I did a quick scan of her brain.

I guess even she realized that it couldn't get any worse.

"Your motor cortex has been damaged. I'm guessing that happened when I controlled your movements. I didn't expect it to last or for the damage to show itself now. I'm sorry. You may never walk again."

"It's fine." McKenzie smiled and I was blinded by her radiance. "God willing, I'll still be alive tomorrow."

Denise muttered something under her breath. Instead of getting angry, McKenzie apologized to her for ruining their chances of getting the prize money. In her eyes, if she'd never agreed to train with me, she wouldn't have gotten hurt. Denise brushed a lock of hair behind McKenzie's ear. I tried to ignore the pain in her eyes.

McKenzie gave a laugh that quickly broke off into a long series of coughs. Denise kissed McKenzie's bloodstained lips before shooing me away. Shafi was leaning over Rhea, his arm braced on the wall and a smile on his lips. Tess had moved away from them. She held a caterpillar in her hands.

I watched her for a moment. She raised her hand over the still creature and passed it over its dead body. The caterpillar immediately came alive, crawling past her hand and up her arm. Tess blinked and the creature froze, as dead as a crushed flower. She repeated this process a bunch of times, a smile growing on her face with every success.

I walked over and plopped on Dorian's lap. He immediately wrapped his arms around me and planted a kiss on the top of my head. He inhaled as if trying to memorize my scent—as if the process somehow comforted him. I did a quick sweep of his brain. I didn't have to do much to realize that he was worried.

"What's wrong?" I said, brushing my lips over his.

"I've been texting you," he said expectantly.

"Oh." A smile curved on my lips. "I'm sorry."

I went over to the table near the bed and opened a drawer. Inside was my phone, which I stored away before I left. I picked it up and walked back over to Dorian. I set it in his palm. Realization dawned on his face.

"You left this here?" he said, staring at the phone as if he'd never seen it.

"Yeah." I planted a kiss elsewhere, near the shell of his ear. "What's wrong?"

"I was so worried." He squeezed me tighter. "I was afraid that I'd lost you. I was afraid that you wouldn't come back."

"I'm here." I ran my hands through his hair, my nails scraping his scalp. He made a noise close to a growl in the back of his throat. "I'm here…"

"Say it," he said, pulling away to look at me.

"Say what?" I said as a coy smile wriggled on my face.

It didn't last long. Jacques's face flashed in my mind, casting a shadow over me. I had to tell him.

"Tell me you love me."

"I love you." I planted a kiss on his mouth, his nose, his cheeks, his eyelids then trailed a line of pecks up and down his stubble-flecked jaw. "I love you so, so much—more than anything."

"Good. I love you, too."

"Dorian?" I pulled away and he opened his eyes to reveal want swimming in their depths. "I have to tell you something."

"Later." His voice was a command that swept through the room. "Everyone out!"

Everyone left without a word. McKenzie's wheelchair squeaked as she was wheeled out of the room. I kissed Dorian as he rolled over me, pressing me into the bed. Micha's face flashed in my mind's eye. It was official.

I would never hurt another person like this again.

CHAPTER THIRTY-THREE

CONFESSIONS WITHOUT A PRIESTESS

D orian pinned me with an animalistic stare as he pulled off his clothes. I froze as I felt his nakedness. He reached out and ran his hand down the length of my body. Back and forth he went before stopping over my breasts. My back arched as he felt my chest through my battle armor.

He took my armor off in one swift movement and peppered small kisses across my chest. Finally, he stopped and took on of my nipples into his mouth. I groaned, throwing my head back as a strangled cry tore itself from my lips. He repeated the action on my other breast, humming in the back of his throat. I was strong but there was only so much I could take before I succumbed.

He peppered kisses down my body before stopping at the apex of my thighs. He looked up and gave me a wicked grin. I bit my lip as his tongue met my clit through my underwear. I cried out as he went to work, stroking his tongue in a lazy circle. I reached down, grabbed his hair, and pulled him closer.

He moved faster and faster. It didn't take me long to begin to climb up that familiar mountain of ecstasy. I felt his hand move up and in a quick flick of the wrist, he'd torn off my underwear. I looked down to watch him and when I saw his face buried in me, I lost it. All the different frustrations bubbled up and exploded; the orgasm rocked me to my very core as I threw back my head and screamed.

Dorian was next to me in seconds, angling his naked body over mine to where he covered me without crushing me. His mouth fell on mine, and he thrust his tongue into my mouth aggressively. I tasted my own juices on his mouth and was surprised by how sweet it was. Dorian ravished my mouth, his tongue unearthing every crevice as he claimed what was already his. I dug my nails into his back, trying to draw him closer.

Dorian brought his hips closer, just barely brushing my entrance with the tip of his manhood. I groaned in frustration as I tried and failed to pull him forward again. He just barely pushed the tip in, held it there for a second and then pulled away.

It was time to take things into my own hands.

I twisted my hips and flipped us over. It was my turn to smile as I took control. I hovered over him for a second, taking in all the feelings stirring between us. Then I sunk down on him slowly, relishing the feel of him inside me, the fullness. He groaned and from over a year of getting to know his body, I knew that it was a sound of pleasure and need.

I raised up and pushed back down repeatedly, already having established a rhythm. Small grunts of encouragement fell from Dorian's lips as he grabbed my hips. I built my rhythm, moving faster and faster. A sigh tumbled from my lips as I felt that familiar build. I could tell that Dorian was close by the way he made me go up and down, his hands yanking on my hips in an erratic manner.

I leaned down and whispered in Dorian's ear.

"I'm yours."

Then I bit his ear. That was all it took. He twitched inside of me before filling me with his seed. I clenched around him as my own orgasm rocked through me, milking him for all he had. Then I pulled off slowly and collapsed next to him.

"I love you," he said, kissing the space behind my ear.

"I love you, too."

He touched the hair on the nape of my neck. I shuddered as he touched a soft spot at the base of my neck. He tickled me there, drawing an involuntary laugh from me. I felt bad, wrong, guilty laughing when I'd wronged him so. Dorian hummed in the back of his throat. I froze, wondering what he was thinking.

"Your hair glows, like fire."

"Fire…"

That was the way people described the hair of the Flaming Gift: my mother.

He kissed the back of my neck, murmuring, "It's beautiful."

I curled into Dorian and fell into a deep sleep.

* * *

My head was on Dorian's chest. His hands were in my hair, running his lengthy fingers through my fiery red locks. The words of truth gnawed at the inside of my stomach, and I tried to pretend that they didn't hurt me.

"I love you," said Dorian.

I died a little every time he said those words. To distract myself, I got up and parted the drapes before bending to open the window. Dorian gave a low whistle. I quickly moved around the room, picking up a pair of jeans and throwing them at my husband. I kept his shirt for myself as I threw on a clean pair of underwear and then put on his black t-shirt.

The smell of sex was heavy in the air. Hopefully it would air out soon. I got in bed and kissed Dorian a little while longer, glad to have this moment alone with him. A darker part of me whispered that I was only buttering him up. It was really the opposite.

I'd do anything for him if he kept kissing me the way that he was.

"So," Dorian said as he pulled away, "what did you want to tell me?"

I gave him one more lingering kiss. I was trying to tell him that I loved him. I was trying to tell him that I didn't mean to hurt him. Above all else, I was trying to tell him that it was far in my past. When I pulled away, he stared at me, and I knew that he knew that something was wrong.

"I did something awful."

"You mean while you left?"

"No." I swallowed. "Before that..."

"When?"

"With Jacques."

A dark look crossed his face. "I told you. That wasn't your fault. When you think of these things, you have to be honest. That way, I can accommodate you."

"But what if it was all my fault?" I swallowed. "What if I welcomed it?"

"What did you do—dance on his grave?" Dorian gave a laugh. He ran his fingers across my ribs, drawing a laugh from me. He had a smile in his voice as he said, "I trust you. Tell me."

I began to cry.

"Please," his voice shook as he tried to maintain control, "explain."

So, I did. I told him of the game that I had inevitably lost. I told him of how I once believed I was special and how my world had been rocked when I quickly came to the realization that I was not. Not because I wanted to be used in such a manner. But because I thought I was above the abuse, higher than any of Jacques's slaves, as he had once told me. Dorian just listened quietly, not saying anything. Then, finally, he asked if he could hug me.

When I nodded, he hugged me gently. "Don't blame yourself."

"But...but I—"

"Listen to me. You were a child. A literal child. And he used that against you. You didn't know what you were doing. And it was up to him as an adult to keep you in a child's place. He made demands of you that I wouldn't even make of an adult woman. Listen to me: you are nobody's whore. And you don't owe anyone sex, whether you kiss them or eat their food or live with them or anything."

That's when I broke. Tears poured down my face as a deep, pained groan built up and untangled from my throat. I wasn't proud of the part of me that was relieved as his face folded in understanding. Dorian didn't mind any of that as he pulled me close and put my face in the crook of his neck. I didn't deserve him.

I cried for what felt like hours. Dorian made a rocking motion that I sometimes did with the baby. When I wiped my eyes, I was surprised that I didn't feel small and helpless. Dorian kissed my cheek, the area still wet from my tears. I was confused and small but once again, not helpless.

Lost but not broken.

"Are you mad at me?"

"I'm really not."

"Even though it's all my fault?"

"I'm not mad. If you knew what the world was like when Jacques ran it, you'd see that you are not unlike many of his ex-slaves. That was part of how he got you. He tricked you into believing that you were special. Attention is a powerful thing. Many men use it to manipulate women, and children, too. But don't ever think that just because you kiss someone, you have to follow through with sex. It's just unfair to yourself."

"So, I'm not a whore?"

He looked like he wanted to cry and punch something at the same time. "You were a child."

At first his words didn't help. They made me feel worse. Dorian told me to lay down and pulled the covers over me. I couldn't help but think of the time that I took care of him and felt that our roles were now reversed. He was the best husband that a woman could ever want.

Dorian went to the bathroom and came back with a hot, wet towel. He wiped the mess off my face, murmuring soothing words the entire time. I didn't realize that I was shaking until he got into bed with me and wrapped his arms around me. In his embrace, I realized that I had nothing to be ashamed of. I'd made some mistakes—all humans did—and we were only going to grow stronger from them.

"You know," Dorian mumbled, "I can't really say that I'm surprised."

"What do you mean?"

I poked my head up from under the covers. My husband smiled and smoothed the hair back from my forehead. I gave him a weak, watery smile.

"I just mean that you've been locked up inside that mansion a good portion of your life. You never really had a chance to be around boys or girls your age. So, it makes sense that you at first willingly came to him. Fucking sicko bastard. He knew what he was doing, isolating you like that."

I twisted the covers in my hands. "Can we talk about something else?"

He nodded and smiled. "Of course, baby. Anything."

A sudden thought, one that I had thought briefly before, popped in my head, so I asked it. "What was your first like?"

"You remember how I told you of her...?" he looked up at me shyly. "The woman that introduced me to sex?"

"Your dad's friend?"

"She wasn't really his friend. More of a prostitute that he hired so that I could have my first time. For a long time, I wasn't interested in girls...at all. And my dad got worried. He arranged for me to lose my virginity, so I could be ensured to give him the airs he felt he deserved. He bought her, gave her to me. I remember, I was so scared...I thought I was gonna hurl. But she was very gentle with me. She showed me what to do, how to do it, even how to take off a girl's bra with two fingers. We grew to be great friends when I was older. That is...before she died..."

"You loved her?"

A tear streaked down his cheek. "What can I say? She was my first.'"

"And your father...he had her killed when you tried to run off with her?"

"No. He just wiped her existence off the Earth, made it so no one remembered her. Even now, if I don't concentrate, her face appears... fuzzy. Like I'm looking through a lens with smudges on it."

"Oh my Goddess, Dorian, I'm so sorry." I diverted slightly. "Did you drink with them around—your parents, I mean?"

"My dad drank. We had a lot of parties where I was unsupervised. When I was thirteen, I started sneaking into the wine cellar. I didn't think that...that I—"

"That you would become an alcoholic?"

"Yeah." He got out of the bed, stood, and stretched. "Are you ready to let everyone back in?"

"No." I said immediately, pulling the pillow that he slept on into my lap and inhaling. "I love you."

"I love you, too."

I sighed as I set the pillow back down. I'd eventually have to let them back in. I walked into the bathroom, ran a quick bubble bath, and stripped down. I sank into the water until it went past my chin then yelled for Dorian. Immediately knowing what I wanted, he undressed and got in next to me.

We had a splash fight in the water, giggling like two little kids. We washed each other, laughing and smiling. When we did get out, both of our skin was wrinkly. We put on our clothes quickly. When we were done, I opened the door and called everyone back inside.

I was tired of getting in the way of my own happiness.

CHAPTER THIRTY-FOUR

A POLARIZING ARGUMENT

McKenzie sat in the bed with her book in her lap. We were all gathered around her. Every now and then Shafi would mutter that Denise shouldn't even be in the room since this concerned magic and she was Mortal.

I kind of agreed. Don't think that anyone was prejudiced. It was just that it was true. Magic was a complicated practice even among its users. This would go way over Denise's head.

"Guys, she's fine," McKenzie said for what seemed to be the millionth time. "I've taught her everything I know."

"You shouldn't have. Putting us all in danger like that..." Tess said, agreeing with Shafi. "You could get us all killed—"

"Look, do you want me to open the damn book or not?" McKenzie snapped.

"Fine." Tess flicked her hair in irritation. "Have it your way."

"Thank you."

McKenzie flipped open the book.

We waited a few minutes while she skimmed the table of contents. It was rather impressive, really, that she found what we were looking for so quickly. After all, the book held a lot of information. She turned the book around so that we could all see the picture of the man raising his hands to the sky. I shuddered at the memory of the unfamiliar sight.

"It says here that this condition is called *Immortale Potentum*—"

"Wow." I rolled my eyes. "That's a very creative name."

Tess sniggered. A laugh slipped from my lips. McKenzie began to close the book. At all our shouts of "NO!" she opened the book back up. She gave us one more warning glance that said this was our last chance.

"The Immortal Power is achieved when a Gifted human receives powers from an Angel. It is a very rare sight to behold and is often seen of as a record-breaking achievement of some sort."

Everyone stared at me in shock—even Denise, who was usually serious. I swallowed. I'd achieved true immortality? How? I looked at McKenzie and nodded. She looked back at the book, and everyone followed suit. McKenzie's brown hands shook as she flipped the page.

"True immortality can only be achieved through one way. You must drink the blood of an angel after taking the Immortality from another human. It was thought that this could be achieved by forcibly taking the blood or blackmailing the angel into giving you some blood. This is not the case. The angel must willingly give you the blood and must be doing it for the betterment of the world and not the receiver or the angel itself."

"Holy shit—"

"This is a rare occurrence. That is why there are only eight people that have achieved true immortality—"

"Make that nine—"

"Those are the Elders, who were directly chosen by the first, Alice, to watch over the rest of the magical world after she was given the final punishment for sharing the secret of God's Magic. Alice is also a true immortal since she is to live and suffer for all eternity. It has been tested and confirmed that this true immortality also includes invulnerability. You cannot die from illness, battle wounds, or kill yourself; you will never age. It is quite odd since you can no longer use runes to conjure things. This is thought to be so that you can use your immortality to live humbly and change the world for the better—the mission that Alice could not complete."

"Who gave you their blood?" Tess asked, staring at me as if she'd never seen me.

"Micha."

"Is he still around?" Shafi exclaimed. "I want to be a true immortal, too! Think of the people I could heal—the lives I could save."

"Screw that!" Tess hissed, elbowing him so that she could be closer to me. "Think of the people that we could unite."

"Actually," I rubbed the back of my neck as a blush crept upon my face, "he's dead."

"WHAT?"

"I kind of killed him." Before they could riot, I looked at McKenzie. "Please, keep reading."

She nodded and kept on.

"There is one more thing that puzzles magic folk, whether true immortals or not. Two of the Elders have Gifts. As we've seen with Alice, a true immortal, it seems that when you gain true immortality, your powers increase more than tenfold. They evolve rapidly and are very hard to control. That is why a few have refused becoming true immortals—because they didn't want to hurt people."

"These mofos are crazy," Dorian muttered.

"What else does it say?" I said, leaning forward as power hummed under my skin.

"That's it…" McKenzie looked up at me, giving me the same look Tess had. "You understand what this means, right?"

"That I won't have to worry about ever getting cancer?"

"You have to drop out of the competition."

"What the hell?" Tess looked as if she wanted to smack the other woman. "Why would she do that?"

"That's out of the question." Rhea said.

"I'm not going to," I snorted. "That'd be stupid."

"But that's cheating!" McKenzie cried as she threw down the book. "You're not playing fair!"

"You let an insider in and got us all sucked into your mess," I hissed, the mean side of me flickering on. "*That's* not fair. I'm going to win this competition. If I didn't know any better, I'd say that you wanted me to drop out because *you* can't compete."

"What?" McKenzie shook her head. "That's not true!"

We all stared at her. She began to cough again, and the scent of blood quickly filled the room. She had every right to be upset—I'd stolen her dreams in one fell swoop. And now I had an advantage that she needed now more than ever. An idea struck me.

"McKenzie, the fate of the world is hanging in the balance. I *have* to do this. But now that I think of it," a smirk curved on my lips, "don't we have enough money, Dorian?"

He nodded, catching on quickly.

"We don't need the money." I gave McKenzie a grin. "Why don't you and Denise take the money? You guys could start over, just like you said. No more living on the streets—just happiness like you two wanted."

"What?" Tess took a step forward. "What about the rest of us?"

"You guys don't need that money. They're *homeless.* They need this. You all haven't been persecuted the way they have. Besides, I ruined McKenzie's chances of competing—"

"She wouldn't have defeated you in the semi-finals, anyway," Tess hissed. "You're a true immortal, remember?"

"Well, I didn't know—"

"It doesn't matter if you knew! You would have fought, and she would have died. You don't think I have problems, too? I've got a daughter at home. I wanted to enter and win that money for her, you know. You ruined that. Do you know how expensive it is raising a child?"

"Of course I do!" I was yelling now. "I have a son, too, you know!"

But truthfully, I didn't. Dorian provided everything we could ever need and more. Still, a part of me said that she was angry because she believed that I took her daughter's future away.

"You don't know!" Tess shook her head. "You just threw away a million drachmas—money that you already have! I can just tell by looking at pretty boy over there that he's grown up with a silver spoon in his mouth. You're rich now—even before you had your son—so you *don't* know how it is to raise a kid on a budget."

"That's not true!" Dorian snapped, rolling his eyes as if he knew. "When I ran away, I—"

"YOU RAN AWAY!" Tess screamed, driving her fist into her palm. "You *chose* to leave."

"Well, you chose to sleep around and get pregnant, same as I did," I said. "You aren't getting—"

"I didn't choose this!" Tess shoved me. "I was raped!"

Stunned silence filled the room. Tess turned and stormed out, the door closing behind her with a bang. I felt like the biggest jerk in the world. I'd assumed the same way that people assumed about me my entire life. I'd passed judgement on a woman that I barely knew. What kind of person did that make me?

Not a good one, I knew.

"McKenzie," I whispered, "would you mind?"

She smiled and nodded. McKenzie and Denise would split the money with Tess. Half a million should be enough to sedate everyone's needs.

Dorian was quick to agree with me.

"You made the right choice."

Then why did I feel like I hadn't done enough?

CHAPTER THIRTY-FIVE

TESS'S TRUTH

I flew over the mainland of the Maeora, searching.

I found Tess huddled up under a tree at the base of the canyon. She should have been cold even with a jacket, but I was guessing that her anger kept her warm. The canyon no longer held resilient flowers. It looked as if a drought had hit it. It looked like a wasteland.

The flowers were brown and dried up, curling into themselves. Even the cries of the animals had gone silent. My best bet was that she killed a majority of those off, too. Either that or they sensed danger. If it was the latter, they were smart to flee before they ended up like the flowers.

I walked over to a nice untouched patch of grass and sat on it. Tess was either blind or very good at pretending not to notice people that she didn't like. After a good thirty minutes or so, I moved a bit closer. She didn't lash out or make me momentarily experience the sensation of death—even though it wouldn't really hurt me.

"Go away," said Tess.

"McKenzie and Denise are going to split the prize money with you."

"..."

"This is where you hit the ground groveling and I say, 'You're welcome, peasant.'"

"That's my line," she said as a smirk twisted its way onto her lips.

No sooner than it appeared did it fall away.

"Look, I—"

There was the sound of a branch cracking. Both of our heads snapped up at the same time. Not even fifty feet away was a grizzly bear. It sniffed the ground with its wet snout. I froze as its head flew up.

It cocked its head at us as if it was deciding whether it was a good idea to eat us straight out or maul us to death and *then* eat us. Don't quote me—I don't excel at bear/human interactions. It took a step forward. I quickly retreated into my mind, hoping for the mauling to be quick. But then I remembered that I wasn't alone and tried to telepathically tell Tess that we shouldn't move.

She either didn't get the message, didn't care, or wanted to die a slow and painful death at the hands—I mean, *paws*—of this grizzly.

As she stood, a slow grin wormed its way onto her face. The bear dipped its head and let out a snort. Tess cracked her knuckles and took a brave step forward. It was like watching a scary movie at the part when that dumb girl was about to open the closet, she just heard grotesque moans coming from five seconds ago. I wanted to look away, but I couldn't!

She seemed to somehow stand taller. The bear took a couple more steps forward. Then the grizzly stopped and cocked its head as if puzzled. Tess's eyes glimmered and I immediately recognized the look. It was the look that she gave me when she was threatening to make me feel death all over again.

She gave the bear that oh so loving 'come at me' glare. The bear, sensing that it was outmatched, turned away. As the bear disappeared into the trees, my mouth practically hit the floor. Tess calmly walked back over to her former spot and plopped down as if nothing had happened. I waited a good ten minutes for the bear to come back for its Happy Meal, but it never did.

"How did you do that?"

"I've always been able to do that," Tess said, those dark shadows returning once more. "Ever since I was three and killed a mountain lion with my bare hands…"

"You didn't!"

"You're right—I didn't. But stuff like that *has* happened before. One time I was visiting my cousins in Amoria, and I ran into this moose and—"

"You were scared of a moose?" I tried not to laugh. "Those things—"

"Can be very aggressive," she said, dead serious. "It came at us like it was going to charge. I just felt this sudden power inside of me in the face of death—as if death was calling me to control it. I honestly felt like if I touched the moose, it would die. The moose ran away as if it knew that, too."

"Look, Tess—and I'm not saying this because I'm scared—but I really am sorry. I didn't know what happened to you. It explains a lot. I understand where you're coming from…better than most. But that's no reason to be mad at the world, and treat the people around you terribly, either. If you want to be angry, be alone. Raising a kid like that…it's not good."

"You sound like you know what it feels like. On our way here, in the jet, you said that you were homeless. Were you ever—?"

"Yes…it was a while ago…it…nothing."

Rape. Raped. Why couldn't I say it? Was it that taboo? I looked at Tess helplessly.

"Rape," Tess finished with a frown. "I used to not be able to say it, either. When I told my mom about it four months later was when I first said it. She took me to the doctor straight away, worried that I might've caught something. She never looked me in the eye the whole ride there. The doctor said that I was pregnant, and she finally looked at me and…and it was like I'd died or something."

"My parents died when I was young but if they were alive and knew what happened…I think they'd still support me."

"Lucky you. My mom started working double shifts on both her jobs, saying that she was trying to make extra money for our new addition. I didn't realize that she was avoiding me until she got wasted one night. I asked her why she hated me so much. Was it because of the baby or because I disobeyed her and went to a party where I was drugged and raped?"

"What was it?"

"She said that it wasn't fair. She said that she tried to be considerate, but she just couldn't wrap her head around it. She said that she'd tried to raise me right. She said that she'd told me not to go and I'd disobeyed her. She…she told me that it was my fault."

Holy crud. I really *didn't* know how she felt. The two people that I'd really come out to hadn't even done a fraction of that. They understood, didn't blame me, and helped me move past it. Yeah, it still hurt but I was never punched in the gut for it.

I felt that silence was the best option.

"Then she started throwing stuff at me. She said that she had me when she was sixteen and that she'd warned me about getting pregnant at a young age—as if I'd *asked* for this. She said that she wanted me to have a better life. She said that I ruined it all by going to that party. She said that it would make it tough finding a man that could deal with that, pointing out that my dad walked out on us when I was eight."

"Don't take this the wrong way," I paused, "but in a twisted way, I think she was worried about you. If she loved you, she shouldn't have said such things. But still—"

"No."

"No?"

"I moved out after that and stayed with some friends. She tried calling me, but I never picked up; I even changed my number twice but she kept coming back. My friends eventually threw me out when the baby was close to being due because everyone at school thought that I was a slut, and it was hurting their reputations."

"Did you ever tell them the truth?"

"They should have stuck by me no matter what!" Tess snapped, shaking her head. "I cut them out of my circles even when they tried to come back into my life. I had Kira at the hospital that my mom worked at. I didn't even realize that she worked the night shift there until she popped up in my room. She said that Kira was beautiful— that she looked just like me—and then promised to leave me alone.

"Before she left, she said that she was sorry for what had happened and that she loved me. It took me a long time to swallow my pride and come home…but it took even longer for me to forgive her. She helped me with diapers and stuff like that. I used my job as an actress on *Strike It Rich* to pay for school as I got my GED and later finished college; mom watched Kira when I couldn't—and she didn't complain once. She even pulled some strings when I quit acting and helped me get the job that I have now."

"Your mom sounds like a great person."

"She's still my best friend." Tess hugged her knees as if searching for her mother's embrace. "It took me a while to realize that. Still, I can't help but think that she was right that day. I can't help but think that it was my fault."

"It's not…"

I imagined being in her shoes. Hopping from place to place, having a baby with no one supporting you and trying to mend wounds scratched into your heart by your mother's knife. Then being abandoned by so-called friends, moving back in with said mom and moving past all of that that to forgive her. Tess may have been the best person out of all of us because if I was her, I would have broken a long time ago. It sounded like she'd been broken and still had the strength to put herself back together.

"No wonder you're so angry."

"Life sucks sometimes. I guess I forget that other people have issues, too."

"We all do that." I nudged her. "Especially me."

"Yeah, I know." We shared a laugh. "Do you want to know what I thought when you came to my job?"

"That I was the devil incarnate?"

"No, I've already got that spot filled," Tess joked. "I thought that you reminded me of myself. I could see the look in your eyes that I saw every day in the mirror. You'd been broken, betrayed, and beaten by life but you still got back up. I thought 'she's a fighter just like me.'"

"I'm nowhere near as strong as you. I've gotten this position of power and all I've done is lash out at everyone. The only thing I'm good at is fighting. I guess that's because I've been fighting all my life—fighting to survive, fighting for respect, and fighting for my own approval, too. I guess I've just forgotten how to stop."

"That's funny," Tess said with a sly grin, "it sounds like you don't like it when he stops."

"What do you mean?"

"You know, when Dorian kicked us out, the five of us just went down the hall. You two were so loud. From the sounds of it, you guys have—"

"And the moment is dead! Thanks for that. It was getting a little too mushy for me, anyway."

"No problem." She punched my arm. "Is this the part where you beg me to come back to the room because everyone misses me?"

"Actually, it's been pretty peaceful without you," I said, shrugging.

"Wow, and they say I'm a bi—"

"I'm just kidding. I think we all understand each other a lot better now. No one will object if you decide to rejoin us."

She nodded and stood. The wind stirred. Just like that, a thought struck me. I thought of Tess's weight and my own strength. I could take down men twice my size in seconds.

I could easily carry her.

"Have you ever wanted to fly?"

"Well, let's see. We came here on a jet so—"

I unfolded my wings. They glowed with a soft bluish pink hue in the moonlight. Tess paused midsentence, her mouth dropping open. I saw her eyes sparkle with envy. This made me grin.

"Think of this as my formal apology."

"Can you give me wings?"

"Do I look like a can of Red Bull to you?"

"Then what are you going to do?"

"I'm going to carry you."

She raised an eyebrow. I ran to the other side of the small patch of land. I told Tess to hold as still as possible. Then I ran forward, feet pounding the Earth, and grabbed her. With a couple of strong beats, we were off the ground, hovering over the treetops. Flying free felt more than awesome.

It felt amazing.

"You're stronger than you look," she said in a quivering voice, staring at the ground.

"Are you scared of heights?"

"I was just on a jet not even a few weeks ago," she hissed but it was missing the same venom.

"I think we need to go higher if we're going to clear the treetops and—"

"No!"

"Then, we're off…"

I flapped in the direction of the Rose Court. It was nice to know that there was someone like me. It was also nice to be reminded that anger was never without a cause. I still walked the path of revenge but that didn't mean that I had to abuse my friends verbally and physically on the way there. After all, there was no love in abuse.

Maybe that was the flaw in my thinking all along.

CHAPTER THIRTY-SIX

EXPERIMENT

A week later, I was in Doctor Larson's office. I was running on a treadmill with three different monitors hooked up to my body. Unlike most monitors, two of them were infused with magic. There was one normal one measuring my heartrate. The other two were going through a bunch of functions for one goal: to measure how much magic was being emitted from my body.

I ran as hard and fast as I could. The heart monitor began a steady climb up. Pretty soon it passed a hundred. That's when the magical monitors started going wild. I quickly lost focus due to all the noises.

With that went my control.

Purple electricity shot from my body in all directions. Doctor Larson and Dorian hit the floor. The magic monitors made a noise close to a computerized scream and caught flame, smoke pouring from their sides. In seconds, I'd torn the monitors from my body and extinguished the flames. When that fun was over, I turned around and sat on the medical bed, a thousand thoughts racing through my head.

The most prominent was this: Would I ever learn self-control?

"The only time I've ever seen magic this strong," said Doctor Larson, "is in demi-demons, Nephilim and the Elders."

"Technically, I *am* Nephilim," I said.

"Since when?"

"Since now." I didn't elaborate. "What do I do?"

"I know just the thing. I always keep a spare in case the Elders need a replacement."

He turned and left the room. Dorian sat on the bed next to me and took my hand in his. His hand was so cold, like the ice-filled tundra Amoria, yet it was warm like an African savannah. But then I realized that the coolness was the possible eventuality of my newfound powers and not his essence. Before I could get lost in the sensation, Larson had already returned.

He held something out to me. I took it in my hands, my powers a second heartbeat under my skin. He'd brought back two bracelets. They were both a deep black like the rock that Keres was chained to. I slipped them on and immediately felt my powers quiet from a scream to a whisper.

"I made these for the Elders, who have achieved true immortality. It took me years to perfect them. At first, they would completely lock away the Elders' powers until they took them off. On the second edition, they would make the Elders feel drained and the wearers would sleep for days. This third edition is available to anyone who needs them. It makes your powers calm, but you can still access your powers fully if you want or you can keep them on a lower setting."

"How do they work?" I said as my tail flicked in excitement.

"When a magic-wielder has an overabundance of magic, they usually produce elevated amounts of the hormone known as Majik, which is the hormone that is unique only to magic-folk. Because of this they usually experience irritation. This is a way of your body trying to trick you into attacking someone so that you can release some of that energy."

I already felt calmer. Doctor Larson saw the look on my face and smiled.

"These bracelets reduce that hormone along with slowing down the ones that produce the magic so that you have more control over yourself and your powers."

I fought the urge to hug Larson. There was always an answer when he was around. I really appreciated that.

"You're a genius!"

"Is that all?"

"Yeah." I grabbed Dorian's hand in mine. "Come on, love. I've got a tournament to win."

* * *

With my powers under control, Kimmy and I rose through the ranks quickly. In less than 3½ weeks we'd faced off against Kikyō and Javier. In the third to last round, the teams were switched. Somehow, I ended being paired with Kikyō. To me, this was a good thing since I liked two things—strength and a challenge—and Kimmy was neither.

I could hear my friends screaming in the stands and I felt a fresh wave of guilt. As if I were playing football with a vase, it seemed that I had a knack for breaking people before I could make use of them. Keres grew inside of me, her darkness spreading like a wildfire. In the end, I saw no reason to hold back as I almost murdered Wynonna and Latasha before making my way to the second to last round.

I was power.

I was greed.

I was merciless.

"All right, folks!" The announcer was beside himself with excitement. "Are you ready to scream?"

The crowd did just that. Kikyō unfurled her wings behind her and gave a large flap. I did the same, wanting her to know from the start that she did not have the upper hand. I heard a voice cry for the battle to hurry up and start. When I looked up, Martin Sawyer was sitting like a king in his throne, watching me as if I were the grand prize.

We took to the sky in an instant. She charged at me with outstretched hands, ready to end the battle that hadn't had time to begin. I was no different and I wasted no time in killing her.

I came at her like a hurricane, all fists, and teeth. She crashed into me like a boulder, automatically reaching for a senbon in her hair. I grabbed her hand and yanked as hard as I could. There was a loud *pop* and Kikyō let out a pained scream. In her moment of weakness, I acted.

My tail snared around her ankle, almost like a thing of its own. I yanked her closer and wrapped my arms around her shoulders as if I were trying to hug her. Then I flipped us over, folded in my wings, and sped towards the ground. We got closer and closer and as soon as we were mere inches away, I called on the training that Micha gave me and pulled up. Kikyō crashed to the ground, blood pooling around her as she lay deathly still.

"We have a winner!"

CHAPTER THIRTY-SEVEN

BLACK SEA

I was now on my way to fight the Black Sea.

I thought of Tess, who wanted to fight so badly. She, like I, wanted to expel her anger in physical activities. But I knew that if I let her show her true strength—expose her Gift—she would annihilate us all. At least I was a contained mess. McKenzie and Denise were still recovering from McKenzie's heart problem. Rhea was still heartbroken over Micha, but she also seemed to have taken a liking to Shafi. The only ones who seemed perfectly fine were Shafi and Dorian.

"Why are all the people that surround me so..."

"Broken?" said Dorian.

"Yeah."

"Broken people find broken people," he shrugged, "so they can fix each other."

"You would've made a really great artist," I said looking at him in a newfound light. "A lot of great artists have mental health issues. You could use your manic episodes to your advantage. They could be an inspiration when all those thoughts are going through your head!"

"I haven't painted in years…" Dorian said, shaking his head.

"Who cares? I've seen your work. You have a gift that has nothing to do with any sort of magic. I bet if you'd done that instead of drinking so much, you would have ended up a lot better off. Just believe in yourself."

"You sound like you're in a TV show." He made googly eyes at me. "Just believe it hard enough and all of your wishes will come true!"

"Well, it's true," I said, fighting down a blush.

"Speaking of believing in yourself, how do you think you're going to do?"

"I'm gonna smoke him!"

"That's my girl!" Dorian kissed the top of my head. "I've noticed that you've gotten a lot more confident these past few weeks."

"Really?"

I hadn't noticed.

"Yeah. I think that when you face down Jacques, he's not even going to recognize you."

"I hope so…"

"There's only one thing that you need to work on," he said, pausing as if bracing for a hit.

"What?"

"You're a bit of a hot-head."

"What?" Rage boiled in the bit of my stomach. "I am *not* a hot-head!"

"Yes," Dorian said, "you are. You've gotten in a fight with almost everyone you've met since I've known you. You don't listen to people's opinion if it challenges yours. You need to remember that we are all your friends. Try to ease up a bit, okay?"

"Larson said that it was my magic."

"Yes, I was there."

"It's not my fault. I can't—"

"You can always help it."

"Are you saying I'm a bad friend?"

"I'm saying that you're a bit…intense."

I heard a chorus of agreements echo behind me. I turned to see Shafi, Tess, Rhea, McKenzie, and Denise behind me. The wheels of McKenzie's wheelchair quietly squeaked as she rolled forward; I wondered why I hadn't noticed her before. She was proof that I was a bit, as Dorian said, 'intense.' After all, I had gotten overly excited in a fight and messed her up.

I would have to work on that.

We were nearing the arena. Everyone showered me with words of encouragement. The only one who didn't was Tess. Rhea told her to cheer up and stop being such a Debby downer. After a quick skim of Tess's thoughts, I found out that she didn't say good luck because she didn't think I needed it. She thought that I could do it all on my own without any outside force.

"Thanks," I said, nudging Tess.

As if she could read my mind, she gave me a nod.

My party quickly took their seats in the stands. I stood in the middle of the arena, my senses on overdrive. My powers were on their lowest setting, a small hum under my skin. My tail flicked behind me in excitement, almost like a whole other being on its own. Above it all, I could hear Keres in the back of my mind, hissing like some sort of snake.

Suddenly, ancient tribal music played loud and strong. The focus of the screens redirected from my eager smirk to a dark tunnel. The Black Sea was making his way through the tunnel, his eyes shining with a soft glow. My tail flicked behind me and as it did, I felt a small twitch in my emotional state. Keres's voice only grew louder and that's when I realized that there was something very wrong.

He took a step. The drums struck like thunder. He took a breath and the wind shifted with him. It was kind of poetic in a way—or at least it would have been if he hadn't been such an asshole. I took a deep breath as I took him in.

Khalil did not look like a man who would one day help save the world. He was much like the Black Sea—raging, overwhelming and toxic for all close enough to feel his wrath. He moved towards the center of the arena like an actor taking center stage. He swept down in a low bow for his cheering fans, who devoured us both as if we were the last bit of entertainment on Earth. Khalil gave the cameras a smile that never reached his cold, dead eyes.

How did he *ever* become a Horseman?

"Are you ready for the fight of your life?" cried the announcer.

The crowd became even more frantic. I glanced up in the stands, an odd feeling sweeping over me. I was afraid that I wouldn't see my friends again. I felt a pair of eyes digging into my back with the large shovel named greed. I turned to see Martin Sawyer watching me, his eyes saying that he was expecting me to bring him more money than he could spend in a lifetime.

The match began. Khalil raised his hands, and a maelstrom of water came rushing towards me. I could see where he got his title. Electricity crowded under my skin due to the looming threat, just begging to be released. As the storm surrounded me, I dug deep and found something that I certainly wasn't searching for.

Keres was waiting for me.

In a matter of seconds, I was inside of that dark place. I was chained to that rock and no matter how hard I tried to move; I couldn't break free. Keres was standing outside of the prison, a twisted smirk on her face. Her tail twitched in glee. As it did, mine mirrored its action.

"I want to have some fun," said Keres, "and I think I know how."

"How did I get in here? What did you do?"

Black spots dotted my vision. I began to feel drained, as if the obsidian was stealing my life force. Keres stood taller with each passing second. The snakes still wound around her body, hissing in glee. My vision began to blur, and I struggled to make out her shape.

"Silly girl. Did you really think that I gave you that tail as a parting gift?" Her mocking laughter dug its talons into my skin, making my body shudder with anger and humiliation. "That tail that I gave you has slowly been stealing your energy and feeding it to me."

"You can't go out there..." I gasped as a knife of pain drove into my gut and twisted. "I have...to win...the tournament."

"Maybe in the next life," said Keres and she was gone.

It was like I was inside of a security room, monitoring all the footage. Yes, it was exactly like that except that I was trapped in the room, tied to the chair by rope and unable to call for help because my tongue had been cut out. I—or to be more accurate, *Keres*—raised our hands as the water closed in. A voltage of electricity—the strongest I'd seen yet—flew from our body.

Our face was all over the screen. The Black Sea didn't look so emotionless anymore, his face, for lack of a better word, flabbergasted. Martin Sawyer was leaning forward in his seat, panting like a dog. We charged forward, pulling back our arm as electricity danced around our fist. We were five feet from the Black Sea, then four, then three, then two...

His hand flashed out. He caught our fist in his own, that familiar haughty smirk returning to his face. He looked so much like Jacques in that moment that I wanted to cry and scream at the same time. A crazed smirk twisted on our face and as it did, Khalil's slowly faded. I knew why in a matter of seconds.

Electricity ramped up and down our body. The Black Sea cried out as voltage after voltage ramped through his body. His back arched and in an instant, he was on the ground, jerking around as his internal organs were fried. Smoke poured from his skin and from his lips, and from his nose and eyes poured a fountain of blood.

I felt the mental manifestation of my mouth muscles twitch as Keres made our lips twitch up into a triumphant grin. I was surprised that she'd ended it so fast. Maybe she *was* stronger than me. My shock was quickly replaced with disgust. A murmur of fear and discomfort rippled through the crowd.

Keres ran her tongue across Khalil's dead face. I could taste the blood in our mouth, bitter like a mouthful of salt. Once she'd lapped up most of the fluid, Keres stood and pumped her fist in the air. The crowd quickly switched from shock to amazement. They rose to their feet, stomping and screaming battle cries as our face flashed on the screen, dubbing us Champion of the Rose Court.

In a matter of seconds Martin Sawyer was in the middle of the stadium, placing a crown that looked to be made from golden thorns on our head. Dorian and the rest of the party ran down into the stadium. They looked cautious and kept their distance.

It was a wise move on their part.

"What a victorious day this is!" Martin Sawyer cried as his mouth stretched in a taut grin. "We have a new ruler!"

The crowd screamed their praise.

Keres turned our head and as she did, I felt her mistrust. Our eyes skimmed over Dorian, who was watching us with that look that said he knew something was off. Dorian didn't kiss or hug us but instead glanced at Martin Sawyer. We turned just in time to see Sawyer pull out a remote. His thumb hovered over a red button, a grin slashing his face in two.

"I had a feeling that someone would defeat the Champion!" He screamed, loud enough for even the crowd to hear. "Let me tell you a story. Years ago, my wife was murdered by one of our Gifted slaves—a beast who used his Gift to prey on innocent women."

The crowd quieted down, sensing that something was amiss. The camera zoomed in on Martin Sawyer's face, which was suddenly filled with rage. I couldn't help but get the feeling that we were in over our heads—that nothing could be *this* easy.

"You said a Gifted," said McKenzie, "as if we were foreign to you. You're one of us."

"I'm not one of you disgusting animals!" spat Sawyer. "Ever since the day of my wife's murder, I vowed to destroy every magical human I came across. That's why I built this arena—to lure in fools such as yourself and purge the world of your infected race!

"I knew that I couldn't do it alone, but I had no one to help me other than Khalil, who is now nothing more than a failed experiment. I needed a way to make the Gifted suffer but I couldn't figure out how to do it other than pinning you all against each other. Then, about three months ago, a man approached me. He said that he knew of my game and my story."

I had a pretty good inkling as to who this man was.

"He said that he could deprive the Gifted of what my wife had been deprived of—a second chance! He said that the Gatekeeper was coming and that with her came a tide that would wash all Gifted clean and ensure that they all would never be able to see the face of the God. He warned me of the new Champion—he said that if she didn't die in these games, she would ruin all my work. He said that she would make it to where you all were—"

"You do realize that Jacques is a half-demon, right?" I heard my voice say as our mouth twitched in a sneer.

"Of course I know that! But he said he'd renounced his ways and wanted to join my cause. That's why—"

"He was playing you." Keres said in my voice, although it was slippery and came off as dishonest. "I used to be his slave. He was using you to get to me. He doesn't care about your petty crusade—he only cares about getting revenge on me for leaving him."

"Your lies mean nothing," Sawyer said as he backed away. "The truth rains from the sky!"

The Marks on my arms began to glow. A shadow instantly streaked across the sky. It landed on the ground in a crouch. The angel stood and we looked into the face of Lisette. Around the angelic woman's neck hung a red amulet that was slowly turning black. The blonde silently took it off and gave it to Keres.

"You know that army you mentioned?" I said, momentarily in control as I put on the necklace. "I think I'm going to need it."

"I'm sorry! There's a battle going on. The demons have reached *Sora,* and the battle is turning into a massacre. Sadly, we're on the losing side. The Creator has called every single angel—Battle Angel or not—to fight."

"I thought you said that the Army of the Creator would descend to help me in my time of need!"

"Don't worry!" cried Lisette before she spread her wings. "Sometimes one warrior has more force than an army of soldiers. Besides, you have the Horsemen with you!"

"How do I seal Jacques?"

"Not sure!" she flapped her wings. "But you'll find a way!"

She gave two strong beats with her wings and then streaked across the sky. Our wings fluttered open, and I could tell that Keres was glad to be using them. Our tail swished in anticipation. I'd wanted to destroy Jacques myself. At least from this angle I could still watch as the life slowly bled from his eyes.

That's when the sound of a helicopter came. We looked up to see a helicopter hovering over us, a long black rope hanging from its open mouth. Down that rope came Jacques, a smirk on his beautiful, ugly face. Keres took a step back and I felt fear trumpet through our heart.

Suddenly, I was back in control of my body. Jacques came ever close and as he did, my tail flicked and disappeared with a strange light—I couldn't believe the magic that Keres implanted had been locked away so easily. Electricity poured from my body in waves. I had one shot—

And I was going to make it count. As if the universe agreed, I felt the force of everything around me lift me up. I flapped my wings and took off with all the power in the world in each beat.

So fast…it's all happening so fast. Can I do it?

I reached into my holster and grabbed the Dagger of Truth. Jacques smirked and with a twist of his body, he dodged the attack. I flipped midair and landed on the ground in a crouch. Jacques swept the hair from his face with a flick of his pale wrist. I was going to cut the damn thing off.

He lunged at me with a swipe. I backed away, a grin crawling onto my face. He moved forward again. I took a step back, balancing my weight so that I didn't fall. Back and forth we moved, locked in a deadly dance.

I don't know how long we fought.

Seconds?

Minutes?

Hours?

Days?

Weeks?

Months?

Years?

Maybe even forever…

Or perhaps it took no time at all…

One second, he was running at me, that beautiful face of his marred with all its insanity. I thought of my parents and then Grant. We'd all lost the ones we loved, and my former Master was one of those losses. But then Jacques gave me that haughty look that he always gave me before he beat me, and I felt nothing for him other than hatred and an incurable hunger for his end. Everything froze and all I was not prepared for what happened next.

He hung in midair. I glanced around myself and noticed that everyone was frozen other than myself and Dorian.

What was going on?

I heard footsteps near the entrance of the stadium. Dorian walked towards me, surveyed me, and then took my hand in his. Together we faced the seven young, flawless figures marching toward us single file. They had black cloaks on, and each moved with a grace that must've taken hundreds of years to master.

I instantly knew that these were the Elders.

The one in the front—a handsome Israeli guy with a chiseled jaw—held his hand high. I realized that he must've been the one to stop time. Dorian fell in a bow and motioned for me to do the same. I glanced at the Elders and shook my head. I refused to kneel before another man ever again.

"You have done well, Gatekeeper," said the one in front.

"Yes," mumbled his companions.

"You have also caused a few problems."

"Yes," they all agreed.

"What did I do?" I shoved an angry finger at Jacques. "He's the whacko who started all of this!"

"Was that when he took you in or when he tried to kill your son?"

I felt Dorian tense beside me. That pulled me up short. I'd almost forgotten about that little incident in all the chaos. Now it was front and center in my mind, filling me with a bubbling rage so profound that I could scream. I swaggered toward Jacques, ready to end his existence in one strike.

"You are not to kill him. If you do, he will just reincarnate," said the first one. "You just have to seal him away."

"No." I growled, slowly turning back to the Elders. "I *need* to kill him."

"That's against the Creator's design."

"I don't care."

"Seal him away," said the Israelite. "There has been enough blood shed today."

"I don't give a flying fuck! I'll chase him in any life. He took everything from me. He beat me. He humiliated me. I'm going to do the same to him."

"No."

I looked at Dorian, who took my hand in his. He eyes held some kind of hidden meaning. I tried to fight his influence, but I was powerless. I felt a sudden calm, like a warmth bubbling in my stomach as if I'd drunk alcohol while lying in the hot sun. I just wanted to breathe.

I took the position that I was in before. I knew that I could move closer while time stood still but to me that would be cheating—I wanted to act on my own time. Time unfroze but the Elders remained in their spot, watching silently.

I came at Jacques with a ferocious growl. He dodged my first attack. I tackled him, hoping to try from a different angle. He opened his arms and we toppled to the ground, limbs flailing. I was on top of him in an instant, ramming my fist into his face over and over.

He twisted his hips and we rolled together. He was on top for a moment before he stood up. I watched as his form rippled like water, shifting before becoming something new. His skin was as black as the obsidian on the bracelets I wore, as shiny as marble and as hard as diamonds. His teeth were sharpened to delicate points, he had two curved horns, and his mouth was caught between a sneer and a grin.

He reached out to push me and I fell towards the ground. He stood over me and pressed his boot on my chest. He pressed down and I. Couldn't. Breathe. I grabbed his leg and rammed a voltage up his leg. He didn't even flinch, but I was granted instant passage into his mind.

I instantly knew what he was going to do next. As soon as his foot lifted, I rolled to the side. Then I pulled the dagger close before driving it into his leg. He gave a howl of pain and for a moment, I scared myself by how much I enjoyed it. He turned around and swiped at me—

But I was already on my feet, backing away.

We moved in a deadly dance, circling as we each swiped with our respective weapons—a dagger and fists versus teeth and claws. He was like the demons that I faced before—all animalistic instinct and nothing else. I had the element of surprise on my side.

After all, he couldn't even fathom an outcome that wasn't in his favor.

"I trained you! Do you really think you can outwit me, you stupid, pathetic little girl?"

Sticks and stones...

He spun in a kick that caught me in the chest.

May break my bones...

"I have more than a hundred years of experience. You're just the useless, ignorant child that was too weak to save her parents."

But words can always hurt me...

Something changed in me. I lowered my hands, letting him knock me to the ground. He straddled me, pressing his knees against my chest. I began to wheeze but still, I did not fight him. He leaned closer and even though there was a smile on his face, I knew he felt nothing.

He didn't hate me and Grant because he loved us, and we got away. He hated us because we slipped out of his grasp. He hated us because we refused to submit to him.

He hated us because in his eyes, we were a battle that he had lost.

"You are nothing but a bug under my boot." His breath smelled sickly sweet as it went across my face. "You are nothing but a failure—a whore...!"

He couldn't control me anymore. I pushed him off, drawing a gasp of surprise from him. A smirk crawled on my face as I stood and watched him fall.

"Suck on this, asshole!"

I flashed toward him with a ready hand, as fast as light. I swiped out with the Dagger of Truth, catching him in the chest. Before Jacques could burst into a million little pieces, I raised the amulet and pressed it to the wound.

A cry of rage and pain immediately fell from the demi-demon's lips. A dark howl of wind built up in the sky, threatening to blow us all over. Something shifted in the universe, making room for another dark soul that would be locked away for all eternity. The amulet turned black and when I glanced back up, Jacques was gone. But he'd left behind a black object that now sat on the ground beeped.

Beep. Beep. Beep.

It was a homing device.

Suddenly, I felt the wind blow back from my face. I looked up to see another helicopter hovering over the stadium. From the opening on the side of the helicopter came thousands of children, their eyes gleaming in malice and their arms overgrown with muscles they shouldn't've had. I glanced at the stands.

And they all had my gleaming red hair and Jacques's fathomless black eyes.

In an instant Tess, Rhea and Shafi were at my side. Denise and McKenzie stayed in the stands, one lame and one unable to feel the call. The child soldiers flooded the arena, feeling familiar for some unknown reason. Tess reached out and grabbed one of the children. He dropped to the ground.

"Dude, those were kids!" cried Shafi.

"Those aren't children!" I cried as I sent a wicked bolt at one child. "They are servants for the Ordained. We have to kill them, or this fight will never end!"

I didn't mention what I knew: these were all my children, borne from the eggs that Jacques had stolen from me when he took out Aiden. After he raped me. In the moments between desperation and despair.

Rhea ducked low, her fists flying at faces that were closer to the ground. Shafi went behind a child and put her in a sleep hold. Dorian's limbs were loose as he dodged each attack before delivering his own blow. Of course, he was a master of the Drunken Fist. Still, everyone fought valiantly as heroes should.

But that heroism was short lived.

I felt it building in me like rolling thunder. This power was greater than anything I'd felt before. I felt no remorse for what I was about to do because all I wanted was peace.

Ergo, kill them to maintain peace.

I knew from the light around me that I was glowing. I faintly heard Dorian yell for everyone to get down. The universe shifted again, this time to make way for what I'd set in motion. Thousands of sparks exploded from my body, hitting each soldier, and making them fly back. They got up quickly, but I could tell by the way they gripped their sides that they were hurt.

As one, they came at me. They overtook me like a wave and in my mind's eye flashed the faces of all my friends. This was no time to play or be the leader that everyone despised. This was the time to take names and kick butt. I let them cover me, sure of what I had to do.

I closed my eyes. A deep hum filled my chest, and I knew that my power was quickly mounting. I focused on the bracelets on my wrists, commanding them to ramp my powers to the max. I felt my body slip away and it was like I could feel all the light and electricity around me. I was not just emanating electricity from my body.

I was electricity itself.

It started with a twitch. Then a flinch. Then a small cry of pain that evolved into a shout. As my presence filled every pore of their bodies, light came from their eyes, noses, and open mouths. I rooted myself deep inside them, dug my claws into the very essence of their beings and then quickly expanded.

The children flew away from me. Their lifeless bodies jerked on the ground, full of electricity that they could not contain. As I went back to my physical form, I was surprised how unnatural it felt to be in such a solid state. Distracting me, Dorian got up and took my hand; just like last time, everything froze. We looked at the Israeli leader, daring him to find an issue with something else.

I'd just saved the world, after all.

"You have vast power. You have a part in this universe that you are unaware of."

"I sealed away the Ordained and destroyed his army." I crossed my arms. "I've done my part."

"Your true part is yet to come," said Lord Helios.

And with a flash of light, the Elders were gone.

To Be Continued…

Author Handles:
@RuquayyaSajjida (Twitter)
@ruquayyasajjida (Instagram)
@ruquayya999 aka Ruquayya (TikTok)

www.ingramcontent.com/pod-product-compliance
Lightning Source LLC
Chambersburg PA
CBHW070617260626
47161CB00007B/2468